Stinging Fly Stories

Stinging Fly Stories

Celebrating our first 20 years 1998-2018

Edited by Sarah Gilmartin and Declan Meade

The Stinging Fly

A Stinging Fly Press Book

Stinging Fly Stories is first published simultaneously in paperback
and in a special casebound edition (400 copies) in April 2018.

Introduction copyright © 2018 Sarah Gilmartin

Selection copyright © 2018 Sarah Gilmartin and Declan Meade

FIRST EDITION

ISBN 978-1-906539-68-9 (casebound)
ISBN 978-1-906539-69-6 (paperback)

The Stinging Fly Press
PO Box 6016
Dublin 1
www.stingingfly.org

Set in Palatino

Printed in Ireland by Walsh Colour Print, County Kerry.

The Stinging Fly Press gratefully acknowledges the financial
support of The Arts Council/An Chomhairle Ealaíon.

CONTENTS

Introduction

Once upon a time, in the not so distant past, I was asked for my favourite short story writer by an enthusiast of the form. Chekhov, Munro, Carver? Or perhaps it was one of our own. Edna, Joyce, Lavin? Put on the spot, the only writer I could think of was Roald Dahl, whose stories I'd read many times over for their wit and fiendish plot twists. It was not the right answer.

Hooked on novels from a young age, I was a latecomer to the short story but one of the great things about the form is that you can catch up quickly. A decade or so of reading means I'm ready to take on that enthusiast, should I ever meet him again. Writing about debut authors for *The Irish Times* for the past four years has brought plenty of emerging short-story writers my way, many of whom feature in *The Stinging Fly*'s vast bank of nearly four hundred stories. Established in late 1997 to publish the best new Irish and international writing, the magazine has been a holy grail for fledgling writers over the last two decades.

When Martin Doyle and Fintan O'Toole approached me to write about new fiction for *The Irish Times* in 2014, there were similar intentions: to review the best—and sometimes the not so best—debut novels and collections being written by emerging Irish and international authors. It is hard to summarise what I've learnt from my time both as a reviewer and co-editor of this anthology, harder still to pinpoint patterns in so many stories. Fiction, by its nature, presents myriad worlds with infinite possibilities and it has been my pleasure to delve into the lives of diverse Irish characters, young and old, as they navigate their various paths. If there is something that links the fictional worlds I've come across as a reviewer it is a yearning for meaning and connection: from affairs in the south of France, to modern immigrants surviving the Australian outback, to a lonely man and his one-eyed dog on the run in rural Ireland.

The same can be said for the stories in *The Fly*'s archive, whose value is often less in what the story happens to be about and more in how the story gets told and how it makes us feel as readers. Occasionally, themed issues have guided content to an extent, but the magazine is first and foremost a space that allows writers to write about whatever they want. The blank page is full of potential and the short story is a grand old form for putting that potential to the test.

A story in *The Stinging Fly* is a proud moment for any new writer. It is also a calling card that gets the attention of busy agents and publishers. Many authors who appeared in *The Fly* early in their careers—Sara Baume, Kevin Barry, Colin Barrett to name a few—are now internationally acclaimed. But despite a back catalogue that most publishers would kill for, the magazine's mission remains the same: publishing new writers, new writing.

The style and scope of the stories in this anthology are not easily categorised. Writers, both emerging and established, are always nudging at the form. Some tweak tradition, others aim to blast it apart. A good story creates a unique world that intrigues the reader from the outset. Éilis Ní Dhuibhne, a master of the form, sums it up as a space that is difficult to leave: 'You don't want the story to end. You love the texture of it, its language, its characters, what is happening in it. You enjoy exploring its depths, its layers, its everything. This is the most important aspect of the story: its being.'

Not wanting a story to end is a bittersweet thing. The first read draws us into the experience, may even leave us temporarily marooned. But finishing a story also brings the pleasure of reflection. Then many of us will go back in again, finding new details with each visit: the older Ireland portrayed through a Club Milk wrapper in Danielle McLaughlin's wonderful 'Night of the Silver Fox'; a mother frantically searching for gifts for her children in Leona Lee Cully's 'A Sin to Tell the Naked Truth'; the teenager in Kevin Curran's 'Adventure Stories for Boys' who feels 'the hard texture of a stray dog's paw' as he holds his father's hand in hospital; the stunning coastal imagery in Sean O'Reilly's 'All

Day and All of the Night'; the atmosphere of malaise in Mary Costello's heartbreaking 'Things I See'; the description of a lonely soul in Claire Keegan's 'Dark Horses' as 'a man who has drunk two farms'.

In our meetings over the year this anthology was put together, I have come to understand something of how a publisher like Declan Meade chooses the stories for his magazine and beyond. The power of a short story lies in writing that makes fictional worlds read true, writing that creates intimacy between the reader and characters 'living' on the page. The stories in *The Stinging Fly* are about anything and everything. The ones that excel draw us fully into an experience, scratching away at the surface to explore what lies beneath.

There are too many stories here to give a breakdown of each one, but singular experiences abound. Kevin Barry's quietly momentous tale of a Limerick outsider who takes on the pack in 'Last Days of the Buffalo'. The liver-punch of an Irish shindig in Danny Denton's 'Cana Wedding'. Carys Davies's severely isolated, terrified new wife in 'The Quiet'. The physical deformities that manifest because of familial discord in Nicole Flattery's 'Hump', with its killer opening line: 'At seventy, after suffering several disappointments, the first being my mother, the second being me, my father died.'

While most of the stories focus on a single moment of crisis in one character's life—the lonely voice calling out—the isolation of whole communities can be glimpsed through stories of marginalised individuals. Lisa McInerney's 'The Butcher's Apron' shows a disenfranchised town, 'a spine of pubs, chippers and dentist surgeries'. The narrator in 'Let's Go Kill Ourselves', Colin Barrett's first story to be published in the magazine, realises he no longer cares about his old town and his old friends on a visit back for Christmas. In Michael J. Farrell's 'Pascal's Wager', on the other hand, it is an inherent sense of community that comforts the residents of a nursing home as they argue over the afterlife. This sense of connection, or lack thereof, is the fulcrum around which the forty pieces in this diverse collection spin.

Although many of the stories look back in time and away from Ireland—Nuala O'Connor's 'The Boy from Petrópolis', Philip Ó Ceallaigh's 'The Beast', Nora Pyne's 'Jeopardy'—they are still relevant today, even as they transport readers to different eras and mind-sets. Not every author published in *The Fly* archives would agree that their stories have stood the test of time. There was much fun, and some horror, in the correspondence with now established writers cringing at the idea of having their early work showcased once more.

When the first issue of *The Stinging Fly* came out in March 1998, Ireland didn't have all that many outlets that focused on new and emerging writers. Two decades on, it is heartening to see a much more vibrant literary scene with an array of thriving magazines. *The Dublin Review, Crannóg, The Moth, gorse, The Penny Dreadful, Poetry Ireland Review, The Dublin Review of Books, Banshee, Southword, Tangerine* and *Winter Papers* are just some of the titles publishing the best new writing out there today. Much has been written in recent years about the resurgence of the short fiction form, particularly its renewed popularity among publishers. In Ireland, Declan and his talented team of editors have had a big hand in that uplift. The editorial policy of accepting open submissions, encouraging new writers and welcoming fresh approaches has helped create the conditions that allow the form to flourish.

The Fly's influence has not been limited to fiction. Budding poets, flash fiction writers, illustrators, playwrights and essayists have also found a home. It is testament to the quality of the magazine that despite having to read four hundred stories, I often found myself distracted by other content. Mary Morrissy's essay on Maeve Brennan, a Nick Laird poem on 'immoderate grief', a flash fiction issue edited by Nuala O'Connor, Colum McCann's ode to New York, song lyrics by Paul Muldoon and an interview with Claire Keegan towards the beginning of her career are just some of the pieces I found myself drawn into along the way. Whatever the form—reviews, essays, interviews—a love of writing and reading shines through.

From Frank O'Connor's lonely voice to Lorrie Moore's love story, Edgar Allen Poe's single mood to Mary Lavin's large deal of detection, many great practitioners of the short story have given their own definition of the form. In her introduction to *The Granta Book of the Irish Short Story*, Anne Enright calls it 'a place to keep things real'. It is as good a summary as any, a succinct definition for a succinct form. It seems particularly fitting for the stories that have featured to date in *The Stinging Fly*, a period that saw Ireland flourish economically in the late nineties, hurtle into the boom of the Celtic Tiger years, crash back to reality in 2008 and attempt to emerge from the debris ever since. The stories the magazine has published chart many different Irelands, though the down times certainly win out as fictional backdrops. This is perhaps unsurprising for a form that deals so well with the desperate situations of ordinary people.

The economic transformation of Ireland in the last twenty years has coincided with huge social change. The first issue of *The Stinging Fly* came out in 1998, five years after the decriminalisation of homosexuality. Divorce for heterosexual marriage had only been legal for two years. The most recent issue of the magazine publishes in an era where Ireland has the honour of being the first country in the world to have legalised gay marriage by popular vote. We are a long way from the lonely protagonist of Keith Ridgway's achingly beautiful story 'Andy Warhol', a young man who must leave Ireland for New York to figure out his sexuality: 'All I want is the men who want me.'

In other areas we have not travelled so far. While stories in the archive on forced adoptions and the shaming of unmarried mothers hark to an older Ireland, we still live—as of publication—in a country where thousands of women each year travel abroad for abortions. Exporting or burying our problems, whether in a personal or public capacity, is an Irish trait that preoccupies many of the writers in the magazine down through the years.

It is a coincidence that this anthology comes out the same month as the referendum on repealing the Eighth Amendment in the Irish constitution. It is not a coincidence that so many female writers have emerged in Ireland in the last two decades, and that their voices are finally being listened to on important issues. Outlets like *The Stinging Fly* have given opportunities to women in a country where the literary gender balance was heavily skewed for most of the 20th century. There is still some way to go but there is at least more reason for optimism now. Without any conscious effort, nearly two-thirds of the stories in this anthology are by women.

The whole point of magazines like *The Stinging Fly* is to help new voices break through. Declan, along with fellow editors Aoife Kavanagh, Thomas Morris, and the recently appointed Sally Rooney, have viewed the magazine as a developmental space where writers are offered guidance, feedback and support through the publication process. Rookie mistakes are par for the course, just as they are with some of the first novels and collections I read as a reviewer. Trying to cram too much into one book or story is probably top of the list, followed by slippages in voice and authenticity while trying too hard to dazzle with linguistic flourishes. The stories in this anthology are not meant to be perfect. They are bright bullets stopping us in our tracks for their short duration, and if we're lucky, sometimes much longer than that.

When Declan asked me to co-edit this anthology, he said he needed someone to blame for the stories that didn't make the cut. Those hundreds of worthy contenders saw us argue back and forth for months. It is my hope that the stories selected here truly represent what *The Stinging Fly* has achieved in its two decades to date. If not, you know who to blame.

Sarah Gilmartin
Dublin, April 2018

Stinging Fly Stories

Let's Go Kill Ourselves

Colin Barrett

Attempting to light a wet cigarette can bring a man to the verge of tears. My last Marlboro had been struck by a flake of snow as I went to tuck it into the corner of my mouth, soaking it through. I'd spent the following five minutes applying the flame of my disposable lighter to its sodden end, to little effect, and my gloveless hands were beginning to turn a bright, raw pink. It was below zero, and the snow was still coming down, in heavy, wet, moth-sized plumes. I checked my watch but there was no watch attached to my wrist. I brushed my hands through my hair and remembered I was a person.

I was standing at the rear of the Pearl Hotel bus shelter in the empty heart of Dunvale town on a dead Friday night. End of December, end of the year. Plexiglass enclosed me on three sides; a fluorescent bar embedded in the shelter's ceiling jittered above my wet head. My battered duffel bag was propped in one corner, freighted with a semester's worth of dog-eared notepads, a three month accretion of foul smelling clothes, and the latest, exorbitantly annotated translation of Blaise Pascal's *Pensées*, on which I had a paper due at some point in the new year.

I didn't notice the car until it was nearly on top of me. I heard it approaching that last, ponderous bend before the road straightened out through Dunvale village. The street was empty in both directions and glittering with a fresh layer of frost. The car, a compact, spearmint green Pinto, came out of the bend very quickly and veered suddenly out into the opposite lane. The driver attempted to correct, but it was too late; what had probably seemed a fractional and entirely proportionate adjustment in the moment it was made brought the Pinto straight into the redbrick wall of The Pearl's car park, directly across the road from where I was standing.

By this point I'd aborted the ignition of my cigarette (though it still clung like a scrap of bunting to my lips) and was rubbing my hands together and shifting from foot to foot in an effort to get my circulation going. Maybe ten minutes had elapsed since I'd limped from the submarine humidity of a packed Dublin bus into Dunvale's chill air. I was home for Christmas.

The dogs of nearby households, jolted from their canine slumbers, sent a chorus of barks into the ensuing silence. I could make out footsteps in the distance, and somewhere nearby, the rush of the Mule river. I remembered the stories I'd heard as a child, about the old Dunvale farmers; how they were reputed to bring their clapped out donkeys—the ones that could no longer hack their daily allotment of donkeywork—to the shore of the river; how they beat their haunches with rods or willow-switches and drove the poor creatures into the water.

The wreckage steamed and hissed in the snow. I picked up my duffel bag—long habit meant I never left it unattended—and crossed the road. Snowflakes splatted against my jacket, leaving dark stains like the photo-negatives of stars. The car was a mess. The front axle had jarred loose and chewed its way partially free of the chassis; the wheel on the far side had punched through the Pinto's frame and buried itself in the innards of the engine compartment. I could smell smoke in the air.

As I approached, the passenger door screeched on its hinge. A figure clambered out, took two unsteady steps towards me, then stopped. He just stood there, and it took me a moment to realise that he was looking at me. We were probably both trying to figure out who was who's apparition.

Of course, was my first thought, *of course it would be someone you know.*

Back in secondary school, at the start of every lunchtime hour, myself and my friends—D, Brian Brennan and Sean Timlin—would rendezvous across the road from the school's front gates, by the Mule bridge, and head uptown together. This was in fourth year, when we still permitted Matty Crollis to hang out with us. He was the joke, the butt, of our gang; the short-breathed, pudgy kid you could dependably pick on with no fear of reprisal, and he was always somehow the last to arrive. When I saw him approaching—slouching down St Carmichael's oak-lined drive—I'd jab whoever was standing closest to me and nod in his direction.

'Shite. Here he comes. Quick: before he gets here. Let's go kill ourselves!'

And with a big smile on my face I'd mime jumping into the Mule.

It was a few weeks before the end of term, and the five of us were standing outside Luther's, a bar with a pool hall attached and a favoured haunt of ours. D had just dispatched the rest of us in a best-of-three-frames snooker tournament (save for Crollis, whose ineptitude with a cue was such that we no longer allowed him to participate in our knockout games). We'd squandered our lunch money and were digging through our back pockets, hoping to dredge up enough loose change between us for a bag of chips.

A raggedy brown and white springer spaniel was cruising the pavement for scraps. It wandered over to our group and began to snuffle excitedly at our hands and pockets. Its coat was matted with stalactites of dirt and its tongue hung from its jaws like a sodden pink sock. It stank like a heap of used bath towels, and was clearly a stray. Timlin snatched playfully at its glistening black nose. He leaned in low to the side of its head and said 'Fuck off,' but said it very softly and evenly, like an endearment. The dog went to lick his face and he gently cuffed its jaw. D finished counting the change we'd poured into his hands. 'We're 20p short of a large curry cheese. Feck sake.'

Crollis had been watching D futilely count up the coinage.

'Look, lads, me Mam gives us a fiver on Fridays. I've enough money to buy us all a bag of chips,' he interjected, 'I mean ye can get me back next week or whenever.'

We turned to him, and crowed 'Fuck off!!' in unison.

'I just beat everyone's arses at pool, I'll buy me own fucking chips!' D jabbed Crollis's shoulder, indignant. Crollis went pale. 'I just thought—'

The spaniel had circled back behind Crollis, and just then began nosing at his trouser pocket: Crollis took a step back, screamed 'Fuck off!' and brought his foot right up into the dog's midriff. It lifted off the ground a little bit, then scrambled yelping down the street.

'You *prick*!' Timlin snarled, shoving Crollis.

'What!?' he screamed. Tears were welling in his eyes, and his cheeks were beginning to go purple.

'You… *apologise to that fucking dog!*' Timlin roared. Timlin was a sweet, generally temperate guy, but big, with a big guy's predilection for the physical stuff when he thought it was called for. With a languid sweep of his arm he grabbed a fistful of Crollis's oversized duffel coat and spun him into Luther's blacked-out window front. Crollis's glasses clattered to the pavement.

'Apologise for what to the dog! It's a dog! I just wanted to buy yez chips!' Crollis pleaded. He was crying now. Timlin kept his arm held out, at the end of which Crollis's purple face squirmed and writhed like a snagged balloon, his glassless eyes reduced and scrunched, Chinese with distress. Brennan put his hand on Timlin's shoulder.

'Leave it, Sean.'

Timlin let Crollis go.

Crollis bent over and picked up his glasses. He kept his head bowed as he rearranged them on his face. Hacking and spluttering, he pinched the bridge of his nose and tried to compose himself. Timlin spun on his heels.

'C'mon, let's go.' The four of us went to walk away. From behind us a sob was stifled and a small voice said, 'Wait up a sec, lads.'

I turned back first. I'd never done anything like it before, but Crollis had opened himself up in a way none of us were equipped to resist or bear. I made a fist and aimed for his bloated, tear-streaked cheek.

After that, Crollis stopped hanging around with us. He started taking increasingly circuitous routes to and from the chipper, in part to avoid us, in part to simply kill off the hour. On the rare occasion he encountered us coming the other way along Dunvale's main street or crossing the Mule bridge, he would look straight on and through us, the wind blowing into his round stoical face, a parcel of soggy chips tucked under his elbow, like a jilted lover with his bouquet of wilted flowers.

I hadn't seen Crollis in half a decade, since our grad ball I'd guess, but he looked the same, more or less, standing before me alive and apparently intact. He was still short, more stocky now than pudgy, with the same sandy brown hair maintained in a severe part, which even after the crash was only marginally disarranged. The lenses of his glasses were fractured, the frames hanging at an angle from his face. His cheeks were purple. 'How are you?' was all I could manage after a pause. 'I mean, are you okay? Matty—'

'...Tweedy,' Crollis smiled, then looked back dreamily at the car he'd just extricated himself from. The snow was still coming down.

'I think Duckie's dead,' he sighed. 'I think Duckie may very well be dead.'

Duckie, it turned out, was Duckie Reape, a low-level drug dealer from 'back the park,' 'the park' being the bad side of town, 'back the park' being the baddest part of that prenominate patch. Duckie wasn't dead, but he had shattered his collarbone, cracked three ribs and lacerated his liver, and was strewn, unconscious, over the Pinto's steering wheel, his shaven scalp studded with shards of glass from the cracked windshield.

A member of staff up at The Pearl had had the wherewithal to make the emergency call. A firetruck, ambulance and a couple of squad cars duly arrived. Crollis and Duckie were strapped to orange stretchers and carted off to the county hospital. One of the guards took a brief statement from me as another three improvised a cordon. My mother, who was late to the bus stop because my youngest brother had vomited up his dinner just as she was about to come collect me, slowed the Corolla to a crawl as I recounted what happened. In the kitchen I inched through two beers and related the event for a second time to my da. I went to bed on a mattress on the floor of my childhood bedroom—commandeered in my absence by the next eldest—fighting off a curious sense of elation.

I bumped into Crollis a week later in Luther's, the night before I was due to head back to Dublin. I was hunched in a corner by the pool tables, out in the renovated and expanded back room. Nobody was playing, and the rows of unblemished green baize shone like miniature municipal parks. An AC/DC *Best of* clanged and chugged at a low volume from the jukebox. D was propped on a stool beside me, another of the seasonally returned college diaspora. We were watching the regulars our age come in, trying to figure out who we knew, feigning vagueness. I sipped my pint and danced around an admission of my patent relief at how far and how easily we had drifted from these poor, landlocked, timelocked fuckers. D, I'm sure, was thinking the exact same.

'These boys never change. Although they've got fatter, some of them,' D said finally.

Crollis just appeared at my elbow. He had a pint in one hand, a bird gathered up in the other.

'Well, lads. This is Imelda—Imelda, Scott, D. Scott here was at the crash. He saw poor Duckie fuck his mam's '96 into that brick wall.'

'Yez were lucky. You were lucky,' I corrected myself. As far as I knew, Duckie was still in traction in Castlebar General, but rumours had already begun to circulate regarding his level of sobriety the night of the crash. This wasn't something I was going to ask Crollis about, nor how he had ended up becoming affiliated with such a character. He said nothing to my remark, just looked from me to D, sucking with steady vehemence at the head of his Guinness, like it was a wound filled with venom.

'You don't look too bad anyway,' D said.

'Ah, I'm walking y'know. I learned my lesson though.'

'He has,' Imelda leaned in queasily. Her breath was weathered and tangy, perfumed with nicotine, vodka and lime. Two slabs of sapphire had been painted in the hollows above her hazel eyes. I was trying to place her, and with a twinge of erotic nostalgia recalled her (or someone very much like her) at fifteen or sixteen, in braces and pigtails, one of the many convent girls that took my bus home, on whom I might once have nursed a crush.

A moment passed, but neither she nor Crollis felt the need to elaborate on the nature of the lesson evidently learned. 'Well,' Crollis said finally, looking out over our heads towards the front lounge. The light caught his cheek, the faded burgundy of a bruise. I realised he wasn't wearing his glasses. We ceremonially clinked our pints and Crollis, Imelda in tow, sauntered off.

Later the barman shooed a fresh one in my direction, and when I asked him who bought it, he cocked a thumb towards Crollis. He was standing in a circle of people out by the front of the bar, enmeshed in conversation. When I bought him one back (the barman easing its trembling breadth along the burnished bartop, through a forest of planted and leaning elbows), Crollis, after a polite interval, had another beer dispatched my way. We went at it like that for a while, engaging the barman with those terse nods only bar staff can properly perceive and decode, shuttling drinks back and forth, as if each one were an apology or a refutation, perhaps even a kind of exhortation to the other to stop, to stop, to simply and finally stop existing.

Last Days of the Buffalo

Kevin Barry

An indisputable fact: our towns are sexed. Look around you. It's easy enough to tell one from the other. Foley's town, for example, is most certainly a woman—just take in the salt of her estuarine air—but she's not a notably well-mannered or delicate woman. She is in fact a belligerent old bitch. You wouldn't know what kind of mood you'd find her in. And so he storms out, every afternoon, and slams the door after himself.

He walks the trace of a creek that takes him into countryside. Today the creek is particularly foul, there is either something very rotten in there or something very alive. Foley walks by and sniffs at it but he has no great interest. This is an enormous, distracted, heavy-footed creature we're dealing with. He's jawing on his thoughts. He's remembering the knockdown fights with his father in the street.

These are the dog days of summer. The country feels heavy. There's a lethal amount of growth and he's pollen-sick from it, Foley, the last of August pulses in his throat. He can see across the estuary to the malevolent hills of Clare. Do hills brood, as they say? Oh they sure do. Foley's massive hands are dug into the pockets of his outsized jeans and the hedgerows tremble with birds. Foley's eyes are watery, emotional, a scratched blue, and they follow the caked dry mud of the pathway. Along the verges there are wild flowers—pipewort, harebell, birdsfoot trefoil, grass of Parnassus, all so melodious sounding it would turn your stomach—and they bloom and shimmer for Foley but he won't give them the satisfaction.

His father sang 'Sean South of Garryowen'. His father sang 'Dropkick

Me Jesus'. His father sang 'The Broad Black Brimmer Of The IRA'. A roof-lifting tenor the old fucker had and unquestionably a way with the ladies.

Dogs somewhere, and the bored drone of motorway traffic, distant, like the sound of a dull dream, also chainsaws.

And he walks the trace of the water, Foley, and he comes within the shadow of the cement factory. The grasses and reeds are dusted grey from the factory's discharge. This is the type of country that would redden your eye and Foley knows it all too well. He spent seventeen years at the Texaco out here—it was, for a time, an ideal confluence of beast and task.

At the start, it was just two pumps beside a dirty little kiosk for the till. Midwestern rain hammered down on the plastic roof. Electric fire, a kettle, a crossword and Foley might have been in the womb he was so cosy. He near filled the kiosk. He was prince of the forecourt. He knew the customers by name: the boys from the cement plant, the Raheen businessmen, the odd few locals. Foley was pure gab in those days. He'd talk shock absorbers, chest infections, four-four-two. He'd talk controversial incidents in the small parallelogram the Sunday gone. But word came through and there was quickly great change. Statoil bought out Texaco and the kiosk was bulldozed. An air-conditioned, glass-fronted store went up, with automatic doors and cooler units. Foley found himself with colleagues. The next thing they were squeezing him into a uniform and sticking a bright red hat up top. Then they started fucking about with croissants. Then they put in a flower stall and started selling disposable underwater cameras—the better, presumably, to document the coral reefs of the Shannon. Foley went to the supervisor.

'Come here I want you,' he said.

'Yes?'

'I want to get one thing clear,' he said. 'Just for my own information.'

'Yes?'

'Are we a petrol station? Or are we an amusement arcade?'

'I must say your tone is slightly…'

'Don't mind tone. Are we a supermarket?'

'Now listen…'

'What the fuck are we?' cried Foley. 'Are we Crazy Prices?'

'There's no need for your tone, I find it…'

'I'll give you tone!'

He lunged for him and that was that. Don't come around here no more, they told Foley, and it was the end of the seventeen years.

Foley was six foot five on the morning of his fourteenth birthday and half as wide again. This is the original brick shithouse we're talking about. He was a clown of a child. His father informed him daily he was fit for Fossett's. There wasn't a school jumper could be got in the town to fit him. The best his father could do was a chandler on the Dock Road that stocked a heavy-duty v-neck designed for vast trawlermen sent to face the wrath of the Irish Box. Foley at fourteen wore it to face the Brothers. In cold weather, the rad in the classroom would seize up and to free its workings it needed to be hit a wallop and this became Foley's job. The teacher would roar down in a hoarse, booze-scratched voice:

'Foley! Hit that rad an auld slap, boy. You're good for something anyway, you big eejit.'

And he'd slug across the floor, Foley, and the other boys would do the Jaws music—dah-duh, daaaah-duh, daaaaaaah-duh—and he'd wind up the shoulder, take a swing at the thing with an opened palm and it'd gurgle back to life from the pure shock of force.

Quiet awe would swell in the classroom.

The shovelers call from the reedbeds but they could stand up on tippy-toes and sing Merle Haggard and Foley wouldn't pay the blindest bit of attention. He's thinking about the time he had the fucker down and a knee on his throat and he could have closed that windpipe lively but no, what possessed him but he let the bastard go.

He has been told he should try accentuate the positives. And certainly, it hasn't been Crapsville all the way. He has had small blessings. He has never, for example, had to journey through the regions of romance. That would have been on the rich side. Of course there are sugary men who will croon that love, at length, shines on each and all of us—woo-oooh! woo-oooh!—but no, thanks be to God, love never came next nor near Foley. Not that till he was twenty-six or twenty-seven, and six foot ten in the full of his growth, the big ape, not that he didn't maintain a glimmer of hope: maybe, oh just maybe... This was a young man listening to enough country and western music to believe just about anything. But he never tried to foretell the detail of it. He never tried to picture it actually come true. Was she really going to float down from the starry sky and put in an appearance on O'Connell Street some Saturday? Walk up to the big tank called Foley and tap him on the shoulder? Settle down and raise enormous children? It wasn't going to happen, and it never did, and it was sweet relief to give up on even the notion.

He walks on. There has been an unpromising start to the new season—two draws and a loss—and black squalls cross his brow when he thinks of the remarks that have been made. Do not say the wrong thing about Manchester United in the vicinity of Foley. Then the storm clouds will gather. Then you'd want to leave a wide berth. He wears the number seven jersey that says 'Cantona' on the back. It's the biggest size the mail-order people can do but still a tight fit. See him of an evening, sat on the corner stool, there in the shadows, with the dry-roasted nuts, and the pint glass like a thimble in his hand. It would go through you, if you were unfortunate enough to be in any way soft-natured.

He follows the creek, goes past the factory, and the creek begins to quicken once it rounds the bend that leaves Mungret behind. Ahead of him on the pathway there's a distraction. On the last high bank of the creek there are some boys gathered and as he approaches them he grows wary because he can see the shimmer of their gold in the afternoon sun. They wear streaks in their hair and dress shirts in bright colours. They have alert brows and startled eyes. There are six of them, no, seven, there's eight of them, count, nine? Travellers.

'Story, boss?'

'What's the story, big man?'

'Some size of a creature we've on our hands here, boys. Look it!'

They stand in a half-circle to block the pathway but they keep switching position, they keep dancing around the place, it's as though they're on coals, and their voices have hoarse urgency.

'Where you headed, sir?'

'Are you headed for the hills, I'd say?'

'Come here I wancha? Where do they keep you, do they keep you in a home?'

'What brings you out this way, sir? And what size are you at all, hah? If you don't mind me asking, like. You must be seven foot tall?'

'Tell me this and tell me no more. What size is the man below? The women must think it's Leopardstown.'

'Now listen,' says Foley. 'That's the kind of talk I won't abide.'

'It has a tongue!'

'Ah come here now and go easy. Where do you live, fella? Are you inside in the city? Are the Health Board looking after you?'

They move in closer, and the talk changes to a confiding tone.

'Listen. You'd do us a turn, hey? You see what it is, we're short a few yo-yo for a game of pitch 'n' putt below in Mungret.'

'Pitch 'n' putt my eye,' says Foley. 'You fellas are no more playing pitch 'n' putt.'

'You're calling us liars?'

A leader emerges. He spreads his arms like he's nailed to a cross and he looks to the sky in great noble suffering and he bellows from deep:

'Hold on, boys!'

It should have been obvious who the leader was. His shirt is of the richest purple and his hair is the most vivaciously streaked. His gold shimmers in the sun and he slaps a stick off the ground.

'Hold on, boys. What we're dealing with here is no old fool. You're right, sir. We are having nothing at all to do with the pitch 'n' putt. Truth be known, there is a tragedy we're dealing with. Martin here—the runt—Martin's mother is laid out below in Pallasgreen. Misfortunate Kathleen! God rest her and preserve her and all belongin' to her. And the situation we're after been landed in, through no fault of our own, we're short the few euro to wake her right. So help us out there, boss, will yuh? Martin is in a bad way.'

'I'm bad, sir,' says Martin. 'I am bad now. And I guarantee you there'll be prayers said.'

'Shush now,' says the leader, and again he slaps the stick off the ground, but Foley just smiles.

'Out of my way, gentlemen,' he says. 'I'm going to walk on through.'

The leader slaps the stick again and exhales powerfully through his nose.

'We're not getting through to you, hey? Put your hand in the pocket there and help us out, like.'

They dance around him again, they swap and jostle with each other, they have terrible static in them, but Foley doesn't move, and Foley doesn't speak. The leader comes a step closer.

'Who the fuck do you think you are?'

Foley smiles.

'Look,' he says. 'We're off on a bad footing. Can we not be civilised? Can we not calm ourselves? Look. I'll tell you what. Will you shake my hand?'

The leader smiles. Negotiations have been smoothed. He opens his face to Foley. He is a reasonable person.

'Of course,' he says. 'Of course I'll shake.'

Foley closes his hand softly around the boy's hand then and a cold quiver passes between them. It's the feeling in the hazel switch when it divines water, and it's the feeling that comes at night when a tendon in the calf muscle has a twitched memory of a falling step, and it's there too, somehow, in the great confluence of starlings, when they spiral and twist like smoke in the evening sky. Foley holds the boy's hand and the feeling sustains for a single necessary moment.

'You were born the fourth son in a lay-by outside Tarbert,' he says, 'and you'll die a wet afternoon in the coming May. The way I'm seeing it, a white van will go off the road at a T-junction. A Hitachi, if I'm seeing it right. And I can tell you this much, Bud—it ain't gonna be pretty.'

'What you sayin' to me? What you sayin' to me you fat fuckin' freak?'

The leader shucks his hand free and takes a step back, and the others step back too. Foley, arrogant now, draws a swipe through the air, as though he's swatting flies, and he walks on through. For a while the traveller boys follow and they taunt him from a distance but he knows they will not make the decision.

The creek dwindles to its outflow, and the estuary has an egginess, a pungency. The lethargy of swamp gives way to the slow momentum of the Shannon. From across the water, the hills of Clare look on unimpressed. You would be a long time impressing the hills of Clare. A path branches off from the creek and from here you can follow the river back into town and it's a weary Foley that turns onto the branching. Sweat pours from his armpits and stains the number seven shirt that says 'Cantona' on the back. Oystercatchers work the rocks, most efficiently, and the lapwings are up and gregarious, but Foley doesn't want to know. He limits his thoughts to each step as it falls. His heavy head lifts up now and then to find the town come closer, and still closer.

It is more difficult to look back. At the way Foley Snr would come home in the evening, take off his workboots, slap his fleshy paws together and do the hucklebuck in the middle of the floor. Twist the hips and pout the lips: ladies and gentlemen, a big hand now for the west of Ireland's answer to Mr Jerry Lee Lewis. He'd manhandle the missus. He'd make slurping noises at his supper. He'd bounce the big child on a giant's round knee.

'Is the water on? Have you the water on at all? How am I supposed to get washed?'

'Where you going, Dan?'

'Out! I'm headin' for the plains, Betsy. I'm gonna make me a home where the buffalo roam.'

Later she'd throw plates into the sink with such venom they'd sometimes smash. She'd smoke a fag, have a long chew on the bottom lip, then get on the phone and give out yards to a sister. Later she'd roar at the child and her brow would crease up as she plotted an escape. Later she'd weep like a crone because she was lonely. Dan'd be down the Dock Road, doing a string of bars and getting knee tremblers off fast girls in behind chip shop walls. Dan'd be going to dances out Drumkeen and swinging them around the floor, making husky promises beneath the candy-coloured lights. He'd sing 'Are The Stars Out Tonight?' as he walked them home. He'd play Russian hands and Roman fingers.

But the way it happens sometimes is that pain becomes a feed for courage, a nutrient for it: when pain drips steadily, it can embolden. She worked up the courage and left him, and left the young fella, too. It was a Halloween she went—Foley was dunking for apples. He was near enough reared, and he was the head off his father. She moved to Tipp town, or was it Nenagh, and fell in love with a bookmaker there and died a happy woman. The lights went down on the Foley boys. They didn't get on. Violent confrontation was the daily norm and the worst of it, like in a country song, was when Foley started to win.

*

He hits the suburbs of the town and takes the Dock Road into the heart of the place. He steps away from the water and enters the grid of her streets, and his mood improves. He has before him the consolations of routine. He will go to the shade and dampness of the basement flat, where mushrooms have been known to grow from the walls. It is not much of a place to lay your head, no, but it is near the bar where they are used to him sitting in the shadows. (Lou Ferrigno, they call him there, but not to his face.) It's near the place he buys the fish. It's where he braces himself for the afternoon walks by the creek, and we all have our creeks. He will put eight mackerel in two frying pans and fourteen potatoes in the big pot. He will turn on the television and go to page two-two-zero of the text to check on the football news. He will sigh then and stretch and take the keys of the car from the saucer by the door. At eight o'clock, precisely, he will turn the key in the ignition, put his size seventeen to the floor and he'll switch on the two-way radio.

'Fourteen here, base. I'm just heading out.'

And Alice at the base will say:

'Okay, Tom, can you pick up in Thomondgate for me? The Gateway Bar. Sullivan.'

'Uh-oh. What kind of a way is he?'

'He doesn't sound great, Tommy.'

'I'll see what I can do.'

And for eight hours he'll pinball all over town—Thomondgate and Kileely, Prospect, Monaleen—and there is a sort of calmness in this and calmness accrues, it builds up like equity.

Maybe Foley will pick you up some night. You've had a few at The Gateway, or you've taken a hammering at the dogs, or you're stood in the rain with bags at your feet outside the Roxboro Tesco.

'Busy tonight?'

'Ah, we're kept going, you know? It's busy enough for a Monday.'

And you'll take him for an easeful man, a serene giant at the wheel of a gliding Nissan. Sometimes even the briefest touch is enough: you hand him the fare and he hands back the change and you feel the strange quiver, its coldness. He can tell precisely, in each case but his own. The town will lie flat and desolate and open to all weathers.

Fifty Year Winter

Sara Baume

My father's dog and my mother die within three weeks of one another.

It's the worst winter in fifty years, so the TV meteorologists say, with their scales and charts and artificial cheer. On the slender balcony of my fifth floor apartment in the financial district, there's a granite birdbath with three granite sparrows stuck to the rim, and every morning I chisel around the circumference and turn the ice out onto the decking, and the frozen discs rise several storeys without melting, into a toytown of twinkling tower blocks. In the absence of scales or charts or cheer, I measure the winter in frozen birdbaths.

My mother dies first, on the second Sunday in Advent, although the dying had started way back in the summer, with a lance of strange pain above the left collarbone, like 'the jab of a tin whistle' is how she described it to the oncologist, as casually as though jabbing people is what tin whistles had been invented for. It jabbed her first beneath the fuchsia hedge on a blistering afternoon in July, and it doesn't end its jabbing until the middle of a winter so cold that the leaves of the fuchsia turn to mush and the hedge is frost-damaged beyond repair.

My mother's last breath is small and sharp, and it makes a sound like the squeak of a strangled tin whistle, as though she'd always known it would.

I'm standing on the cracked concrete slabs of the graveyard, between the polished granite and Celtic crosses, the plastic bouquets and green glass gravel, when I realise it will be just my father and me for Christmas this year, and the dog, of course, who is not dead yet.

All my life my parents have lived in a village on the south coast called Ballycotton. In summertime, tourists clog up the narrow main drag and queue along the pier to cast their feathers to the mackerel and slog the cliff trail in single file. But, in winter, Ballycotton is restored to the locals. The ice-cream man disables his jingle, the windowsills of the Bay View Hotel fill up with dead bluebottles, and blackberry briars engorge the cliff trail.

The house where I was raised is crowded with bookshelves and worm-eaten furniture. The radiators are rusted, the wallpaper is dappled by mould, the sofas chuff clouds of dust whenever you sit on them and the books fall apart at their sellotaped spines as you pick them up. My father is tall and craggy-featured and has a particular affection for damaged things. He likes the stuff he owns to arrive second-hand and already possessed of personal history, the more tragic the better. Much of his stuff has its home in the garden, from sun dials and swan-shaped flowerpots to every fabric and shape of birdbath. On the front lawn facing the sea, there's even a commemorative bench that bears the name of a man my father has never known.

His dog, adopted through some animal welfare society, is stumpy and coarse-coated. Even though I've always found him to be sweet-natured, there's something about my father's dog that irks me, something disconcertingly human-like in the way he is forever raising himself up, resting his front paws on chairs and knees and cupboards to perch neatly upright atop his two back legs. Sometimes when he yawns he makes a noise which sounds like he is saying the words 'I am', like he is beginning a sentence he never finishes. The dog is called 'Fella', and I've never yet remembered to ask whether the name came about because my father saw the disconcerting streak of human in him too.

It's the worst winter in fifty years, so cold the back road to Ballycotton turns to a channel of black ice overnight and the potholes freeze into mouse skating rinks, solid as clear brick. By the time my mother dies, the tarmac has frozen and thawed so many times that great chunks of road split into rubble and tumble to the ditches. On the morning of her funeral, neighbours trudge over the broken ground to attend the service. They stop in the churchyard and prop themselves against the railings to clap snowflakes from their mittens, to peel socks and unshackle bicycle-chains from around their boots.

'She was such a good woman,' the priest says, having never laid eyes on my mother's face until the night of her wake, until after the undertaker has done a job with his paints and balms and powders, and the face in the coffin looks nothing like my mother anyway.

My father locks Fella in the greenhouse for the reception. He gives him a squeak-toy but we know he will not play with it. Fella never wags his tail or plays. He takes fright at the slightest of sudden noises and cowers whenever he meets a new person, squinting his eyes as though they are about to slap him for no reason at all.

I drive the three hour trip back to Dublin the same night, to the wall-mounted microwave and the bubble-eye goldfish and the recycling bin overflowing with expended tram tickets. I lie on my leather sofa and look around at all the beige-coloured things that constitute the adult life I've built for myself. I say to my goldfish, 'How is it that the gravediggers managed to reach down six feet through the frozen soil?' But he doesn't answer.

I don't go into work the next morning, nor any of the other mornings, even though I know it's the restaurant's busiest time of year, and in the absence of anything meaningful to do, I scrape the black gunge from between the shower tiles, I throw out the dead plants on the balcony, I reunite all my loose socks and roll them into married balls. I phone my father every day to check how he's doing and make half-hearted plans for December 25th. I try my best to make my voice sound higher than my spirits.

'How are you doing?' I say. But my father never really answers.

'Fella misses her,' he says instead, 'he waits outside the bathroom door, he doesn't understand why she never comes out.'

On the last posting day before Christmas, I find my P45 in the downstairs letterbox. I carry it back upstairs and dangle it over the recycling bin, and then I feed it to the expended tram tickets.

It's the coldest winter in fifty years, so cold snowmen everywhere live far beyond their expected life-spans, standing staunch against each fresh fall, their twig-arms only a little droopy, their coal-eyes only a little sunk. Without scales or charts or cheer, I measure the winter in snowmen.

On Christmas Eve, I pack the car and drive the ice and salt and grit road out of Dublin and down through the midlands, heading south. I try to kill the journey by counting fairy-lighted trees behind front-facing windows, a game I'd played as a child. But most of the road is motorway now and most of the houses that line it are too faraway to make out decorations. As I turn off onto the back road for Ballycotton, it's smudgy dark and beginning to freeze again. For the last several miles, I drive unnecessarily slowly. Bit by bit, the countryside beyond my windscreen dissolves to a mass of rolling shadows beneath a sky full of white flecks, and I realise that in spite of the winter's intense coldness, it hasn't actually snowed in a couple of weeks, since the last time I was home, since the night of my mother's wake. And I think how banal, how predictable it is that it should snow now, on Christmas Eve.

Sitting at opposite ends of the kitchen table, my father and I eat supper together, and it's only once I've mopped the last of the sauce from my plate that I notice Fella is missing, that I feel the vibration of my father's leg twitching through the bockety floorboards. We're talking aimlessly about rain and motorways and Christmas trees and sometimes his sentences trail off, but it isn't exactly as though he has forgotten what he's saying, but as if he's trying very hard to listen for something very quiet without appearing to.

'He just hasn't been right lately,' my father says, 'and this afternoon, he looked to be let out, and so I let him out, and he hasn't been home again since.'

'He knocks,' my father says, 'when he wants to go out, then again when he wants to come back in.' And low down on the back door, I can see where the paintwork has been worn clean by the knocking of Fella's blunted claws.

At half past eleven my father rises from his chair and, in wordless announcement of bedtime, measures milk into a saucepan and spoons powdered chocolate into two mugs. As the surface of the milk is steadily thickening into skin, I look around at my mother's collection of cook books and souvenir fridge magnets, at her mug still tea-stained and hanging from its branch on the mug tree, and the blue loops of her handwriting still scribbled across December on the kitchen calendar. Then I look at Fella's sullied dish beside the pedal bin, his basket of gnawed wicker beneath the stairs. My father leans against the kitchen counter top and together we watch as a tumbleweed of moulted fur gusts past us over the weathered floorboards, caught by the breeze of a misaligned draught snake.

Upstairs, my childhood bedroom is a junk room now. There are neat piles of sealed boxes and then loose piles of things still waiting to be boxed. Interspersed with my chipped knick-knacks and scrolled posters, there are the unfamiliar objects my father has been free to accumulate in the almost-decade since I moved out: a mahogany whatnot, a conked out metronome, a whole assembly of unpainted gnomes.

Lying on the flock mattress of my old bed, wrapped up in the rainbows and Care Bears of a faded duvet, I stay awake all night watching the view from my window, just like I did as a child, every Christmas Eve. Sometimes I'd see an aeroplane and believe its tiny coloured lights were those of an approaching sleigh. But tonight, the sky is utterly empty. There is only the perfect view of the unbending bay, stretching from the roof tiles across the harbour to the anchored trawlers floating in the black gap, to the lighthouse and the open sea.

It's the worst winter in fifty years, so cold fish die in the ponds and sheep lie down and blend into the fields, icicles like crystal stalactites swing from the branches of trees and clank tunelessly in the wind. And this is how I measure it, in dead carp and treeicles.

It's the Christmas the phone rings early in the morning, and I follow my father into the hallway to answer it.

'Yes?' he says into the receiver, 'yes…'

Then he just stands beside the coat rack and nods. My father nods without saying anything, as though the person on the other end of the line can see right down the wires and into the hallway and somehow know that he is nodding. He stands beside my mother's tweed jacket still hanging where she left it on her hook. It even has her brown wool scarf tucked inside the collar, as if her left-behind clothes were sneakily trying to reconfigure themselves back into my mother.

'Thanks for letting me know,' he says after a few minutes, and hangs up.

Then he walks past me and back into the kitchen. He is stooping slightly, almost as though he is carrying a tree trunk slung across the points of his shoulder blades, a great invisible log that is softly forcing him closer and closer to the ground.

'That was Malcolm Harty from the corner,' he says. 'Fella's been found. He's lying on the rocks at the bottom of the cliff, along the trail beneath the place where there's a sheer drop and no fence to close the path in. Malcolm saw him. He ran in a clear line towards the edge, and then straight off, fast, as though he knew exactly where he was going.'

I stand up and rest my hand on my father's sleeve. There on the kitchen floorboards with the soles of our feet to the fissures and furrows and pocks inflicted by child and man and woman and beast across all of my lifetime, between the souvenir fridge magnets and the tumbleweeds of moulted fur, I realise I have not deliberately touched my father since childhood, and suddenly everything about the gesture feels somehow choreographed and strange. And so, I pull away.

Instead I just watch as he steps into his wellington boots and dons his shabby raincoat, as he rummages beneath the sink for a black bin-liner. I just watch as he starts towards the gate through the misting sleet. And there on the concrete steps of the front door, beneath the lintel and its sorry string of unlighted bulbs, I think about how in recent months he has held himself like a man pinned beneath a tree trunk, how it is only since my mother started to die that my father started to stoop.

It's the worst winter in fifty years, so cold all of the rain solidifies to balls or flakes or slush, then smothers the streets and roofs and lawns, so cold that the earth sets like cement and gravediggers everywhere have to thaw the ground with a heated grave blanket before they can attempt to reach six feet deep. It's the worst winter in fifty years, and between the cold hard walls of my soul, it's the winter which feels fifty years long. It's the winter my mother dies and the winter I lose my job and the winter my father comes back up the driveway on Christmas morning carrying a black bin-liner bulging full of dead dog.

And while we should rightly be basting the turkey and peeling the sprouts and listening for the knocking of Fella's small paws against the back door, it's the Christmas my father and I stand outside in a flowerbed in the sleet, chipping a shallow hole through the hard earth at the feet of the commemorative bench, and stopping every now and again to look off away over the unbending view of the bay, to where the lighthouse is pulsing its red beam: a soft flash through the gloom, and ten seconds later, a soft flash again.

Ten seconds and three shovels, without scales or charts or cheer, this is how I measure it.

Grace at the Wall of Death

Maria Behan

'You've got to go in there,' Cal said. 'It was the best thing at the carnival last year.'

The shiny hysteria in his eyes reminded Grace of Hamu, the skydiving pig whose performance had been their first stop that night. Hamu hadn't done much for either of them—in fact, they'd talked about calling the ASPCA—but the Wall of Death clearly had been a transcendent experience for Cal.

'I thought they'd die,' he gasped. 'I thought I'd die. It's violent, it's sick… you'll love it.'

Grace studied the poster for the Wall of Death. Well-muscled hunks—one of them sporting an eye-patch—rode motorcycles up the walls of a ring. Puffs of exhaust curled prettily from the Harleys' tailpipes as the bikes hung parallel to a floor that seemed to sparkle malevolently, awaiting gravity's assistance to pulverise man and machine.

'The freaks you're paying to see aren't long for this world, and chances are they'll take a chunk of the audience with them when they go,' Cal continued. 'It's so awful, it's exquisite. And if this one biker is still in the show, you're in for a treat. He's positively magnificent: not handsome, strictly speaking, and his nose is huge. I don't know if it's his mindless courage or the ciggie dangling from his pouting young lips, but it's a slice of heaven when he rides up the side of the pit towards you, risking your life and his.'

'Okay,' Grace said. 'I'll take a look, just to check out this heartbreaker. But it's your treat—and I sure as hell don't want him aiming that bike at me.'

'That's what you say now,' Cal said, laughing.

The two of them walked over to buy tickets from a well-used blonde selling 'I Survived the Wall of Death' T-shirts. Feeling superior and a bit envious, Grace wondered what the woman had been through to achieve her worn sensuality.

Cal and Grace parted black felt curtains that stank of exhaust and went inside. They climbed a set of stairs and joined a few dozen others who were leaning against a waist-high barrier formed by the top of a pit about 25 feet deep. Its smooth wooden walls were topped with criss-crossed steel cables intended to keep errant bikes from careering into the audience.

A door at the base of the pit opened. Out came a paunchy man with multiple tattoos that looked as if they'd been etched in the jail yard.

'Ladies and dudes, on behalf of the California Hell Riders, I welcome ya to the Wall of Death,' he began. He was wearing leather chaps and his grey hair was tied in Willie Nelson pigtails.

'As you'll soon understand,' he announced, slowly pacing the pit's floor, 'it's impossible for the brave men you're about to see to get health insurance. So we've set up a special fund, based on donations from the audience. And the Hell Riders ain't lazy. If ya hold your one-, five- or hundred-dollar bill over the edge during the finale, they'll come 'n' get it.' The barker indicated a few random spots where audience members might stand at the edge of the pit and proffer money. His wan gestures reminded Grace of a retirement-age stewardess pointing out emergency exits on the fourth shuttle flight of the day.

'And now,' the barker said, his voice rising to convey a morsel of enthusiasm, 'lemme present the desperadoes of the Golden State, the scourge of the Catalinas, the bane of civilised men and women everywhere… the California Hell Riders.'

Grace thought these last words should have been accompanied by an apocalyptic racket as a swarm of Hell Riders rumbled into the pit. Instead, a thin man strode in. He was young, probably around 19, wearing black jeans and a white T-shirt. A blue-and-white gingham bandanna was tied on his head pirate-style.

'Let's hear it for Robby,' the barker tossed over his shoulder as he left the pit. There was a smattering of applause and a wolf whistle, courtesy of Cal.

'That's him,' he whispered. 'That's my Hell Rider.'

Grace didn't say anything to dampen Cal's high spirits as his eyes consumed his Rider, but she wondered how long it would be before they were out of the Wall of Death and she could devour something herself—say, fried dough slathered in maple-flavoured syrup.

Robby bowed, then walked over to a dirt bike half the size of the Harleys in the poster outside. He straddled the bike, turned it on, and gunned the motor. The noise grew louder as he began circling the floor of the pit, deafening as he picked up speed and mounted the wall. For the first time, the audience cheered.

He guided his bike up the side of the wall, four feet, then ten, before settling in at a comfortable height about halfway up the pit.

'It gets good now, Grace,' Cal said. 'You wait and see.'

Robby swung his legs around so both were on one side of the bike. He leaned back on the seat, his feet pointing toward the floor as the bike circled the wall parallel to the ground at fifty miles an hour.

Grace believed that centrifugal force was like religion: one moment of doubt and you're lost, flung into oblivion. Robby, who slowly separated a Marlboro from the pack in his shirtsleeve, clearly had no such fear. He lit the cigarette nonchalantly and the crowd hooted its approval, throwing fresh butts and dollar bills.

Cal nudged her with an elbow.

'When I'm right, I'm right,' he said, grinning.

Turning to check Robby out more carefully, Grace had to admit that was true. She decided Robby looked like a homely version of the young Elvis. The torso under his T-shirt was compact yet impressive and Grace admired his tattoo, a snake slithering across a wiry bicep. He was the type she went for when slumming in her fantasies, though she usually chose an unshaven hero whose sandpaper chin would rub all her soft places raw. Robby's sallow skin was smooth and glistening, as if he'd shaved for the performance—or wasn't old enough to have a beard.

He came back down to earth and two other Hell Riders, the barker and another plump, 40-something ruffian, emerged for a tandem act. As Robby sauntered towards the doorway, Grace pulled a dollar from her pocket. She tried to send it his way, but it fluttered ineffectually to the bottom of the pit.

Despite the imminent doom of the two new riders, who skirted innumerable smash-ups as they rode the Wall, Grace felt unmoved by the proceedings. That changed when Robby returned for the finale.

The bikers cut their motors and the one who doubled as the barker announced, 'Ladies and gents, the three of us will now scale the Wall of Death at the same time. This is where that health insurance comes in handy, so if ya'd be good enough to hold out your bills, we'd be pleased to come up and collect them.'

The three bikers mounted the Wall. None of them seemed to have a set cruising altitude; their paths kept crossing randomly and precariously.

A woman with mascara-matted eyelashes thrust a dollar into Grace's hand. 'Go on, it's a blast,' she said with bullying hilarity, pushing Grace toward the rim of the pit. Grace sheepishly thanked the woman and held the money out.

An eagle sighting a telltale flash in the stream, Robby swooped in her direction. He looked in Grace's eyes, rather than at the dollar or the safety cables. Shit, she thought, he's going to kill us both, but I'll die happy. Robby glanced down shyly for an instant, then locked on Grace once more before spiriting the bill out of her hand with delicate accuracy. She regretted his precision, since it meant their fingers hadn't come into contact.

She was seared by Robby's much-obliged-ma'am courtliness. And impressed that he could convey it riding a dirt bike up a wall and straight into her face at forty miles an hour.

'So are you ready to ride a Hell Rider?' Cal asked as they walked from the fume-choked Wall into the windy September night. She and Cal were practically strutting, their gestures enlarged by horniness and a sense of adventure.

'Jesus, you have a way of cutting to the heart of the matter, don't you?' Grace replied, straightening the elastic that held her strawberry-blonde hair in a pony tail.

'Yes or no?' he persisted.

'I guess I'd give him a spin. I don't even have to ask you.'

'No, you don't,' he said with a grin. 'Shall we cap off this magnificent evening with a night-cap at The Den?'

'It's full of lowlifes,' Grace said.

'We'll fit right in then.'

To reach the exit, Grace and Cal had to thread through a tight row of booths. Plenty of attractions—the Guess-Your-Age Sage, the rifle range, the Crucible of Strength—remained open. The show was leaving town that night, so the carnies were burning up their reserves, flaring up in one last display calculated to pry a few more worn dollars from the fun-stupefied residents of Lima, Ohio.

A vicious-looking youth with a crew cut homed in on Cal.

'Can't let your woman go home empty handed, can you?' he shouted, gesturing towards some stuffed animals lined up behind him.

An array of squashed or elongated faces—a winking piglet, a poodle with heart shaped red eyes—stared out at Cal and Grace. Globs of stray glue marred the beasts' ill-sewn canvas pelts.

'All you have to do is aim the water pistol at the clown's mouth and pop the balloon,' the barker went on, rubbing a zit-ridden chin.

Cal and Grace studied the scene. Three people stood with water guns raised, poised to compete for the dubious trophies. The combatants were two teenagers who looked like they might be a couple and an older man with a port-wine birthmark that pooled from the left corner of his mouth like a cartoon speech-bubble.

'No thanks,' Cal said.

He exchanged glances with Grace and the two of them walked off quickly. 'What's the matter?' the barker shouted after them. 'Isn't she worth it?'

A preserve for second-hand smoke, The Den was loud and packed with meaty men in bent-bill John Deere caps. Some were accompanied by even heftier women who'd topped themselves off with teased meringues of hair.

The most interesting Den denizens were the unaccompanied women who dotted the crowd. They tended to be thinner, with streaky dye jobs, drawn expressions and good legs. These women reminded Grace of the one selling Wall of Death T-shirts. She had probably slept with some or all of the Hell Riders—rutting in buses, trailers and tents from Bean Blossom, Oregon, to Laconia, Pennsylvania.

'Will I look like that in a few years?' Grace asked, pointing to a black-haired 40-year-old whose shoulder blades sliced at the edges of her halter top.

'No such luck, doll,' Cal said with an evil smile. 'You haven't had enough sex.'

They ordered two double Jack Daniels and sat in companionable silence until the liquor sent warm feelers into their bloodstreams.

'I suppose you've had enough sex to achieve blowsy 40-something splendour?' Grace asked.

'I don't want to brag,' Cal said. 'But I'll bet I've been with twice as many men as you have. How many is that, anyway?'

Grace reflected on the trickle of men in her life: Walt, the earnest premature ejaculator she'd dated in college; Stewart, whom she had married in the mistaken belief that spinsterhood would be worse; and Joe, a horny but otherwise unremarkable tension-reliever she'd resorted to after her divorce three years ago.

'Five,' she said.

'Hmm, worse than I thought,' Cal said. 'Make that three times as many men.'

Grace and Cal's bourbon-stoked giggles were interrupted when a middle-aged man banged into the back of their barstools. Sunburned and sandy-haired, he looked like most of the men in the bar, except his baseball cap was on backwards in an inexplicable home-boy flourish.

'Did I hear you correctly?' he said.

'This is a private conversation,' Cal replied, shifting to try to close the man out. 'Just let me ask you one question,' the man continued, pushing his weight forward so his distended belly pressed against Cal's back. 'Are you a goddamn homo?'

He jerked his head and sloshed his drink for emphasis. Rusty yellow liquid, likely a whiskey sour, splashed on Grace's white shorts and bare leg.

She down looked at her lap, then up at Cal. His pupils were huge, his jaw was working, and she could see he was going to erupt. Something— pride, whiskey, the Wall of Death's afterglow—was driving him towards recklessness.

'Why don't you head back to the farm, homey,' Cal said. 'The lady and I would like to be alone.'

'I don't think you want to be alone with no lady,' the man replied. 'Am I more your type?'

'Sorry,' Cal said with a taut smile. 'Maybe another night. I'm too exhausted from drilling your father.'

Grace and the drunk both let out a similar sound, a sort of whoosh. Then there was silence, as everyone—including the drunk himself— waited to see what he'd do in response.

'You, fairy boy, you have no business in here,' he said finally.

'You're right,' Cal said, standing up. He turned to Grace. 'Let's head home and leave these decent folks to swilling beer and vomiting in the urinals,' he announced loudly. 'And that's just the ladies.'

Shit, shit, shit, Grace chanted in her head during the long march to the door. If they made it out, she'd lecture Cal about his technique for winning friends and influencing homophobes.

Ten feet from the exit, Grace felt a hand on her shoulder. She froze.

'So we meet again,' came a syrupy voice behind her. The humid breath propelling it fluttered the hair at the base of her neck. Grace turned around.

'Robby,' was all she could get out.

'I'm afraid you have the advantage,' he said, extending a hand to shake hers.

Finally, they'd touched. She felt the calluses on his fingers, the power of his grip as he gave her hand a squeeze before releasing it.

'No, Robby, I'd say you have the advantage with Grace here,' Cal said.

Christ, she thought, did he ever know when to shut up? Tiny drops of sweat sprung from every one of Grace's pores. She looked back at the drunk, who was glaring in their direction.

'Is that so?' Robby said.

'What?' Grace asked, distracted.

'Do I have the advantage with you?' He looked at her expectantly, then lowered his eyes. It was the same gambit he'd used in the Wall of Death, but this time his gaze trailed down her body.

Grace's sweat and adrenaline began to compete with other, equally urgent, secretions. She couldn't think of anything to say.

'So your name's Grace,' Robby said.

'Yes.'

'Pretty name for a pretty lady.' He offered her a cigarette.

Ignoring Cal's snort, Grace grabbed a Marlboro and accepted ignition from Robby's lighter. It was shaped like a panther's head; when he pulled back the ears, the flame shot out its mouth.

Grace looked back towards the drunk at the bar. He was talking heatedly with three friends and all of them were glaring their way.

'Yes, I'm Grace and I'm pleased to meet you,' she said. She took a long drag on the cigarette. 'But we've got to go.'

'Really? You're leaving?' Robby asked with a stage pout.

'Yeah, sorry, got to fly.' She turned to Cal. 'You ready?'

'Okay, Grace, if you're sure. Or I could head off on my own and you could stay and have another Jack with Robby here.'

'No, I better get you home safe.'

Sitting behind the wheel of her Taurus, Grace felt wrung out. Cal was quiet, too. For the first few miles, all the headlights in the rear-view mirror seemed menacing. Once they got close to Dayton, the tightly packed bungalows started to close in around them and they felt safe.

'Grace?'

'Yeah?'

'What are you thinking?' Cal asked.

'Nothing,' Grace said.

'Come on, talk to me.'

Grace lit another cigarette and cracked the window. 'I couldn't just have sex with him backstage at the Wall of Death or in his smelly trailer or wherever we'd do it, could I?'

Cal didn't say anything.

'Could I?' Grace repeated, her voice climbing towards shrillness.

'Ah, Grace,' Cal sighed. 'You could. I would have.'

'And that's why we're at this particular juncture, isn't it?'

They laughed and Grace started to feel better. Visions of Robby's dirty nails raking down her back were punctured by images of the morning or even the moment after, when she'd feel absurd and alone.

'You and I have to make a pilgrimage,' Cal said as Grace turned the car into his street.

'Like to Lourdes?' Grace asked.

'No, to Coney Island. I went to the sideshow there when I was a kid,' he said, fishing around in his jeans for his keys. 'A guy called the Human Blockhead pounded wooden pegs and nails into his nostrils. There's no blood or anything, and he's so happy doing it, it's an affirmation of life. I think he's still there.'

'Maybe we'll go next summer,' Grace said, pulling into the driveway. The headlights illuminated a gnome with its hand raised in salute, the pride of Cal's lawn ornament collection. 'I'd like to see that.'

Finishing Touch

Claire-Louise Bennett

I think I'm going to throw a little party. A perfectly arranged but low-key soiree. I have so many glasses after all. And it is so nice in here, after all. And there'll be plenty of places for people to sit now that I've brought down the ottoman—and in fact if I came here for a party on the ottoman is exactly where I'd want to sit—I'd want to sit there, on the ottoman. But I suppose I'd arrive a little later on and somebody else would already be sitting upon the ottoman very comfortably, holding a full glass most likely and talking to someone standing up, someone also holding a full glass of wine, and so I would stand with my fingertips upright on a table perhaps, which wouldn't be so bad, and, anyway, people move about, but, all the same, I would not wish to make it very plain just how much I'd like to sit there, on the ottoman—I certainly wouldn't make a beeline for it!—no, I'd have to dawdle in and perch upon any number of places before I'd dare go near it, so that, when finally I did come to sit on the ottoman, it would appear perfectly natural, just as if I'd ended up there with no effort or design at all.

Howsoever, I am not, and never can be, a guest here, though in fact taking up the rugs and changing everything around and putting the glasses in a new place—two new places actually, there are that many glasses—does make it all quite new to me, and I have stood here and there sort of wondering what it was all for, all this rearranging, and it seems to me I must be very determined—it seems to me my mind is quite made up about who's in and who's out. With everything changed and in new places I can say to myself, no one has been here yet, not a soul—and now, I get a chance to choose, all over again—I must be very determined after all, to make things fresh and stay on guard this time. Yes, I get a chance to choose all over again, and so why not make use of such an opportunity in a very delightful way and throw a little party, because it is perfectly clear to me now who I will invite and who will not know a thing about it—until after perhaps, there might be some people who were not invited who might come to know a thing or two about it afterwards.

And that's just fine, that's fine by me. After all, isn't a party a splendid thing not only because of the people there but also because of the people who aren't and who suppose they ought to be? No doubt about it, there'll be a moment, in the bathroom most likely—which will naturally exude an edgeless, living fragrance because of the flowers I picked earlier from the garden—when I feel quite triumphant for having developed the good sense at last to realise that people who are hell-bent upon getting to the bottom of you are not the sort you want around. This is my house—it doesn't have any curtains and half the time half the door is open, that's true. The neighbour's dog comes in, that's true too, and so do flies and bees, and even birds sometimes—but nobody ought to get the wrong idea—nobody ought to just turn up and stick a nose in! I wonder if it'll become wild or whether people will stay in range of tomorrow and leave all of a sudden around midnight. I wonder actually if anyone will ask what the party is for. Because of the summer I'll say. It's because of the summer—this house is very nice in the summer—and that'll be quite evident to anyone who asks. Yes! It's for the summer, I'll say, and that'll take care of it.

And sure enough there'll be martinis and Campari and champagne and bottle after bottle of something lovely from Vinsobres. And beautiful heaps of salad in huge beautiful bowls. Fennel and grapefruit and walnuts and feta cheese and all kinds of spread-eagled leaves basking in oil and vinegar. Because of the summer! Can't you see! No doubt there'll be some people who will be curious and will want to take a look upstairs—and perhaps I won't mind at all but I shan't go with them unless, unless—no, I shan't go with them no matter who they are. Sure, I'll say, over my shoulder, go on up and take a look. Be my guest. And, then, not long after they've come down and made this or that comment, I'll find some reason to go on up there myself—I won't be able to help myself—I'll want to try to see what it is they saw I suppose.

I wonder who out of everyone will sit on the ottoman? Well, if you must know, that is not a spontaneous point of curiosity and I don't wonder really because in fact I already possess a good idea—a clear picture actually—of who will sit upon the ottoman. Oh yes, a lovely picture as clear as can be. And as a matter of fact it might be the case that this vision preceded my fantasies about being a guest here myself and artlessly contriving to sit on the ottoman beneath the mirror—I'd go further and say the vision, the premonition if you will, of who exactly will sit on the ottoman very much instigated my fantasy of doing just the identical thing. What kind of a calamity would it now be if as it turned out the person I have very much in mind does not in fact sit upon the ottoman but leans in the doorway, for example? Just leans against the door frame and prods at the door jamb, actually. Would it appear so very eccentric if I suggested to them that in fact the ottoman is a very nice place to sit? Well of course it would, it would be very eccentric, and my friend, and by the way I don't even have this woman's phone number, would understandably feel a little unnerved that I'd singled her out in this way—in this strangely intimate way. Of course I could devise some kind of game that included everybody and involved me appointing each person a place in the room—that could work—that would work—but it would be stupid, even if they thought it was sort of charming and zany I would know it was absolutely bogus and stupid, and how would I live with myself for the rest of the night after that exactly? Still, despite all that, despite how fraught this can all become, I am quite unperturbed—I'm determined you see, quite determined to host a low-key, but impeccably conceived, soiree.

I don't mind asking people to bring things by the way—and I'm very specific. Gone are the days when I make a lot of work for myself—that might surprise you, it surprises me. I'm very forthright on this matter, which is something people appreciate very much in fact because, naturally, people are short on time and they can't allocate time to trying to work things out like what to bring to other people's parties, it's a minefield, and even if you do have time to give to working such things out the fact is there is always an anxiety that what you finally select to bring is a real clanger. It never is a clanger, not really, but who wants to sit in the back of a cab with a bowl covered with tin foil in their lap wondering if what it contains is going to be met with melodious condescension—who needs any of that? Give people a specific request and they arrive feeling pretty slick and raring to go. Not that the requests are issued in haphazard fashion of course—I know perfectly well who to ask to supply the cheese for example, and who to contribute the bread. It's easy to notice what people enjoy eating, and from there it's reasonable to infer that they'll endeavour to procure the finest examples of whatever comestible treat it is they have cultivated a particular fancy for. And, naturally, there'll be one or two you let off, simply because, gusto notwithstanding, they've never demonstrated any discriminating interest in what they eat. They'll probably rock up with hash and breadsticks, and quite possibly a dim jar of drilled out green olives, and people who stay late will horse into the breadsticks and the following day there'll be shards of breadstick all over the floor, ground to a powder in places, where people have stood on the bigger shards while talking to people they don't usually talk to, or even when dancing about perhaps. I always enjoy the day after in fact. Slowly going over everything from the night before until it's all just so. Everything in its place: awakened, accomplished and vigilant.

As it turned out he came and she didn't. They couldn't get a babysitter you see. He came on his bicycle and his face was incredibly flushed, which he seemed to be enjoying very much. Indeed, it is nice to be flushed, whatever way it happens. I can't recall what he brought with him, which surprises me—I've a feeling it was something that needed to be kept flat because I seem to remember that the minute he came in the door he was anxious to look inside his rucksack. It was a tart, I remember now. That's right, he took a tarte normande from his rucksack and it was perfectly intact—and there was a bottle of Austrian white wine too with a distinctive neck which I put in the fridge right away and I don't think I opened it until much later on—the neck was distinctive you see and I remember putting my hand around it again quite late, it was really chilled, possibly too much. There was lots of wine, more than enough, and I was pleased about that, in addition my friend with tenure brought beer and a bottle of my favourite gin, which was unexpected and very kind because that particular gin is astronomically expensive. Everyone came with something thoughtful in fact and now and then I'd bring some chicken wings out of the kitchen, or one of those pizzas that have such beautifully thin bases some people presume they're home-made, and everyone already knew each other more or less so I could do whatever I liked and didn't have to worry about whether so-and-so was enjoying themselves because anytime I looked around there wasn't anyone who looked left out, but then it's so small in here it would be pretty difficult for anyone to look left out even if they felt it.

For a long time a man sat on the ottoman, I don't remember which man and perhaps it alternated. I just remember jeans and boots, and of course that wasn't at all what I'd had in mind. Quite often I'm terribly disappointed by how things turn out, but that's usually my own fault for the simple reason that I'm too quick to conclude that things have turned out as fully as it is possible for them to turn, when in fact, quite often, they are still on the turn and have some way to go until they have turned out completely. As my friend who lives nearby frequently reminds me, that part hasn't been revealed yet. My fascination was short-lived in any case, perhaps it lasted a fortnight, less, and it was only brought about in the first place by a blouse she wore one day—the collar, to be precise. The way her head was bowed, actually, just above the collar. So that I could see the roots of her hair, which was parted and pulled back. She was flipping through a very thick fashion magazine. One hand flipped through the magazine and the other hand was up near her face—near her chin—near her collar. What must it be like, I thought, to stand there like that, flipping through a fashion magazine? That shows you how determined I was, how utterly determined, to overhaul everything, to convince myself anything at all was possible—and obviously I must have thought that it must feel really terrific, standing there like that, flipping through a fashion magazine, wearing discreet earrings and a diaphanous collar.

Well really, I get so carried away.

The following day I took my time and returned everything gradually. There were lots of crackers and grapes left over, and some nicely slumped cheese. In fact I discovered all sorts of things here and there. Including a small bag of jelly babies on the windowsill. There's bed linen inside the ottoman by the way—some of which I've had for years.

Ten Days Counting Slowly

Jennifer Brady

Day 1

So, this is our holiday resort. And here is the residents' beach upon which a man in Speedos wrestles with a sun-lounger. The legs will not unfold. He thumps belly down on it anyway, his arms disappearing into the sand. He may well be the man who chooses me later, despite the woman. And here she is, all holiday breasts and wet hair, which she now wrings out on the sole of his foot, for a bit of laugh, and what fun! He reaches behind him, a rump of fat gathers on his left shoulder blade as he latches a claw firmly around her ankle. She shrieks, straddles his buttocks, bastes his skin with oil. There are muffled noises of approval from him, laughter from her. It is all working. It is great. She is making, as most women do, a *job* of making the holiday a success.

And a success it will be. I am that woman.

I am that woman with that man.

Day 2

And I assume most couples are like this?

'Michael? This is *my* side of the bedroom. This (point, point) is *yours*.'

'I hear ya, I hear ya,' he says to the remote control.

He is looking for whatever channel it is on Latin TV that has the horny goodies for free.

'Damn thing,' he says.

The screen will not produce a picture. The screen will only produce options that say 'no signal' when he presses the buttons.

Or, most couples are like this when the gleam of unification has gone. MichaelandClaire, doubleincomenokids are back to being Michael.

And Claire.

Five years ago, I did not shudder at the sight of his athlete's foot cream. Now, I feel discomfort to the point of nausea at the open display of remedies that allude to rot of any kind.

Day 3

Because smearing the good germs on decay doesn't work, although you dish out the relationship syrup nevertheless. *Yes hon, no hon*. It's all such a giveaway, that goo. And what about the infidelities? Not only the ones we know about, but those that we don't? Did he, or did he not, have sex with the teenager in the yeehah hat in Greece while I was laid up with an infectious eyelid? Did I, or did I not, have a liaison with the safari guide in South Africa while Michael was rigid in a hotel room with an ingrown hair? And these are only the holiday detours.

Okay. Say we wanted a baby, abandoned the thought of marriage, skipped ahead to the main issue of *progeny*. Would I catch this wilting bull at the perfect moment of my own fading cycle? Because maybe something happens to a man when he has passed a certain age. He becomes, perhaps, a 'nicer guy', flaccid even. I myself am pushing forty and feel the pipe and slippers draw near, the eggs running out.

I sit on the balcony with a bottle of airport tequila, a shot glass for decency, and the more I drink, the more I am able to sum it up: some couples will never end up together, and out of those, the ones who have no courage, end up 'ending-up-not-together,' slowly. Riddle-me-ree. This could last a lifetime.

The sun nods its fat head over whatever ocean I am looking at, and wouldn't you know it? The world is rosier on the other side, just as it was rosier here when I was back home. From the bedroom, Michael shouts, *I get it, it's fucking analogue.*

Day 4

The bedroom is his. The balcony is mine, and it is here where I sit and drink and watch. He sprawls on the fault line of the mattress zipper snapping like a dog at aeroplane treats he throws in the air for the challenge. He tucked these secret eats away in a candid moment of foresight, despite the queasiness he experienced on the flight. In between munches his mouth falls ajar.

This is it. This is what the end is. Looking at someone you love and seeing someone you hate. He sucks his breath in and redirects a belch through his nose. He yawns and scratches his balls. His hand rests on his penis.

The thought of taking it in my mouth.

Yet, that I will do at some stage before the ten days are up. I turn my attention to the beach and what do I see? Another couple, of course. Too happy to bear. Or maybe not? This time, the man sits on the edge of the jetty. The woman sits behind him, her legs taut and spread in a V, her toes skyward, agonisingly graceful. This is the way a dancer sits, as if moments of repose are, and should be, a ballet exercise. The man might be skimming stones, if the beach was of that ilk, but it is not. As it is, he imagines the leapfrog of his aim, and his hand is slightly closed on a non-existent pebble, his wrist twitching rhythmically. From behind they are a monster-match of collusiveness. But up close who knows? They may not be not touching at all.

Day 5

Even a fight would be better than this. Then, thank God, there is one. It starts on a walk to some remote, but touristy village in the baking heat where he sweats and complains of an itchy arse crack. I complain about him complaining, although I myself have an itch in a compromising spot that I do not whine about. Then we get lost. It is his fault, of course, but then he tells me it is my fault. Stupid women. You can't trust them with a map. And you can't! We row over the map with such volatile and irreconcilable opinions that he jumps on a bus alone, and I sit in a café that is playing *No Woman No Cry*. When I return to the apartment the row continues. I wallop him across the head, he thumps me in the chest and the force of it lands me on the floor, proving to the team of women in my head that all men are wankers. They are, aren't they? It is in that spot we finally 'do the deed' with the relief that the argument has spared us. It has spared us the pretence of genuine desire and it has proven that at least the muscle of sado-masochism can be flexed when you simply cannot go through it any other way.

Now we are free to get on with our books, TV, drink, thoughts.

From my balcony I watch the sun go down. At my right foot lies the cause of the disagreement earlier—the map. There are bald patches on the streets and coastlines are eroded where the print has rubbed off.

Day 6 (morning)

Michael is in his nut-huggers wrestling with a sun-lounger. The legs will not open. He flops down on it anyway. I wring my hair out onto the sole of his foot. He reaches behind him, and latches his hand around my ankle so tightly I suck in my breath with pain.

Michael!

Just give us some oil will you?

Fuck you.

I sit on him and rub the sun lotion in, dragging my nails down his back as hard as I can. Red tracks appear where the nubbles of his spine are at their highest. A barman arrives with our cocktails, winking at me as he sets them down on the little sun table.

Day 6 (evening)

Michael sleeps in the apartment. It is a bad dose of sunstroke, we believe. I sit at the bar—rather, I sit in the sickly whiff of pineapples and coconuts, slashed and juiced for the cocktails that will be the excuse for my behaviour later. The barman picks up a bell beside a dish of quartered limes and rings it. Holidaymakers appear from nowhere, and make their way, Pavlovian style, towards the bar.

'Happy Hour,' he explains to me with a companionable smile, as if we are already lovers.

I watch him twirl spirits in the air: gin, tequila, vodka. His talents please him. I can tell by the efficient way he eyes it all up, this crescent-shaped bar, his world. I will not know him long enough to despise all of this. When he smiles I see that his left canine tooth, through neglect or genetic misfortune, is cornflake coloured. No tooth—or a big manky gap—would be better than this. But, I will never have to live with this glitch, so it is forgiven as I order my two-for-the-price-of-one cocktails, no ice.

*

Day 6 (late evening)

It is over (or nearly) with Michael.

This is what I tell the barman anyway. It is the only way to remain decent if this infidelity is to happen. Unfortunately, with barmen, you have to wait till their shift is over before you can nail it.

'Nuther-one-bites-the-dust,' I say, just loud enough to be heard. I will ham up the drunkenness, get some sympathy, bring him in.

'Oh come on, lady,' he has the American twinge to his accent that non-English speakers pick up from TV. He could be from Sweden, Mexico or Israel, 'You seemed pretty happy earlier.'

This is a backfire.

'If you knew what I put up with there,' and for a few seconds I am genuinely melancholic, for now it makes perfect sense to me: I am turning into a whore if I do not find the courage to get out. That is all that is stopping me from getting married to someone I might actually love, and having two children.

'He seemed okay to me.'

The barman is on Michael's side? This is not what I expected, no sly glint of an ally here. My blood turns nasty.

'Walk a mile in my shoes.' I make sure that the tone is full of self-pity. My world is a mess and I don't care anymore if I have crossed the line between flirting and drowning (my sorrows, that is).

'Walk a mile in *theirs*.'

'Sorry?'

'Do you ever think it might be you?'

I do not know what to make of this. Yet, I feel a grudging admiration for whatever woman he loves.

'Listen, amigo, stick to what you know,' I say, pointing at my glass.

He twirls the bottles in the air. One of them falls with a smash to the ground. I have made him nervous then. I have spoiled his little show. Good. There is a cheer from the customers. Now see him stoop to clear up the spillage. I lean over the bar to watch. He looks up at me. He is no longer smiling.

Still Day 6

Last orders. I tell the by-now-unfriendly barman why I will not have sex with him.

'S'not because your tooth, s'because…'

'My tooth?'

'S yellow.' I smile over the salted rim of the margarita glass.

He shakes his head in disbelief.

'I'm not looking for sex. Not from you anyway.' He says this under his breath, but I hear it.

'Of course you are. Don't all barmen work in these package joints for sex? It has to be the *only* perk of the job?' I drain the glass. I am an arsehole and I don't care any more who knows about it.

'That's rough, lady.' He pours alcohol into a metal cocktail shaker. Shakes and pushes a fresh cocktail towards me. 'On the house,' he tells me.

I've had four cocktails by now. Two Pina Coladas, two Margaritas and now this, another one. A fifth is too much, but, fuck it, I must sustain inebriation to justify my actions. I gulp the drink down, crunching the ice cubes on my teeth without flinching.

Day 6 (even later)

And I would like to say that he had the integrity, or that I did, but we are human after all, and I climb the stairs with an aching vagina, actually stinging with new wounds, *torn,* as is the way when you are not ready, or not really interested. That's two rips in the last two days.

The TV is still on when I walk into the apartment and judging from the romping on it, the unsavoury channel has been located at last. But he sleeps, and like most men, he sleeps like a child. There is something I cannot resist about a sleeping man and I touch his face and kiss his forehead and whisper so many sorries that I am beheaded with grief and consider the balcony, but it is only two floors up, no good. Instead, I stand on it and confront the stars and the moon, really look at them, and the barman's words come back to me.

Ever think it could be you?

There is a warm breeze out, certainly no need for a cardigan, yet a shiver moves through my body and washes up in my teeth with an unexpected chatter. I pull the doors shut and go to bed finding comfort in the triangle-shaped space around Michael's bulk.

*

Day 6, no, Day 7

Three or four in the morning. Every muscle, every joint aches. I am aware that Michael is not beside me. Is it over then? Has he already gone? I lever myself out of the bed, fall, pick myself up and feel my way in the dark, down the split-level floor on my hands and knees until I reach what I think is the sofa, and instead feel Michael on the sofa. I pat my hand gently on what must be his jaw or chin, because I can feel his stubble and a stab of regret nags me, as if I will only ever feel this in my dreams from now on.

'Are you okay?' I say.

'Not me. You.'

'What?'

'You stink.'

Just when I am thinking I deserve that comment, I realise he means it, literally. The stench of my own wind smacks me in the nose. It fills the apartment. My stomach is leaden, as if I've swallowed a sack of mauled copper coins. I heave myself back to bed and lie on it, breathing carefully through my nose. The mosquito net smells too much like washing powder, the perfume off it is hideous. I can hear it too. The mosquito. Is it *in* the net then? The small of my back feels like there is a plank of wood jammed in it and it is splitting in two. I pull myself from the bed. My buttocks ache. I am going to throw up. No, the other. What's it going to be?

Both.

I swap from toilet, to sink, to toilet, knickers in limbo around my knees. I go back through my mind rewinding details of every morsel that I have eaten to see what did it. My throat clicks as I remember the cocktails, the ice cubes, slightly smelly, as they were crunched up in my mouth. I had even thanked that barman. Anytime, he had smiled. And it occurs to me I thanked him for the sex too, just like that. *Anytime.*

Day 8

I sleep all day. On and off. Another night passes. I am like a slab in the bed.

Day 9

I feel good again and strangely not even hungry. Michael is already up.

He looks shattered. I remember that he must not have slept much in the past few days. I put my hand on his arm and rub the hairs there, thinking at the same time: this is the arm I know, the arm I am used to, thank God for this arm.

'Listen,' I say.

'I know,' he cuts me short, 'we keep avoiding it.'

Day 10

We are wishing the beach goodbye before the coach picks us up for the airport and already, when I turn my head to the apartment block, I can see the cleaners on the balcony making the place ready for the next couple who will watch TV, fight, pummel each other to the brink of rape, drink and laugh too—because we enjoyed it, now that we are leaving, at least that is what we will tell ourselves when we get back home. But before we start revising it, we must have this moment of solitude to ourselves and I don't want to see any part of Michael's face, not even his profile, in case I recognise the agonies that might be inching their way towards the thin line of his mouth. So, I sit behind him with my legs stretched out in a V so I can embrace him clinically.

Silence. His hand is slightly closed on a non-existent pebble, his wrist twitches now and again, and now his hand moves sideways and rests on my shin. What is he thinking of? The son he could have? The one-bed apartment he will purchase in the commuter belt if we break up and need to sell the house? Nothing?

I tilt my face downwards into the small space of air between his back, my chest, and try to feel it, *what* it is between us, if there is anything. And there is something all right, but it is muffled, sort of stagnant, something not good, not bad, just banked and dry, something you imagine could only exist in the space between the two panes of glass on a double-glazed window. You'd have more trouble crossing that space than the sea before us, which is a desolation already too big to contemplate. But it is gone for now, whatever the moment of courage was the day before. Nothing has been said, yet, and if you put a spin on it, *courage* might mean the other: staying together, and there is still a chance that we can make it, yes, there is still the possibility that we have made it. Again.

Danny

Lucy Sweeney Byrne

Lucy is sitting on a flaking, purple chair outside the cultishly popular health food café in her local town, half-listening to a theory on how to live one's life well ('the simple things!') that her father has already expounded in detail the day before, and the day before that, when she gets the text from Aisling; Danny has tried to commit suicide. She's only there because her father offered to pay for lunch, and she finds it difficult to turn down offers that are free, especially if they pertain to food, or sex. This was, naturally, just food.

Lucy finds eating with her father unpleasant, because they've already said all of the things they have to say to one another, and new things aren't occurring quickly enough to sustain further conversation. Or, they've said all of the things they're capable of saying as father and daughter, which is about .001% of the things they hold. Still, she does find him easier to talk to than most people. She also finds it unpleasant because her father eats with great haste, as though at any moment he expects a bell to ring and his plate to be swept away. He only ever uses one piece of cutlery, the fork, and when he tries to scoop up the last scraps, he knocks food off the side of his plate, which makes her want to reach across the table and slap his munching face.

It's Lucy's fault that she and her father live together. She's twenty-five, and refuses to accept adulthood in any responsible, fiscal capacity. Because doing so looks, from her admittedly ignorant perspective, shit. She works little, and not well; much like the way she exercises, or plans for the future. She makes enough money to not die, and to drink wine on Fridays (supermarket wine).

Her father is talking. 'It's important, to be happy, I think, to wake up every day with something you're looking forward to, some kind of treat...'

Lucy watches him as he scans the seating area for people he knows. He loves chatting to people, though he pretends to hate it because she does and he feels obliged to be more like her. Lucy regrets that she makes him feel this way. Sometimes she treats him as though he's an imbecile. And he's not. There are simply things she wouldn't discuss with her father. He is a staunchly logical and literal man. She'd never discuss her thoughts on contemporary art or philosophy, or attempt to describe the conceptual framework of the novel she's working on. He'd think it was contemptible bullshit. And he'd probably be right, which is another reason she wouldn't discuss it with him.

'You need to have balance in life, you see. It's important to work, I think, to have worked hard, for your sense of worth, for your little reward at the end of the day. For it to feel *earned*...'

Lucy's father is a drummer and to him everything has a rhythm, which can be worked out, if you just take a moment and listen properly. He's aware of the existence of metaphors and symbolism and subtleties, but dismisses them as the refuges of the weak and pretentious. He sees this as a stance shared by comic greats such as Woody Allen and Larry David; denouncers of all things excessively heartfelt and hifalutin. She thinks he's mistaken. But there'd be no point arguing. And, besides, winning for Lucy (because she naturally assumes she'd win) would really be a loss. She does love her father, and so wants to help maintain some of his self-protective walls. She believes this is what we do for our loved ones: fortify their delusions.

Unfortunately for her, Lucy can't help but share her father's loves, and his dismissive attitude to the wishy-washy world of art and the expression of *feelings*, and so she is a torn-up, Frankenstein's monster of a person, filled with immiscible contradictions and self-loathing. She goes to poetry readings in basements in the city, and scoffs and yearns in equal proportions until her insides feel like curdled milk. Afterwards, in small low-lit bars, she listens to painters and writers discuss the nature of artistic inspiration, and feels a contorted, knotty despair; a reaction to her intense desire to both contribute earnestly to the discussion and simultaneously beat them up and take their lunch money. A sort of socio-creative masochism. But as this seems to be how all great artists are posthumously described by their biographers ('conflicted'), Lucy hopes this means she has a fantastic novel lurking inside her.

'You can be just as happy with a small thing as a big thing, in life, you realise. A good cup of coffee can be as good as a holiday, if you just look at things the right way…'

For Lucy, conversation with her father is like walking through a minefield they both know well. They're in no real danger; they can choose whether to misstep or not, and sometimes she deliberately does so, just to see the dazzling fireworks of guts when it all blows up. Lucy supposes that this is what is referred to as being close to someone. So close that their muted nasal breathing becomes a constant irritation, like Chinese water torture.

As they sit in the sun over their freshly emptied plates (alas), and Lucy's father wisely sermonises, nodding in agreement with himself, she interrupts, to tell him the news she's just received: that a friend from her younger years—Daniel, do you remember Daniel? He would have been at the house a few times?—has tried to commit suicide. He's in a coma, in a hospital, somewhere on the outskirts of Boston.

But then, of course, Lucy's father wouldn't remember Danny. All of those pimply, hunched male friends were just a blur to him, to be treated with distrust. Potential defilers of his daughter and robbers of his DVDs and CDs, filing past with their heads down, up to Lucy's bedroom to drink and smoke weed and talk loudly about Tarantino films or the sound quality of vinyl until last bus-time.

His immediate reaction is to be annoyed that Lucy was looking at her phone, but because of the gravity of the news, he checks himself. 'God, that's terrible.' 'Yes, it is.' She reads the text aloud, processing:

Hey, so I've bad news. Danny tried to kill himself. He's in a coma, water damage 2 his brain or something. This is all coming from Sarah thru Jen, so bit vague. Apparently he fell off a bridge!? So awful :(

Fell off a bridge? Even after opening with the shocker of it being a suicide attempt—people love telling shocking news as a rule, Lucy thinks, as long as it isn't their own—Aisling still chose to use the word fell. Too real to say jumped, maybe. Or were they—his friends and family, his girlfriend Sarah—holding out hope that it had been an accident? That he'd wandered onto a bridge and stumbled off, Laurel-and-Hardy style?

Lucy's father lets out a 'how terrible' sighing sound and sits back in his chair. He rubs his mouth with one hand, while the other hand cups the first hand's elbow, which she recognises as the pose he unconsciously adopts when faced with something serious, and wishes to convey an appropriate physical reaction. 'God. I can't believe it,' Lucy says. Although really she can and does believe it.

Lucy finds herself wishing she'd kept in closer contact with Danny. She attempts, furrowing her brow slightly, to conjure up her already faded memories of him. Sessions, parties, cinema trips. Bus rides, swigging cans, shouting and singing down the back, on the way to gigs or nightclubs in the city. His dark brown eyes and sallow skin. His love of drugs, and his unwillingness to ever concede a point, no matter how clearly wrong he was. When they were fifteen, sixteen, Danny had been the guy they could always be sure would do the dare. One night he'd gone to the nearby petrol station totally naked and bought chewing gum. That had blown their minds.

Now that Lucy thinks about it though, there was definitely a sadness to him. Those black eyes, always up for anything, could be unnerving to be around, especially towards the end of a night. But maybe she's inventing that now; making a poetry of him, based entirely on this attempted suicide. Maybe that 'sadness' was just evidence of the fact that he was always, *always* high—or just bored, or preoccupied. Maybe he was just hungry. But then, he has now tried to commit suicide. He's in hospital with water damage to his brain. So he probably was sad and maybe you could see it. Maybe, Lucy reckons, it's just that if you see a sadness in the dark depths of someone, it's unlikely you'll tell them. Or even give it that much thought.

Lucy and Danny were never that close, but he'd been good friends with her ex. They'd been in a mediocre post-punk band together. Danny played bass. Lucy had always thought he was good-looking, if not especially bright. And besides, he was shorter than her. Now Lucy wishes she'd been closer to him. She regrets not having taken some opportunity to kiss him. In the corner of a party someone had thrown because their parents were away for the night, or down the fields in summer, away from the light of the bonfire. But why? She'd never considered it before, so why now? Why does she suddenly regret they weren't closer? So that she could have helped him? Somehow prevented this? Talked him down from that bridge over the phone? Lucy has never been the type to do that anyway.

It's not that she wouldn't care, she reassures herself. She just wouldn't know what to say. It'd be so real, like live TV, she'd have no time to think of the right answers. Besides, she is not the person anyone would call. Except maybe her father, but he is far too practical to lend much thought to suicide. To Lucy, the sudden image of her father standing on a bridge considering the murky depths below is so absurd that she smiles, in spite of herself. She looks at him absent-mindedly as he scrolls through his phone, pretending to check for work emails but actually perusing Facebook. There is a line of white foam from his cappuccino in his moustache. This gives her satisfaction and she says nothing.

Lucy wonders if she wishes she'd been closer to Danny, so that she could be more directly involved in what is an undeniably intriguing occurence? The thought makes her uncomfortable. She shifts in her seat. Danny, by falling off that bridge, has inserted himself as a violent interruption into the flow of unremarkable events that Lucy's life is turning out to be. He has done a real thing. A significant thing. It's something all of their mutual friends will remember now, forever. 'I think it was when I was in the last year of my Masters, yeah, living in Edinburgh, the year Danny, off a bridge wasn't it…?'; 'Well I remember I was in the changing rooms in Topshop, uhuh, the one at the top of Grafton Street, when I got the text about Danny…' Lucy would love to do something all of their mutual friends remembered.

Lucy overhears a woman seated behind her tell her huband it's going to rain soon. Her husband grunts. Lucy imagines he might be reading a newspaper. The woman pauses, and then says in an ominous tone that she can smell it coming. Lucy shifts in her seat and folds her arms. Sure enough, at that moment shadows fall across the café's outdoor seating area and she hears the first droplets land, spattering the grey cement between the tables. The woman says, 'Ha, look now, told you!' and her husband says nothing. Lucy's father contracts his body, hunching his shoulders slightly and scrunching his nose. He is ready to go, but awaits her cue.

Lucy sits still. Although she is keen not to become cold or wet, she feels obliged to take a moment to think about Danny. She feels it would be indecent to get going too soon. It's probably already odd, she realises, that she hasn't even cried a bit. She tries very hard to think about him. To really consider the boy she knew. Danny, with whom she danced in stuffy, crowded living-rooms, talked with on train platforms and played basketball with on the courts behind their old primary school. She tries to picture him now, lying unconscious, on a lung machine (that breathing thing, whatever on earth it's called), with water swilling around his brain. A tiny creature in a sterile hospital room in the wide-open, sprawling United States of America. But she can't get to him. She is sitting here with her father outside this café growing cold and Danny is off somewhere, far away, and she can't get anywhere near him.

She watches the speckle-feathered thrushes fight for the last crumbs of scone on the table next to hers. The tanned, dark-haired waitress bustles over to gather up the plates and cups, shooing the birds with her dishcloth. Lucy watches her father as he attempts to catch the waitress's eye. He leans forward and back, trying to enter her line of vision, hand poised to wave. He has been shamelessly flirting with her for over three months now, and she has resorted to pretending not to see him, or responding in her native Spanish, feigning confusion. She escapes inside, and he wilts slightly, before resignedly turning back to the table.

Lucy can't imagine Danny doing it. Actually stepping off, falling through air. She wonders what it felt like. She could never ask him. She wonders how they got him out of the water. She wonders who found him and how they got word to his family. Would they be flying over to him? Would he definitely recover? Would he have brain damage? Would Sarah stay with him, if he does? Lucy breathes heavily in and out through her nose, frustrated by the lack of information given in Aisling's text. She frowns as she scrolls down through it again. No, nothing more.

She tries again to reach for Danny. She closes her eyes and pictures his physical body. His chest rising up and down, each of the thick, dark hairs of his eyebrows. She wonders if his skin would feel cool or warm, were she to lay her hand on his arm, his cheek? She wonders would they have washed his body? Would someone have lifted and sponged his heavy limbs or run their soapy fingers back and forth through his hair? Or would he still smell like the river?

But Lucy can't seem to concentrate hard enough on any of it. He slips away from her and is replaced by the rain, the cold, the taste of coffee in her mouth. She knows it happened, but feels nothing to correspond with the knowledge. The fact just sits there in her mind, a lump of nothing. If she were shown a photograph of Danny, maybe. Or if she could listen to his mother or his girlfriend Sarah talk about him. Could see them tearing up. Then the reality of the image, their emotion, would surely seep into her. Lucy doesn't consider herself unfeeling. She reads poetry. She cries at sad films and Trócaire adverts. Recently she'd sobbed watching a television show about mistreated dogs. Her father had rushed into the living-room, afraid something terrible had happened.

But now, nothing. To Lucy, Danny's just a notion. She feels no more than she would feel were he a stranger she'd read about in the newspaper, or a story heard on the radio. She checks inside herself, has a feel around, but there's nothing there, no matter how much she wills it. She'd love to be moved by this. She would give anything to be shedding tears, to require comfort, and to actually mean it. This is exactly the sensation Lucy undergoes when she watches the news and sees images of death and carnage in foreign places. A strange sudden awareness of the lack of any feelings where there surely ought to be some. The sensation makes her feel a little nauseous and she unintentionally puts her hand to her stomach. Her father glances at her. He probably thinks it's grief.

'I can't believe someone actually went and did it,' is all she manages to say into the pause, as her father fidgets, growing restless, thinking of the next thing to be done in his day, but not wanting to be too hastily unfeeling. 'Yeah. It just goes to show, people…'

And he's off again, full throttle on a tirade of platitudes. Lucy recedes back into her own thoughts, picking up her cup and knocking back the last dregs of her coffee, nodding at moments when she senses a pause requiring affirmation. When he has finally finished imparting wisdom, Lucy—as a conclusive statement which works sufficiently well to mask that she wasn't listening—says, 'It's all just too terrible to think about,' to which he agrees, nodding, 'Yes, yes.' Wise words all round.

There's a moment of silent respect. They linger, half gone already, thinking of the evening ahead. Large drops are falling regularly now, sploshing on the purple table and leaving dark round stains across her father's shoulders. An old man who had been sitting at a table near theirs sighs theatrically, picks up his mug and walks inside, holding his folded newspaper over his head. He gives Lucy an eyebrow arch and smile, as though to say, 'Typical rain, aye?' Lucy looks past him. She wonders what she should do about Danny. Send a card to the hospital? *Hi Danny, heard you fell off a bridge, hope you're feeling better, and that the weather is nice in Boston, xox.* A sad animal with a bandage on its head. *Get Well Soon!* Probably not.

She breathes deeply through her nose and sits up straight. Time to go. Her father is off to pick up a six-pack of Guinness before meeting a few friends to jam. They are hoping to stage a gig in the town hall: songs from the eighties, with all profits going to a charity. They haven't decided which charity yet, but Lucy's father is leaning towards cancer. As well as drumming in the band, he's been asked to sing a few songs, and so has been practising around the house, slapping his hands on the armrests along with the music or humming under his breath.

Lucy had intended to return to the library after lunch to keep 'researching her novel', which seems to involve a lot of online reading about atemporality and Taylor Swift's childhood. That morning she had typed 'Lena Dunham success how' into Google. But she quickly allows herself the excuse of this upsetting news to go home and watch a film curled up on the couch instead. She reasons that even if she doesn't, on the surface, feel upset about Danny, deep down this has no doubt affected her greatly, and so she ought to take the time to sit with it and 'mind herself'.

That night Lucy sits idling on the couch while the end credits of *The Odd Couple* roll up the television screen. She has completely forgotten about Danny. She texts Aisling:

Hey gurrrl, we should defo get brunch in town on Sun after Sat night. We cud go 2 the Rumbelly, sure it's jst around the cornr frm K8's place!x

Just as it sends, a text comes through from her father:

Hey Lu, told the lads wat hapend to ur friend. We thought it might be gud to do the gig 2 raise money for him? Wat u think? Hope u'r ok, it's very hard. Luv dad, x.

Anxiety rises in Lucy's stomach. She had completely forgotten. Her father had been talking about Danny, and making plans to help, and she'd been thinking about the weekend. She worries that Aisling will get her text and be disgusted at how she can think about something as trivial as brunch when their childhood friend lies fighting for his life all alone across the Atlantic. Lucy feels ashamed. She starts concentrating as hard as she can on Danny, out of guilt, as punishment. As she's rinsing out her teacup and returning the biscuit jar to the shelf and brushing her teeth and pissing and washing her hands and face, she tries again to picture him. She wonders if he's bruised, or if anything is broken, or if, from the outside, he simply looks like he's sleeping.

As she cleans her retainer, she wonders again why Danny did it. What was going through his head? What was the last straw, for him? Was someone rude to him on a train? Did he have a fight with Sarah? Did he get short-changed for his groceries? Or had it been growing in him, slowly, all these years? She wonders if there's anything she could have done differently, anything a bit nicer she could've said. Then she thinks how egotistical it is of her to think she could've made any difference at all, and she sighs, pointedly. She pauses. Why can't she feel anything *real* about this? What's wrong with her? She looks in the mirror forlornly, but it's no use. No tears come.

He must have felt so alone. He probably pictured Ireland and allowed himself to see all his old friends here having a great time without him. Like people in a Swedish insurance ad or something. Which isn't the case. People are just mildly unhappy everywhere, Lucy thinks. Geography doesn't make a difference. Although, of course, it can make things worse, if you're somewhere war-torn or disease-ridden or something. But when it comes to melancholia, she imagines one place is as good as the next.

She wonders if Danny had been drinking. Lucy thinks that if she ever tries to commit suicide, she will definitely have been drinking. Did he think about how they'd react? The 'folks back home'. As he was walking to the bridge, or planning it in bed the night before, lying awake in the dark, slightly too hot in the close, Boston summer—did it cross his mind? What did he think they'd feel, all of them back here? Did he think it would make a difference? Lucy composes a reply to her father, saying yes she's okay, just shook up, finding it tough, but that the gig sounds great.

She resolves, as she presses the send button, to be heavily involved, to do lots of fundraising, to really be at the forefront in helping Danny. She pictures herself on a picket line with her fist raised, shouting passionately. She is wrapped up in gloves and a scarf and there is a poster of Danny's face strapped to the barrier before her. She will become his champion and will make sure he gets all the help he needs to get better. People will wonder at her generosity and Danny's mother will personally thank her, grasping both of Lucy's hands, tears welling in her eyes. Maybe, afterwards, she could even write a book about it.

Also, she resolves she will be kinder to her father from now on. He is a good person. She's too hard on him. Maybe he is wise, and she's the imbecile. She will buy him lunch next time. She will listen when he speaks. Then, as she is shutting the hall door, Lucy receives Aisling's reply:

Eeeh YES, sounds brill. Also, what'r u wearin Sat? Can't tel how dressy to go, stressin bout it all day… PS Just 8 an entire bag of jelly snakes :/

Deep Fat

Colin Corrigan

What's this?

Billy stood in the doorway staring down at the kitchen table. Marge placed a glass of water next to his plate as the kids scrambled onto their chairs.

Fish fingers and chips, said Edie, who was eleven and loved answering questions.

Billy sat sideways on his seat. He picked up a dry, skinny chip and looked at it.

Mam says we're not allowed have proper chips until you get a job again, said Dara, who was thirteen. Marge sat down opposite Billy to her plate of steamed broccoli and carrots.

These are proper chips.

Billy bit the end off the fry in his hand. It tasted like... no, it didn't have a taste.

Use your knife and fork, said Marge.

Don't talk with your mouth full.

The kids looked at Marge, then Billy. He dragged his legs under the table and shook salt onto his plate for twenty seconds, then vinegar. He picked up his cutlery and sliced a corner off a fish finger. He chewed, and swallowed, and put the fork down on his plate. He reached for the Chef red sauce and squeezed it over his chips. The bottle sputtered and rasped.

There's more in the press, said Marge.

Billy stood and went to the cupboard. Inside was a litre bottle of Kandee. He closed the door and sat back at the table. As he ate, he counted in his mind all the reasons why he used to love Fridays.

The graphic was big, blue and red: there were fourteen days of the January transfer window remaining. David Beckham might be moving to Spurs after all. Billy squirmed in his armchair as he tried to reach the itchy spot between his shoulder blades.

Marge walked into the room, dressed in shorts and a running vest with matching head and wrist bands.

I'm going for a run, she said.

Okay. See you later.

Why don't you come with me?

He laughed.

I'm serious. The fresh air will do you good.

I'm grand here, thanks.

She caught her ankle in her hand and held it tight against her arse, reaching out at the air with her other hand to keep her balance.

We can just walk, if you like.

Maybe next time.

She jogged on the spot, looking down at him. She stretched her other thigh, kicked out her leg, and did three star jumps. The dishes rattled in the dresser. He turned his attention back to the telly. He heard the front door close, and saw her run past the front window. The ads came on: Guinness, Renault, Dustin Hoffman selling that new Sky channel.

Up in the attic, behind boxes of Christmas decorations and video tapes, Billy found the deep fat fryer. He tried to wipe off the dust but it was stuck solid to the dried-in grease. They'd got the fryer as a wedding present from someone, and they'd used it a bit when the kids were younger, but Billy hadn't seen the thing in years. He hauled it down to the kitchen and put it on the counter.

He boiled water and scrubbed away as much of the greasy scum as he could. He peeled a few potatoes and chopped them into thick chunks. He found half-empty bottles of vegetable oil and Flora, which together almost filled the fryer, and he plugged it in and waited until the red light went off. He poured the chips into the wire basket and lowered them into the oil. They sizzled loudly. He smiled.

Every few minutes he spooned out a chip to check on its colour.

They took ages to cook. Eventually, when they looked to be about the right shade of golden brown, he lifted out the basket and spilled the chips into a big bowl. That's when he heard the front door bang, and Marge walked into the kitchen.

What are you doing?

I've made chips.

She wiped her finger along the oil-spattered worktop.

I can see that.

He raised the bowl to her face. She looked like she couldn't decide whether to laugh or not. He raised the bowl another inch, and she picked one out and bit into it. Her face scrunched up like a felt puppet, and she turned away from him. He put the bowl down and tried one himself.

It was crispy on the outside, but still hard in the middle. He gagged, but forced his jaw to keep chewing. A bitter oily taste swilled around the raw, soapy lumps of potato. Bile surged up his throat and he rushed to the sink and spat into the basin.

When he turned around, wiping his mouth with the back of his wrist, Marge stood looking at him, an empty oil bottle in each hand.

Billy didn't have a clue how the best chips in the world came to be cooked in Ireland by Italians, but no chip he'd ever eaten from a place that wasn't called something like Luigi's or Borza had even come close. They must, he reasoned, have some secret recipe, a method handed down from one generation of immigrants to the next.

Why don't you google it?

Dara was tapping away on the computer in the corner of the living room. Billy leaned over the back of his chair.

Like they're going to put stuff like that on the internet.

Within five minutes, Dara had told him that the chippers parboiled their spuds before frying them, and that they used lard instead of vegetable oil; that parboiling meant half-cooking the chips in boiling water before they were fried; and that lard wasn't available in Irish supermarkets anymore, but could be found in the Polish stores. Billy clapped his son on the back of his head.

And is there one of them shops near here?

*

That night, Billy lay in bed with his eyes open. Once he got the lard, he thought, there would be no stopping him. Next he would move on to onion rings. He liked the ones that were whole slices of onion, so that they were actually more like discs than rings. He wondered what the Italians made their batter out of. He thought he remembered hearing that they put beer in it. That would be an excuse to open a can before six o'clock. He smiled. After he had mastered the onion rings, he would move on to fish. Cod, or haddock maybe. Fish was good for you. And battered fish was delicious. Then he was walking home from his office on a Friday evening. He could feel the weekend like a warm breeze behind his back, and he stopped into Ezio's. The place was packed: people, like him, just out of work; a gang of student types; a pair of twelve-year-old girls. The insides of the windows were all steamed up. When it was Billy's turn to order, the Italian man behind the counter smiled at him in recognition, like they were old friends. Billy wondered if this was Ezio himself. He watched the other lads working in the background.

The skinny guy shovelled chips from one metal tank to the next, and they landed with a satisfying thunk. The fat fella poured another plastic bucket of chips into the oil, and they sizzled: whoosh! At last Billy's food was ready. Ezio winked as he handed him his change.

Billy walked out into the lamplit fridge of an evening. He tried a chip first. It was thick and soft, with just the right level of crispiness. The coarse salt bit, the special brown vinegar kicked. This, he thought, is how it's done. He moved on to the fish. The crunchy batter melded perfectly with the juicy white flesh of the haddock. Wonderful. He wolfed down the whole fillet before returning to the chips. He made an effort to eat them slowly, one by one, to savour them. Then Marge rolled over in her sleep and knocked the bag into the road. A bus gusted by and its wheels smushed the chips into the tarmac. Marge jogged along after it. He called her name, but she didn't turn around. She kept on running away.

Twelve days of the transfer window to go. David Beckham's move to Spurs was definitely not going ahead, though he might train with the team for a few weeks. Marge came into the room with her free weights and perched on the arm of the couch. She began working her left biceps. Billy glanced across at her.

I'll look after dinner tonight, if you like?

She looked at him.

You can put your feet up for once, he said.

What's brought this on?

Ah, nothing.

She looked at him.

You're going to get that fryer out again, aren't you?

Billy turned back to the telly. Marge kept looking at him.

They'll be much better this time, he said.

Oh yeah?

Dara found out how to do them properly.

Dara's thirteen. He can barely burn toast.

It was on the internet. It's all about the lard, apparently.

Lard?

You can get it in the Polish shops.

Marge moved on to her right biceps.

With the money you're wasting on your experiments we could all eat out at the Shelbourne.

They'll be much better this time, he said.

I'm doing pork chops and vegetables tonight, she said. Feel free to help me if you want to.

Billy shook his head and stared at the telly. The ads came on: Guinness, Renault, Dustin Hoffman selling that new Sky channel.

At half past four, Marge went out for her run. Billy watched her go past the front window, jumped up out of his armchair, and rushed to the kitchen. Then he paused and took a deep breath. He had to be careful. It was important to get this right. He poured the oil from his first attempt down the sink, and replaced it with the six blocks of lard Dara'd got for him. He took the printed list of instructions from his pocket, and smoothed the paper out on the worktop. He chopped up the last few potatoes and dropped them in a big pot of boiling water. The kids came home and he sent them upstairs to do their homework, but they wouldn't go. They kept watching him from the kitchen doorway. He told them they could play their Wii if they wanted, so long as they were quiet, and he shut them into the living room. Ten minutes had already gone by, and he drained the chips from the water.

He put them in the fryer at two hundred degrees, and set the countdown timer on his phone to twenty minutes. He got the pork chops out of the fridge and put them under the grill—chops were just like rashers, he reckoned, except they'd take a bit longer to cook. He set the table for four, making sure the knives were on the right side, forks on the left. He turned the chops. He put the oven on at low heat and stuck in four plates to warm. His phone went off, and he turned the fryer up to 210° for another two minutes, to add that final crispiness. Shaking off the grease, he spilled them into a big dish lined with kitchen paper, and patted them dry. He took the chops off the grill and put one on each plate from the oven. He turned back to the chips, added salt and loads of vinegar and let the fumes waft up his nose.

Then Marge came home. He met her at the kitchen door.

I know you're going to want to kill me, but I swear it'll be worth it.

She looked at him.

I've done the pork chops too, he said.

When was the last time you saw me eat chips, Billy?

That's just because of your diet or whatever.

It's not a diet, it's a fitness plan.

One plate of chips won't kill you. Come on, they're getting cold.

He leaned into the hall and shouted to the kids that dinner was ready. Then he began to serve the chips from the dish onto each plate. Marge gripped him by the elbow and pulled him over to the sink. Air bubbles were gurgling up through a thick coagulated pool of oil around the drain.

Shite, said Billy.

Marge looked at him.

I'll sort it out after, he said. Let's just sit down and eat.

Now he took Marge by the elbow and led her to the table. The kids were already in their chairs, looking up at him with their mouths open. He made a crescent of chips next to each chop and brought the plates to the table, then took his own seat.

Alright, he said. Dig in.

They sat looking at him. He laughed.

I'll be the guinea pig, so, he said, and he picked up his cutlery. His fork penetrated the chip easily, and his knife slid through exactly as it should. He blew the steam away and folded his lips around the fork, pulling the chip clear of its prongs. His jaw moved up and down as his teeth ground through the potato. His tongue rose and scooped the mush to the back of his mouth, and he swallowed. And then he swallowed again.

It was definitely an improvement, he thought, much better than the last batch. Compared to the last batch, this was far, far better. And yet... he swallowed again... they weren't quite right. A sour aftertaste lingered on his tongue, and a greasy film lined the inside of his cheeks. No, he thought, no. They weren't right.

His family was looking at him. Behind them, black smoke was billowing from the deep fat fryer. He jumped up and rushed over to turn it off. The smoke kept coming. He went to pull out the plug and noticed that the bottom of the net curtain had caught fire. He ripped it off the rail and threw it in the sink. It landed in the pool of oil and orange and yellow flames blazed up from the drain. Marge came running over with the fire blanket. He grabbed it from her and tried to smother the flames. Smoke rose up into his eyes and nostrils and he coughed and choked and turned away. Edie started to cry. Dara stepped towards him and then stopped. Marge stood in the middle of the floor. They were all looking at him.

I just wanted a nice plate of chips, he said.

He pulled the fire blanket out of the sink and flapped it against the smoke still issuing from the fryer. Inside, the lard bubbled and spat. The lard was supposed to make all the difference. His hand was clenched into a fist. He had followed the instructions. They were all looking at him. He had done everything he was supposed to do.

He plunged his fist into the fryer. He heard them scream, Edie, Dara, Marge. He heard the sizzle: whoosh!

Things I See

Mary Costello

Outside my room the wind whistles. It blows down behind our row of houses, past all the bedroom windows and when I try to imagine the other bedrooms and the other husbands and wives inside, I hear my own husband moving about downstairs. He will have finished reading the paper by now and broken up the chunks of coal in the grate. Then he will carry the tray into the kitchen, carefully, with the newspaper folded under his arm. He will wash the mugs and leave them to drain; he will flip up the blind so that the kitchen will be bright in the morning. Finally, he will flick off the socket switches and pick up his bundle of keys. Occasionally, just, he pauses and makes himself a pot of tea to have at the kitchen table, the house silent around him. I know the way he sits, his long legs off to the side, the paper propped against the teapot, or staring into the corner near the back door, pensive. He drinks his tea in large mouthfuls and gives the mug a discreet little lick, a flick of the tongue, to prevent a drip. When I hear his chair scrape the tiles I switch off my lamp and turn over. Don is predictable and safe. Tonight he is making himself that last pot of tea.

There are nights when I want to go down and shadow him and stand behind his chair and touch his shoulder. My pale arms would encircle his neck and I would lean down so that our faces touch. Some nights between waking and sleeping I imagine that I do this but I stand and watch him from the kitchen door and I am aware only of the cold tiles under my bare feet. There is something severe and imperious in Don's bearing that makes me resist. He has a straight back and square shoulders and black black hair. His skin is smooth and clear, without blemish, as if he has many layers of perfect epidermii. Beside him, with my pale skin and fair hair, I am like an insignificant underground animal, looking out at him through weak eyes.

Lucy, my sister, is staying with us for a week. She is sleeping in the next room and when she tosses I hear the headboard knock against the wall. I get up and stand at the window. The light from the kitchen illuminates the back garden and the gravel path down to the shed. When I am away from this house I have to let my mind spill over into this room before I can sleep. I have to reconstruct it in the strange darkness of another room before I can surrender. Its window bears on the old fir trees looming tall and dark beyond the back wall. There is the house and these trees and a patch of sky above and these are my borders. They pen me in and I like this. I cannot bear large vistas, long perspectives, lengthy hopes. When we first came here Don wanted us to take the front room; it is west-facing and sunny and looks onto the street. He likes to hear the sounds of the neighbourhood; he likes to know there are lives going on around us. Some nights he sleeps out there. This evening he told me I was intolerant.

Tonight I long to be alone. I would walk around the carpeted rooms upstairs, straightening curtains, folding clothes, arranging things. I would lie on the bed and inhale Don's scent on the pillow and this contact, this proximity to him, would be enough to make me nervous and excitable, too hopeful. Sometimes when Don and Robin are out and I am alone in the house I am prone to elation, swept up in some vague contentment at the near memory of them. I let myself linger in their afterglow, and then something—a knock on the door, a news item on the TV, the gas boiler firing up outside—will shatter it all. Lately I have become concerned for our future. It is not the fact of growing old, but of growing different. Don gets impatient if I say these things and I see his face change and I know he is thinking, For God's sake, woman, pull yourself together.

I go into the bathroom and the light stings my eyes. I splash water on my face. He will hear my movements now. I rub on cream and massage the skin around my eyes and cheek bones. My eyes are blue, like Lucy's. There are four girls in my family and we all have blue eyes.

I go out on the landing and lean over the banisters and check the line of light under the kitchen door. I pause outside Lucy's door. I imagine her under the bedclothes, the sheet draped over her shoulders, her hair spilling onto the pillow. Lucy is a musician; she plays the cello in an orchestra and this evening she played a Romanian folk dance in our living room. Robin was in her jammies, ready for bed and afterwards she picked up Lucy's bow. Lucy let her turn it over carefully and explained about horsehair and rosin and how string instruments make music and she showed her how to pluck a string. Then she whisked her up into her arms and nuzzled her and breathed in my daughter's apple-scented hair.

'Have you thought about music lessons for her?' she asked me a moment later. 'She could learn piano, or violin. She's old enough, you know.' Before I could reply she brought her face close to Robin's. 'Would you like that, Sweetheart—would you like to play some real *mu-sic*?' Robin giggled and clung to Lucy like a little monkey. They sat on the sofa across from me. A bluebottle came from nowhere and buzzed above my head.

'I don't know,' I said. 'She's already got so much going on. And she's only six.' I watched the bluebottle zigzag drunkenly towards the uplighter and for a second I was charged with worry. Every day insects fly into that lighted corner and land on the halogen bulb and extinguish themselves in a breath.

'Don't leave it too late, Annie. She's got an ear, she's definitely got an ear. I said so to Don today.'

She carried Robin upstairs then and they left a little scent in their wake. It reminded me of the cream roses that clung to the arched trellis in our garden at home. No, it reminded me of Lucy. I think she has always given off this scent, like she's discarding a surfeit of love. I wonder if all that wood and rosin and sheep gut suffocates her scent. I think of her sitting among the other cellists, her bulky instrument between her knees, her hair falling on one side of her face, the bow in her right hand drawing out each long mournful note, the fingers of her left hand pressed on the neck of the instrument or sliding down the fingerboard until I think she will bleed out onto the strings. I watched those hands today as they passed Robin a vase of flowers. She has taught Robin to carry the flowers from room to room as we move.

*

I turn and tiptoe into Robin's room. The lamplight casts a glow on her skin and her breathing is so silent that for a second I am worried and think to hold a tiny mirror to her mouth, the way nurses check the breath of the dying. She is a beautiful child, still and contained and perfect, and so apart from me that sometimes I think she is not mine, no part of me claims her. Don has stayed home and is raising her and she is growing confident. Often at work I pause midway through typing a sentence, suddenly reminded of them, and I imagine them at some part of their day: Don making her lunch, talking to her teacher, clutching her schoolbag and waiting up for her along the footpath. I have an endless set of images I can call on. This evening as I pulled into the drive Don was putting his key in the door. The three of them, Don, Lucy and Robin, had been for a walk. It was windy, they had scarves and gloves on and their cheeks were flushed. Lucy and Robin laughed and waved at me as I pulled in. I sat looking at them all for a moment. Now I have a new image to call on.

If I ever have another child I will claim it—I will look up at Don after the birth and say 'This one's mine.' I have it all planned.

After dinner this evening Don took the cold-water tap off the kitchen sink. He spread newspapers and tools over the floor and cleared the cupboard shelves and stretched in to work on the pipes. He opened the back door and went out and back to the shed several times and cold air blew through the house. After a while there was a gurgle, a gasp, and a rush of water spilled out along the shelf onto the floor. He jumped back and swore. Robin was in the living room watching Nickelodeon and Lucy was practising in the dining room. I had been roaming about the house tidying up, closing curtains, browsing. I had stepped over Don a few times and over the toolbox and spanners and boxes of detergent strewn around him.

'What's up?' I asked finally. His head was in the cupboard. 'What are you at?' I pressed.

'Freeing it up,' he said, and I thought of the journey these three words had to make, bouncing off the base of the sink before ricocheting back out to me. 'Did you not notice how slow it's been lately?'

I leaned against the counter. The cello drifted in from the next room, three or four low-pitched notes, a pause, then the same notes repeated again.

'Wouldn't the plunger have cleared it?' I watched his long strong torso and his shoulders pressed against the bottom shelf. He drew up one leg as he strained to loosen a nut. His brown corduroys were threadbare at the right knee and the sight of this and the thought of his skin underneath made me almost forgive him. The cello paused and then started again and I focused on the notes, and tried to recognise the melody. Lucy favours Schubert; she tells me he is all purity. I have no ear and can scarcely recognise Bach.

'Is that urgent?' I asked.

'Nope.'

'Can't it wait then?'

I imagined his slow blink. Next door Lucy turned a page. I sensed her pause and steady herself before raising her bow again. A single sombre note began to unfurl into the surrounding silence and when I thought it could go on no longer and she really would bleed out of her beautiful hands, it touched the next note and ascended and then descended the octave and I thought this *is* Bach, this is that sublime suite that we listened to over and over in the early months of the pregnancy, and then never again, because Don worried that such melancholy would affect his unborn child.

'Can't you do these jobs during the day, when there's no one here?' I blurted. A new bar had begun and the music began to climb, to envelop, again.

He reversed out of the cupboard and threw the spanner in the box. 'What the hell is needling you this evening?'

'Shh. Keep your voice down. Please.'

It was Bach, and I strove to catch each note and draw out the title while I still could, before it closed in.

He began to gather up the tools and throw them in the toolbox. 'Jesus, we have to live.' I stood there half-listening. The music began to fade until only the last merciful note lingered. I can recognise the signs, the narrowing of his eyes as he speaks, the sourness of his mouth when he's hurt and abhorred and can no longer stand me, and when the music stopped I longed to stop too, and gaze at him until something flickered within and his eyes met mine and we found each other again.

He leaned towards me then and spoke in a low tight voice. 'What's wrong with you, Ann? Why're you so fucking intolerant?'

He slumped against the sink and stared hard at me and I looked out at the darkness beyond the window. I heard Lucy's attempt to muffle our anger with the shuffle of her sheet music and cello and stand. I longed for her to start up again, send out a body of sound that would enrapture, and then I wondered if he had heard it, if it had reached him under the sink all this time, and if he'd remembered or recognised or recalled it. *What was that piece,* I longed to ask him, *that sonata that Lucy played just now, the one we once loved, you and I?*

I thought of them, Lucy, Don and Robin at the front door earlier. They had all been laughing. Who had said something funny? Robin is sallow like her father, with long dark hair, and some strands had blown loose from her scarf. Don was laughing too but when he saw my car he averted his eyes and singled out the key in his bundle. There was a look on his face. I have seen that look before. It is a dark downcast look and when he looked away this evening perhaps he was remembering another day, the day that I was remembering too.

Robin was newly born and Lucy, having just finished college, came to stay for a few weeks, to relieve us at times with Robin. I had wanted a child for a long time and now, when I recall them, I think those early days were lived in a strange surreal haze. At night, sleepless, I would turn and look at Don in the warmth of the lamplight, his dark features made patient and silent by sleep, and I would want to preserve us— Don, Robin and me—forever in the present then, in that beautiful amber glow.

I had gone into the city that day and wandered about the parks and the streets, watching my happy face slide from window to window. Light-headed, euphoric, I bought cigarettes and sat outside a café and watched people's faces and felt a surge of hope. An old couple came out with a tray and sat down, hardly speaking but content. Young girls crowded around tables, flicking their long hair and chatting to boys. I lit a cigarette and bit off half of the chocolate that came with my coffee, saving the rest for later, to disguise the cigarette smoke on my breath. I had not smoked for years and the deep draw spiked my lungs and the surge of nicotine quickened my heartbeat and made my fingers tremble and I closed my eyes and relished the pure intoxication of it all.

Suddenly I was startled by a pigeon brushing my arm and landing at my feet. It fluttered and hopped on one leg and then I saw the damaged foot. There remained only one misshapen toe and its nail, ingrown, coiled tightly around the leg, swollen, sore, unusable. I met the pigeon's round, black empty eye and thought of the word *derelict* and it seemed like the saddest word I had ever encountered. Two more pigeons landed close by and pecked at crumbs. And then a gust of wind—tight against the street—blew in and tossed napkins and paper cups and wrappers from the tables. My chocolate, half-eaten in its gold-foil wrapper, blew to the ground. My pigeon hopped over and pecked at it and I smiled at his good fortune and then, in panic, thought that Don would now smell the cigarette when I got home. I checked my watch and remembered Robin and her tiny clenched fists and her moist eyelids, and wondered why I had ever left her. I went to rise and a terrible racket of flapping wings and screeching started up at my feet. The others had come after the chocolate. They had cornered my lame pigeon. 'Shoo, Shoo,' I called at them. I waved my arms and tried to rise again but with my shaking hands and my clamorous heart and the terrible screeching of pigeons, I fell back into the chair.

Later I fled the city, trembling, and drove fast towards the suburbs, with Robin on my mind and a sinking feeling that I might not see her again.

At the front door I reached into my pocket but found no key. I looked in the living-room window. Robin was asleep in her Moses basket. She was there, safe, and she was mine.

I walked around to the back of the house. The old fir trees were pressed flat against the sky and everything was still. The neighbourhood was silent and the birds and the dogs and the children's street play were all absent, or that is how I remember it, as if all living creatures had sensed danger and fled, as they do on high Himalayan or Alpine ground before an avalanche. The back door is half glass and Don had his back to me. I raised my hand to knock on the glass and then I saw Lucy, in front of him, wedged up against the counter. He stood over her, leaning into her, with an arm on each side of her and his palms flat on the counter. He was spread-eagled; he had her cornered. Her body and face were hidden from me; her hands moved on his shoulders, and then her fingers touched his neck, and her legs in jeans emerged from between his. I looked at the back of his head, at his thick black hair, his square shoulders. He was wearing a check shirt I had given him at Christmas, and his dark brown corduroy trousers. He moved his hips and his thighs, grinding her, and I thought: she is too small for him, he will crush her. But I underestimate Lucy.

And then he stopped moving and tilted his head, as if hearing something. He turned his face to the right and I slid back. All he would have caught was a shadow, like a bird's, crossing the back door. I walked lightly around to the front and sat in the car. Later I rang the doorbell and pretended to search for something in the boot. And things started to come out and move again. A jeep drove into the cul-de-sac and a child yelped and cycled his tricycle along the footpath. An alarm went off at the other end of the street. Finally Don opened the door.

'I forgot my keys,' I explained quickly. He looked at me, that too calm look.

'You should have come around the back. Robin might have woken with the bell.'

'Did she sleep the whole time?' I asked, and we looked at each other for a terrible moment and neither one of us heard his reply.

Now I hear his movements below and I become anxious. He is locking the back door. I have a sense of being in both places now—there, below with him, and here in the bed. My heart is thumping and I am far from sleep.

And then suddenly I am exhausted from the effort of tracking him. My bed is too warm, too familiar, like a sickbed. I am agitated, and I twist and turn and lie horizontally and try to use up all the space and I remember a childhood illness, a fever, and my mother's voice in the darkened room, saving me. And now I want Don here, I want the memory of him here. I want him beside me so that I can find the slope of his body and lie against it. I want him to reach across the wide bed and draw me into his arms. I want him to lay his large hand flat on my belly and press gently and feel desire flood through me. I want to be silent and dreamy and view this room, this sky, everything, from a different angle. I want to be shielded by trees and lie against him and sleep.

'You asleep?'

I did not hear him come upstairs. He has stolen upon me before I am prepared. He approaches my side of the bed but stands back a little. His voice is soft and defeated. I open my eyes and look at him. I am waiting for some sound to rise out from inside me, a few words to send across this short distance that will not disappoint. He waits too and a long look passes between us and I know something has spoilt, and then he moves away and starts to undress. And for the first time his undressing, piece by piece, is too intimate and crushing and revealing and I close my eyes and weep.

He goes into the bathroom and closes the door. In a moment I hear the flush and the brushing of teeth. When he returns he walks around the room and hangs up his clothes, unplugs the hairdryer, tidies away his shoes. Now and then he clears his throat in a precise, emphatic way. He does this when we argue—he appears occupied in his task, untouched, untroubled, aloof. He does it to distance me, to reduce me, to make me think, *This is nothing*. And I am left wondering—do I magnify everything, do I magnify the words and the pain and the silences? Do I?

He reaches for a pillow and for a moment I think he is going to take it to the front room. But he gets in beside me. He sits with his arms folded, looking from him, and I can feel the rise and fall of his chest. I wonder at his thoughts, at those clear thoughts I imbue him with, at his certainty, at how he seeks always to unscramble things when all I can summon is silence, and how I will never know him but always imagine him. Outside there is the occasional flapping of our clothes on the clothesline, and then the faint distant whistle of the wind, as if it has moved off and left our house alone tonight. And I think this is how things are, and this is how they will remain, and with every new night and every new wind I know that I am cornered too, and I will remain, because I cannot unlove him.

A Sin to Tell the Naked Truth

Leona Lee Cully

Okay, but you can't stay the night.

As soon as she says this, she feels emptied out. She looks away from him, into the mirror behind the bar.

You've done this before, he says. What other rules have you in mind?

He has a lopsided smile, and deep lines around his toffee-coloured eyes. She gazes at their image in the mirror—he's holding her hand, kissing her neck, whispering French obscenities into her ear. Her torso is twisted slightly away from him, as if she were more interested in the drink behind the bar than him. He has silver strands in his hair, and his eyes are narrowed with lust. She notes that the dull blackness of her hair is unflattering in the harsh light, and that her roots betray the original mousiness of her hair. In order to distract from the roll of fat around her waist she has too many buttons undone on her blouse, revealing her pale, soft cleavage.

He tries to kiss her lips, misses and grazes her cheek. The scratch of his day-old stubble arouses her. She turns away from the mirror, and smiles at him, caresses his bare forearm. His skin is smooth and sallow. A fierce heat flares inside her, then it flickers out again. He is too handsome for her.

Her glass is empty, so she takes a sip of his wine.

That's okay, help yourself, he says.

The smell of the wine revolts her for an instant. Her sense of smell has been heightened these last few days. Chlorine in the water. The ammonia reek from a toddler with a dirty nappy in the lobby. The Sauvignon Blanc they are drinking tastes and smells as sharp as cat's piss. Yet this man, whose smiles she has returned for the last two days, has no smell at all, not even a whiff of aftershave, as if she had conjured him up, a chimera to flatter and cajole her.

The hotel is arranged like a Benthamite prison, with a tiered central panopticon of octagonal floors and balconies. From six flights ups, you could see them kissing at the bar below. Or you could hurl yourself from any balcony, and crash dramatically down onto the grand piano in the lobby. Not that they care who sees them in this city of strangers. Partners, children, duty, carefully packed away in their luggage for this night.

They are both drunk, biding their time now that the chase has all but ended. She stares out of the tinted glass windows of the hotel bar as he continues to describe in English and French what he wants to do to her.

Across the street there are two H&M stores, a Zara and a C&A, and right outside the hotel bar is a section of the Berlin wall owned by the hotel. You get a hammer and chisel, protective goggles, and a porter to help you carve out and buy a piece of history. She was shocked, and then dismayed by her own naivety. Everything is for sale, isn't that the business she has found herself in, mangling language and creating images to instil false desire in people.

He orders her another glass of wine. They compare the souvenirs they have purchased, carefully omitting mention of spouses. Talk of children is allowed, but only for the briefest of moments. They agree that every city, every conference, throws up the same problem of where to find a toy shop.

At lunchtime, in a frantic search for toys on Friedrichstrasse, she had stumbled upon Checkpoint Charlie. Actors in fake army uniforms posed for photographs with tourists. Behind them a replica of the guardhouse of the former Allied-controlled border crossing between East and West Berlin. History emptied out, a vast array of simulacra to be purchased or photographed. Knots of tourists perused the text and photographs on the outdoor exhibition hoardings that attempted to explain the suffering those streets had witnessed. Then they turned away to browse through the stalls selling fake memorabilia of the Cold War. She couldn't bear the travesty of it; she imagined the appalled ghosts of those murdered trying to escape Communism as prisoners once again, tethered to this no man's land of ersatz memory.

On the way back to the hotel, she walked past one familiar chain store after another. She could be in Dublin, or any city in Europe, and only the knick-knacks in her bag (*I Love Berlin* pencils and model Trabant cars) reassured her that she had indeed entered a different city. This old city sewn back together, modernised and homogenised by commerce. She can't summon a feeling for the city: it's too spread out and slippery, it seems to have no centre.

Seized by a fit of rebellious depression, she decided to skip the afternoon session of the conference, the men in identical suits, the handful of women dressed just like her in black skirt, white blouse, and heels. She had no desire to listen to an earnest young woman talking about 'Online Sales and Marketing Solutions'.

For a moment she considered visiting the Topography of Terror, or the Gropius Bau museum. She stayed on Friedrichstrasse, and chose the benumbing pleasures of a department store over the piety of consuming history and culture like fast food. The Galeries Lafayette department store was a panoptic echo of the hotel, a dizzying array of luxuries, concession stands, and floors spiralling upwards to a glass dome. She drifted around the circular halls, eyes watering from the perfume samples that lingered in the air. On the third floor, she stopped to look at swimsuits. She wondered if she could brave the hotel pool, plunge her fleshy body into the same water as the taut, tanned girls she imagined haunted the bowels of the hotel where the spa breathed out its steamy scented oils. No, she couldn't face it. She would treat herself to some new underwear instead.

An *Agent Provocateur* concession stand greeted her at the entrance to the lingerie department. A girl, about eleven years old, with long brown hair, stood in front of a mannequin. She looked puzzled as she examined the female doll, and bit into her ice-cream cone. The girl scrutinised the contraption of black leather belts, studs, and nipple pasties that perverted the doll's plastic nakedness, as if she were eyeing up her future. The girl asked her mother something in German. The mother replied in a no-nonsense tone, examined a frothy pink bra, discarded it, and continued browsing. The little girl followed her mother past hold-up stockings, control underwear, padded bras, and stopped to examine pink plastic hearts in a box. She asked her mother another question. The mother took the box out of her daughter's hand, and moved her along.

She stood in the spot vacated by the girl. She wondered what she might look like in the playsuit, and wondered at its name. A suit for pleasure, the opposite of the working clothes she wore—or just more of the same. She knew it would turn her on to wear it, to play the prostitute, play with the porn stereotypes, take pleasure from violating her own rage at them. Her husband would say, you look like a whore, you're a mother for God's sake, you look ridiculous, and he would laugh at her but still want to fuck her. The same man who sighed with relief the night of their wedding, and said, now we can stop pretending, and the jolt of fear in her when she realised what he meant.

The sales girl laughed at her shock when she told her the playsuit cost three hundred euro.

'Women don't buy these with their own money,' she said and winked. 'You get the man to buy them for you.'

She left empty-handed.

While her colleagues sat through 'Increasing Sales in European Markets', she wandered around the antique stores nestled underneath the S-Bahn track that ran between Friedrichstrasse and Hackescher Market. Fine bone china in delicate flower patterns. Glass decanters, soda spritzers, and ornaments in deep blues, bright reds, mouth-watering yellows, nostalgic greens. Intricate Art Deco jewellery, silver spoons, old photographs, vintage handbags, soft leather gloves, worn top hats, yellowing spats, gabardine coats, and porcelain dolls with horror movie faces. The stolen, lost, pawned, abandoned luxuries of the bourgeoisie. She couldn't help thinking of gold fillings, and children's shoes, piles of clothes, mounds of bodies and bones and skulls.

Nauseated, she left the gloomy shade of Georgenstrasse. Back on the main street, in the glare of the sun, she walked towards the river Spree. She crossed the bridge, and went deeper into East Berlin where graffiti and street art replaced, or at least vied with, brand logos. Artists' studios, trendy bars, and organic restaurants with ubiquitous spray-painted exteriors housed in glamorously decaying buildings. Several barefoot girls walked the streets, bicycles in tow. So many people, so white, so young, some of them Irish, pursuing dreams of art installations, and best-selling novels, and exciting love affairs.

She walked around a courtyard where artists worked and displayed their wares. The sound of welders and hammers and laughter echoed through the network of alleys. She took a picture, on her phone, of an ugly metal sculpture of a mechanical bird-woman. Her own shadow zigzagged across the blurry shot, almost as deformed as the sculpture itself. Overcome with embarrassment at her boring work clothes, and by a fierce longing, she had to leave the place at once.

She went into a bar, ordered a Pilsner, and lit a cigarette. Smoking branded tobacco in a bar gave such a sense of transgression it was pitiful. It was Saturday, late afternoon, and the place was crowded. A Bulgarian boy sat beside her and said hello. They chatted about their countries, and then Berlin, with the ease of foreigners in an anonymous city. He told her about a sort of fake protest march held every summer in Berlin, which is ordered and police-sanctioned, and releases some tension but rarely any violence, and never any change. The police allow large amounts of drugs for personal use. Prostitution is legalised but only for registered, native German women. You pay your fees to the city, and are assigned your spot on the street.

Is all that true, she asked.

Yes, I think so, he said and smiled. He was like a cherub, blonde and dimpled, but with sad eyes. He said he hated his job, and missed his home town in Bulgaria, and the girl he left behind.

Someday I will go back home and live there.

Could you go back there, after this city?

I love my country. And my girl. You gotta have love right? There's no point in living otherwise. You love someone and your country too, don't you?

She felt stricken, deficient in comparison with the boy who could talk so easily of love, and of a country he loved.

I don't love it. Well some things I used to love about it, but I can't remember them now. I never left it because I never had the money, and then I married and had a family when I was quite young.

You fell in love when you were young, he said and smiled.

I don't know if you'd call it that. It was just the thing to do.

You married without love, he asked, as if this were a crime.

You don't understand what it's like. What it was like.

What do you mean, asked the boy.

I never learned to talk about love the way you do. You have to put a good face on things, don't make a fuss, keep bad things hidden. It's like it's a sin to tell the naked truth.

Well, many people are like that, you know, and it is not so great here either. In Berlin there's a lot of racism and unemployment, and poverty, especially amongst Muslims.

*

Hours later she leaves the bar, kisses the cherub goodbye on the cheek after he tries to kiss her on the mouth. Goes back inside the bar to retrieve her children's gifts. Outside again, she deciphers her map, and walks towards Hackescher Market to get a tram back to Friedrichstrasse and her hotel.

Despite her beer-haze, the smell of sewerage overwhelms her. Why is she so sensitive to smell all of a sudden? The light fades quickly, and the streets are suffused with a purple dusk. The weather is abnormally hot and sticky; prelude to a summer storm. She turns a corner, and sees the legally registered prostitutes standing defiantly on the street. They all wear high-heeled boots with platform soles of clear plastic, like portable pedestals. Their working uniform of corsets and bodices and shorts and stockings are so familiar from pop culture that they look like extras from a music video.

There's one girl so young and pretty and distressed looking that, at first, she has to look away from her, but her gaze returns to her again and again. The girl paces back and forth like a trapped animal, her brown hair brushing her shoulders. Her tiny waist is compressed into a lavender basque, and she has thin shoulder blades as graceful as a dancer's. Two men pass her by, and insult her in an unfamiliar, but universal, language. She shakes her head at them, frowns, and continues to pace restlessly.

She turns away from the girl, and walks on. Further down the street, older women strut more confidently, follow men, literally soliciting them. She catches the eye of a woman with blonde dreadlocks, red lips, a red corset, and red boots. The woman stares back at her with hatred in her eyes.

Don't pity me, you bitch. We're all the same, all in this for the money, she imagines her thinking. And she thinks, yes, we're all slaves, working for companies and countries who own us body and soul. They allow us fake decadence, fake rebellions, regulated fun, and the city sells sex like a supermarket. A city cosies up to you and tempts you into shops, cafés, controlled underwear, watered down SubDom playsuits, into gated apartments like prisons, then into suburbs and families, passivity, houses with 2.4 kids, and husbands who dream of fucking schoolgirls, porn queens, your best friend, the babysitter, his best friend—anyone who isn't you, who is new, fresh flesh. She longs for some vague freedom, for the erotic, just to be fucked again, used for a moment, and never mind the reality, the agony of bad sex, soulless sex, wilting awkward dry drunken sex. She longs for the erotic beauty of her fantasies, as she longs for riches, and physical perfection, and ultimate happiness.

She gets a tram back to the hotel, tripping on the steps, sitting down too heavily on the seat. Neon flashing past, the glimmer of blues and pinks on the dark river. Then she is back in the hotel, sitting at the bar with the French man, so drunk, but part of her is aware, watching, bemused. She tucks her bag of souvenirs under her bar-stool.

They work quickly—he holds her hand, she smiles, they chat, and she shows him the presents she bought.

He kisses her briefly.

Are we going back to your room, he asks.

Okay, but you can't stay the night.

They leave the bar, and kiss again in the lift, their bodies reflected to infinity in its mirrors. Her hotel room is cold, air-conditioned into numbness, and he turns the heating up without asking. Turns to her, and strips her of her clothes so quickly she is naked while he is fully clothed. She likes this, but wants to feel his skin, opens the buttons on his shirt, and kisses his hairless chest, gently bites his nipples. He doesn't make a sound but when she opens his trousers she sees he is hard, circumcised, his pubes waxed symmetrically. She hasn't shaved or waxed but he isn't complaining. She talks to him and kisses him but he is silent, unsmiling, and he doesn't want to kiss her back.

His hand is rubbing hard and fast between her legs.

She is dry but aroused, a voyeur of her own experience.

I'm not wet because I've had too much alcohol, and it's all going too fast, she says.

He pushes her back onto the bed, removes his clothes. He is beautiful naked. She wants to drink in the beauty of his body, slowly like a glass of ice-cold champagne.

Slow down, please, I want to look at you, she whispers.

He takes a deep breath, lies on his back, and looks at the ceiling. She recognises guilt in his silence, in his avoidance of kissing, and thinks, okay, I can play the whore.

She straddles him and slides onto his prick, liking the slight roughness. Already she knows she won't come no matter what they do, she can't share that with him. She caresses the smooth taut skin of his arms, rubs her cheek across his waxed chest.

He's holding her hips now, trying to get her to move faster, harder, and she sighs and moves off him.

What, he says.

Let's try something else.

He flips her onto her back and spreads her legs, then grinds his palm into her.

Shit, you're bleeding.

Am I?

Blood all over his hand, streaming down the inside of her thighs. She can smell the ferric tang of it. Her period has come early, heavily, and with it that heightened sense of smell that had bothered her all day.

Sorry, she says, and smiles.

He isn't disgusted, and this encourages her. She leads him to the bathroom, turns on the shower, and invites him in. He's still hard, undaunted. Now they stop pretending that this is anything other than strangers using new bodies for pleasure.

He fucks her from behind but keeps slipping out because there is so much blood—and, she thinks, because she has had three children. He kneads her breasts, her generous belly, and then she knows what she wants him to do. She can't say it but she can show him. She stops watching, loses herself in the dizzying freedom of sex with a stranger.

I want you to fuck me up the ass, a voice she doesn't recognise says but it emanates from her, and he groans and holds her hips and pushes gently, expertly inside her.

Her first time, and she gasps with pleasure, with the strangeness of it, like entering a parallel universe. She can smell her blood still. He doesn't make a sound, barely murmurs. He moves inside her, and she feels like she is on a drug, her senses hyper-alert, but not orgasmic. A different league of pleasure.

Then he stops though she would like him to go on. He gets out of the shower, and washes his prick carefully at the sink.

He puts a towel on the floor, and motions for her to go down on her knees.

Please?

She gets out of the shower, and still wet, and dripping blood, she kneels and licks him, sucks him, scrapes her teeth lightly against him, uses her hand and mouth to bring him close to climax, then she lets go, and stands up.

I can't. You finish and I'll watch, she says, and she feels suddenly hollow, overcome with exhaustion.

He closes his eyes on her. She looks at their reflections in the mirrored bathroom, their bodies separate, multiplied, grotesque, comical. He works his fist, and comes without a sound, the white pearls of semen adorning his flat, brown belly. They don't speak when he is finished. She gets back into the shower to wash, while he goes into the bedroom. As she finishes showering, he comes back into the bathroom.

Where have you hidden my trousers, you witch?

His eyes avoid hers, his voice is frantic.

She is horribly aware of her nakedness, covers herself with a scratchy hotel bathrobe, and follows him into the bedroom.

I can't find my trousers, he says again, accusing her.

She wishes he would laugh, and she says with a smile, Well, I haven't hidden them, but he doesn't want to share the joke.

She helps him look, and finds the trousers hidden in the creases of the duvet, hands them to him. He dresses quickly, and goes to the door.

Are we all right, he says, but he's not looking at her.

Sure. Don't worry about it.

He hesitates for a moment, then leaves.

She turns off all the lights and lies on the bed and tries to feel something. All she can muster is a nagging awareness that she is bleeding into the pure whiteness of the bathrobe, that she should do something about it. She listens to the hum of the air conditioning, to shouts below on the street, to the crash of a glass bottle. The faint red glow of the standby light on the flat-screen TV is the only illumination in the room. She has the feeling that someone is watching her, that if she could see through the walls she would find a pair of eyes in there, the ghost of someone.

She has forgotten to call the children to say goodnight. The bag of souvenirs is still tucked under the bar-stool downstairs.

Adventure Stories for Boys

Kevin Curran

I pulled the yellow curtain behind me and never even noticed the lack of a swish.

'Alright, Da,' I whispered, soft, cause I was kinda afraid to disturb things. For one, I was on the bounce and didn't want to alert anyone to my presence, and two, the place felt like a library.

'Yer looking good, Da, yeah,' I said, easing my schoolbag to the ground and lifting the plastic grey chair around to face the side of the bed. I scraped myself in, knees up against the mattress and took a breath. Got myself together, like.

I found my da's hand—the one not bruised and hooked up to tubes—down by his side and rested my wrist on the cold metal rail. I lifted his fingers, just held them while I rested my thumb on his palm. I was always surprised by the warmth and feel of my da's hand. There was a roughness there like the hard texture of a stray dog's paw.

I had no memory of ever holding my da's hand before. I was what, fifteen. I'd no memory of holding anyone's hand. Other than Holly's when I had to bring her to school. But that didn't count. She had to or I'd bate her.

I quit inspecting his fingers and looked at his face.

'Sorry I'm late,' I said, 'it's not my… I had to go to class.'

It seemed with every visit I was discovering something new. Today it was his stubble. Normally he was freshly shaved. I remembered his line from a few weeks before the accident, mumbled while he was checking his foamy face above the bathroom sink, the razor about to draw down on his cheek, his eyes all bloodshot and dark, staring hard at his reflection, 'If you're feeling rough as fuck, son, never let them bastards know.'

A distant trumpet of daytime television played over the ward. A slight breeze from somewhere swayed the curtains, but couldn't budge the heat.

'Ma says she's been getting calls and shit.' I paused. I was trying to stay all upbeat like they said I should. Keep things positive. But it wasn't easy. 'She's telling me I haveta go in or the courts will be on and, like, then there'll be more trouble.'

A trolley and its rinky contents stopped outside our yellow enclosure. A voice—the nurse's muffled instructions—filled the gap in a big thick country accent.

The hair on me da's face was growing high on the cheekbones. Like something out of *Dawn of the Planet of the Apes*. He wouldn't have been impressed.

'So, yeah, Da, I went to a class.'

I gave his fingers a gentle squeeze and withdrew my hand and leaned down for my bag. I took out my only book and some cold toast I'd fleeced from Breakfast Club leftovers nearly two hours before. I settled the book on my lap and said, 'Where were we, Da?'

But I couldn't concentrate. I was drained. Absolutely bollixed. So instead, I said, 'I met a girl off the train yesterday, Da.'

And so, to fill the silence, I went on and told him about how the earphones were in and I was lost dealing with the awful bang of hunger when I heard Taylor call after me. I just strolled on, head down, trying to adjust my walk to stop the instep on my converse from wearing through to the socks.

'Hey Rory, Rory!' she shouted and suddenly she was there with her big giddy face beaming beside me, her cheeks pinched pink like one of Holly's old dolls we'd left abandoned in her bedroom.

'Hiya,' she mouthed.

I took out the earphones. She smelled fresh and clean, like Hubba Bubba.

'Hi,' I said, returning my eyes to the path, trying hard not to pull a redner.

She stood too close, but. My school shirt smelled like shit after Ma hand-washed it in the sink and dried it on the radiator in the bathroom in one of her manic fits.

'Ye need to turn yer music down,' Taylor gushed. 'I was calling ye for ages. I saw ye get off the train and followed ye over the wall. I had no ticket either so ye saved me. Were you on the mitch too?'

She was almost skipping with the excitement of it all. We were surrounded by suits and hands pocketing weekly tickets and cars reversing out of spaces. The train sounded so loud and sluggish pulling away from the platform.

'Yeah.'

She giggled and nudged me.

'Where'd ye go?'

'Eh, I, the usual place.'

'Usual place? Oh yeah, you do this a lot, don't you.'

'Suppose.'

She stopped walking. The crowd had thinned out.

'I used to think you were, like, a nerd.'

I shrugged it off, but still felt the sting.

'You going home?' she said, a glint in her eyes, the final word a little too rushed. The earphones clicked softly in the palm of my hand and I looked to the blue sky for an answer. She was exhausting.

'Suppose.'

'I'll walk with you then.'

And she waited for me to lead the way.

'I nearly missed the train,' she went on, her face lit by the horror of such a possibility. 'My ma would've been ringing the school if I wasn't back by five.'

I just nodded, watching our shadows ripple like ghosts before us over the path.

'She's mad like that. Stupid bitch. Though me da wouldn't give a shit if he found out. He's grand. What's yours like?'

I looked up to read her face. There was nothing only her wide eyes and stupid smile. 'Me ma's strict but me da is...'

I trailed off and Taylor giggled nervously and blurted, 'They're all the same. Do you know Shauna Boylan's da? She lives a few doors up from you. Like, directly behind my house. I can see into her back garden from my bedroom and everything, like. Her da does be out there naked. The state of him. Freak.'

And so it went for the next five minutes of walking, me nodding along to Taylor's shite talk until we reached the estate. It was still bright and sunny and there were kids out on their bikes pulling wheelies and circling lazily in the middle of the road. Taylor stopped at the corner beside the 'Drive Slowly Children Playing' sign and stretched up on her tippy-toes and peered down the row of houses.

'Looks like you're in the clear. Your da's van isn't there.'

She was nibbling at her bottom lip eager for something. I gave her nothing. So she said, 'See ye around then, and maybe the next time ye go on the mitch ye can give us a shout, yeah? What's your Snapchat?'

I went, 'Eh, I'm...'

'Mine's Taylorbyrne56. Add me.'

And she giggled and hunched over her phone and started typing while she walked away.

I watched her go and then craned to look where she'd just looked. See what she had seen. I lingered on the empty driveway a while. Thinking about the fading patch of oil near the porch from his work van. When I was sure she was gone I put my earphones in and felt myself disappear. I turned away from the road, the driveway, the kids' laughter, and started back towards town, to the empty hours ahead.

'Member we used go the cinema, Da?' The memory pushed forward a giggle cause right under it a sob was waiting to burst through. My da's chins were doubled up like Jabba the Hutt's, his eyes closed, his face frozen like Han Solo's in *The Empire Strikes Back*.

The nurses had said it was good for him to hear our voices. And since I was in no mood to read, I just kept talking shite.

I told my da the film had been cat and right at the end, when the lights had come on and I'd looked up from fixing my runners, the cleaner lad with the brush and pan was sweeping behind me.

'Excuse me, our...' the lad called. The dull soundproofing of the theatre, mixed with the earphones, dampened the young lad's voice and I didn't turn round.

I'd a good head start and so got into the lobby before the pan and brush appeared from behind the screen door down the hall. A girl in a red shirt was at the counter sifting through a thin set of twenty-euro notes for Wednesday night's takings.

'How many for Screen 3?' the young lad called, slightly out of breath.

I scarpered through the neon colours and echoing movie trailers on the HD screens, feeling an awful bang of hunger from the warm smell of popcorn. The girl looked up from her count, confused, and strained into the computer screen, 'Eh, three.' She tapped the screen. 'No, four. Four. Why?'

I didn't hang around for his answer.

I laughed when I told my da. I'm sure he would've laughed too. After he gave me a bollicking about not paying for the ticket.

Still the book lay heavy on my lap, and still my da lay there, the rhythm of his breathing the only constant in my life. And still I couldn't bring myself to read to him so I said, 'It was one of those days yesterday. Non. Stop. All I wanted to do was keep my earphones in and my head down.'

I looked around for a sup of water. My mouth was so dry.

'So I have yer one wrecking my head, and then your man from the cinema running me outta the place, and then, guess what, Da? I had me first pint.'

Once I'd got around the corner from the cinema I slowed down to pull my jumper over my head. The earphones managed to stay in and I kept my head straight, my stride consistent as if walking to a steady beat. My shadow stretched out and disappeared when I moved away from the streetlight, only to be replaced by two more mumbling and cursing silhouettes from behind.

I kept walking up Main Street, head down, until I got to the heavy oak door just up from The Front Bar. I shifted my bag on my shoulder and waited for the shadows to pass. The polished lustre on the gold handle had faded since morning. Once I thought the voices were gone, I went to open the door but my feeble attempt at a pull saw an arm stretch over my shoulder. I followed the arm and saw Martin Maughan smiling down on me. His cracked lips and freckly nose were nearly touching my face. The earphones were taken out and the hiss of Main Street and the whoosh of passing traffic filled the silence and I said, 'Thanks,' and Martin nodded for me to go ahead.

And so we stepped into the claustrophobic hush of reception—the plush red carpets and polished oak cases, trophies and black-and-white pictures of Gaelic and hurling and football teams from the town. No one was at the desk—thank fuck—and Martin leaned down to whisper in my ear.

'They serve you in here too?'

It was only then I saw what must've been Martin's da standing behind him, concern digging at his brow.

'I've never tried before,' I said.

'Are ye meeting someone then, lad?' Martin's da asked, stepping forward, tucking his shirt into his jeans, the question thinning his lips.

'No.'

Martin and the da exchanged a look, as if I'd just confirmed something, and the da's face immediately opened up and he threw his head back and blew out a small, surprised laugh. 'Well, you're here now, lad, so ye may as well go for a pint.'

I said nothing, did nothing.

'Come on inside,' the da said, clapping his hands together. 'I'll get ye a pint.'

The stairs past the front desk to the first floor were lit in a low yellow. I had no money on me. I never had any money.

We sat in a corner, hidden from the bar by a stained-glass harp with honey strings and a red shamrock on its body. Martin scrolled through his phone.

'You on Facebook?' he said.

I just shook my head as the da arrived back with a Guinness and two golden pints held tight in the triangle of his hands.

And so I took a timid sup, testing the weight of the beer on my tongue. It was rank, but I managed not to gag.

'Do you drink here much?' I said, just to say something.

Martin nodded, 'Now and then. They do know me from the boxing up in the function room.'

'This lad brings in the crowds so he does,' the da announced, licking the froth off his top lip. Martin nodded proudly.

'Wait'll I tell ye about this lad here, Da,' Martin said, 'real quiet lad, but always on the bounce.'

Up until that day I'd been convinced no one had noticed.

'It's the quiet ones ye haveta watch,' the da said.

'What class are we in together?'

'Can't remember,' I whispered and we chuckled.

'French,' Martin responded, smiling at his recall.

'Par-ley-voo fuck off,' I said.

The heads of the pints rippled with laughter. I felt satisfied with their approval. Cheap too, but, like I had to perform for my drink.

Their glasses were raised again. I wasn't sure how much to swallow at each lift, and how quickly, so I followed Martin's lead. Only a few gulps in and my stomach was feeling hollow and my head a bit dizzy.

'Don't suppose you'll be here again tomorrow morning?' Martin said.

It was like I'd been sucker punched. They had me cornered. I didn't know where to look. 'Tomorrow morning?'

Their beermats stuck to the bottom of their glasses. They both took a long, long gulp of their pints. I didn't follow.

'The school awards, Rory. They're on upstairs in the function room.'

The da held out his Guinness. 'This lad here'll be getting sportsman of the year. Won't ye son?'

They clinked glasses.

'Oh,' I said, trying to keep my head steady. 'No. No award for me.' And I took a quick sup to catch up with Martin and hide the relief.

The harp darkened and the woman from reception appeared over our table.

'Out,' she snapped and to make things as painless as possible, I just ducked for my bag and mumbled, 'See ye,' and legged it.

'The lad deserves a break,' was the last I heard from Martin before I went through the door into reception.

'What ye make of that, Da? Me first pint,' I whispered.

The memory embarrassed me and after a while of just sitting there in silence I ducked out and found a small plastic glass and filled it with lukewarm water from a jug at the bottom of the ward. Got myself together, like.

I went back in after a while and moved the chair close to the bed again and took my da's hand. The book was resting on my lap. I'd nothing more to say. I certainly didn't want to talk about that morning. He certainly didn't need to hear it.

Ma and Holly were gone and I'd slept in again and even though I was rushing to get to school for period two, I'd stalled it at our front door with its silver 201 until I'd felt the earphones in my bag. But it was only after the door had clunked shut that I realised I'd left my keycard and coke bottle filled with water beside the bed. The light above the handle clicked from green to red and I knew I'd be parched for the day.

The lift was in use so I went down the hall towards the stairs to reception and there, like something from a nightmare, at the function room double doors, was one of the new teachers and a row of maybe twenty students all lined up in twos against the wall, going from the function room back to the stairs. All the conversations stopped and the faces went blank. If I'd had time to think I probably would've taken an almighty redner, but I just put my earphones in and forced myself to keep walking.

The teacher started tapping the toe of her high heel when she saw me approach.

'And where do you think you're going?' she said

I powered on past her.

'Excuse me,' she said, 'are you helping with the awards? The function room is here.'

I gave her a glance—that's all she deserved—but didn't stop.

Her voice went up a notch. 'I'm talking to you. Where do you think you're coming from?'

All the eyes looked to their crests, their school shoes, intimidated and awed. I walked by and made the stairs before anyone had a chance to say anything.

The worn hardback trembled on my lap. The corners of the glossy cover were dented and curled, the cheap cardboard lurking under the golden title marked by my da's work stained hands.

The book was all I took with me. Ma had put everything, absolutely everything we had of worth up on Gumtree to cover the rent. And when that month was up and we got no deposit back, anything unsold that we couldn't fit in suitcases was left behind. Left behind like we'd evacuated our lives without warning—posters still on walls, jackets still on hooks, soggy tissues still under pillows, dolls still on beds, books still on shelves.

The ward was unusually quiet. I'd been silent for too long, so I pulled on the silk strip of cloth just like my da used to, and opened the book at the end of our last story. I took a breath and got ready to read.

Her voice shocked me with, 'I'm sorry, love, no phones or electronic appliances so close to the equipment,' and I slammed the book shut, freaked. I copped where the nurse was looking and put my hand to my ear and realised I hadn't taken the earphones out.

'Oh, sorry,' I said, like a little kid, and since I'd been caught off guard,

I pulled the empty jack out of my pocket and held it up and said, 'I don't have anything to plug them into.'

There, the truth was out and I was exposed. All she did was press her lips together and nod as if to say, 'Isn't that nice?' and finished what she had to finish and left me there feeling the familiar burn on my cheeks.

The earphones clicked around in my hand like painkillers. The new noises of the ward started to press in. The curtains looked real flimsy all of a sudden.

'Who'm I kidding, Da?' I said, a defeated laugh escaping into the high ceiling. The earphones had helped me ignore them, but as much as I tried to convince myself otherwise, people's words were getting through. The reality of it all was getting through. It was constant. Day after day after day. Ignoring them had me shattered. Taylor didn't need words, she was obvious. The girl in the cinema had asked the lad with the brush and pan who I was and he'd told her what I'd become. Martin and his da had talked about me before I got to the hotel entrance, and a girl's voice that morning at the function room—just as I ran down the stairs—had explained to the teacher they'd had a special assembly about me.

My da's stubble was dark, his face was pale. I thought of his eyes looking at me through the mirror while he'd shaved before work. They had been exhausted. He had been exhausted.

I opened the book and said, 'Where were we, Da?' wishing, really, really, really wishing today would be the day he'd answer back.

The Quiet

Carys Davies

She didn't hear him arrive.

The wind was up and the rain was thundering down on the tin roof like a shower of stones and in the midst of all the noise she didn't hear the rattle of his old buggy approaching. She didn't hear the scrape of his iron-rimmed wheels on the track, the soft thump of his feet in the wet dust. She didn't know he was there until she looked up from her bucket of soapy water and saw his face at her window, his pale green eyes with their tiny black pin-prick pupils blinking at her through the glass.

His name was Henry Fowler and she hated it when he came.

She hated him sitting there for hours on end talking to Tom about hens and beets and pigs, filling his smelly pipe with minute pinches of tobacco from a pouch in his cracked sheepskin waistcoat, tamping down the flakes with his little thumb, lighting and re-lighting the bowl and sucking at the stem, slurping his tea and sitting there on the edge of his chair like a small observant bird, and all the time stealing glances at her and looking at her with his sharp eyes as if he could see right through her. It filled her with a kind of shame. She felt she'd do almost anything to stop Henry Fowler looking at her like that, anything to make him leave and clear off back to his end of the valley. It felt like the worst thing in the world to her, him looking at her the way he did.

He was looking at her now on the other side of the glass, blinking at her through the falling rain. She wished she didn't have to invite him in. She wished she could send him away without asking him in and offering him a cup of something, but he was their neighbour and he had come six miles across the valley in his bone-shaking old buggy and the water had begun to pool around the brim of his old felt hat and drip onto the shoulders of his crumpled shirt. It was bouncing back up off the ground and splashing against his boots and his baggy serge trousers. She would have to offer him a chair by the stove for half an hour, refreshment. A cup of tea at least. She wiped her soapy hands on her skirt and went to the door and opened it and called to him.

'You'd better come in, Mr Fowler. Out of the rain.'

Her name was Susan Boyce and she was twenty-six years old.

It was eight months now since she and Thomas had sailed out of Liverpool on their wedding day aboard the *Hurricane* in search of a new life. It had excited them both, the idea of starting from nothing. They'd liked the razed, empty look of everything on the map, the vast unpunctuated distances, and at the beginning of it all she hadn't minded that the only company was the sound of the wind and the rain and the crackle of the dry grass in the sunshine. At the beginning of it all, she hadn't minded the quiet.

She hadn't minded that when they'd arrived in the town they'd found nothing more than a single dusty street. No railway station and no church, only an empty hotel and a draper, a dry goods store that doubled as a doctor's surgery, a smithy and a pen for market day. She hadn't minded that when they'd ridden out twelve miles into the parched country beyond the town they'd found rocks and gum trees and small coarse bushes and the biggest sky she'd ever seen and in the middle of it all their own patch of ground and low, fallen-down house. She hadn't minded that there weren't other farms nearby, other wives. She hadn't minded that there was no one but Henry Fowler, who lived six miles off and had no wife. No, she hadn't minded any of it and wouldn't now, she was sure, if things with Tom were not as they were.

Now she wished there was another wife somewhere not too far away. Someone she might by this time have come to consider as a friend; someone she might be able to bring herself to tell. But there was no such person. There was her married sister in Poole who she could write to, but what good would that do, when it might be a year before a reply came? A year was an eternity; she didn't think she could last a year, and even then, she wasn't really sure she could get the thing down on paper in the first place.

Once, a month ago, when she and Tom had gone into town and he was off buying nails, she'd got as far as the black varnished door of the doctor's consulting room in the dry goods store. She'd stood there outside it, gripping her purse, listening to the low murmur of a woman's voice on the other side of the door and she'd tried to imagine her own voice in there in its place and she couldn't. She just couldn't. It was an impossible thing for her to do. What if the doctor said he had to speak to Thomas? What then?

If there'd been a church in town, she might have gone to the priest. A priest, she thought, might be an easy person to tell; but even there, she wasn't sure what a priest would say on such a matter. What if he just told her to go back home and pray? Would she be able to tell him that she'd tried that already? That every night for more than half a year she'd lain in bed and prayed till she was blue in the face and it hadn't worked? Anyway it was a waste of time to think about a priest because there wasn't a church for a hundred miles. It was a godless place they'd come to. Godless and friendless and only Henry Fowler's wizened walnut face at her window at nine o'clock in the morning, poking his nose into her private business.

Well, she would not sink under it. No she wouldn't. She'd experienced other setbacks in her life, other disappointments and shocks of one sort or another. It would be the same with this one, she would endure it like anything else, and wasn't it true anyway, that in time all things passed? This would too. There was a remedy, in the end, for everything. She just had to find it.

When she and Fowler were inside she told him that Tom had gone into town for salt and oil and needles and wouldn't be back till nightfall. Fowler nodded and asked if he might tip the water from his hat into her bucket of soapy water.

'Of course,' she said—cold, prim, barely polite.

She invited him to sit, and said she would boil the water for some tea.

At the stove she busied herself with the kettle, wondering what he wanted, why he'd come. She wondered if he was going to sit there and look at her in that way of his that made her want to get up and go somewhere away from him, into a different room, behind a door or a wall or a screen, so he couldn't do it. Somehow it made everything worse, being looked at, especially by someone like Henry Fowler. She'd rarely seen anyone who looked as seedy as he did. She wondered if he'd been a convict.

He'd visited them three times before now, once not long after they'd arrived and then again a few months after that, and then a third time just last week. Each time he'd come wearing the same grimy outfit, the same crumpled shirt and ancient sheepskin waistcoat, the same greasy serge pants, the same bit of cotton rag about his thin neck. The only thing she noticed that was different about him today was that he seemed to have brought nothing with him; whenever he'd come to visit them before, he'd always brought some kind of neighbourly gift. The first time it had been a quarter pound of his own butter, the second time a jar of pumpkin seeds. Last time, a loaf. This time his small weather-beaten hands were empty; today Henry Fowler seemed to have brought nothing but himself.

He was forty-five years old—a small, scrawny-looking man with bow legs and rough brown hands no bigger than a woman's.

At sunrise he'd stood with one of those hands resting on the wooden rail of his rickety veranda at the far end of the valley, watching his new neighbour's black horse and dray moving slowly along the road in the direction of the town, wondering if the handsome husband was travelling by himself—if the young wife would be alone there today.

It was six months now since he'd watched them come in on the same road with a pile of furniture tied onto the dray. Since then he'd seen her three times. Three times he'd gone over there with a neighbourly gift. Three times he'd walked about outside with the husband, admiring the progress they'd made. The beets and peas and beans, the potatoes and the fat new pigs. The two hundred chickens, the cow. Three times he'd sat with the two of them inside the house drinking tea and for weeks now he'd been spending the evenings sitting on his veranda and looking out across the grassy desert towards their place.

Susan. That was her name. Susan Boyce. For weeks he'd been thinking about her and practically nothing else. Her stiff, cold, proud-looking face, the closed-off, haughty way she had of speaking to him, the way she couldn't stand him looking at her.

When he could no longer see the dray on the horizon, when it had disappeared completely from view, he went inside for a while and then he laced up his boots and put on his hat and climbed up onto the seat of his high sloping buggy and set off along the track down the valley to her house.

He sat now, at her table, tamping the tobacco into the bowl of his pipe with his little thumb, watching her at the stove.

It's true that Henry Fowler still had the look of a convict about him. He had the look of an old sailor too, and of a fairground monkey someone had dressed up in a pair of pants and a waistcoat and an old felt hat. He was small and sun-wizened and ugly and as he sat now, listening to the wind and the rain and the snuffling of Thomas Boyce's pigs and the crackle of the fire in the stove and the simmering of the water in the kettle on top of it, he was sure he could also hear the beating of his own heart.

The fact is, Fowler was even more nervous now that he was here than he'd expected to be.

His sheepskin waistcoat creaked; he didn't know where to begin. He'd rehearsed everything before he came, had stood for an hour or more before the mirror looking at his own half-naked body, and it had all gone smoothly enough. The words had come without too much difficulty. Now, looking at the other man's wife standing at the stove with her slender back turned towards him, they escaped him.

He took a few quick puffs on his pipe and decided the best thing to do would be to undress.

He took off his waistcoat and placed it over the back of the chair, unknotted the grimy square of cotton he wore folded around his throat and laid that on top of the waistcoat. He undid the buttons on his crumpled linen shirt until the whole thing was hanging down from the canvas belt that held up his trousers, and at that moment Susan Boyce turned. She turned and screamed and dropped the teapot, and covered her mouth with her hand.

Henry Fowler's narrow pigeon chest was lumpy and shrivelled like the map of some strange unknown country. It had a kind of raised border all around it that was ropey and pink; inside it the skin had a cooked, roasted look to it—it was blackened and leathery and hard, like a mummy's, or a creature that has lain for a thousand years in a forgotten bog.

He turned. Three dark triangles the colour of ripe Victoria plums decorated his shoulders; below them and covering most of the rest of his back was another dark shape, also plum-coloured—the puckered print of something large and round.

Low on his hip, just above the canvas belt that held up his trousers, there was a firework splatter of a dozen deep, wrinkled divots.

'My wife,' said Henry Fowler, the words finally coming to his rescue, 'was bigger than me.'

Looking down and behind at his own ruined body he explained how he'd got his blackened chest (a jug of boiling water from the copper), the three dark triangles on his back (her smoothing iron), the big round brand beneath them (the frying pan), the divots (the red-hot poker), and then with his voice dropping very low he told Susan Boyce that there was something else too, below his canvas belt, but he would not show her that. No. If she wanted to guess the worst thing a bad-tempered wife might do with a pair of sharp-bladed dress-making shears, then she would have it.

Susan Boyce said nothing, only looked.

'She is under the beets,' said Fowler quietly—one night when she was sleeping he'd stabbed her through the heart with the sharp stubby blade of a paring knife and carried her outside and buried her with all her things: her skirts and her clogs and the pins from her hair, her frying pan and the jug from the old copper, her iron and the poker and the cutting-out shears and everything else she'd ever owned or touched that reminded him of her and might make him think she was coming for him again—anything that might make him think he could hear the clatter of her furious clogs charging towards him across the hard clay floor.

In town, he said, he'd put it about that she'd run off and left him.

Susan Boyce looked at him.

Her face was still, without expression, and Henry Fowler thought to himself, *I have made a mistake. I am wrong about it all.*

He had been so sure before but now that he was standing in front of her with his waistcoat over the back of the chair and his neck-cloth lying on the seat and his shirt-sleeves hanging down like a skipping rope between his knees Henry Fowler said to himself: *I have watched her here in this house, moving about in her shawl and her plain high-necked gown, passing behind his chair and pouring his tea, and I have caught the scent of something that isn't here, and when he returns tonight she will tell him what I have told her and he will fetch a few of the men from town and they will come with their shovels and dig under the beets and they will look at the marks on me and I will tell them how I got them and they will look at each other and remind themselves that Henry Fowler is nothing but a seedy old convict with a bit of land to his name and they will shake their heads and call me a liar and then they will hang me.*

He began to scrabble between his bandy legs for the cuffs of his shirt, telling himself that as soon as he was dressed he would climb up into his old buggy and head off back up the valley and once he was home he would think about what to do, whether he should sit there on his veranda and wait until they came for him, or if he should leave tonight and go somewhere they wouldn't be able to find him, or if he should come back in the morning and talk to Boyce and explain things to him in his own words so he would understand. He bent to the chair where he'd laid his clothes and picked up his neck-cloth, looped it behind his dipped head and pushed his arms into the sleeves of his dangling shirt, and he would have left then, probably without saying another word, probably just reaching out for his hat and heading for the door, but by the time he'd raised himself again and looked up into the room to where Susan Boyce was standing, she had begun to unhook her bodice.

She was loosening her skirt and pulling her chemise over her head and undoing the tapes of her petticoats and then she was letting the whole lot slide to the floor around her feet on top of the broken remains of the teapot and its lake of cooling water until she was standing before him in nothing but her woollen vest and her cotton drawers, and then she was taking those off too. She did it quickly, hurriedly, as if she thought she might never again get the chance to show him, as if she thought, even now, he might not be on her side.

She looked smaller, without her clothes, different in every possible way, turning in front of him, displaying the split, puffy flesh of her thighs and buttocks, the mottled green, black and yellow of her belly, the long, weeping purplish thing that started under the hair at her neck and ran down the back of her like a half-made ditch. She came towards him, stepping through the puddle of tea and over the piled-up heap of her things. She took his small brown hand and lifted it to her cheek and closed her eyes like someone who hadn't known till now how tired they were, and then she asked him, would he help her, please, to dig the hole.

Cana Wedding

Danny Denton

On television screens, in the houses that still have power, families and housemates and people alone watch footage of the destruction. Predicted to be the most powerful storm since the nation's records began, it is the tail of a Category 3 hurricane that has decimated parts of Mexico and the Revilladego Islands. Here, trees come down along primary roads and wild boreens. There is already a death toll, the first note of its staccato passage struck in South Leitrim, an elderly man favouring the promise of a pub and the local news over the danger of the gales. He is gone forever now, buried into the lane by an old yew. Further south, two people are married in the eyes of God. They say that the hotel would probably be closed—the church too—but because of the recession they must take what business they can get. The cars should never have ventured beyond the driveway, they say, but still they move in slow train along the abandoned dual carriageway, from country chapel to four-star city centre hotel. From backseats the wedding party cheerfully ask the drivers to sound the horns—even as they glance nervously out the window, watching for a swaying tree or a cow lifted on high like in the film—but the klaxon call is lost in the howling as they descend into the vacant city sprawl, each car rocking from side to side.

Chip bags, cans, plastic bottles, newspapers, polystyrene cups, wrappers, pens, cardboard, fruit skin, cartons of various design: all kinds of debris is chased up the Mall as the cars park outside the hotel. An empty shopping trolley shudders across the road to clatter into the curb and fall, sliding then in the direction of the river.

'Fuck this,' John says to his suited friends, and he is the first to force his way from the car.

John knows most here, old classmates, but he was probably invited to this small wedding only because he attended both stag parties, the first in Prague and the second, for those who couldn't travel, in Wexford. As he opens the door the gale rips at its hinges. He struggles to counter that power and his suit jacket flutters, suddenly panicking, wanting to be anywhere but on his shoulders. Slamming the door he makes for the troop of staff who have gathered inside the glass-fronted lobby, and look out, dazed.

As two porters let him in, the current bursts through the lobby like a tantrum, scattering flyers and brochures from the marble reception counter. A vase topples from its plinth to be caught by a young, surprised waitress.

'Fair play to you!' John digs his hands into his pockets, pinching his thighs, embarrassed now that he is the first. He should have at least escorted a lady; anything would have been better than the selfish dash for refuge. He stands among the uniforms, looks out with them to the wedding cars and remarks at what a crazy thing they have all done. 'We should all be at home!'

'None of us'll ever forget this day,' the manager says, an edge of excitement in his Northern accent. He'll tell this one forever.

Outside, some tiles come off a roof and we feel that the world for all its sins is truly coming to an end. When the first car moves off John is stricken with fear, again pinches his thighs. They're calling the whole thing off, going home without him. He leers giddily at the two porters. 'They're leaving!'

The porters smile.

Ribbons cling to the bonnet of the Rolls Royce, are a frantic blur as it turns a wide circle, coming up onto the pavement and lining up about two feet from the doors. Making up for his earlier lapse in etiquette, John pushes his way out and opens the back door. Puts a hand out for Josephine Kelleher, neé Kelly, who wears a simple ivory dress. A girl of twenty-seven, with curtains of dark hair, Josephine was the first dance John ever had. A slow set at a rowing club disco, aged eleven maybe. She steps out now and smiles at him as if he is a total stranger. Says, 'Thanks,' and places a hand on her head to keep the hair right. Says, 'Dear God!'

It should have been Cian Kelleher chaperoning her like this, would have been, had John not stepped out with his stupid smile and fraudulent bravado. Cian was a year ahead of John throughout school, had always that enviable quiet confidence. He never needed anyone's attention, never had to talk himself up. Even his wife fell into his arms. A toolmaker now, John cannot look him in the face as he follows after his wife and the Rolls Royce moves on.

The second car follows suit. Relieved parents finally arrive, in the company of the priest and a sole surviving grandparent. They remark yet again on the weather and the fact that they are almost the only ones here over forty years of age. They are grateful for these two seeds of conversation. Next come bridesmaids and groomsmen, and the people with whom John shared the fourth car. JJ strides up and asks, 'Can we get pissed now?' Soon the lobby becomes a quiet place again and, in a small function room in the belly of the building, away from the howling winds, the bar is set upon by twenty-something-year-olds.

'By Christ,' John says to JJ at some point, 'what kind of omen is it for the holy union of our own two friends?'

John finds himself watching Orla, a cousin of the bride, as she stands alongside him at the bar, chatting. Her eyes are set apart, large brown eyes, and she has a strange kind of boxer's nose. She is, by all related accounts of her, a drunken lunatic. He watches for signs of this, excited deep down, and sees the proof in the way she looks unashamedly into people's faces as she talks to them, in the way that when she puts her gin and tonic down it is left in limbo, leaning from beer mat to bar counter. The glass is neither here nor there, and the nervous potential energy is thrilling. John is attracted to her in a way he is not attracted to the mother of his boy.

'Look at us,' JJ is saying. 'Twenty years ago this is the schoolyard. We'd all be here bar a few. We'd be playing soccer with a tennis ball.'

John knows how this one goes. 'And now we're marrying.'

'Fuck,' says JJ. 'Christ.'

JJ has piled on weight since those school days, addicted to the meat he gets at a staff discount from O'Sullivan's. He sups his pint fondly. He often does a great trick where he joins his hands behind his back and takes a full pint of cider up in the grip of his teeth. It has even been recorded and committed to the internet for anyone to see.

Paddy too has a trick: he can't sing, which makes it all the mightier when he straps his tie below his receding hair line and climbs aboard a table to belt out a full and perfect recital of *We Didn't Start the Fire* at the top of his lungs. Then there's Boris, who'll fall asleep anywhere after five-to-seven pints. At John's own twenty-first birthday party, on a December night, Boris was found under a Ford Mondeo in the car park, at four in the morning.

Why don't I have a trick? John asks himself. Why am I always in the crowd for these things?

'And now we're all builders,' Paddy is saying.

'And teachers.'

'And butchers and accountants and painters.'

'And bankers and doctors.'

'And IT people.' JJ points a finger.

I don't have a thing. John tries to appear nostalgic. I mingle. I say things that make people pleased with themselves. I go on the internet all day and then repeat what I've learned. But nothing marks me out. He finishes his drink and raises it to his gang. 'More of the same?'

'Fuck, yes.'

'We're all grown up now,' Paddy concludes.

'We're the fabric of society,' Boris recites.

'The future,' John adds. They toast themselves.

They drink a few pints more before they are seated at round white tables. We are all drunk, John believes as he pulls a chair, believing it in the way a man does after four pints of stout, in the way that life has become an epiphanic thing, in the way that JJ's gesture, as he speaks with a brick of a hand on Boris's bony shoulder, is in some way symbolic. Orla, the artist, takes her seat next to him, giving him that broad smile, her soft nose the north star of his vision. She shakes his hand in a single pump, her fist small even in his average, unweathered hand. He sees his own clipped nails, thinks of his days at the computer calculating risk, saying words down the phone like *streamline, credit, internal*.

'You're one of the locals?' she asks, lifting her glass.

'For my sins, I admit to knowing this crowd,' he replies, hoisting his own.

'Cheers.' Her voice crackles as if she's already smoked too many cigarettes.

'Cheers.'

JJ laughs. 'Cheers!'

'Let's get slaughtered,' Paddy says.

JJ is all grin, spinning empty side plates. To Orla: 'No date?'

'He'd only slow me down.'

'Ahow! You're out to get your hole so?'

Orla raises her eyes to the ceiling drapes.

'Don't mind this oaf.' John fidgets with his pint.

'Sure if I get a good offer.'

Paddy comes around the table, red-faced, big-eared and joyful, gets down on one knee, pumps Orla's hand and says, 'Patrick Leonard at your service,' and the whole table is released into laughter.

JJ holds court at the table, talking about wedding presents. Meats and vegetables are served. He has given to bride and groom a set of kitchen knives and chopping boards. He tells them all how important it is to have good blades.

'Do ye like meat?' he asks the ladies present, and there is lusty mirth again, that of men enjoying their laughter, falling about like maniacs. Wine arrives, the storm pushed to the back of the mind now.

Some devour their food, some only poke at it with their fork. The wine is finished off; they order more. Blaming the storm, the hotel is now down to red only. It is poured and enjoyed, and no one worries about the disruption to the delivery schedule. John asks Orla what kind of stuff she paints. Paddy tells them about computer games and John stops him to point out how infantile their generation has become.

'Our fathers were working hard and raising families when they were twenty-five. Look at us talking about games!' This, full in the knowledge that he can pass an entire day at online poker.

Bending to retrieve his fallen knife, he sees Orla's stockinged calf under the table. Even with his mouth full of mashed potato he wants to bite a chunk out of that calf. Suddenly it is later and they are discussing pornography.

*

'It's great to see so many young people here today.' Mr Kelleher seems afraid of the microphone. He isn't ancient himself, maybe not far beyond his fiftieth year, tall, grey-haired, another quiet man, speaking in metronomic sentences that betray his recollection by heart of a memorised speech. 'Ye are more educated, more talented than us that came before ye, and ye are all, especially you, Cian and Josey, a credit to your parents. And remember these compliments when it's time to care for us old fogies.' The jokey plea is more touching because of the speaker's satisfaction in the well-rehearsed punchline. There's more, but most have already tuned out.

Deborah calls from Fuerteventura and he takes the phone out to the corridor to hear her better. Tells her he misses her. The three of them are having a ball, she says—her mother is not getting on her nerves at all actually—and when he speaks to his son he tells him he loves him. She asks about the storm, worries. 'I'll see you in a week,' he says.

The servers clear the cutlery and crockery until the plains of tables are populated only by clusters of glass. The wedding party lines the perimeter of the laminate wooden floor and watches the happy couple take their first dance. There are no rehearsed moves here, no flamboyance, only a slow shuffle. Cian and Josephine mirror each other's comfort.

John watches Orla dance with another cousin. She bounces her hips from side to side. Her legs are pale, shimmering, and he feels a deep hunger.

'No prisoners,' Paddy decides, and the talk goes like this until they are dancing themselves and trying to make fools enough of themselves to be charming, throwing arms and legs, doing twists and pumping fists and sweating, sweating, and going to the bar for more drink and shouting louder and louder all the time to get each other's attention.

John and Orla rant about some show they both enjoyed as kids, some painting he likes and wonders does she know, some important point about the state of play in the property market, some complaint about the banks, some story about how he plans for the future with his partner and son, some moan about how much he hates his job, how she's living her dream and how they were all meant for better than this, some borrowed anecdote about a friend who kidnapped a midget. And he's thinking about wedding mornings in the family home—the getting dressed up, the gel in the hair, the fixing of the tie in the mirror, the watch, the socks, the waiting for others, the fingering of the lapels, the open door letting the air in and just waiting, waiting, waiting to be walked out of. And still in the front of his mind he's thinking about Orla, her mouth, his room upstairs, about the vacant spaces all around them to lie down into. He's got his arm on her shoulder and then around her shoulder and she's punching his chest with her tiny fist when he mocks her. He's telling her how much he loves his girlfriend, how his little boy is learning the alphabet. Then they're on the dance floor again and he's holding her two clammy hands and they're rolling off each other and everybody is reeling, the place heaving like a ship in the storm.

A crowd has gathered. 'JJ! JJ! JJ! JJ! JJ! JJ! JJ!' Hands pinned behind his back the glass comes up, always seeming like it's about to slip from his lips. The nectar drains away until there is only a clear pint glass upturned, seeming to balance on his chin, and he bends then to let it back on the table and everybody is applauding hysterically. Paddy dances on a chair, beating the air with his fists. There is talk of smoking joints from someone's bedroom window. Pills are reported to be going round, nobody knowing the names of these things anymore. Boris watches, hands in pockets, a dopey, gleeful smile across his face. Despite wanting Orla so badly, John knows that he loves Debbie. His own Debbie. Tomorrow, he would regret it—if it were to happen—and here she is downing red wine in front of him, an ecstatic observer of life, her eyes and mouth saying, 'Yes! Yes! Yes! Yes! Yes!'

He is happy to find the bathroom empty. Staggering into the cubicle, he bounces off the wall, the toilet seat, the cistern. After letting down his trousers he prepares a handful of toilet paper on the cistern and then, facing the wall, relieves the urge. It is over quickly. Twitching culmination of ecstasy, he drops the sodden paper in the bowl and rights his trousers. Tucks the shirt and loosens. Thoughts of his absent partner flood him with tenderness. Deborah, he says. Debbie. The room spins.

On exiting the cubicle, the vision of the white tiles soothes him. He smiles. JJ comes in the door. 'HOOOOOOOOOOO!!!' John cracks up. JJ is pissing in the urinal and singing and John shakes him by the shoulders so that his piss will fly. JJ roars but pisses on and John falls about in convulsions and then some lad is laughing alongside them and now they are talking football.

In the wedding hall people pose for photographs, postures ludicrous and sincere. John emerges from the bathroom and realises the beauty of the room. Fairy lights adorn the long curtains and ivory drapes billow about a huge chandelier. Spotlights strobe the dancefloor, making holograms of the dancers. Everything reels and then Orla is there again.

'I was wondering where you went.'

She takes him by the arms.

JJ winks.

There are bottles of red wine still on the tables, tables that are lonely Shinto gods now, the chairs all pulled away from them. Orla arrives with a tray of blue shots and the group winces when they empty them. Someone else returns with more.

'Where does all the drink come from?' The shirts and tongues hang out; the eyes have lost all focus. Paddy's tie is on his head.

'We are the generation that remembers life before the mobile phone, before the internet. '

'Where did all the fucking drink come from?'

John dances with Orla, a glass of red wine in his hand, the liquid swirling in the glass. Funny how it moves like that. Some of it lifts out of the glass, defying gravity, spilling onto her dress. It's magical how it happens, but then she's looking at the wine stain on her chest and rubbing at it. He apologises, mumbling, and she laughs as she tilts a dollop of her own red wine onto his shirt. 'Now we're even!'

'Even?' He pours wine onto her legs, where it runs over her knees.

She shrieks. People look serious, then they laugh.

She empties a glass over his head. Lads around them are dancing with each other like lovers, hugging and cheek-kissing and mock-humping. Orla puts her hands to her mouth, shocked and amused at what she has done. JJ is hysterical about it all so John throws what's left of his glass into JJ's face. The dumbfounded look comes into the butcher, the widening of the eyes and O-shaped mouth. Orla is bent over, crying tears of joy, when JJ empties the contents of his own glass into her hair. Then she is shrieking again and someone else gets involved on her behalf, throwing a clear liquid onto JJ's shirt. It is as if John has only blinked and suddenly everybody on the dance floor is pouring alcohol over everybody else. Bottles of the Shiraz have been retrieved from tables and are poured liberally overhead. The floor is a shallow, bloody pool. JJ gets Paddy in a headlock and decants a half-bottle through his hair. Orla slips screaming on her arse. Some people still dance to the music, throwing their arms around and embracing the drink dispensed over them as rain after a drought.

The elders look on with awful faces. Paddy dives chest-first across the wet surface, crying, 'Slip'n'Slide!' John is tittering, tittering, tittering and still pouring whatever drink he can find over friends and strangers, sloshing some of it into his mouth, the rest over shoulders and backs. Three porters are trying to break it up but they're getting doused themselves. John sees Boris asleep at a table, head buried in folded arms; a full bottle is emptied out of John's happy hands.

The lights come on and the music stops. People drenched in wine run about like children in a gory water fight. There is a brief fight, soon broken up. The bar has been shut down and John and JJ trawl the tables for leftover drink. Someone says the guards have been called. Some men are pulling off heavy red shirts; one cousin is down to a pair of underpants, standing by the top table with his hands on his hips looking crossly about him. The two newlyweds are nowhere to be seen. The women begin to disappear into bathrooms and bedrooms.

'We'd be thrown out but for the storm,' someone says.
'The army's out for it.'
'For fuck's sake, we're not at war!'
The manager is telling people to go to their rooms. Anyone not staying is to assemble in the lobby.
'We'll have to pay for this damage.'
'Battle fucking Royale!'
'How the fuck did this happen?'
'It's only a bit of craic for Christ's sake.'
'The thing is that it's the random mutation of non-random cells.'
'Let's nobody lose their cool.'
'Who started it? For fuck's sake, who started it?'
'That's how you do it now.'

'There's no fucking taxis.'

'Of course there's no taxis. There's no anything out there.'

John understands none of this. He rocks there dead-eyed. He thinks about the Stanton account. About the Panini machine on the corridor outside his shared office. Then there's the wine drying on the faces and arms, filling the shoes. He's suddenly hungry.

'Has anyone food?' he asks. 'Has anyone any grub?'

In the lobby the manager stares, his arms folded.

Then John wanders corridors alone, in a dream within a dream, passing numbered bedroom doors. Down an echoing staircase with a yellow block wall. The little glass windows of service doors, all locked, show him kitchens and stores where he could eat if he could only gain access. A fire escape. He pushes the bar and goes out. Fuck them all.

The howling winds barrel down the dark side street. All becomes clear where it was muddled and dimmed before. The door won't open again to let him back in and he is bullied along by the wind. He lets out his tongue and turns his head sideways to catch the currents. In moments his clothes are dry. He could eat a horse. He could eat the chunks of slate and masonry that litter the streets, the fast apocalyptic clouds above him too. Tie flying in his face, he takes out his phone to call someone but fumbles and drops it, watches as the pieces are sucked away down the pavement.

'Fuck!'

His words too are swept away before he has a chance to hear them.

'FUCK YOU!'

All the wine, he thinks, shuddering in the cold gale, the cold gale pulling and dragging out of him.

By the river he grips the railing to stop himself going over. A million white waves ride the black water. He misses his son. I could eat the riverbed, he mutters to himself, enjoying his mute voice and the wind rattling through his head. I'm too hungry to go on. In the far distance he sees an army truck moving slowly, lights on full. He will buy the boy a remote control fire engine for his birthday. He is swept along in the direction of a bridge that shines neon on the river. A property sign flies out of the darkness and past him, hitting the railing only a few feet away, tipping up and sailing out over the river where it splashes into the dark again. The new city hall looms, a lit-up window-and-steel wedge on the cityscape. He's so hungry, he could eat city hall. He could mangle the whole fucking country, the storm and all, his hunger a void. He wonders whether hunger might be his thing. Staggering along, he wishes he was anywhere else: back at the hotel with everyone, home in bed alone, or on a beach in Fuerteventura, watching the boy build sand castles, comforting him when they are washed away by the tide, scurrying to help him begin them again. More than that, he wishes that he was no longer hungry, or that he could be certain about even one thing.

To All Their Dues

Wendy Erskine

Mo

Three types of beauty salon: the pristine Swiss clinic set-up where the staff might as well be in scrubs; tart's boudoir with a job lot of gold leaf and damask; and then the retro parlour with a few framed fifties pin-ups. Mo had tried something different. Tropical. An InvestNI start-up loan and a bit of money she'd saved bought her a tiny shop unit and some second-hand equipment from a liquidation auction. On the two-week start-up course they'd said about how you'd to achieve a total concept with it all working together to create brand synergy—the waiting area, the music, the décor. She had got a mate to do the painting. She had in mind a Caribbean paradise but when he'd finished it looked like a coffee shop off the Damrak. Would you like a quarter with your eyelash tint? Today's double-sell! The lights on dim and it didn't look so bad. The total concept got abandoned. The bowls of sand and shells in the waiting area should have been a good idea but people were always sticking their hands in and making the magazines gritty. After three days of *Classic Reggae: The Soundtrack to Jamaica* on repeat Mo retreated to the usual gentle ambient sounds and filled the bowls with boiled sweets.

What they said on the course didn't matter anyway because it was all about the quality of the treatments. Treatments were reasonably priced—allowing for a careful margin—and methodically executed. Nails, waxing, facials, bit of massage, fake tan. One treatment room. Total reliability: no day-release wee dolls messing things up. She was in the place for 8, ready to start at 9 and she was there for the rest of the day, six days a week. Mo was starting to get regular clients, which was good. When she opened she'd put an advert in the local free paper with a discount voucher (15%: enough to create a positive vibe) and that had got things started well. She wasn't fully booked at this stage—there were gaps in the diary—but she had known that this was how it would be for at least the first six months.

This morning Mo arrived at the same time as usual. The butcher next door was putting out his sign, a wooden cut-out cow, as Mo put up her metal shutter. Then she went through her routine: kettle on first, switch on the wax pot, light a few of the scented candles (black coconut). You needed to take away the smell of the bleach that lingered from the night before when the whole place had been washed down because ammonia wasn't very ambient. Switch on the heat: important this, although it was expensive. The place always needed to be warm because people felt awkward enough stripping down to paper pants for a tan and they didn't need to be freezing as well. The electric heater made a racket but no one had ever complained. Listen to the answer machine, turn the sign to open and finally, finally make the cup of tea.

Mo was reaching for the milk when there was a shatter of glass. She came through from the back and saw a hole in the window, a circle about two inches wide, and coming from it silver spokes that were tinkling as they crept further towards the edges of the window. Beside the table with the celeb magazines, a shiny red snooker ball had just come to rest. Mo heard the cracking of the glass, stared down at the ball, then looked at the window. Through the hole the road looked darker. She put the ball on the counter and went next door to the butcher's.

Did you hear that? Mo said. My window's just been put in.

The butcher shook his head, continued moving some meat from one tray to another. Shit, he said. That's not good. Do you need a number? For a glass place?

Yes, I do, said Mo. I can't believe that just happened.

Desperate like, he said.

I can't believe that just happened!

A woman came into the shop and he turned his attention away from Mo, did the what can I get for you my darlin?

Waiting at the bus-stop outside the salon were a handful of people.

Did you see what happened there? Mo asked them. My window's just been put in.

An old fella shrugged. A boy in school uniform didn't take out his headphones.

Yeah, a man said. Car pulled up and the window went down and they threw something. Drove off quick. Did anybody get hit?

Nobody got hit, said Mo. It was just the window that got wrecked.

Bad state of affairs, said the man. Nuts.

Mo's first client of the day, in for an eyebrow wax and an eyelash tint, never commented on the window.

Blue black? Mo asked.

Blue black, the woman said.

She had taken her shoes off to lie on the bed and they sat neat in the corner, sad little comfortable shoes. Mo mixed the dye in the glass vial then smeared the Vaseline over her eyelids and under her eyes, positioned the semi-circles of paper under her bottom lashes. That window. Unfair so it was. The woman's eyelids fluttered as the dye went on, cold and wet.

That's us, said Mo. I'm going to leave you for ten minutes to let that take. You warm enough? Mo pressed two cotton wool pads on her eyes.

Oh yes, said the woman, lovely.

Good then, said Mo, and she closed the door on the woman lying blind in the dark.

The man from the glass place said he couldn't come out until tomorrow but Mo supposed that was probably as good as she was going to get; she knew that even with the insurance this was going to work out expensive, one way or another. It wasn't a total surprise it happened, she had been expecting something or other. And shouldn't she be thankful that it wasn't something worse, good that it had happened when there weren't any clients around. That fella would call in soon again, she knew it.

Mo went back into the room.

All okay?

Yes, just nodded off, said the woman. Can I stay here the rest of the day?

Mo laughed as she cleaned off the dye, firmly and precisely, and then she handed the woman a mirror to look at the transformation. Before: eyes like a rabbit's, pink and fair. After: it's all the blue black. The woman made her mirror face, an ingénue smile even though she hadn't seen sixty in years.

Oh now that's great. That's great.

The eyebrow wax took seconds, a few swift strokes. Mo mentally calculated her pay per second.

As the woman went out, the butcher came in. Here you might be needing this, he said. We had a bit left over. And he held out a length of glass repair film.

He put it on with only a couple of bubbles rising.

Kids, huh? the butcher said.

Kids, said Mo. That's good of you, I appreciate it. That's great.

Just pay it, he said. Ain't really that much, just pay it.

She hadn't spoken to him before beyond hello. She didn't talk much during the day. Alright, if it was nails, you're facing the person and it's ignorant not to, so you have to talk, but people want to keep it light, holidays and work-dos and new shops that have opened in the town. Other treatments, people just need you to shut the fuck up so let them head off to wherever they want as the cotton wool sweeps over them or your hands smooth their skin with cream. Oh there were questions you could ask if you wanted to, bodies that begged for someone to ask why, what's all that about. That long thin scar, running along the inside of your thigh, lady in the grey cashmere, what caused that? Those arms like a box of After Eights, slit slit slit, why you doing that, you with your lovely crooked smile, why you doing that? The woman with the bruises round her neck, her hand fluttering to conceal them. Jeez missus, is your fella strangling you? But you don't ask, why would you?

Mo had done enough talking, done enough listening. The call-centre job she had done at night while getting the beauty qualification had a boss called Eamonn, a man from Donegal in a velvet jacket. The pay was very poor, he had told her, below the minimum wage, but for every thirty seconds over ten minutes you kept people on the phone you got a bonus. Plus you could work all the hours you wanted pretty much, right into the night. Theresa over there, he pointed at a woman drinking tea from a flask, Theresa earns more than I do. There was a choice: either the sex line or the fortune line. Irish angle on both: guys getting off talking to colleens or women having their future decided by Celtic mystics. The other new girl said, what's with the Irish stuff? I'm not telling some fella I'm Irish when I'm not. You'll just be on the phone, the man from Donegal had said. It'll just be the accent. Which for most people, regardless of your own local distinctions, is Irish. But I'm British, she said. I'm from the loyalist community. Eamonn had looked thoughtful. No, he said. No. That's just too niche. Loyalist psychic readings. Loyalist girls wanting to talk to you now. No, my sweetheart, you are Irish to your fingertips and if you don't like it then that, and he pointed, is the door. She had stayed though and so had Mo. And what would you say, asked Mo, if you were speaking to the fellas? 'Work away there', 'keep working away there' and 'that you finished?' I'm sure you can manage something better, Mo, he had said, if you want to earn any money. Mo was put on the fortune telling. No knowledge of anything spiritual required, said Eamonn. Just keep it sensible and lengthy. If anyone is in severe straits give them the number of the Samaritans. But only after a while.

You could feel them sometimes, people's hopes, even though all you wanted to do was just get on with your job. People looking at their faces, seeing a crumpled version staring back at them, hoping that the dermabrasion was going to make them feel like the time when they were thirty and they told that funny story at their sister's party in that restaurant and everybody laughed. For all this stuff you had to work neatly and quickly: people got nervous if you were hesitant or unsure.

Mo rolled the snooker ball in her hand. Not good. She imagined sitting down in the police station, those concerned faces when she explained what was happening, the offer to make her a cup of tea, the feigned surprise, the commitment that they would do something about it, then nothing, maybe the worse than nothing. Just pay it, the butcher had said. Ain't really that much. Well it really wasn't that much: you could recoup it with a late-night opening. But but but… that would be just the start of it. You could just see the sorry little tale taking shape: next thing it's a friend of mine's daughter needs a job, lovely girl, very keen, all those qualifications in beauty and you don't need anybody but you have to take her, and then the next thing is she arrives, hard piece, lazy-assed piece, and you are stuck with her loafing about and all her friends coming in for mates' rates. The guys next door were paying the money though and Christ knows who else on the road.

Maybe it wasn't any different to insurance. That's what the fella was implying. When he had come in before he had introduced himself and he had shaken her hand. Kyle, he said his name was. There was something about him that let her know that he was not some bloke coming in for a voucher for his missus, the only reason men came to Mo's place. She wasn't doing male treatments, no thank you, she was not doing back, sack and crack, not when she was working by herself, no way. The way he stood there, cock of the walk, like he owned the place.

With this situation there was no a, b and c. It was difficult to know what to do. That was what was wrong with the phone-line, idiots wanting advice from spirits or the runes or the stars and yet it was obvious what option they should take. Kick him out! Get out of the flat! Go to a gym! Go to the doctor! Tell her the truth! Give in your notice and look for another job! Can you not understand?

One woman had phoned up about her new dream fella who just didn't get on with her ten-year-old son, had hit him quite hard one time, although fair's fair, the son had been bad, beyond cheeky. Her fella had said that the son was gonna be a problem big-time before too long and she was just so worried about the situation and wondered if she should put the son into temporary foster-care, you know just temporary. Couldn't go back to being on her own again.

Pretty obvious what you should do love, isn't it?

What? the woman had said.

I said if you aren't thick as shit it is pretty obvious what you need to do, huh?

Silence on the end of the line.

People like you don't deserve to have kids. You hear that? The stars are saying that, and all the spirits in the spirit world, I can hear them coming through very clearly and they're saying you're a fuckin tool.

Mo didn't need the job any more anyway. She'd got the beauty qualification and the money saved and she was all set: a, b and c.

The next client was a full-body spray tan. Mo showed her into the cubicle where she had laid out the paper pants. White—if it was Marilyn-white, dense and creamy—was beautiful. But people weren't ever Marilyn-white, they were lumpy and mottled. Tan helped but everyone wanted it too brown; never mind the different calibrations Mo offered, they always went for the top intensity. Mo liked doing the spray tan. You needed skill. It wasn't just point and go.

What happened your window? the woman asked, shivering a little as the tan spray moved across her tits.

Mo shrugged, concentrating on progressing to the woman's shoulder blades. Not entirely sure, she said. Young ones messing. It'll be sorted tomorrow. Hopefully anyway.

Terrible, the woman said. A place was burgled the other week.

The man, Kyle, held the door open for the woman on the way out. It gave Mo a shock to see him standing there. He wore a leather suit jacket and held a briefcase that could have come from a game show, the prize bundles inside. He put the briefcase on the table and rested on the counter.

Problem? he asked, nodding towards the window.

It'll be fixed by tomorrow, said Mo, and she started fussing at one of the shelves, aligning moisturisers.

Kyle sighed slowly, shook his head. Not good, he said. This road isn't what it used to be.

Yeah, said Mo.

The other week, he said, I was only trying to help. Seriously. This situation is just what you are trying to avoid.

Through the broken glass and the cellophane Mo could just about see a man outside, leaning against a car. She said nothing but put her hands by her sides because shit they were shaking.

You live round here? he asked.

No, said Mo. Well, not that near, she said.

Yeah, you do, said Kyle. House with the white door, number 32. Is there any point in being stupid? he said.

Mo thought of her white door.

He spread himself out in one of the seats. You see, it's like this, he began. It's all about community. Communities don't run themselves. Businesses like yours, they're vulnerable, you see what I mean? There's a lot of people out there who are not nice people and all we are really doing here, you know, if I'm being honest, is offering you our help. As a member of the community.

I know what community means, said Mo.

You do? said Kyle.

I know exactly what community means, said Mo.

On the shelf by the window there was a line of OPI nail varnishes, running the range of colours of the spectrum, twenty of them. Mo watched as he used the back of his little finger to push from the left so that the varnishes fell slowly on to the tiles, one at a time. All twenty bottles, one at a time.

Only two actually smashed, a coral and a hot red.

You need to watch it, he said.

Mo swallowed. That leather jacket would be wipe-clean.

It'll need to be in an envelope, Kyle said. And it'll be a Friday.

On his way out he turned round. And you'll also be giving me a Christmas and Easter extra. Plus something over the holiday.

I'm talking money, he said. Fuck sake don't flatter yourself love.

Hey, she shouted after him, when she knew he couldn't hear. Hey, big man! You left your ball!

Another late night it would have to be then. Nothing else for it. In the appointments book she ruled the line for Tuesday down to the bottom of the page.

Kyle

The cemetery sloped down the side of the hill. Although it was big, there was rarely anyone there during the week and it was always cold up there, looking over the city. The older graves had granite surrounds and marble chips, some kept white with squirts of bleach, but most were green and mildewed. Kyle was at the lower section, the newer space, where the graves were less grandiose—just headstones side by side. He was nervous walking towards it. Over the past year there'd been the time when it had been spray painted with red loops—you wouldn't have known what it said, if it said anything—and then there was the day when someone must have taken a sledge-hammer to it. They'd knocked off a great lump. Scum, pure and simple. The worst time, and Jesus this was the worst time, was when somebody had shat on the side of the tombstone. They'd smeared it across his name, David Ian Starrs, and when Kyle saw it he was disgusted to the pit of his stomach. He had only been wearing a T-shirt and he took it off, run it under the tap at the bottom of the graveyard. He attacked the stone with a fury and thought about the sound of cracking bone and the way a lip swells.

T-shirt had been stinking. He couldn't see a bin so he just bunched it up and threw it a couple of rows away where it landed on an urn.

There's a fella's feeling the heat, said a fat man who was getting a bunch of flowers out of the back seat of his car.

What did you say? Kyle went over to him. What did you just say?

Nothing mate. The man held out his hands and shook his head. No offence. It was just, you know—and he pointed at Kyle's bare chest—feeling the heat.

Kyle grabbed the bunch of dog daisies and shoved them into the man's face, right into his mouth. He was making a choking sound and the flowers were falling apart but he still kept pushing.

Who the fuck do you think you are? Kyle said, genuinely inquisitive. Like who?

He didn't tell Grace about the man and the flowers but he told her what had happened to the grave this time.

Who's responsible for doing that? she had asked.

Don't know, he said, but he knew it could be several different people, several different groups. Davy's funeral had actually been on the TV, well the local news at six in the evening, but by the later news something else had replaced it. Afterwards they had sat in the bar with Davy's three little children marauding around and the two practically identical ex-partners. But today the grave was fine and nobody had touched it. Kyle traced the golden lettering with his finger.

Grace had said that they were going out for their dinner that night but he had not been enthusiastic. Well, we're going, she had said, and that's that.

Why? he had asked.

Just are. It's bring your own, so if you want to, bring your own. It's just new opened. I met the guy who runs it's wife.

Do we have to?

Yes.

Well, I got stuff to do. Tell me where it is and I'll just meet you there.

Kyle's stuff. A diverse portfolio. He had heard somebody say that once and he had liked it so he used it. Things had been better though: money came in well enough most of the time, but it wasn't always easy to maintain control. The taxi company, such as it was, did all right delivering the after-hours what have you, and then there was the shop and the mechanics that he had a main cut in. Most places were still paying up, as were the small dealers, but nothing felt secure. What was it? It was just—maybe it wasn't any different from what it had ever been and it was just him. Davy going had been terrible. That coroner:

heart attack brought on by steroid abuse, no way was Kyle having that. Why wasn't everybody having heart attacks then if that was the case? Basically the enemy was everywhere and there wasn't anybody left to trust except Grace who he did trust even though she probably disapproved of everything. Once, when there was a situation, she had been taken in for questioning for a day and a half and she had said nothing. In fact, one of them had said to him, you're punching above with that one Kyle. There were Hungarians on the scene now, they smashed up one of the bars and they were making inroads into things. And your woman, lippy fuck, going on about community the other day, oh I know about community, should've fire-bombed the place. Might still. The sort of people that were coming up now, they weren't the same. Boys were stupid, the ones who would have been part of it in the past now went to university, cleared out.

But maybe it was just him. That was why he was going to try this place, against his better judgment. A flyer had come through the door about it but it was far enough away for very few people to recognise him. It was above a dry-cleaners. He'd been past the other day to see what it looked like, the Class A Hypnotherapy. Just a staircase up and then some net curtains. Looked a dump, but if it worked it worked. Nothing else—and he had tried a lot of stuff—had made any difference.

The waiting room was a small white cube and on the wall there were testimonials from people who had been successfully treated at Class A Hypnotherapy. There was some ponce who he had never heard of saying that Class A had cured him of his stage fright and that he was ready to do a summer season in Blackpool for the first time in years. Fella looked a fruit, him and his nerves. Fuck him and his nerves. And then there was some student who had written to say that her troubles had cleared up thanks to yeah yeah yeah. There was a candle oil burner and the place smelled of a plant and the music was like you'd get in a Chinese. Kyle lifted out the candle and burned along the edge of one of the brochures on the table, setting fire to an inch or so at a time, and then blowing it out. When he'd done round the whole brochure he blew out the candle.

He heard voices, somebody coming out of the room and going down the stairs, and then a man appeared in the waiting room. Geoff, he said, extending his hand. Very pleased to meet you.

Kyle stood up.

And you are, he got a diary out of his pocket, you are—

Marty, said Kyle.

Well Marty please come on through.

The Chinese music was still on the go in the other room and there was a beige sofa where Kyle was told to sit because there needed to be a consultation before any treatment could begin.

We need to fill in a questionnaire, said Geoff. Your other name, Marty?

Kyle thought for a minute. The only thing that came to mind was Pellow.

Pellow, he said.

Alright, said Geoff, as he filled the boxes. Marty Pellow. Address?

Look no, said Kyle. Never mind my address. Are you gonna just get on with this?

I do need your GP's name, said Geoff with an apologetic smile. Who would your GP be now, Marty?

Arches, he said.

Right you are, said Geoff, writing in The Arches Medical Centre. So, he said, admin done, what brings you along to us today?

Kyle shrugged. Just the usual.

Geoff continued to look at him, his pen poised. Just what, Marty? How do you feel?

Alright.

You feel alright. What would alright be on a scale of 1 to 10?

Jeez. Seven out of ten, Kyle said. Maybe an eight.

Now that, said Geoff, is really quite good.

Yeah, so? said Kyle.

If most days you feel seven, maybe an eight, then why, Marty, have you come to see us?

There's only you here, yeah? asked Kyle. Why you keep saying us? Why you keep saying that when it's only you?

People come to us for all sorts of reasons, Geoff continued. Some want to give up smoking say, others have a specific fear, of flying perhaps, or maybe they feel nervous thinking about a particular event.

Kyle's face showed his opinion of these kinds of people.

And then there are those who come to us because they experience high levels of anxiety, manifest quite possibly in panic attacks, sleeplessness, obsessive-compulsive disorders—

Alright, said Kyle, don't be telling me any more about these people, I don't care. Could we just get on with whatever it is you do like, you know, maybe now. If that's convenient.

Geoff indicated a chair over in the corner. You sure you want to continue, Marty? he said. There's not a lot of point in continuing if you feel this isn't for you. The will must be there.

Well, he wasn't expecting it to be a man swinging a watch on a chain and saying look into my eyes but this was just a chair with your man perched on the desk, but then the chair reclined, like a La-Z-Boy, but so far back it wasn't a telly you were watching, it was the ceiling. There was a black spot on the ceiling. The man had gone out and come back with a blanket and a cushion that had been heated up.

Kyle threw the cushion on the floor. I don't think we'll be needing that, mate. He kicked off the blanket. All this shit would you just make a start here?

Geoff started to say the spiel. He was reading it off, you could tell, the way he was savouring every word. Something about a beach and the sun shining: yeah, he could imagine the beach, he could imagine a few hot birds in bikinis, okay well now they were starting to get off with each other. Well, that was pretty all right to think about, but Geoff said *Focus* really loud and then he was back to the room, listening to that voice of his going on about different parts of the body. That Chinese music was still on the go, the ribs and the black bean sauce, wee doll bringing over a sizzling dish, you spinning that revolving table. Mandarin City. Cueball ate the fortune cookie at the end, bit of paper and all. How the fuck was I meant to know, he said, give me yours and I'll eat it as well. That was a while ago though, some laugh, that fella was long gone.

Geoff was saying to think about contentment, when you felt in control, and Kyle is in the old front room where their dad is lying half on, half off the rug and the blood from his mouth is pooling on the floor. A couple of weeks before Davy had asked, you know the way I'm fourteen and you know the way you're thirteen? You put us together do we equal a man of twenty-seven? Must have put it into their heads they could swing it—and they did because when the old fella hit Davy full on the face the two of them laid into him and there he was on the floor. Still dangerous because they couldn't afford for him to get either one of them alone, but even that would only be for a certain period of time because they were getting stronger and his boozing was getting worse. Pathetic him lying there. Felt good to see the legs collapse from under him, pathetic the way he tried to appeal to them through the blood. Davy! And then, Kyle!

Even their ma was pleased. She said oh what's the world coming to, and all of that stuff, but she was happy and they knew it. She put a tea towel over his head. And that was what Kyle was thinking of, that was a good day.

Try to take a snapshot of that contentment, focus on a detail of that scene if you can, said Geoff, are you focusing Marty, on something specific? (Yes: the blood on the floor way darker than you'd think.) Can you do that, Marty? That's good. Good. You are going to hold that in your mind as a motif of happiness that you can refer to. You holding it in your mind?

I am, said Kyle.

And how are you feeling? asked Geoff.

Okay.

You're feeling good? asked Geoff.

Okay, said Kyle.

Hold that image and know that you are the same person who can achieve that contentment again, whenever you want, Marty.

But no, Kyle thought. No. Because Davy wasn't here and that made everything not the same. What the fuck was he doing lying with a blanket round him on a chair above the dry-cleaners listening to this pure shite, how bad had things got that this was what he was at?

Right, that's it. Over, that's enough. Will you move this fucking—he tried to push himself out of the chair—this fucking—

Geoff spoke calmly. The initial session can sometimes be a little underwhelming. Next time—

There'll be no next time, said Kyle. That's it.

Geoff took an invoice from a pad at the desk, calmly filled it in, and handed it to Kyle.

You got to be having a laugh, he said. Eighty quid to lie back in a chair and listen to you reading a script off a page, well I do not think so. Here, he hoked around in the pocket of his jacket, that'll do you, and he handed him a fiver. You are making easy money, pal, let me tell you with this fucking caper.

Geoff watched from the window as Kyle got into his car, slammed the door shut.

Kyle Starrs, he said aloud.

The restaurant had had a refit since it had been the burger bar. There were now white tiles and pictures from local artists. Every table had a couple of tea lights and a posy in a jam jar. Grace was already there, sitting at the table. Kyle came in, clinking with bottles.

Can I take those for you? the fella asked.

Kyle lifted out two bottles of Moët, and a bottle of Courvoisier.

One of those over in an ice bucket, he said. What? he said to Grace.

Nothing.

It's bring your own, yeah?

It's bring your own.

Well, then. What's the issue?

She sighed. Doesn't matter.

It's bring your own and I've brought my own. Jesus Christ.

The young man brought over the menus.

I'm actually quite hungry, Grace said. Haven't eaten anything all day.

Well, order whatever you want. Here, what's the hold-up with the drink? Kyle said. Oi! Mate! He pointed to the table. Drink?

The fella came over, apologetic. It's just that, we don't have any ice buckets yet. We're only open, I mean, we're only just open so not everything's quite right yet.

Grace smiled at him. No problem, she said.

Hick joint, said Kyle when the waiter had gone. Don't think much of this place.

Wise up, Kyle, Grace said. Just leave it for goodness sake.

The fella came back with the champagne, glasses and an improvised ice bucket in the form of a vase. Oh, not for me, Grace said when, having filled Kyle's, the waiter went to pour her a glass. I'm happy with this. She pointed to her tonic water.

Right you are, he said.

When the fella moved to the next table, Kyle poured Grace a glass of champagne. Cheers, he said.

I don't want any, Kyle. I said to you.

God, a glass won't kill you.

I don't want it.

There was no enjoyment in drinking by yourself. That voice of hers killed him. Always calm. He once had said to her, you know who you remind me of? Clint Eastwood.

That's flattering, she said.

I know it is, he had replied.

But she could make you feel like nothing. She wasn't impressed by much: a five star would mean as much as a two star. Jewellery she wasn't into. Not interested in fancy places, well that was obvious when you took a look round here. They could have been in the town at somewhere where you got treated really well, where there were plenty of people about to see you out and about. He knew fine rightly that she knew about the various other women over the years, but she never made a scene. He wouldn't have minded her being bothered, full-on furious, he wouldn't have minded if she'd punched and slapped him. Even that one time when your woman that he had seen on and off for a few months came round to the house to make a row, she had just said, a friend of yours to see you, and gone out of the house. Did your woman ever regret that one, but Grace never mentioned it again other than to say, please try to avoid that kind of thing, Kyle, because I could do without it.

The young fella was over asking them if they had decided what they wanted. Grace said she would have the pulled pork and Kyle said he wanted the steak. He hadn't looked at the menu, but he wanted the steak.

Well done, he said. I like it, you know, really well done.

The fella went away and then came back. It's just, he said, it's just that the chef says that it's a minute steak.

So what? Kyle said.

Minute steaks are meant to be cooked quickly. That's what the chef says, he added carefully.

No, said Kyle. Well cooked. End of.

Grace leaned across the table. They're only saying that if you want it well done, it's likely to be tough because minute steaks need to be fried quick.

Did we come out for a cookery lesson? Did we? Minute steak. What a load of shite.

The woman appeared at the table. We're sorry about the steak situation, she said. Maybe there's something else on the menu that you would like to choose.

No love, said Kyle. I've made my order, thank you very much.

Were you busy today? Grace asked.

Kyle shrugged. Just the usual. Was up at the grave, he said.

Used to be small, that graveyard, said Grace. It's eaten up most of that hill now. Everybody all together in that graveyard, she said.

Yeah well, said Kyle. Death comes to us all. Grim Reaper.

Does that steak come with sauce? Can't remember, he said. I don't want the sauce all over the top of it. I hate when they do that, slather the sauce all over the top of it.

The young fella came over to top up Kyle's glass of champagne.

You celebrating something? he asked.

No, said Kyle. That guy's doing my head in, he said to Grace when he had gone.

He's just doing his job Kyle, she said.

The steak, when it arrived, was a pathetic specimen, a shrivelled offering.

Well you got what you asked for, said Grace. You can't complain. So don't complain.

Kyle tried to cut it but it didn't yield.

Fucking shoe leather, he said. That's gonna bounce off the walls.

Try some of this, said Grace. It's nice. We'll share it and they can bring us another plate.

So I've come out for half a meal, he thought. I can't even get a proper meal. That ponce, what had he said to think about, what did he tell me, and he thought, yes, it was his da lying half on half off the rug. Davy had wanted to wrap that electric flex round his neck, the one that he used to hit them, but he had said no just leave it, that was enough, enough for now. Sore being hit with that flex.

Grace

The worst was the street-preaching when they stood in Cornmarket on a Saturday afternoon with two speakers, a microphone and a cardboard box full of tracts. If it rained they put the box in a black bin bag. On the rare occasion they went to places like Portadown or Lurgan and Grace didn't mind this so much because there would be no chance of seeing anyone from school. It would be the usual: you'd be cold and you'd get people either shouting abuse or laughing at you, but at least no one would know who you were.

There were things you could do to pass the time. You could count the paving stones for as far as they stretched into the distance; they started square and then, as they got further and further away, became wafers. You could hold your breath until you saw someone with a pink coat. Then you could hold your breath until you saw someone with a green coat. Then you could hold your breath until you saw someone in brown boots. You could do those same things in Cornmarket but you had no anonymity. Three o'clock on a Saturday afternoon there would be all the shrieking laughing crowd from school. Is that not your wee woman from our year? Your wee doll in that big coat? It is her. Feel wick for her. Shout something over but.

Sometimes there would be competition from other groups: fire-eaters, choirs and, now and again, break-dancers who would bring a CD player and turn it up loud until the sound broke. Grace's dad would turn up the preacher's volume and his sound won out because it had an amp. It was a cosmic battle between good and evil right there in Cornmarket, transmogrified into a street sermon versus 2 Unlimited.

An American evangelist had held an old-time crusade in a huge white tent on the O'Neill Road and the very first night he went Grace's dad had some kind of epiphany. On the next evening Grace's mum had one too. They started going to a mission hall that was opposite an old dairy and constructed out of corrugated iron. Women had to wear hats. There were some people who had apparently been very bad like Jimmy Baker who had given his testimony and told everyone about how he had found the Lord after being a gambler and a womaniser and a communist street-fighter. Jimmy Baker seemed so nice, sucking his mints in the back row.

Sunday clothes were uncomfortable in ways you could not have imagined. The tights were always too small and the good wool skirt scratched. The label on the nape of the jacket was stiff but it was stitched right in so you couldn't cut it out. The hat was like a pancake. There were lots of ways you could wear a beret, Grace's mother had said.

Yeah and every one of them stupid. The shop windows showed bright clothes, tight clothes. You walked past people, women, and they were all like the drawings in the maths book with the compass, soft concurrent semicircles. Grace's clothes, bought at charity shops, were chosen for their amorphous quality. Her mother talked about 'good' materials, wools, gabardine, camel hair, durable and decent. The girls in her class used tampons. Grace's mother thought tampons tantamount to rape.

The preacher was called the Reverend Dr Emery. Everything he said was in groups of three. Sin, despair and iniquity. Our Saviour past present and future. A strong, hot, welcome cup of tea, available at the back of the church after the service. The long, boring, repetitive service. You could stare at the Reverend Dr Emery in the pulpit until he doubled and became surrounded in black light and then you could look at the ceiling and see his outline in relief against the white-washed beams. You could make bargains with the Lord. I will believe if you make your woman there's hat fall off. She scratches her neck. Split second when you think it might happen. Hat stays on. You could listen to tales from a mostly Old Testament world of hard justice. You could listen to his lamenting tone: oh why is the world filled with such evil? You could think: I don't know if I believe this.

Then the Carson family started coming. They were tall, thin people, a husband and wife, who had been in Malawi for many years, mostly working on bible translation but involved in other projects too. Their own children had long left home but they fostered kids, short term, and they had plenty of room in their big double-fronted house with the overgrown garden. First there was a boy, about ten, who had a hearing aid and a green coat. Grace wondered if he could hear what the Reverend Dr Emery said; he mouthed the hymns like he was dubbed. Then there was an older boy, although he wasn't there for that long, whose head was always cocked to one side; oh aye right, it said. Then there was a girl who overlapped with him for a month or so, fat with a pale face. Grace's mother had said, why don't you go over and talk to her after church, so Grace had tried but the girl hadn't asked her anything back. Grace shifted from foot to foot until it was time to go. And then there was the next one who had a clump of hair dyed pink. After one of the bible readings she shouted out, Amen! and then started laughing. There was embarrassed, irritated shooshing. Later, Grace's mum said, I think that girl's a bit lacking. Shouting out like that. People don't shout out like that in our church.

She did it with an American accent, said Grace.

She's a bit lacking.

But that didn't stop Grace's mother asking her to go round to help the girl, Kerri, with her schoolwork.

Why? said Grace. It didn't go well, speaking to the other one.

This is a different girl. She needs help with her schoolwork.

Why can't Mrs Carson help her?

She's busy. You're going round tonight. I said to them that you would.

Like I'm the genius.

Don't be cheeky, Grace, her mother had said.

Mrs Carson said the bedroom was the first door on the right at the top of the stairs. Should she knock? Grace wasn't sure.

Hello, she called.

What you want? the girl Kerri said from inside. And then she came to the door. What you want?

I'm meant to help you with stuff, said Grace. That's what they said for me to come and do.

Who?

Them.

What stuff?

School stuff.

I don't go to school, Kerri said.

Then why did they send me?

I go to a centre.

They said I was to help you.

Well, I don't want any help, Kerri said and closed the door.

But her mother sent her back again the next night. Sometimes it's necessary to persevere. We need to do what we can where we can.

Not you again, Kerri said, opening her door when Grace knocked. Behind her everything was round the bed like a magnet: clothes, magazines, dirty tights with the knickers still in them, cans of coke. You could smell body spray but mainly smoke. Did the Carsons not notice?

Did you not get the message last time? she said. Why you here again?

Mrs Carson called them downstairs. Kerri screwed up her face. On the dining-room table there was a book with a rabbit on the front cover and a worksheet. The other kids were playing out in the garden, even though it was raining a bit. Mrs Carson said, Kerri, I want you to remember the talk we had earlier. You remember? No effort made with work, no allowance. No allowance, no whatever it is you like to buy.

Kerri scowled across the table at Grace. Then she lifted the book about the rabbit and opened it at a random page. Her finger slowly ran under each word and her lips silently formed the words. She read about ten pages like this, with Grace looking on redundant.

Then she sighed, closed the book. Done, she said.

What's it about? asked Grace.

Fucking rabbit, said Kerri. Did you not see the front of it?

Is that what you have to read?

If it wasn't, you think I'd be looking at it huh?

It's a rabbit that goes round doing stuff, she added.

She dropped the book on the floor.

The other one was about a homeless man, she said.

Was it better? Grace asked.

No, said Kerri.

Come on up the stairs, she said. I want to show you something.

Grace thought that Mrs Carson might object but she was involved in doing something in the kitchen and so said nothing. Grace found herself sitting on Kerri's rumpled bed. Kerri was pulling something out from behind her wardrobe. She sat down on the bed beside Grace with a magazine.

Never mind that, look at this, she said.

She opened the magazine at a page where there was a woman lying on a sofa with her legs wide open. Not totally naked: she had on gold platform heels.

What do you think of that then? said Kerri, holding it up close to Grace's face.

Grace said nothing.

What do you think of that?

She turned to another page with two women.

And that?

Never you mind you coming round here to tell me about this that or yon, you don't know it all. Look at it again. Look at this one. They're all at it. All that lot in that tin box just the same as everyone else.

You're not normal, Kerri went on. You're really weird. I seen you sitting there with those two, your mum and dad, all holy holy, and I think god help you. You know Helen Watson who used to live here, well she said the same thing about you. Said you were a psycho.

You're the one who's not normal, said Grace.

Oh aye is that right? I'm not going round like a granny mush fucking mouse. What you frightened of? Burning in hell?

No, said Grace. I'm not going to burn in hell.

Here let me tell you something, said Kerri. Let me tell you something. What year were you born in? What year was it?

1980, said Grace.

1980. So in 1979 you weren't here. Were you bothered? You weren't. So when you're not here again because you're dead, will you be bothered? No. You weren't before—so you won't be again.

Grace thought about this.

Hah! said Kerri. Think about that one. Put that in your pipe and smoke it. Aw, but no, you can't because Jesus says don't smoke.

1979. It was a nothing.

Kerri started reading the description of the woman from the magazine. Here listen, she said. Listen to this. She read it with a big pause between each word, the cadence of a kid, following the line with her finger. Cindy likes Cindy likes—

What? said Grace. What is it Cindy likes?

Kerri puzzled at the word.

Maybe, said Grace, maybe you should stick to the rabbit book, Kerri.

Kerri rolled up the mag and threw it at Grace. Read it yourself, she said.

Grace grabbed it, twisted it tight and hit Kerri across the cheek with it.

I didn't want to come here. Do you understand that?

Kerri came charging across the room, grabbed Grace by the hair and threw her onto the bed, elbowed her hard in the gut. Grace gasped—she couldn't breathe out. But it was easier to hit Kerri than she would have thought; her fist made contact with her stomach, taut as a drum, and she hit her again and again. They fell onto the floor on top of the dirty tights and the dirty plates. Kerri was quick and heavy, the ways she flipped Grace over, twisting her arm up behind her back. She couldn't move and Kerri kept pushing harder so that she thought she was going to be sick.

And then Kerri stopped. She was panting, trying to catch her breath. All Grace could smell was fags and hot fabric conditioner. Mrs Carson must put loads in the washes. Kerri took another handful of her hair and Grace thought she was going to get hit again but instead Kerri's mouth was soft although you could taste the blood like a coin.

At home Grace's mother was sewing a hem.

All go well? she asked.

It was alright, Grace said.

There are some booklets you could take round next time. There's those new ones that were sent from the States.

Sure, said Grace.

Her mother's hand stretched the thread taut, did a final double stitch and cut the thread.

When they were next in church there was a big empty space at the end of the pew where the Carsons sat. Kerri wasn't there. It was the same the week after and the week after that. After church Mrs Carson said that she was grateful that Grace had helped Kerri along a bit, but that she had gone back to live with her mother now. They come and they go, Mrs Carson said. This is for you, she said. She gave Grace a folded up piece of paper with an address and phone number on it. The frill of a spiral bound page torn off. Big bubble writing: written with careful deliberation, nearly pressed through the page. She kept the paper even though she knew that she was never going to phone or call round. She couldn't imagine it: going to the pictures with Kerri; going for a meal with Kerri. Sending each other a Valentine: it seemed preposterous.

The next week Grace didn't go to church. She said it was because she wasn't well, but when her mother came up to her room, she said the thing is I'm giving going to church a miss for the time being. She knew that they prayed for her all the time. They sent Reverend Dr Emery round to see her and she sipped a cup of tea slowly while he told her about lost sheep and the prodigal son. He tried to scare her by talking about girls he had heard of who had strayed from the righteous path and who, without exception, had come to a bad end. They would congregate at the front door, there would be whispering and then he would go. There would invariably be a quiet knock on her door. Everything alright, Grace? Her mother would be hopeful. Fine, Grace would nod.

There was pain and there was passion and there was no God. Some people had to wait a lifetime to find out that kind of thing, had to study and read books, gaze up at the stars. But it had been made apparent to her when she was young, it had come all in a rush when someone was whacking her with a porno mag. You might never experience that intensity of revelation ever, ever again.

You lived your life. You didn't expect anything too much. There were holidays and meals and trips to the multiplex and city breaks. There was work in the nursery, which was good fun most of the time. All that intensity was a long time ago now. She loved Kyle and wouldn't leave him. Would he have been like how he was if it hadn't been for that brother of his, getting him into stuff? Good riddance to Davy. Live by the sword die by the sword. Matthew 26: 52. She could remember that. Grace had found out she couldn't have kids. They had tried IVF but it hadn't worked. She had been frightened he would go off with one of the others but he didn't. Doesn't matter, he said. I've got you and that's what matters. Sex was useless because she felt a dud.

She went to church one time, nostalgic for her youth, when she saw a poster for a crusade, but it was a small scale affair that took place in a hall where the floor was marked out for badminton and basketball with coloured tape. All the people were old and had all been saved years ago. There was no singing, only a man and a PowerPoint, but she ended up helping out with the teas because there was something wrong with the urn.

This morning Grace was leaving stuff at the dry-cleaners and then going to the beauty place. She had been there practically every other week since it opened. She had never thought before that she was high maintenance, but now it turned out that she was. She wouldn't have thought of going there if she hadn't seen the advert and the voucher in the paper. The woman was just starting out. Weird little box of a place but she liked it. It was always warm, and it smelled of coconut. The girl didn't say much which was good. The first time she had gone, it had been for a leg wax. It was sore. The woman had said, next time, take a couple of paracetamol before you come. You know what in fact, she had said, take a couple of paracetamol and a brandy. Can only make it better. She had taken neither the paracetamol nor the brandy. The girl's face was sometimes only a couple of inches away from you: you could run your finger along that frown of concentration. That pony tail, you could wrap it round and round your fist, pull it tight. She always looked preoccupied. Grace thought about her all the time. What did other people think of? Lying on beaches? Being in the Caribbean? To do lists? Grace though about the taste of blood, a woman in gold high heels, lying face down on a bed. It was a disappointment every time when the woman said, well that's it, I'll leave you to get ready and I'll see you outside. The dull thud of the well this is all there is.

And here she was again, back for more, sitting waiting for the woman to get the room ready. She looked at the line of moisturisers, the row of nail varnishes, the stack of magazines.

What happened the window? Grace asked when the girl appeared.

It'll be fixed this morning, she said, if the fella ever arrives. Go on into the room, it's all set up, and I'll be through in a minute.

Jessie

Oisín Fagan

I used to be a passenger in Laura's car. I think that was when I was happiest, though you can never be sure about these things. When she wasn't there, her boyfriend and I would drive around instead. Back then I would reach my head out the window and whistle or bark at women who were walking on the side of the road. Shane soon picked up the habit and we became known around town as troublemakers, though we rarely ever stepped out of the car, the car being our sanctuary. I had picked up the habit during my year in Boston when I worked on the sites, labouring for a virile bunch of men who I liked so much I continued wolf-whistling at girls when I returned home. Every time I leant my torso out the window and screamed at a young woman I would recollect fondly the time I spent with those men. But when Laura and Shane were together in the car it was different. It was then that I would lie down on the backseat, just smoking cigarettes and listening to their constant, vicious arguments. I would feel dazed and think maybe hell was just repetition and that when fire bites your heels it is not the burning that hurts, but the fact that there is nothing new in the flames. On good days though, there were no better people to be around. Then we would go anywhere. We would go to Funtasia in Bettystown and I would watch schoolgirls who were on the hop crashing into each other in bumper cars, or we would go to Howth and sit on the pier in the wind and eat expensive, vinegary chips, or we would go to Trim castle and climb on the ruins of the old churches and sit on the soft grass on the banks of the Boyne and lie there for hours. Of course it came to an end soon before I went to England looking for work.

The end came one day when we were in the Tesco in Maynooth, sitting in the car park sharing a strawberry milkshake and listening to Bruce Springsteen. Springsteen's *Greatest Hits* was the only album Shane had in the car and we had never listened to anything else, though it was really only me who liked the album. Laura had just begun to shout at Shane over some spilled ash on the floor when I saw a girl I was interested in walk by going into McDonald's, still dressed in her school uniform. Checking the dashboard, I made the time out to be two o'clock, which meant she was mitching. I whistled at her loudly, forgetting Laura was in the car. The girl's older sister's boyfriend, who I used to go to school with, had told me she'd turned seventeen that February, so there was no risk. She didn't turn around the first time I whistled, so I stuck my fingers in my mouth and whistled again, even louder this time. She still didn't turn around, but just went on through the glass doors into the restaurant. Laura, distracted from her burgeoning argument with Shane, turned to me and said, What the fuck are you doing? I looked from her to Shane. Nothing. What are you talking about? Do you think it's okay to do that? she asked. I could hear the spite in her voice. Ease up, Shane said. Here, I said tiredly, don't be at me as though you've nothing of your own worth harping on about. What? said Laura What did you say? Laura, Shane pleaded. Go easy, he's heading soon.

I could see out of the corner of my eye the girl idly eating chips just inside the McDonald's window, slowly stirring each chip in a shallow pool of ketchup on her tray. Shane and Laura had started arguing about how Shane always sided with me in arguments because I was a man. This might have been true, but she always sided with me against Shane whenever I disagreed with him. I don't know why, but it must have something to do with relationships, which I've never been much good at. At some point, after I stopped listening to them, Laura turned to me and said, You're both pieces of shit. Fuck you, Laura, I said. Whoa, said Shane. Laura was shocked; usually I was quiet during their outbursts. I had gone too far and I could see Shane would have to take issue with what I said, so I made it easy for him. Fuck you both, I'll see you around. And then I pushed the door open and slid out, leaving them both speechless. I was careful to slam the door, and as I walked away towards the McDonald's I could still hear the muffled sound of Bruce Springsteen's voice.

When I went into McDonald's I made sure not to go straight up to the girl so I ordered a coke at the till and sucked at it through the straw for a while, leaning against the counter and watching her from behind. Her name was Jessie and she was in fifth year. I think so anyway. I waited there for about five minutes and then she turned around at last. She saw me and smiled. She walked towards me, teasingly sauntering past to put her rubbish in the bin. Underneath her long school dress, I could see she was wearing a pair of high heels that clacked off the large diamond-patterned tiles. She looked over her shoulder and called at me, grinning: You still acting the pervert, Jim? Watching schoolgirls from a distance? Oh, nothing like that, I was just passing by and thought I might have recognised you, I said, still slurping on my coke. For some reason, I felt good and free. You still riding bitch with your faggot friend? she said. Ha, I laughed back sarcastically. No, that's all done with now. So you got your own car then? she asked, in a way that gave me pleasurable shivers on my neck. Not yet, I answered. But I'm working on it. She was closer to me now and, as though her confidence had vanished in proximity, she had begun to look at her feet. We can still have a gander up the canal, if you'd like? I suggested. Sure, she said. Just give me a minute while I pop off to the loo. Grand, I said, grinning. She walked off and I quickly went to the window, to see if Shane's car was still there. It was, but because of the way the sunlight hit off the windscreen, I couldn't tell if anyone was still inside.

Still peering through the window, I didn't notice Jessie coming up behind me. She pinched my ear. Are you coming? Of course I am. When we went out I put my hand on the small of her back to guide her to the left so we wouldn't be walking past Shane's car. She offered no resistance, so I slipped my hand around her waist. It felt small and warm underneath my hand, even through her blue school jumper. We walked like that down the canal, which was very pretty at that time of year, though Jessie just looked at her feet most of the time. A few times she looked up at me as though she were struggling for something to say. I could tell she wanted to kiss me, but was too afraid, and I began to lower my hand even further. Then, before I got too low, she said, Do you want a joint? Sure, I said, only slightly surprised. Have you tobacco? Uh-huh, I nodded. Let's sit down here, I said, motioning to the grass beneath us. She lowered herself onto her knees, spreading her skirt before her as a flat surface for the rolling. I lay on my back, looking around me.

The grass around us was warm and sweet-smelling. Between us and the canal were lengths of tall rushes that had grown in the shallows of the banks where a solitary swan drifted by from time to time, going back and forth, its gracefully arched neck like a question mark. The only other breathing thing in sight was a middle-aged man in an overcoat sitting on a deckchair further along the canal casting a fishing rod. Both sides of the canal were bordered with ash trees, spaced haphazardly enough to give them the misleading appearance of sprouting up of their own accord without human interference.

I looked at Jessie beside me. She was hunched over so her hair fell in swathes across her small face looking for skins in her breast pocket. I leaned forward and brushed her hair away and kissed the back of her neck. She shivered and I saw gooseflesh appearing on her skin. I guided her cheek with my fingers so she was facing me. Her mouth hung open very slightly and her breath had quickened. I eased her back onto the grass and then I brushed her cheek again with the back of my hand. She closed her eyes and swallowed and I began to kiss her. She worked her tongue slowly at first, but soon her movements quickened against mine. Kissing her was as pleasant as I had imagined it would be, although I was annoyed by her flesh-tinted make-up rubbing off my nose and my eyelashes. Slipping my hand underneath her jumper and shirt, I could feel the small arch of her hips and the slenderness of the white skin on her belly, like the underside of a cat. With my forefinger, I traced playful patterns across her abdomen, each one getting lower, until I could feel the buckle of her skirt, the clasp of which I took between my thumb and middle finger. She giggled and pushed me away, whispering that it tickled. I grinned and, leaning forward again, bit her ear, squeezing the lobe softly between my teeth. She squealed and laughed. As I was about to put my hands beneath her skirt again, approaching from beneath the hem this time, she once again pushed me away, this time more forcefully. Stop, she said. I sighed and sat up, gazing at the canal and resting my chin on my knees. She rearranged her dress and started rolling the joint. I gave her a cigarette without speaking or looking at her. Neither of us said a word. The silence lasted for a few minutes and in that time I saw the man down the canal catch a medium-sized fish, possibly a trout. The fish danced upon the line in its death throes like a haywire puppet on a string. This lasted for a few seconds before the man finally got a firm grip on its slippery body, but only after its oscillations had defied him several times and left him grasping at air foolishly, making him look like a frustrated shadow boxer. Then, rather than unhooking the fish, he ripped the hook out of its mouth violently, so that he must have rent the lower half of its mouth in two. He beat the fish's head off the ground for so long that its body must have been near disintegration. Then, strangest of all, he threw its limp corpse back into the water carelessly, before casting out again. It made me nervous wondering how long he had been doing this, repeating this redundant, violent procedure.

While I was still wondering, I noticed that Jessie had already lit up and inhaled several times. I looked at her and saw she was an inexperienced smoker. She gulped the smoke like she was drowning or trying to prevent herself from vomiting. After she was finished, she handed me the slim joint, burning end first, and lay on her back in the grass. I smoked for a while, staring at the small ripples on the edge of the canal made by the haze of insects that treaded the surface of the water, until I saw that Jessie was staring at the sky with one eye closed and tracing clouds with her finger. She giggled softly from time to time and I thought how she seemed very young now. At the same time, I noticed that with her knees drawn, and lying on her back, her dress had slid up enough to expose a sliver of white underwear. I was about to put my hand on her thigh again, but I thought better of it and went back to staring at the canal. At some point, she asked me: Do you do this often? What? Smoke? I said. Yes. No, she said. Do you do this with girls often? No. I shook my head. You're the first. She craned her neck to look at me. One of her eyes was still closed and there were some blades of grass tangled in her dark hair. No. I mean with girls from school, she said. No, I repeated. The grass in her hair made her look feral and I couldn't stop looking at it. Well, she continued, Stacey says you were going with her a while and you went with a load of ones from sixth year. Well, Stacey's a little slut, I said, and I wouldn't fucking touch her. Okay, she nodded placidly, almost happily, and began to look back at the sky. Stretching her hand out, she said, Give us that. I handed her the ends and she sucked on them deeply and began to cough. I waited until she had finished coughing and I asked, Jess, are you a virgin? What? she said, surprised. I said: Are you a virgin? What do you think? she snorted and put her hands behind her head. I think you are, I said. She laughed falsely. I'm not, though it's none of your business anyway. I think you're full of shit, Jess, I said, pulling a tissue out of my pocket to blow my nose. Fuck you, she said. I laughed and then we were quiet again for a while. She closed her eyes, which had begun to redden, and began to breathe deeply and slowly. I watched her while she lay there on her back, almost asleep, and I lit another cigarette, grinning to myself. Then she began to talk to me again, but it was as though her words were directed at herself, and my presence was incidental. Draping her hands over her face like a fan, she peered through her fingers at me. I don't know why this, along with the slip of her underwear visible and the grass in her hair, excited me as much as it did. And when she began to talk I thought she was opening up to me, which these young girls usually do before they commit themselves to me. They act as though their secrets are the price for their bodies and they feel safer once they've spoken, as though the act of giving makes the receiver as complicit as the giver. But I see through the hypocrisy of it. They know they're lying to themselves. They're lying to themselves through the truth and through me. But I don't mind, because at least what I want is on some level honest, and that's enough. But Jessie was different, or maybe she was just stoned. She started speaking while still peering out through her fingers, as though her fingers were a door and her eyes were peeking through the keyhole.

You used to go to school with Damien? she asked. Yeah, he was in my year, I answered. You know he's going with my older sister. Uh-huh, I nodded. Well, he used to pick me up from school after basketball training. He had a car. Okay, I said, prompting her to continue, though not really interested. She hesitated for a moment. Well, one night, last year. It was raining, I remember, and he was waiting for me outside the gates, opposite the Protestant church. I remember he seemed weird because when I came out he was holding the steering wheel and looking at it, like he was thinking, and usually there'd be music playing in the car, but that night he was sat on his own in the dark, looking at the steering wheel and I knocked on the window and asked him to let me in and he unlocked the passenger seat. I was soaked and it was really dark because the lights were broke so I kept standing in puddles in my tennis shoes cause I couldn't see the puddles at all. You know, because it was so dark? Okay, I said, not knowing where this was going. Well, she went on, I got in and we drove along and neither of us talked. I thought he must've been in a mood or something or maybe he was just concentrating and I didn't mind. I could stand it cause the trip isn't too long. It's like five minutes cause I live just behind the Glenroyal and there was no traffic so it would've took even shorter. But when we were passing the station he said to me, real quiet, he said, I'm gonna rape you and I don't care. I'm gonna fuck you whether you like it or not. I'm going to open your legs and rip off your skirt and fuck you right here in this car. What do you think of that? And I began to shake and I had to hold the sides of the seat to stop my hands shivering and I just said nothing. But he kept talking anyway. He wouldn't stop. He was like the buzz of a machine that won't stop and he kept saying things like, I'm gonna fuck you from behind and you'll drink it. You'll fucking swallow it. You won't like it at first, but you'll fucking love it later. And if you don't, I don't give a fuck. I'll show you. When we reached the house he pulled up outside the drive and I could see my mam in the kitchen window washing the dishes or something. She hadn't noticed us cause he had killed the lights and even when he killed the engine he kept talking with his hands on the wheel, staring at it. I'm gonna fuck your tits till you bleed and you're not gonna tell anyone and if you do I'm gonna fuck you again till you shut the fuck up. I'm gonna fuck you so hard you'll never speak again. I didn't get out of the car. I was shaking so much I couldn't even move. I just looked at the house again and my mam in the window doing the dishes and I began to cry. I covered my eyes, so he wouldn't see and I just cried and cried. I cried for ages and when I looked up he was looking at me and his eyes were sad and he said, I'm so sorry, Jess. I'm so sorry. I didn't mean it, but I could reach for the handle now, I was empty of tears and could move again and I ran out of the car. I didn't even shut the door behind me and I ran up to bed, making sure nobody saw me and I just lay in bed for ages just thinking and not sleeping. I don't know what I was thinking but I promised I'd tell nobody and I've not spoke a word till now and I don't think I'll tell anyone else, cause there's no need.

She stopped at this point and pushed herself up to a sitting position and stared at the canal. She straightened out her dress and I saw that she seemed calm now, tranquil almost. Jesus, Jess, I said. I'm so sorry. I'm so sorry. No, it's grand, she said and gave me a wan smile. You don't get it, she said. You don't get what I'm trying to tell you. I was silent for a while and looked at my shoes. Then she continued in a different tone of voice as though she were taking a different tack: No, the only thing that gets me is that I see him all the time and neither of us says anything, but I'm always thinking. Thinking of what? I asked, trying to seem genuine. I'm always thinking, she said, I'm always thinking, well, will he do it again? And if he would, would it be so bad? What? I said. Would it be so bad, she repeated. Jesus Christ, I said. What the fuck? She looked at me and I could see her soft eyes and her mouth hanging open. My stomach clamped itself into a knot and my heart was hammering my ribcage as I closed my eyes, fighting down a surge of nausea. Look, Jess, I said, swallowing drily in between words, this weed isn't the best and it's working on me something awful. I'm going to head. Are you not going to walk me home? she asked, almost pleading. I waved my hand at her. No, I've got to go. Please, she said. Please. I'm sorry. I didn't mean to… No, no it's grand, I said, standing up. It's just I've got to. I'll see you soon. Bye. I turned around and she called my name, but I had already started walking away.

By the time I reached McDonald's I had stopped twice to kneel down, thinking I was going to vomit, but my retching had produced nothing except for a vile taste in my throat and on the back of my tongue. I felt relieved when I saw Shane's car, still parked where I had seen it last, but when I got up to it I could see the passenger seat and the driver seat were empty and that Shane and Laura had left. I had no keys, but I circled the car again and again, knocking uselessly on the windows. The inside of the car was cloaked in shadows and I thought if I kept looking at the shadows, my friends would appear. I thought about breaking in a window so I could lie down in the backseat and smoke, but instead I lay on the bonnet and smoked a cigarette. Afterwards I started to circle the car again, knocking on the windows and whispering, Laura. Let me in. Laura. Laura. Let me in. I finally stopped. I leant my head up against the window in defeat, my nose and cheeks pressed ghost-white against it, like a flower compressed in a book. Then I whispered one more time, Let me in, before I walked through the empty car park alone, looking for loose cigarettes in my pocket and trying to empty my mind of everything it had ever held.

Pascal's Wager

Michael J. Farrell

Every morning, out of the blackness, a hint of brightness would appear, impossible to say when one gave way to the other. Soon a saffron ribbon would emerge, or some silver lining, or, on days of destiny, bronze. After that it was only a matter of time until the world was up and making mischief.

Ronan looked at his watch. Not yet seven. His pyjamas sported a white crossways stripe like a jailbird. His large angular head hinted at a big bony body under the blankets. The chemo had taken the little hair that was left at eighty. The blue eyes were alert like lights on a dashboard that showed the motor still running.

'Good morning, Malachy,' he said when the watch edged past seven. Ronan had volunteered to double up with Malachy, who had not spoken a word for two years. 'Another foggy one, I'm afraid. Did you sleep well?' He always threw in a question in case a miracle happened overnight and Malachy might be bursting to talk.

Down the hill past the two ash trees was the river—which was why this was called the Riverside Nursing Home—a prudent river that never overflowed. Where it took a turn one could see the water reflecting the bronze sky. The wall was still there, if it was a wall. And where the wall met the water: a boat, if it was a boat.

Someone shuffled by on the corridor. From the distance came the clatter of dishes. 'I'll will you all my worldly goods, Malachy, if you'll just say something.' Ronan scratched his groin. He could stand himself no longer, reached for the mobile.

'I need to urinate.' He knew Starski was on duty.

'Good morning, Ronan,' she said affably. 'You know how to urinate. Or shall I walk you through it, step by step?'

'If you would, please.' But she had cut him off. He eased himself out of bed, sat for a minute to check aches and pains. He had only one crutch, which he used under the right or left wing depending on the spur of the moment. 'I'll be back in a minute, Malachy, don't go anywhere.'

When he emerged from the toilet he got into the faded blue robe. The television set was still asleep on the wall. The wardrobe had a mirror attached, in which the remaining tatters of his ego refused to look at him. On the locker beside his bed was a black-faced clock, a stack of books and more on the floor. Malachy's side of the room was crowded with medical instruments and plastic tubes, one of which was stuck in his nose supplying a sort of life. There was a print of a clamp of wet turf by Paul Henry on one green wall and a calendar on another. It was a hard room to love. He phoned Starski: 'The senior occupant of 244 is moving out. Malachy wishes to be excused.'

'Leave me alone, Ronan,' Starski said. He never risked phoning the other nurses.

In the dining room, Benny and Sara were already eating their bran flakes.

'You're late,' Sara said. She was ninety and counting. She had lost her dentures years ago and no one had ever replaced them. She was in love with Ronan and told him so whenever she could pry him loose from Benny, who in turn was in love with Sara. The three of them stuck together, Benny said, because they were the only intellectuals left in the nursing home.

'The sun came up again,' Ronan announced as he attacked his lukewarm porridge.

'It's tireless, that sun,' Benny said. 'That's several times this week.'

'You're looking debonair, Ronan,' Sara said, 'you must have slept a sight.' She had spilled the milk and it dripped from the table into her lap.

'Thank you, Sara.'

Meanwhile, other residents were wheeled into the dining room. The walls were green like the bedrooms and kissed in places by the sun. The toast arrived. One girl brought coffee and another tea. Life seemed ordinary, Ronan thought, yet every time the sun showed up it instigated enough intrigue to drive the world out of its mind. He pulled out the mobile and dialled expertly with his thumb.

'This is Ronan O'Day, don't hang up. I need to go to confession... I know—I'm sorry, I won't do it again.'

'What did he say?' Benny wanted to know.

'He didn't say anything, he just hung up.'

'By the hokey,' Benny's laugh sounded like a series of hiccups. He wore stylish, gold-rimmed glasses and never left his room except in his blue striped suit and a white straw hat on his round head. 'If I was you I'd report him to the bishop.'

'It's no use. The bishop is running out of clergy and the few who are left have forgotten how to hear confessions.'

'Sure, don't I know. I never bother myself.'

'You're looking debonair, Ronan,' Sara returned to her theme.

'Did I ever tell you about Pascal's Wager?' Ronan asked.

'Tell it, Ronan,' Sara coaxed.

'Just between ourselves, Pascal's Wager is why I need confession.'

'Go on,' Benny encouraged.

'Do you believe in God, Benny?'

'Well sure I do.'

'And have you any proof?'

'I don't need any—haven't I got along grand without proof until now?'

'A God that might send you to hell?'

'Oh, I'm going to hell for sure,' Sara said with enthusiasm.

'Blaise Pascal,' Ronan held up the cup for more coffee and dumped an extra spoonful of sugar into it, feeling expansive, an intellectual among intellectuals. A world of nostalgia drifted up from his days at university when athletic young men and mysterious girls solved ancient enigmas in cafés down Dublin's side streets on evenings that had no end. 'Blaise Pascal was a philosopher, you see.'

'A what?' Sara asked.

'One can't be sure God exists: that's where Pascal came into the picture. Aquinas's five proofs, Anselm's ontological argument, when it comes to real life these are only old wives' tales.' He lit a cigarette. 'Here's the nub of it: God either exists or doesn't exist. If the chances are fifty-fifty, you might be tempted to take a sporting chance. But you'd be on thin ice. Because, if you backed the wrong horse, hell might be waiting on the other side.'

'You're a genius, Ronan,' Sara's head was lolling, her eyelids drooping.

'So if one met God over yonder, with heaven in his right hand and hell in the left, a hell full of burning and regretting that might go on for eternity, one could, to say the least, be in a fix.'

'So long as there's a toilet there, I won't mind,' Benny said and shuffled off.

'But if one has wagered on God's majestic existence,' Ronan focused his full attention on the sleeping Sara, 'then one can face the future with equanimity. If, at the heel of the hunt, we find no one there, we won't have lost anything. We'll just have darkness, which, under the circumstances, won't bother us. But if God is indeed among those present, why, we'll be glad we bet on a winner. That's what Pascal said, back when the world was innocent.'

Sara opened one eye and smiled.

'But there's a catch, Sara, old doll. If we bet on God, we have to stick with the straight and narrow. Don't bear false witness. Put money in the poor box. Go to confession when lust raises its head or we want to kill a neighbour.'

Several crows were perched in the trees beyond the window, sullen and watching. Another couple arrived and a few flew off. They knew a lot from observing people. Certain crows were said to live ten thousand years, and the last thing the world needed was some ornithologist to come along and disprove this for her Master's thesis. Ronan removed the mobile from his robe pocket, put the robe around Sara's shoulders.

'Spiffy pyjamas, Ronan,' Starski passed him on the corridor.

It took an hour to dress. 'It's not us, Malachy, it's time that has shrunk since we were young.' He dialled again. 'Is that Riverside Radio?... This is Ronan O'Day, don't hang up. Aye, the schoolmaster. Am I on the air?... The priest refuses to hear my confession...Very well, I'll be back tomorrow.'

The carers had changed Malachy's sheets during breakfast. They had topped up the liquid in his plastic pouch. Short of a miracle, he would never eat another fried egg. His closed eyes pretended to peer over the fresh white linen. He didn't need to be conscious for his hair to keep growing, and his white stubble. Occasionally there would be an accident under the sheets followed by the odour of sanctity, which the carers took in their stride because they all had hearts of gold.

'Hold the fort, old friend.' He took two extra pills for the pain. He buttoned up the topcoat and slipped out the side door. When the sun came from behind a gable, his pale shadow hobbled ahead of him down the hill. All he could see was a dab of colour in the distance. The only excuse to call it a boat was its proximity to the river. That and a belief in destiny. The bladder was a problem, unpredictable and impatient. When he reached the hedge, he peed with satisfaction on the safe side of the laurels.

A moment came when the coloured object was unmistakably a boat. That still left unanswered questions. Was she seaworthy? Were there oars? Still, one had to take some risks with life.

'It's a boat all right,' he announced to Sara and Benny at teatime. 'You know the routine,' he said to Benny after Sara fell asleep by the radiator. Benny grinned until his face bulged, and saluted in silence.

Back in his room, Ronan phoned again. 'I need confession,' he said without preamble.

'The last time,' the priest said, 'you blasphemed.'

'And if you come over, I'll confess it.' The lonely purr of the phone told him the priest had hung up. 'Did you hear that?' Ronan said to Malachy. 'You'll have to do.'

He brushed his teeth. He turned the bedside light low, lay on his back on the bed.

'It's sixty years, more or less, since my last confession.' He lit a cigarette, placed the ash tray on his belly, blew slow smoke at the ceiling.

'If it's all right with you, we'll skip the preliminaries and go straight to the meat and potatoes.' He glanced at Malachy, who raised no objection. 'There was a girl—that's the part I want to get at. When I was at the university. We were all young—young and foolish, what can I say, but in fairness we were also planning to change the world. Debating about Plato and Nietzsche and Moses and the pope, drinking and smoking and showing off.

'There was one girl, as I say.' How explicit would he need to be? A real priest would probe for the telling little details. 'Everyone said how beautiful she was. I took their word for it, though personally I don't any longer see that it mattered. When word spread that she was pregnant, Nietzsche proved to be of little help. There were no potential fathers rushing forward to claim their prerogatives. And there was no wronged high-cheeked girl to point the finger. She had disappeared. It was easy to disappear because none of us looked very far. The summer exams were approaching. We had futures to think about. We hid behind our books until the storm blew over. Not a storm, either—she could have created one, but only a gentle breeze blew through the space she had occupied in our lives. Word spread that her family had disowned her;

that she was working with the nuns in a laundry in the south. No one accused anyone of hardheartedness, much less of fathering the baby. If there ever was a baby. One morning, it was as if none of us had ever met her or each other. On one ordinary day we became strangers created by this disappeared girl. We walked past each other in silence, taking short cuts to the rest of our lives.

'After the exams I would search for her, I vowed. I would rescue her from that laundry. I would cherish her and marry her just as soon as I found time and got my life in order. If there were a child I would be her father, or his father, even if she didn't look a bit like me. Then one thing led to another, and I started teaching, and I never got my life sufficiently in order to go and find her. I was waiting to have a bit of money, a better job. Above all I was waiting for the backbone to claim a daughter or son already two years old and then three, then ten or twenty. Every year the undertaking grew more formidable. I steered clear of marriage, because if such an occasion arose, I would be forced to search first for the other woman. In the end I felt we were married, wherever she was. An unwritten contract bound us together. I was convinced she had not married either. We were both waiting for the right moment when our lives would finally be in order.'

He threw a glance at Malachy and waited. He didn't expect the usual absolution—that came from a higher authority. But this would be a good time for a few words. Malachy, however, held his peace.

'I'll say one Our Father and ten Hail Marys so,' Ronan said. 'That should cover it.' He prayed them silently, meticulously, as the cautious Pascal would have done. Beyond the window, half a moon was leaning over. It would be throwing light on the boat. Ronan put on the topcoat and tightened the belt buckle. He put on the woollen cap and scarf. He put his wallet in one pocket and toothbrush in the other, picked up the flashlamp, and carried the crutch under his arm, that way it would make less noise.

'Thanks for everything, old pal,' he tweaked Malachy's toe.

He knocked discreetly on Benny's door. Benny wore a large puffy jacket like a tent, and an orange scarf across his lower face like a bandit.

'It's very mysterious, Ronan,' Benny said as they stumbled and slithered down the hill towards the river.

'There's a woman lives on the other side.' He had to tell Benny something.

'Aren't you the sly devil.'

'Keep it quiet, Benny, or Starski will come after us.' They stopped to pee behind the laurel hedge, then they pushed on. She might be on the other side—it was a mighty big world over there. If she ever existed. That would have been the year he was twenty-two. But he couldn't remember being twenty-two.

'Do you remember 1942, Benny?'

'Can't say I do.'

'Me neither.' Ronan felt relieved. That year had never taken place. Sometime he'd search for old calendars or newspapers just to make sure.

'Slow down,' Benny said, falling behind.

On the other hand, there was, according to some, the golden book. What mattered was whether the recording angel remembered the year in question. Pascal's Wager was more than an intellectual exercise. To be quite frank about it, a man with an immortal soul needed to cover his arse.

He looked back at Benny sitting on a stone.

'Take this, Benny,' he handed over the flashlamp. 'If you go back now, you'll be in time for the bran flakes.'

'Goodbye so, Ronan.' Benny's soul had a shorter wing span. They shook hands solemnly.

The moon pointed a finger at the boat. The boat tensed and held together. Ronan unwrapped the chain from around a stone. He shook off old age and infirmity and gave her a push, then a pull, up to his ankles in the dirty water. She moved readily enough, went with him, until it seemed she was pulling him along. There was an oar and then another, stretched patiently across the two seats. Only then did he realise that the boat had been waiting there, year after year, for some codger from the nursing home to grab the bull by the horns and give destiny a last chance. He threw his leg over the side as once on summer days. Pushed with the oar in the rushes. Settled himself on the cold seat. Eased the boat out into the dark water where the silver half-moon danced. And headed for the future.

Up in the nursing home, a few lights had refused to go out. He pulled out the mobile.

'Starski? There you are.'

'I'll kill you, Ronan.' She was affable as ever.

'Benny is safe and sitting on a rock. He'll be home in time for breakfast.'

Before she could respond, he threw the mobile in the water.

Hump
Nicole Flattery

At seventy, after suffering several disappointments, the first being my mother, the second being me, my father died. One evening he gathered the family in his room and asked if anyone had any questions. No one did. The next day he died. At the funeral everyone looked like someone I might sort of know. These strangers told anecdotes and made general health suggestions to each other. I passed out the sandwiches. The sandwiches were clingfilmed and oddly perforated, like they had been pierced again and again by cocktail sticks. I said 'Sambo?' to every single person in that room. It was a good word, a word I hoped would get me through the entire evening. I wasn't strong on speaking or finding ordinary things to discuss in large groups. The place was crowded with false grief, people constantly moving positions, like in A & E, depending on the severity of their wounds. I mentioned that I held his wrist when he passed and through the use of the phrase 'flickering pulse' I was booted up to First Class.

My father told me he regretted not talking more. He felt the time others used for conversation, he filled with snooker or nodding or looking away. He surmised, through a mouthful of diabetic chocolate, that he had only spoke thirty per cent of his life. It was a dismal percentage and I was familiar with what dismal percentages could do to a person. We were spending a lot of time together then, linking arms and being totally happy. I had this one trick I did for him. I'd curl up tight into his bed, under the starched sheets, and peep out at the nurses like I was an old lady. It was a scream. They said I was their youngest patient. I laughed and asked them to leave the pills in a tidy arrangement on the bedside locker. My antics gained me a certain level of recognition and infamy in the retirement home and, at times, I could feel my father almost bursting with pride. We both agreed it was the perfect trick for the occasion of his near-death. I was good at gestures, but it was only in that function room when I spoke my sad-but-true stories in my fragile tone that I finally got the appeal of talking. I thought this is what I will be now: a talker. My job had taken a sinister turn and I had started to keep an eye out, like you do for a new lover, for other things I could try. There weren't many. All jobs seemed to contain one small thing I just could not do. It was maddening.

I told a number of stories about my father that evening. I was there, but I wasn't. My mind was mainly preoccupied with what I could do in my new life as a talker: I would be both stylish and intelligent but also deeply affecting in my conversation. When that room of strangers looked up at me I did not know if I wanted them to cry or to clap.

It was in the shower where I found it first. I had moved into my father's old house, and sometimes would shower sitting down on the stool that was installed for comfort or, if I was feeling up to it, I would stand. The bathroom was filthy with intermittent flashes of what looked like the colour peach. On sitting-down days, I often crawled from one side of the room to the other. I could get away with this because I lived alone. It must have been a standing day as I realised I was a lot closer to the taps than I used to be. I was a lot closer to the hair on the taps. I was stooping over like I was playing the Old Lady in a celebrated stage production, except I was all scrunched up and very naked. I pressed my fingers below my shoulders and felt it shifting, unfurling. The hard roundness of it—like a golf ball or a marble. I dressed myself quickly, being careful not to catch sight of it in the mirror. When I stood on the train that morning, my fingers gripping the rail above, I could feel it growing beneath my skin like a second layer of flesh.

I worked in an office outside the city and we all had the appearance of people who had been brutally exiled. We shed our city selves but, lacking imagination, we had nothing to replace them with. Between the forty of us, I think we could have made a complete person. I had been there six months and it was probably the longest position I ever held. None of it mattered but I liked to pretend it did. If someone came in I might say 'Come in!' That was it. That was the whole script.

It wasn't exactly spiritually fulfilling. Often, I was so bored I couldn't hold a conversation. I walked around cubicles abandoning sentences. Whenever I entered the kitchen area, my colleagues left quickly and without warning. I think they were jealous because my desk got the most direct sunlight. I didn't understand them at all. I had a habit of thinking I was very unique and interesting.

My one friend spent her days on the phone to the refuse collection. There had been a dispute over the bins, no one knew who started it, but the rubbish had not been collected in six weeks and it was not a time for chit-chat, idle or otherwise. I wanted to tell Paula about my discovery, ask her had she noticed anything different about me, but all she did was place her hand over the mouthpiece of her phone and mutter 'Sorry'. She had married young and was squeamish about all sorts.

I used my mornings to investigate what was wrong with me. I opened several internet tabs, each one containing something possibly wrong, and explored them all. In the afternoons, my boss came and sat at the edge of my desk, like a hip teacher, and tried on being a thoughtful man. He was always trying to sell me things that were allegedly good for me—almond butter, aloe vera juice, himself. His face was stupidly handsome and so symmetrical it made me roll my eyes to the ceiling. He wasn't perfect though. I noticed he had a hidden aggressive streak and, at times, I suspected he was responsible for the absent bin men. Also, he was not someone I went to for love and affection and he was maybe better dressed than I would have liked. I had a lot of problems with him. He was obsessed with success. I felt I was under constant inspection, and he had a way of looking me up and down like I was a CV full of errors and misspellings. He was older, but it was hard to pin down anything precise. We went to a lot of dimly-lit restaurants. Anytime I thought I got a handle on his age, he ordered another bottle of wine and it was gone again. We talked mostly about the office, the flies that we couldn't get rid of, the people we disliked, how we physically had to wrench ourselves out of bed in the morning. Afterwards we would go back to his and he would attempt one of his two-and-a-half moves. He always fell asleep with both hands on my shoulders like we were in a conga line at a party. Conga, conga, conga. Honestly, I hated him.

At first, I worried about it a lot. The worrying made my food come up and up. I came to resemble my father in the early days of his illness; I was surprised when I caught sight of my concentration-camp legs. 'How do they support me?' I wondered. I had no idea but I got high and giddy on the engineering of it. At lunchtime, I ate outside with Paula. The smell of the office forced us into the cold and we sat together shivering over our lunchboxes. Paula's lunch was made up by her husband and always contained the correct amount of protein and carbohydrates. I can't describe the empty, whooshing feeling that went through me when I saw those food combinations. When I found the courage, I asked Paula if, at any stage of her life, she felt herself moving closer to the ground? If the chewing-gum stains on the street were any clearer to her than they used to be?

'I think I'm becoming a hunchback,' I confessed.

Paula was adamant that I was not a hunchback, that my fundamental problem was that I used people to feel attractive. Paula wasn't interested in turning heads. She didn't want men to look at her. Anytime a man looked at her she just picked up the phone and called the refuse collection. I think she was in love with the person on the other end of the line. Their conversations tended to be about Art and Beauty and not about bins at all. In a short space of time, Paula became quite a dangerous woman to know. Slowly, I moved my desk three inches away from hers.

At the weekends, I compensated by overeating. I went to nice places and flirted with the waiters. I bought books on pressure points from charity shops, some of which were highly complex pop-ups. I read these books or I rested them, two at a time, on my head and walked the length of my father's house. As soon as I moved in I realised this house was a mistake. It was too big for me and the stuff I owned shrank by comparison. It looked like I had a wardrobe of baby clothes in those giant, oak cupboards. If I couldn't sleep in one room I just moved to another. It wasn't as suffocating as I needed it to be. Sometimes, I just sat in a tiny space on the sitting-room floor and ran my fingers over those fake 3D backs. It was like seeing a photo of myself with every flaw removed. Often, I played with my father's collectibles. It wasn't a large collection, just two ceramic children, a boy playing the flute, a girl smiling encouragingly, and a shell in which you could hear the sea. I moved the children around the mantelpiece and marvelled at their serenity. I turned them to face outwards; I turned them to face inwards. There wasn't much else to do. I listened to the seashell like it was my last hope.

My boss described the house as 'weird'. He said the whole set-up was 'weird.' Except me. I was cute and he liked to tickle me under the chin, and then take off his clothes. He guessed something was wrong with me lately: in the way I sipped my wines, the way I sat upright and desperately still. He raised the question of me making myself sick.

'Only during the week,' I said, cheerfully, touched by his concern.

We were giving up. Previously, he had listed out my faults with amazing conviction and I truly thought that brought us closer together as a couple. I had no discernible direction in life, I didn't want anything, I was stupid and entitled. Suddenly, he acted as if he didn't care whether I knew these things or not. Instead, he said, 'Okay I'm going to make myself come now,'—as if removing me from the whole act was a sort of kindness. All that was left to talk about was what we'd do to the bin men if we ever found them. Our last night together I folded up my blouse and asked him to perform a thermal massage on my back and growing hump. He refused. Several weeks later, he called me into his office. There had been complaints from anonymous staff. I was never at my desk. He said it was imperative an assistant be at his or her desk.

'Where exactly are you?'

At home I was learning how to self-massage and was feeling pretty fulfilled. I had no interest in my job anymore but I tried. My concentrating face required more effort than genuine concentration. The organisation of the face, the setting up of the features, was exhausting. Afterwards, I often lay down on the cold tiles of the office bathroom floor and didn't move for hours. On normal days I did my job correctly, I counted and pointed and made pleasant popping noises with my mouth, but now there were no normal days. My boss suggested time off. To grieve.

He said I was a brilliant assistant but my father's death had affected me deeply. Take a holiday, he said. I muttered something about the restorative properties of the sea and went home to my sitting-room with its battered, springless couch. Before I left, Paula gave me one of those insincere half hugs. I smiled, thinking of the polite phrasing of the email that was probably sent around informing everyone of my departure.

Without work, I had hours and hours to fill. I performed difficult bending exercises. There was a futility and pointlessness to the whole procedure that I found particularly moving. These exercises had a sighing soundtrack I provided. I skimmed over articles on graceful posture: Pretend to be brimming with self-confidence. Pretend to be a movie star. Pretend to be a human being. At night, I tried to forget about it. I stayed out, alone. On the way home, drunk, I took bits of songs I heard in taxies and applied them to my own life. For the first time ever, I was meeting people. Full of my own brazen ugliness, I was just walking out into the night and finding them.

I considered myself pretty tolerant of people and open to new experiences and ideas. I didn't often seek out experiences but when they were presented to me I usually liked them. I took the new people out to meet college friends, beautiful sad girls who dressed like widows and claimed the world had crushed them, cruelly, like 'matchboxes'. Most of the new people were shy in their company. The men, usually men, often older, never joined in. They just looked at me like that was what they were supposed to do. It was unnerving. They smelled like crackers, sometimes crackers and cheese, sometimes crackers and another substance, but there was always a distinctive cracker smell in the air. My friends had their jackets on before they finished their drinks. I felt I was being thought of as 'inappropriate' and, in response, dug out dry skin from my scalp and discarded it on the floor beneath me. The men sat still and silent as dummies.

'What do you want from all this?' the girls asked. I didn't know. I was never a big dreamer. Maybe someone to wave at who feebly waves back? These women thought of me as typical: not tragic enough, but still capable of pulling stunts that lowered the calibre of their beauty. I counted the number of times I had touched them all, appraised their imperfections, cheered at their hickeys and sex bruises. It occurred to me that I could never ask any of these women to pour aromatherapy oils over my back, gently and without judgement. They would never rub their hands along my spine and check for signs of roundness whilst making soft reassurances. They were there for me in the ways they should be, at the funeral they formed a neat cluster and discreetly cried, but that was where it stopped. I wanted them to say: 'Thank you, thank you so much for everything you have done for us and our self-esteem.' I wanted them to cheer the fuck up. They didn't cheer up though and they didn't express gratitude. They just wafted out of the building and I straightened my back at them. The men continued to stare at me like I was an item of significant interest.

I needed these friendships to go somewhere. I made certain alterations to my lifestyle for these old men. I dusted, I tidied away my father's collection, I cleaned out my bathroom cabinet so it resembled the cabinet of a woman who had very little to worry about. I saw myself making these slight adjustments. I watched as if it was an instructive montage about how a person can take purposeful strides in their life. The music that accompanied these scenes was sassy and upbeat. I suddenly gave a shit and it suited me.

My father used to ask if I cared about other people at all and the correct answer was 'Yes'. I did. I cared, I cared, I cared. I had healthy friendships in mind. Things should have been easier when I got the men alone but they never were. I wanted them to talk, to tell me everything, about their families, and the minor incidents that destroyed them, and maybe the moments they had ruined by doing or saying the wrong thing. What then, what then? But, nothing. Their eyes just roamed around like they were searching for something better beyond my head. Of course, they were all seized by a singular fear when I began my striptease. I guess it was because I was always more involved in the tease than the strip. I liked jokes, death jokes, single-girl jokes, and was shocked when these didn't lead naturally to a friendly situation.

Sometimes, when the fingers were flying over the front of my blouse, I thought: 'This is hilarious. No, actually, this is an illness. This inability to take anything seriously. I should get money from the state.' Afterwards, I compensated by lying. I'd been let go, I'd been promoted, I do this, I do that, who cares? In a second of stupidity and weakness, I told one of them about my developing hump. I may have curled up on his chest and cried. I may have beaten his chest lightly with my fists. He promised that if we stayed together he would love me all the same. He wasn't begging but he nearly was. After he left the house, in the half-dark, I caught him on the street, kicking a taxi. It was an embarrassing situation.

The time came to return to work but I couldn't do it. It wasn't so much the job as the confusion and frustration that went with it. Standing and sitting and breathing in the stale air of people who despised me—I couldn't face it. I rang up HR and told them my boss made a pass at me. I said I hoped it accounted for some of my odder behaviour in the few weeks before my departure.

HR asked: 'What happened?'

I said: 'Well, he brought me into his office.'

HR said: 'Of course, he did. He's your boss.'

I said: 'He sat across from me at the table.'

HR said nothing.

I said: 'He leaned quite far across the table.'

HR said nothing.

I said: 'It was a very small table.'

I was granted a further two weeks holiday, fully paid. I decided to use that money to invest in my future. I visited various chemists and I had a lot of questions. 'Is it more politically correct to say: I have a hump or I am a hunchback?' The counter girls made funny clicking noises with their teeth and I pined for my own lost work noises. They prescribed yoga classes which promised to straighten my spine and make me wholesome at the same time. Things were too trippy for me in that tiny room and I found all the goodness smothering. Anything could happen in that blissed-out state and that seemed idiotic and negligent so I stopped going. A backscratcher appeared in my room, leftover from a previous life when back-scratching was something to look forward to. I slept beside it, and at night, it extended its long-armed sympathies towards me. When I woke up beside that disembodied hand, I didn't feel so bad. I went to a general store which felt illegal and like I was breaking a code—my friends and I were fonder of expensive, specific things. In the queue, fly-swatter in hand, I asked myself if I looked like a sophisticated person. I didn't. I closed my eyes and imagined hitting the hump downwards with tools and quiet prayers. In the lamplight of my luckless bedroom, I delivered fast, brisk strokes to the centre of my back. I found it hard to keep a straight face.

I saw a chiropractor. I made that choice. A solid man who searched his hands up and down my back as if looking for someone to blame. He was tall and boring and told me he went canoeing at weekends. I asked, 'How many tall men can you fit in a canoe?' which sounded like the beginning of something, a riff or an innuendo, but was a real and genuine query. The gap in my canoe knowledge was huge and overwhelming. I told him I imagined my hump would be a large square shape, like a heavy schoolbag full of difficult homework. He frowned and flipped me over. He didn't look like a chiropractor at all. He looked like a hippie, or a child's lazy drawing of a hippie. All he could offer was drugs and hand-holding, neither of which I wanted. Before I left, he gave me a tissue and said, 'In case, you get upset.' I would never get upset in that sort of room with that sort of man, but I stuck the tissue in my sleeve for safe-keeping. After that, there was nothing, just wide-open spaces, like the reception desk and the world. On the way out, I passed a girl with a neat bob and thought: That's me. I could be that girl. I could be a girl with a bob. She asked if I needed to make another appointment. I told her to schedule me in every month for the foreseeable future and to adopt an air of discretion when she greeted me at the desk. I did not expect to be treated vastly differently, I was a standard hunchback, but a smile or kind word might ease a burden. The bob put her hand over her mouth like a silent-movie actress. Where do they even find these women? She steadied herself on her chair as I shuffled away.

My life, and what I did with it, became a sort of mystery then. I reorganised my father's collection, I called Paula and heard the phone ring out and out, I took an aversion to the shower tray. I removed traces of my father from his own home. I needed it so that he wasn't my father, that I didn't know him, that I had never even heard of him. I wrote my boss a letter. It was titled: 'I'm Sorry'. Prompted by this letter he rang me and said he was sorry too and let's meet, let's be two sorry people in the same room. I dressed up for it. I took my time. I wanted him to wait and I wanted to be the thing he was waiting for.

In the lobby of the cinema he was nothing like I remembered; angrier, shorter. He looked like a small town I might live in and die. He told me there had been a confrontation with the bin men and he had been fired. His arm was in a cast. During the film, anytime he turned towards me, the cast rubbed off my face. Afterwards, we stood on the street and I thought he was going to kiss me or grab me or do something obvious. Instead, he pulled my hand and placed two of my fingers on his bare neck. 'Can you feel that lump? Right there?' I rubbed a small swollen mark from where the shirt of his collar had been closed too tightly. 'That's cancer, I think. It's cancer more than likely.' I agreed that it probably was cancer, that he had caught it early. He asked me if I wanted a drink and I said no, thank you. It was important to me that I was polite.

When I left him, I felt a happy relief. I thought of night classes, the sea, re-decorating.

Return

David Hayden

On my last day, the day that is upon me, the big lady with the flowery apron will arrive and bustle about, preparing the room, making every surface shine white. She will leave without talking to me. I will never know her name. She will never speak mine.

Edith.

I will lie comfortably on the bed in my nightdress, as I do today, looking at the cannula in my hand; smaller than I was, as small as I once was. Summer will reach me from the courtyard through the window's narrow opening on the slow moving scent of the gum trees.

Out of the inner dark they begin to show themselves.

Daddy is wearing his long black overcoat and stands turning his hat in his hands. Mummy's perfume arrives next, tea rose, and then I see her in a yellow summer dress, her hair pinned up in loose rolls. She moves forward and the bag that she holds crackles. Daddy takes the loop handles and begins to remove small parcels neatly wrapped in shiny gold and brick red paper.

'For later,' he says.

Mummy hugs me, presses me, speaking close to my ear so that I cannot understand her.

'You've been gone such a long time,' is all I can say at first. 'Where did you go?'

Mummy stands back from me.

'We've missed you too.'

She sits on the bed and smoothes down the coverlet.

They become still, so quiet that I think they might go away again.

Then Daddy speaks.

'Don't you remember? Mummy and I took the train from Victoria to Dover Marine and caught the ferry. We were going to France. We rented a car in Calais and made for Paris. The hotel was seedy but charming. The perfect place. We went dancing; the floor was so small that we filled it on our own. I don't think I've ever felt so close to your mother as on our last evening in Paris.'

The colour leaves Mummy's face, her features fade away; her large brown eyes gaze into mine.

'We began to drive south heading for an appointment with an agent at Toulouse to discuss properties in the Lot Valley. We had received advance details about a number of places and your mother and I were particularly keen to look at an old mill house near a village called Vayrac. There was a small cottage with several large buildings with potential for conversion, a generous stand of walnut trees and, as one might expect, a tributary of the Lot river running through the grounds. The surrounding area, we knew, was beautiful and, as yet, unspoiled by people like us grubbing around for rural idylls. I was sure that we would spend many happy summers there.'

Daddy reaches into his coat but finding nothing he withdraws his hand and pats his chest at the empty pocket.

'I was driving down a long poplar-lined road when I noticed the sky changing colour and a hissing began that I thought for a second was the radiator overheating, but which, I soon realised, was a fine orange dust skittering over the windscreen. I could feel the wind pick up behind us, and the hiss turned to a gush and the wheels' revolutions began to soften. The fields, the farms, the fences began to blur and sink and the trees sagged under their colourful burden. The air in the car remained cool and fresh but the world outside grew wilder and redder. Eventually we could see nothing through any window and I had to accept that we were no longer moving.

'The steady patter of falling dust soothed and lulled us, and your mother and I fell asleep, separating into our dreams. On waking we found that we were buried, the car packed in a warm mass of fine desiccants. Your mother turned on the overhead light and I rummaged in the glove compartment for something to eat, though neither of us was hungry. I found a travellers' tin of boiled sweets. I suggested that we talk about something, Paris or you, and your mother said…'

'I believe this is a marvellous opportunity for us *not* to speak, Darling.'

'Admirable woman. So we sat and listened to the slight shiftings of the dust, breathed the dry air and waited. I ventured that it might be a good idea if we were to turn the light out to conserve the battery but your mother said…'

'I can't see what difference that will make. We're not going any farther.'

'Yes. You see, it didn't matter. I had a hip flask filled with a good, single whiskey, which I've always preferred to malt, and we dined on that and boiled sweets whenever the desire came on; which wasn't often. Nature didn't impose any further inconveniences on us and I began to be aware of how very tired I had become, and when I was certain that I was free, I submitted to a feeling of blissful release that I had never before experienced, and I slept and slept.'

'So very tired,' says Mummy.

'We were woken by a rushing, collapsing sound. Straight ridges were appearing in the matter pressed against the windows, visible by the yellow light that still flickered above. The wind had risen and was, in turn, raising our car out of its sandy captivity. The air grew frantic all around us and the particles lifted and flew, who knows where.'

'Heavenwards,' says Mummy, her mouth twisting but not smiling.

'I started the car and we continued on our way to Toulouse but when we reached the agent's offices we found that they were closed. It was then that we turned around and came back home. I'm sorry that we missed so much. There was nothing that we could do, Darling.'

Daddy takes out his pipe and sucks a few times to check the air flow before getting a floppy leather pouch from which he brings out rough pinches of tobacco that he pushes into the pipe's bowl. His teeth click on the stem as he focuses on the crossed red circle of a sign that reads 'No Smoking.' Daddy slips the pipe into the side pocket of his overcoat. I turn my head with some difficulty and I smile at him and he grins back like a naughty boy.

'What happened was more like this, Sweetie,' starts Mummy.

'We ran for the balloon which was rocking in the wind, despite the guy ropes, as if it were being pulled by an invisible hand. The rain lashed down. I was so glad that I was wearing the sou'wester that your father bought me. The mud was sucking at my boots and slowing me down. Your father pulled me by the hand and I nearly fell over but we reached the basket and clambered inside before, with one enormous heave, the balloon leaped off the ground and lunged for the sky leaving the pilot—or whatever they're called—waving on the ground. I did feel sorry for the fellow.

'The sky grew bigger and bigger as we fell towards the clouds that tossed icy rain onto us, and then suddenly we broke through, still rising, out into brilliant sunshine. I can't tell you how marvellous it was to be bathed in that warm, buttery light. But before long the sky grew paler and weaker, turning white then darkening blue before we came up into the outer blackness where the stars shone all about like... like nothing but stars. It wasn't nearly as cold as you might imagine and we continued to fall towards the moon.

'We landed softly enough but in a tangle so that it took us a while to crawl out. We had the place to ourselves. At first I thought that everything looked the same, but once my eyes became accustomed to the conditions I began to discern, in the seeming uniformity, a captivating variety of form. Your father and I went for long walks, there wasn't a whisper of air and the land was easy under foot. We camped under the basket on a tartan rug, which was adequately comfortable, and time passed in that manner.

'One morning we were standing facing home when a light breeze rose up and began to play around us. Your father realised what was happening sooner than I and began to untangle the ropes and set the basket straight, and by the time the gale was truly up we were crouching inside, braced for the ascent. The balloon re-inflated like a great red lung and pulled us back to Earth. The air gyred as we plunged into the atmosphere and I lost my emerald cloche hat; a favourite of mine, such a pity. The storm abated, the balloon floated down pacifically and we debouched onto the strand. Your father and I were ravenously hungry so we walked up to the old hotel and ate breakfast; kedgeree and everything. I can't tell you how delightful it was. Then we walked home and here you are, my darling. Home without us. Waiting.'

Mummy never cries so I am shocked when I see her open her clutch purse, take out a perfect white square of linen and dab her eyes and cheeks. Daddy puts his arm around her and kisses Mummy once on the ear. She stops sobbing and returns the handkerchief to its proper place and Daddy talks.

'What your mother meant was that we were at Dotty's summer house party…'

'She does so hate it when you call her Dotty,' says Mummy.

'… and we were all gathered in the sitting room after the outlying guests had gone home and Victor suggested that we play hunt the trophy. Now Dorothy and Victor had set up all the clues beforehand as a special treat so we didn't want to be spoilsports but we did insist, against bitter opposition, that your mother and I would not be split asunder. We took our sheaf of clues and our brandies and set off into the house. We bumped into Gerald and Sylvia in the kitchen, which I understand wasn't supposed to happen, and, of course, Gerry started to moo on about his printing business so we fled to the library where we quickly gathered our wits.

'The theme was fairy tales with each clue taken from a different colour of those marvellous books that, as luck would have it, my mother used to own, and which I had read backwards and forwards before I knew that they weren't for boys.'

Mummy looks as if she might cough.

'Of course, your mother knows the books too. So the upshot was that we romped through the trail, the yellow dwarf, the troll's daughter, Drakestail, the glass axe and so on, until we came to the last clue which came from The Silver Fairy. This was the story of the Sunken Princess who is betrothed by her wicked guardian to a handsome prince who lives in a moss-covered castle deep in the Broken Mountains. The princess travels alone through the swaying trees of a misty forest, her wedding dress shining white, scattered with perfect pearls that glitter like a scattering of tiny tears. The brave girl climbs up the slippery slate ramp and into the castle, her breath curling white through the air and rising away into the darkness. She mounts the steps that spiral up to join a long corridor that leads to another corridor that leads to the icy, airless room that is her bridal chamber.

'The girl approaches. Before her is a vast bed dressed in mildewed yellow satin, surrounded by flickering candles resting in shivering bowls of water, their surfaces starting to crisp over with ice. She sits on the bed then swings her legs up and reclines on the mattress, her chestnut hair fanning over the pillow. The handsome prince enters through a hidden panelled door and as he walks towards her his grey livery falls away, his skin and flesh slop to the floor revealing the livid form of her guardian. The princess looks around for anyone, anything to rescue her but there is no one. 'Room, help me!' she cries, but the room cannot help her. 'Candles, help me!' she cries, but the candles cannot help her. 'Bed, help me!' she cries and the bed begins to ripple and soften, the mattress rises slightly before sinking down, down into the world through the roots of the mountain, down and out and up into a bright orange world and out of the story. The wicked guardian jumps onto the sunken bed and falls down and down and is caught in the fiery heat at the centre of the world where he burns still.'

Daddy coughs and runs his hand through his shining hair.

'So after searching into the dimmest recesses of the house your mother and I finally found a musty bedroom with a four-poster bed, hung around with moth-eaten drapes. We searched for some time but couldn't find the answer and then your mother, the clever thing, suggested that we try the bed. We lay down on the dusty covers, and high over us pinned to the canopy was the answer; must've used a stepladder. I'm sorry to say but we'd had the best part of a bottle of wine each, Darling, and the brandy must have finished us off, because we fell into the deepest sleep, and when we woke up I remember a delicious smell of toasted cinnamon and an unaccountable soft warmth under my back. We sat up and saw the old house fallen, scorched and broken down all around us, and your mother and I lying on a bed of ash without a scratch on us. There wasn't a soul in the grounds and only our car was left of all the partygoers'. I immediately started her up and we came home to you as quickly as we could.'

Mummy turns from Daddy and presses my knee gently; she smiles slowly, her eyes glittering, the colour rising on her cheeks, her face radiant, limitless. I can see the shape and meaning of the whole world hovering over me; loving me. Daddy puts his hat on and takes it off again. I look down at my hands withered and veiny, small and smooth and pink.

'Darling, I would have thought that you'd remember what happened,' said Mummy. 'It had been a dreadful winter and we'd all been stuck inside far too much for our own good and we'd managed to clamber up to March, but instead of the first feeble rays of the blessed dawn of life reaching down to warm our clammy bones, all that came was rain. Torrents, sheets, buckets and bathtubs of icy, dreary rain. Then one Sunday your father put down his pipe, stood up and said…'

'Are we not men? To cower thus squinting under a few pale drops of water. Let us go forth,' says Daddy.

'Magnificent, Darling,' says Mummy. 'So we rugged up and ventured out into the wind-bent world and struggled up to the park. Umbrellas were useless and despite our best efforts we were all soaked to a mush. We made for the Pavilion, squelched in and ordered tea and buns from the poor soul whose office it was to provide for waifs like ourselves. I can't tell you but that it was the most delicious tea I've ever tasted and we felt fortified, emboldened even, to take you outside and attempt some proper fun. Daddy and I brought you to the boating lake, unsurprisingly there was no attendant in view, so we took matters into our own hands and located the most stable looking vessel and your father and I climbed in. One of us must have knocked the bank with an oar because we started to pull away from the shore and by the time we had fitted the oars into the rowlocks we had drifted quite a distance from you. I saw you waving, my angel, and it broke my heart, but no matter how hard we rowed the boat kept moving further away. There was water stretching to every horizon and the only dry land in sight was the bank where you stood and the path that led up to the Pavilion. A current had gripped the boat and was dragging us towards the lowering sky. Your father had had the foresight to bring a bag of toffee bonbons with him so we didn't starve.

'The rain stopped eventually but the water took a long time to fall away. When the flood subsided we found ourselves forked high in the top of a tree. The leaves were fat and glossy, and purple fruit hung in clusters close to hand but we didn't trust them, Darling. We climbed down through knotted boughs and branches, past founts of mistletoe and nests filled with spoons and medals and pocket watches, before shinning down the trunk onto the path. We were immediately jostled by a group of schoolboys in blue jerseys running towards a playing field but in doing so they had turned us in the right direction for home. We walked on and here we are.'

'Here we are,' says Daddy.

The clock ticks with a *suck-suck, suck-suck* and the light dims outside and I close my eyes and remember the day that I stood in the parlour, still and cold, my uncle telling me that they were never coming home. And I open my eyes and they stand there smiling, smiling, and the night will come on and the moon will come out and traverse the sky and the dawn will return and we will stand there together smiling, smiling.

Kennedy

Desmond Hogan

A nineteen-year-old youth is made to dig a shallow grave in waste ground beside railway tracks near Limerick bus station and then shot with an automatic pistol.

Eyes blue-green, brown-speckled, of blackbird's eggs.

He wears a hoodie jacket patterned with attack helicopters.

Murdered because he was going to snitch—go to the guards about a murder he'd witnessed—his friend Cuzzy had fired the shot. The victim had features like a western stone wall. The murder vehicle—a stolen cobalt Ford Kuga—set on fire at Ballyneety near Lough Gur.

The hesitant moment by Lough Gur when blackthorn blossom and hawthorn blossom are unrecognisable from one another, the one expiring, the other coming into blossom.

Creeping willow grows in the waste ground near Limerick bus station—as it was April male catskins yellow, with pollen, on separate trees small greenish female stamens. In April also whitlow grass that Kennedy's grandmother Evie used to cure inflammation near fingernails and toenails.

In summer creeping cinquefoil grows in the waste ground.

He was called Kennedy by Michaela, his mother, after John F. Kennedy, and Edward Kennedy, both of whom visited this city, the latter with a silver dollar haircut and tie with small knot and square ends. He must have brought a large jar of Brylcreem with him, Kennedy's father, Bongo, remarked about him.

'When I was young and comely,
Sure, good fortune on me shone,
My parents loved me tenderly.'

A pious woman found Saint Sebastian's body in a sewer and had a dream he told her to bury him in the Catacombs.

Catacumbas. Late Latin word. Latin of Julian the Apostate who studied the Gospels and then returned to the Greek gods.

The Catacombs. A place to take refuge in. A place to scratch prayers on the wall in. A place to paint in.

Cut into porous tufa rock, they featured wall paintings such as one of three officials whom Nebuchadnezzar flung in the furnace for not bowing before a golden image of him in the plain of Dura in Babylon but who were spared.

Three officials, arms outstretched, in pistachio-green jester's apparel amid flames of maple red.

The body of Sebastian the Archer refused death by arrows and he had to be beaten to death. Some have surmised the arrows were symbolic and he was raped.

As the crime boss brought Kennedy to be murdered he told a story:

'I shook hands with Bulldog who is as big as a Holstein Friesian and who has fat cheeks.

It was Christmas and we got a crate and had a joint.

He said "I have the stiffness."

He slept in the same bed as me in the place I have in Ballysimon.

In the morning he says "Me chain is gone and it was a good chain. I got it in Port Mandel near Manchester."

He pulled up all the bedclothes.

He says "I'll come back later and if I don't get me chain your Lexus with the wind down roof will be gone."

He came back later but he saw the squad car—"the scum bags," he said—and he went away.

A week later I saw Cocka, a hardy young fellow, with Bulldog's chain, in Sullivan's Lane.'

The crime boss, who is descended from the Black and Tans, himself wears a white-gold chain from Crete, an American gold ring large as a Spanish grandee's ring, a silver bomber jacket and pointy shoes of true white.

He has a stack of nude magazines in his house in Ballysimon, offers you custard and creams from a plate with John Paul II's—Karol

Wojtyla's—head on it, plays Country and Western a lot.

Sean Wilson—Blue Hills of Breffni, Westmeath Bachelor.

Sean Moore—Dun Laoghaire can be such a Lonely Place.

Johnny Cash—I Walk the Line.

Ballysimon is famed for a legitimate dumping site but some people are given money to dump rubbish in alternative ways. 'Millionaires from dumping rubbish,' it is said of them.

By turning to violence, to murder, they create a history, they create a style for themselves. They become Ikons as ancient as Calvary.

Matthew tells us his Roman soldier torturers put a scarlet robe on Christ, Mark and John—a robe of purple.

Emerging from a garda car Kennedy's companion and accomplice Cuzzy, in a grey pinstripe jersey, is surprised into history.

Centurion's facial features. A flick of hair to the right above his turf cut makes him a little like a crested grebe.

South Hill boys like Cuzzy are like the man-eating mares of King Diomedes of the Bistones that Hercules was entrusted to capture—one of the twelve labours King Eurystheus imposed on him.

'If I had to choose between Auschwitz and here,' he says of his cell, 'I'd choose Auschwitz.'

As Kennedy's body is brought to Janesboro church some of his brothers clasp their hands in attitudes of prayer. Others simply drop their heads in grief.

Youths in suits with chest hammer pleats and cigarette-rolled shoulders. Mock-snakeskin shoes. With revolver cufflinks.

One of the brothers has a prison tattoo—three Chinese letters in biro and ink—on the side of his right ear.

The youngest brother is the only one to demur jacket and tie, has his white shirt hanging over his trousers and wears a silver chain with boxing gloves.

Michaela's—Kennedy's mother's—hair is pêle-mêle blanche-blonde, she wears horn-toed, fleur-de-lys patterned, lace-up black high heels, mandorla—oval—ring, ruby and gold diamante on fingernails against her black.

Her businessman boyfriend wears a Savile Row-style suit chosen from his wardrobe of dark lilac suits, grey and black lounge suits, suits with black collars, wine suits, plum jackets, claret-red velvet one-button jackets.

Kennedy's father Bongo had been a man with kettle-black eyebrows, who was familiar with the juniper berries and the rowan berries and the scarlet berries of the bittersweet—the woody nightshade— sequestered his foal with magpie face and Talmud scholar's beard where these berries, some healing, some poisonous, were abundant. He knew how to challenge the witch's broom.

John Joe Criggs, the umbrella mender in Killeely, used send boys who looked like potoroos—rat kangaroos and prehensile tails—to Weston where they lived, looking for spare copper.

'You're as well hung as a stallion like your father,' Bongo would say to Kennedy. 'Get a partner.'

In Clare for the summer he once turned to Michaela in the night in Kilrush during a fight.

'Go into the Kincora Hotel and get a knife so I can kill this fellow.'

He always took Kennedy to Ballyheigue at Marymass—September 8—where people in bare feet took water in bottles from the Holy Well, left scapulars, names and photographs of people who were dead, children who'd been killed.

He fell in a pub fight. Never woke up.

His mother Evie had hung herself when they settled her.

Hair ivory grey at edges, then sienna, in a ponytail tied by velvet ribbon, usually in tattersall coat, maxi skirt, heelless sandals.

On the road she'd loved to watch the mistle thrush who came to Ireland with the Act of Union of 1800, the Wee Willie Wagtail—blue tit—with black eyestripes and lemon breast, the chaffinch with pink lightings on its breast who would come up close to you, in winter the frochán—ring ouzel, white crescent around its breast, bird of river, of crags.

On the footbridge at Doonas near Clondara she told Kennedy of the two Jehovah's Witnesses who were assaulted in Clondara, their bibles burned, the crowd cheered on by the Parish Priest, and then the Jehovah's Witnesses bound to the peace in court for blasphemy.

Michaela's father Billser had been in Glin Industrial School. The Christian Brothers, with Abbey School of Acting voices, used get them to strip naked and lash them with the cat of nine tails. Boys with smidgen penises. A dust, a protest of pubic hair. Boys with pubes as red as the fox who came to steal the sickly chickens, orange as the beak of an Aylesbury duck, brown of the tawny owl.

Then bring them to the Shannon when the tide was in and force them to immerse in salt water.

The Shannon food—haws, dulse, barnacles—they ate them. They robbed mangels, turnips. They even robbed the pigs' and bonhams'—piglets'—food.

'You have eyes like the blackbird's eggs. You have eyes like the céirseach's eggs. You have eyes like the merie's eggs,' a Brother, nicknamed the Seabhac—hawk—used tell Billser.

Blue-green, brown-speckled.

He was called the Seabhac because he used to ravage boys the way the hawk makes a sandwich of autumn brood pigeons or meadow pipits, leaving a flush of feathers.

He had ginger-beer hirsute like the ruffous-barred sparrowhawk that quickly gives up when it misses a target, lays eggs in abandoned crows' nests.

A second reason for his nickname was because he was an expert in Irish and the paper-covered Irish dictionary was penned by an Seabhac—the Hawk.

Father Edward J. Flanagan from Ballymoe, North Galway, who founded Boys Town in Omaha and was played by Spencer Tracy, came to Ireland in 1946 and visited Glin Industrial School.

The Seabhac gave him a patent hen's egg, tea in a cup with blackbirds on it, Dundee cake on a plate with the same pattern.

Billser used cry salty tears when he remembered Glin.

Michaela's grandfather Torrie had been in the British Army and the old British names for places in Limerick City kept breaking into his conversation—Lax Weir, Patrick Punch Corner, Saint George's Street.

Cuzzy and Kennedy met at a Palaestra—boxing club.

Cuzzy was half-Brazilian.

'My father was Brazilian. He knocked my mother and went away.'

'Are you riding any woman now?' he asked Kennedy, who had rabbit-coloured pubes, in the showers.

'You have nipples like monkey fingers,' Kennedy said to Cuzzy, who has palomino-coloured pubes, in the showers.

The coach, who looked like a pickled onion with tattoos in the nude was impugned for messing with the teenage boxers. HIV Lips was his nickname.

'Used box for CIE Boxing Club,' he said of himself. 'Would go around the country. They used wear pink-lined vests, and I says no way am I going wear that.'

'He sniffed my jocks. And there were no stains on them,' a shaven-headed boxer who looked like a defurred monkey or a peeled banana, reported in denunciation of him.

A man who had a grudge against him used scourge a statue of the Greek boxer Theagenes of Thasos until it fell on him, killing him.

The statue was thrown in the sea and fished up by fishermen.

In the Palaestra was a poster of John Cena with leather wrappings on his forearm like the Terme Boxer—Pugile delle Terme—a first-century BC copy of a second-century BC statue which depicted Theagenes of Thasos.

John Cena in a black baseball cap, briefs showing above trousers beside a lingering poster for Circus Vegas at Two Mile Inn—a kick boxer in mini-bikini briefs and mock-crocodile boots.

Kennedy and Cuzzy were brought to the Garda Station one night when they were walking home from the Boxing Club.

'They'll take anyone in tracksuits.'

Cuzzy, aged sixteen, was thrown in the girls' cell.

Kennedy was thumped with a mag lamp, a telephone book used to prevent his body from being bruised.

Cuzzy was thumped with a baton through a towel with soap in it.

A black guard put his tongue in Kennedy's ear. A Polish guard felt his genitals.

Kennedy punched the Polish guard and was jailed.

Solicitors brought parcels of heroin and cocaine into jail.

Youths on parole would swallow one eighth heroin and fifty euro bags of heroin, thus sneak them in.

One youth put three hundred diazepam, three hundred steroid, three ounces of citric in a bottle, three needles up his anus.

Túr, Cant for anus.

Rispún, Cant for jail.

Slop out in mornings.

Not even granule coffee for breakfast. Something worse.

Locked up most of the day.

One youth with a golf-ball face, skin-coloured lips of the young Dickie Rock, when his baseball cap was removed, a pronounced bald patch on his blond head, had a parakeet in his cell.

Cuzzy would bring an adolescent Alsatian to the Unemployment Office.

Then he and Kennedy got a job laying slabs near the cement factory at Raheen.

Apart from work, Limerick routine.

Drugs in cling-foil or condoms put up their anuses, guards stopping them—fingers up their anuses.

Tired of the routine they both went to Donegal to train with AC armalite rifles and machine guns in fields turned salmon-colour by ragged robin.

The instructor had a Vietnam veteran pepper and salt beard and wore Stars and Stripes plimsolls.

The farmer who used own the house they stayed in would have a boy come for one month in the summer from an Industrial School, by arrangement with the Brothers.

The boy used sleep in the same bed as him and the farmer made him wear girl's knickers.

In Kennedy's room was a poster of Metallica—fuchsine bikini top, mini-bikini, skull locket on forehead, fuchsine mouth, belly button that looked like a deep cleavage of buttocks, skeleton's arms about her.

'It was on Bermuda's island

That I met with Captain Moore…'

'It's like the Albanians. They give you a bit of rope with a knot at the top.

Bessa they call it.

They will kill you or one of your family.

You know the Albanians by the ears. Their ears are taped back at birth.

And they have dark eyebrows.

I was raised on the Island.

You could leave your doors open. They were the nicest people.

Drugs spoiled people.'

Weston where Kennedy grew up was like Bedford-Stuyvesant or Brownsville New York where Mike Tyson grew up, his mother, who died when he was sixteen, regularly observing him coming home with clothes he didn't pay for.

Kennedy once took a €150 tag off a golf club in a Limerick store, replaced it with a €20 tag, and paid for it.

As a small boy he had a Staffordshire terrier called Daisy.

Eyes a blue coast watch, face a sea of freckles, he let the man from Janesboro who sucked little boys' knobs buy him 99s—the ice-cream cones with chocolate flake stuck in them, syrup on top, or traffic-light cakes—cakes with scarlet and green jellies on the icing.

He'd play knocker gawlai—knock at doors in Weston and run away.

He'd throw eggs at taxis.

Once a taxi driver chased him with a baseball bat.

'I smoked twenty cigarettes since I was eleven.

Used work as a mechanic part-time then.

I cut it down to ten and then to five recently. My doctor told me my lungs were black and I'd be on an oxygen mask by the time I was twenty.

I'm nineteen.'

The youth in the petrol-blue jacket spoke against the Island on which someone on a bicycle was driving horses.

A lighted motorbike was going up and down Island Field.

We were on the Metal Bridge side of the Shannon.

It was late afternoon, mid-December.

'They put barbed wire under the Metal Bridge to catch the bodies that float down. A boy jumped off the bridge, got caught in the barbed wire and was drowned.

They brought seventeen stolen cars here one day and burned all of them.'

There were three cars in the water now, one upside down, with the wheels above the tide.

'When I was a child my mother used always be saying "I promised Our Lady of Lourdes. I promised Our Lady of Lourdes."

There's a pub in Heuwagen in Basel and I promised a friend I'd meet him there.

You can get accommodation in Paddington on the way for £20 a night. Share with someone else.'

He turned to me. 'Are you a Traveller. Do you light fires?'

He asked me where I was from and when I told him he said, 'I stood there with seventeen Connemara ponies once and sold none of them.'

On his fingers rings with horses' heads, saddles, hash plant.

His bumster trousers showed John Galliano briefs.

Two stygian hounds approached the ride followed by an owner with warfare orange hair, in a rainbow hoodie jacket, who called Mack after one of them.

He pulled up his jacket and underlying layers to show a tattoo Makaveli on his butter-mahogany abdomen.

'I got interested in Machiavelli because Tupac was interested in him. Learnt all about him. An Italian philosopher. Nikolo is his first name. Put his tattoo all over my body. Spelt it Makaveli. Called my Rottweiler-Staffordshire terrier cross breed after him. Mack.

Modge is the long-haired black terrier.

Do you know that Tupac Amaru Shakur was named by his mother after an Inca sentenced to death by the Spaniards?

In Inca language: Shining Serpent.

Do you know that when the Florentines were trying to recapture Pisa Machiavelli was begged because he was a philosopher to stay at headquarters but he answered,' and the youth thrust out his chest like Arnold Schwarzenegger for this bit, 'that he must be with his soldiers because he'd die of sadness behind the lines?

They say Tupac was shot dead in Las Vegas. There was no funeral. He's alive as you or me.

I'm reading a book about the Kray Twins now.

Beware of sneak attacks.'

And then he went off with Mack and Modge singing the song Tupac wrote about his mother, 'Dear Mama.'

'When I was a child my father used take me to Ballyheigue every year.

There's a well there.

The priest was saying Mass beside it during the Penal Days and the Red Coats turned up with hounds.

Three wethers jumped from the well, ran towards the sea.

The hounds chased them, devoured them and were drowned.

The priest's life was spared.'

They were of Thomond, neither of Munster or Connaught, Thomond bodies, Thomond pectorals.

The other occasion I met Kennedy was on a warm February Saturday.

He was sitting in a Ford Focus on Hyde Road in red silky football shorts with youths in similar attire.

He introduced me to one of them, Razz, who had an arm tattoo of a centurion in a G-string.

'I was in Cloverhill. Remand prison near a courthouse in Dublin. Then Mountjoy. You'd want to see the bleeding place. It was filthy. The warden stuck his head in the cell one day and "You're for Portlaoise." They treat you well in Portlaoise.'

'What were you in jail for?'

'A copper wouldn't ask me that.'

A flank of girls in acid-pink and acid-green tops was hovering near this portmanteau of manhood like coprophagous—dung-eating—gulls hovering near cows for the slugs in their dung.

A little girl in sunglasses with mint green frontal frames, flamingo wings, standing nearby, said to a little girl in a lemon and peach top who was passing:

'There are three birthday cards inside for you, Tiffany.'

'It's not my birthday.'

'It is your fucking birthday.'

And then she began chasing the other like a skua down Hyde Road, in the direction of the bus station, screaming, 'Happy Birthday to you. Happy Birthday to you.'

Flowers of the magnolia come first in Pery Square Park near the Bus Station, tender yellow-green leaf later.

A Traveller boy cycled by the sweet chestnut blossoms of Pery

Square Park the day they found Kennedy's body, firing heaped on his handlebars.

I am forced to live in a city of Russian tattooists, murderously shaven heads, Romanian accordionists, the young in pall bearers' clothes—this is the hemlock they've given me to drink.

The Maigue in West Limerick, as I crossed it, was like the old kettles Kennedy's ancestors used mend.

Travellers used make rings from old teaspoons and sometimes I wondered if they could make rings from the discarded Hackenberg lager cans or Mr Sheen All-Surface Polish cans beside the Metal Bridge.

I am living in the city for a year when a man who looks as if his face has been kicked in by a stallion, approaches me on the street.

'I'm from Limerick city and you're from Limerick city. I know a Limerick city face. I haven't seen you there for a while. How many months did you get?'

Becoming Invisible

Grace Jolliffe

Josie stared at the blackboard, her thin lips parted in disbelief and her eyes half shut in a vain effort to avoid seeing. The chalk drawing looked to her like a squashed tulip and couldn't possibly resemble that place between her legs she knew only as her 'private parts'. Beside the sketch the lecturer had written a list of words people used to describe their private parts—words Josie could not and would not ever use.

Josie wanted to run as far from this place as she could get. But how could she get to the door without everyone noticing and maybe even laughing? She was stuck, trapped by her own inability to move. All she could do was stare at her feet and just allow herself an occasional glance at the offending picture.

She had not come here by choice. She'd been coaxed and cajoled by, of all people, Mrs Summers, who did the floral arrangements for the church. For months after her husband Benny's death, Josie had stayed indoors waiting for someone to tell her what to do. No one had, until one day Mrs Summers had called in, bringing her a bunch of flowers and urging her to visit the local community centre.

'After all, Josie, you're still young at fifty-five and there's lots of things you could be doing while you've still got the chance.'

Josie didn't like to offend anyone so the next day she got the bus down to the community centre and scoured the notice board for anything that didn't involve jumping around in a leotard. 'Self Awareness for Women', one poster said. Josie asked the receptionist if you needed any special clothes and when she said no, Josie signed up.

This was Week Seven and they were 'exploring sexuality'. Josie had been going to pretend she was ill and not turn up but Pat, whose presence beside Josie in class made her feel frumpy and whose hair hung straight in a neat bob, making Josie conscious of her permed grey curls, had laughed.

'Jesus, Josie,' she said 'after three children and thirty-five years of marriage, you can't be that shy. Come on, it might be a laugh!'

Josie didn't think it would be a laugh at all. More like torture, she thought, but Pat was adamant and had even called to the house for her so they could get the bus to class together. On the way, Pat teased and joked. Josie tried to smile and hoped the other passengers couldn't hear Pat's loud, crackly voice.

Pat was dressed in pale blue and wore a large tangerine-coloured crystal around her neck. She told Josie the crystal was a present from her daughter and helped her keep calm. Her daughter lived in a 'New Age Community', whatever that was. Josie didn't like to ask in case it turned out to be some sort of cult or sect, where everyone ends up taking poison or shooting themselves like on the telly. She felt sorry for Pat having a daughter in a place like that but Pat herself seemed quite pleased about it and spoke about visiting her daughter at weekends. Obviously she didn't watch much telly, thought Josie, whose three children had emigrated and who had no one to visit.

Television was Josie's only pastime. Before Benny died they had gone once a week to the local pub. They sat in the corner, eating chips and chicken wings, sipping their drinks slowly to make them last. Benny had been a postman so they'd never been well off, but then they'd never been poor either and had just enough to manage on, provided they were careful.

The woman who ran the course was called Fiona. Josie felt reassured when she appeared behind the desk on the first day, dressed in a respectable skirt and lovely hand-knitted Aran cardigan. The first thing she did was push the desk to one side of the room saying that she didn't want any barriers between her and the women. She chatted to them about herself for a few minutes and then she asked the women to introduce themselves and say a few words about their lives. Josie listened in terror as her new classmates talked, saying things like: 'Hello, I'm Mary Conroy, I've been married for thirty years. I bake all my own bread and I knit jumpers for my grandchildren,' or 'Hello, I'm Jackie Meadows and I used to work over in the Rit-Ex factory before it closed. I did reception and some typing and now I can't find another job.'

Around the room it went. They were sitting in a semicircle and Josie was in the middle. She was only half listening to the women next to her as they introduced themselves. She was busy trying to figure out what to say. She could get the hang of the 'Hello, I'm Josie' part, but what to say after that was a big problem. She hadn't worked since she was a young girl. She didn't bake her own bread or knit or sew. By the time Fiona smiled and nodded to let her know it was her turn all she could manage was: 'Hello, I'm Josie, I'm a widow woman.'

Her words hung in the air as if on the edge of a silent cliff. Fiona continued to smile at her and beckoned for her to say more, but Josie's spit had disappeared and her throat was almost closed—all she could do was stare at her lap.

'It's lovely to have you here, Josie,' Fiona said, and she came over and grasped Josie's hand.

The friendly gesture made Josie's eyes fill a little and she had to blink several times and count to seventy-nine in her head to keep from breaking down. Her hand tingled a little where Fiona had touched it. The woman beside her nudged her and winked and this turned out to be Pat.

After this it got easier and although she didn't quite know what the point of it all was, she started to look forward to the classes, half excited and half terrified. All the subjects were new to her, things like 'Women in a Changing Society', 'Health for Life' and even 'Relationships'. Josie thought that this meant marriage but now she knew it meant lots of things. She began to wonder if she and Benny had even had a relationship. She couldn't remember them ever 'communicating' on an intimate level or discussing their hopes and dreams or fears. Of course, Benny had always known Josie had a fear of spiders and if one appeared in the bath he would remove it with a long-handled brush and shake it away in the garden. He never killed them, he even quite liked them but he fully understood how Josie felt and how she dreaded the thought of one running up her leg and tickling her thigh.

Fiona talked about relating to other people and how some people had more of these skills than others. Someone who relates well to other people accepts them for what they are, listens to them and validates them, Josie learned.

'To validate someone as a person is to make them aware that they are special and unique,' Fiona said, making Josie feel miserable. She couldn't remember having done any of that for Benny.

'I didn't know how. No one told me how. I must have been a terrible wife!' Josie said to Pat during tea break.

'Of course you weren't,' Pat answered. 'I bet you did all those things in your own way. Don't worry about it. It's just a way of talking, that's all.'

Josie had worried, though, and after that particular class she had gone to Benny's grave. Inscribed on the headstone were the words 'Beloved Husband', and Josie had knelt down and stared at the words and sobbed.

However confused these other classes had made her, none of them compared with today's sexuality lecture. Fiona was now in the process of drawing a man's genitals right beside the woman's. Some of the women giggled and some sat quietly like Josie, shifting slightly in their chairs and trying not to look.

'As women we owe it to ourselves to explore our bodies,' Fiona said with a bright, encouraging smile. 'We should begin by examining our vaginas, getting to know them and to admire them.'

Josie squirmed, then rose slightly from her seat. Pat touched her arm and shook her head.

'It's all right. She's not going to make us do it here!'

Fiona continued cheerfully as if she was talking about the price of apples. She talked about orgasms and erogenous zones—neither of which Josie had ever heard of. Nor had anyone else she knew, though, of course, there was always the possibility that they had and they just hadn't told her. Since she'd started this course, it seemed like nobody had ever told her anything.

At the end of the class, Fiona handed them all a leaflet that contained the same drawings as had been on the blackboard. Josie stuffed hers into her handbag and hoped to God she didn't have an accident on the way home. The nurses would think she was awful.

Pat asked her to go for coffee and Josie couldn't think of an excuse quickly enough so off she went. Inside the café, she didn't know whether to sit down at a table or go to the counter and serve herself. Pat took control.

'Sit down over there, Josie, this one's on me. I'll get it while you mind the table.'

Josie sat down and fiddled with the clasp of her handbag. When Pat returned with coffee and two slices of cake, she took out some money and offered to pay her share.

'Not at all, Josie. You can get it next time if you like.' Next time, thought Josie. Now she'd have to come again. She couldn't owe Pat money. She bit into her chocolate cream cake and realised with a shudder of excitement that she'd quite like to come again.

'Here, let's have a look at this,' Pat said, taking the leaflet out of her bag.

'Oh no, people will see. They'll think we're a bit, well a bit, you know… funny.'

'Funny!' Pat laughed, 'of course they won't. People don't care what two middle-aged women like us do. Haven't you noticed? When you get past forty, you're invisible!'

Josie looked around the café. Sure enough no one was looking at them. Not so much as a glance! She thought of all the time she'd spent in the house after Benny's death, waiting for someone to come, waiting for someone to notice, and no one ever did. Except for Mrs Summers, who was middle-aged herself, so she didn't count.

Josie watched a film when she got home. It was one of those detective thrillers. Loads of action and excitement, but the average age of everyone in it was about twenty-five except for one woman, in her fifties, who was accidentally shot because she got in the way. Josie stood up and switched off the television. Benny frowned at her from his framed photograph on the mantelpiece. She turned it round to face the wall.

'Just in case,' she whispered as she climbed the stairs to bed. She lay there for an hour, just staring into the darkness. Then she got up, stretching slowly, and as she did she caught sight of herself in the mirror, her clean white cotton nightdress looking strangely like a shroud.

'Not yet,' she said to the mirror in a firm, loud voice as she covered it with a sheet. Taking her compact mirror and the leaflet Fiona had given her out of her handbag, she thought how nice it might be to be invisible. She could do what she wanted, whatever that might be!

It was difficult to explore with one eye barely open and the other tightly shut. What she could see looked nothing like a squashed tulip, more like a… Well, she couldn't describe it really having never seen one like it before.

Dark Horses

Claire Keegan

In the night, Brady dreams the woman back into his life again. She's out the yard with the big hunter, laughing, praising her dark horse. She reaches up, loosens the girth, and takes the saddle off. The hunter shakes himself and snorts. She leads him to the trough and pumps fresh water. The handle shrieks when pressed but the hunter doesn't shy: he simply drops his head and drinks his fill. Further off, the cry of hounds moves across the fields. In his dream these hounds are Brady's own and he knows it will take a long time to gather them in and get them home.

Waking, he finds he's clothed from the waist down: black jeans and his working boots. He gropes for the clock, holds the glass close, reads the hands. It isn't late. Overhead, the light is still burning. He gets to his feet and finds the rest of his clothes. Outside, the October rain goes shuddering through the bamboo. That was planted years ago to stake her shrubs and beans but when she left he took no mind, and the garden turned wild. On McQuaid's hill, through cloud, he makes out the figure of a man walking through fields greener than his own. McQuaid himself, herding, counting all the bullocks once again.

In the kitchen he boils water, scalds the pot. The tea makes him feel human again. He stands over the toaster and warms his hands. His aunt brought up marmalade last week but there's hardly a lick in the jar. With a knife he scrapes what's left off the glass and goes out, in his jacket, to the fields. The two heifers need to be brought in and dosed. He must clear the drains, fell the ash in the lower field—and there's a good day's welding in the sheds before winter comes on strong. He throws what's left of the sliced pan on the street and starts the van. One part of him is glad the day is wet.

In Belturbet, he buys drenching fluid, welding rods, oil for the saw. There's hardly any money left. He hesitates before he rings Leyden from the phone box, knowing he'll be home.

'Come up to the house,' Leyden says. 'I'm in need of a hand.'

It is a fine house on a hill, which his wife, a schoolteacher, keeps immaculate. Two storeys painted white look out over the river. In the yard a pair of chestnut trees, the horse lorry, heads over every stable door. When Brady lands, Leyden waves from the hayshed. He's a tight man, bony, with great big hands.

'Ah, Brady! The man himself!'

'There's a bad day.'

'Tis raw,' Leyden agrees. 'Throw the halter on the mare there, would you? I've a feeling she'll give trouble.'

Brady stands at the mare's head while Leyden shoes. The big hands are skilled: the hoof is measured, pared, the toe culled for the clip. On the anvil the shoe is held, hammered to size. Steel nails are driven home, and clenched. Then the rasp comes round, the shavings falling like sawdust at their feet. All the while it's coming down, gasps of sudden rain whipping the galvanised roof. Brady feels strange pleasure standing there, sheltered, with the mare.

When Leyden rasps the last hoof, he throws the tools down and looks out at the rain.

'It's a day for the high stool,' he says.

'It's early,' Brady says uneasily.

'If we don't soon go, it's late it will be,' Leyden laughs, his eyes searching the ground for nails.

'I've to get me finger out; there's jobs at home.' Brady puts the mare back in the stable, bolts the door.

'You'll come, any road,' Leyden says. 'I'll get Sean to change a cheque and we'll settle up.'

'It'll do another day.'

'Not a hate about it. I might not have it another day.'

'All right so.'

As Brady follows Leyden back to town, a burning in his stomach surges. Leyden turns down the slip road past the chemist and parks behind The Arms. It looks closed but Leyden pushes the back door open. The bulb is dark over the pool table. On Northern Sound, a woman is reading out the news. Long Kearns is there with his Powers, staring into the ornamental fishing net behind the bar. Norris and McPhillips are picking horses for the next race. Big Sean stands behind the counter, buttering bread.

'Is that bread fresh or is it yesterday's?' Leyden asks.

'Mother's Pride,' Sean smiles, looking up. 'Today's bread today.'

'But if we ate it tomorrow wouldn't it still be today's?' says Norris who has drunk two farms. Except for the slight shake in his hand, no one would ever know.

'Put up two of your finest there, Sean,' says Leyden, 'and pay no mind to that blackguard.'

'He's been minding me for years,' says Norris. 'He'll hardly stop now.'

Sean puts the lip of a pint glass to the tap. Leyden hands him the cheque and tells him to give Brady the change. The stout is left to settle, the dark falling slowly away from the cream.

'We got the mare shod, any road.'

'Did she stand?'

'It was terror,' Leyden says. 'I'd still be at it only for this man here.'

'It's a job for a younger man,' McPhillips says. 'I did it myself when I was a garsún.'

'After three pints there's nothing you've not done,' says Norris.

'And after two there's nothing you won't do!' says Leyden, raising the bar. 'Isn't that right, Sean?'

'Leave Sean out of it,' the barman says affectionately.

Norris looks at Brady. 'Is it my imagination or have you lost weight?'

Brady shakes his head but his hand reaches for his belt.

'It's put it on I have.'

Big Sean wraps the sandwiches in clear plastic and puts them in the fridge. Brady reaches out and his hand closes on the glass. The glass feels cold in his hand. It isn't right to be drinking at this hour, and the stout is bitter.

'Have you a drop of blackcurrant there, Sean?'

'What are you doing with that poison?' Leyden asks. 'Destroying a good pint.'

Brady swallows a long draught. 'At least I didn't destroy four good hooves,' he says, finding his voice at last.

Everybody laughs.

'Is that so?' says Leyden, smiling. 'And what would you know? There's nothing but cart horses in Monaghan.'

'Every good cart horse needs shoes,' says Brady.

'They wear around the Cavan potholes,' says McPhillips, a Newbliss man.

'Now we have it!' Norris cries.

When the banter subsides, McPhillips goes out to place the bets. Sean turns off the radio now that the news is over. The silence is like every silence; each man is glad of it and glad, too, that it won't last.

As they sit there, Leyden's nostril flares.

'Which one of ye dug up Elvis?'

'Lord God!' Long Kearns says, coming suddenly to life. 'That would knock a blackbird off its pad.'

Leyden swallows half his pint. The shoeing has put a thirst on him so Brady, not liking to leave with the money, orders another round.

Out in the street, school children are eating chips from brown paper bags. There's the smell of fried onions, hot oil and vinegar. It is darker now and the rain is still falling. When Brady walks into the diner, the girl at the counter looks up: 'Fresh cod and chips?'

'Ay.' Brady nods. 'And tay.'

He sits at the window and looks out at the day. Black clouds are sliding over the bungalows. He thinks again of that night in Cootehill. There was a Northern band in The White Horse. They sat at a distance from the stage and talked. She had a thoroughbred yearling and a three-year-old she thought would make an honest hunter. As she talked, a green spotlight shone through her hair. They danced a little and she drank a glass of wine. Afterwards, she asked him back to the house. *If you bring the chips, I'll light the fire and put the kettle on.* They ate supper in the firelight. A yellow cloth was spread over the table. She put down wicker placemats, pepper and salt, warm plates. The cutlery flashed silver. Smell of deodorant lingered in her bedroom, a wee candle burning, and headlights were passing through the curtains. When he woke, at dawn, she was asleep, her hand on his chest. He was working then, full time, for Leyden. That morning, walking down the main street, buying milk and rashers, he felt like a man.

The girl comes with his order. He eats what's placed before him, pays up, and faces down the street. He has to think for a moment before he can remember where he parked the van. He passes a stand of fruit and vegetables, a bucket of tired flowers, boxes of Christmas cards, ropes of trembling red and yellow tinsel. When he is walking past the hotel, he recognises a tune he cannot name. He stops to listen, then finds himself at the counter ordering a pint. The day is no longer his own. A few more tunes are played. At some point he looks up and realises McQuaid is there, in a dark suit of clothes, with his wife. Sensing him, McQuaid looks over, nods. Soon after, a pint's sent down. On Brady's lips the stout tastes colder than the last.

'The bould man himself! Have you no home to go to?' It's Leyden. He takes one look at Brady, and changes. 'What's ailing you at all, man?'

Brady shakes his head.

Leyden looks over at McQuaid. The waitress is bringing serviettes, knives for the steak.

'Pay no mind,' he says. 'Not a hate about it. The land'll be here long after we're dead and gone. Haven't we only the lend of it?'

Brady nods and orders the drink. Leyden pulls his stool up close and waits for the pint to settle. Brady is almost sorry he came in. When the pint is ready, Leyden puts it on the beermat, turns it round.

'Never mind the land. It's the woman that's your loss,' he says unhelpfully. 'That was the finest woman ever came around these parts.'

'Ay,' Brady says.

'There's men'd give their right arms to have a woman like that.' Leyden says, coming in tight and taking hold of his arm.

'They would, surely.'

The waitress passes with two sizzling plates.

'What happened at all?' asks Leyden.

Brady feels rooted to the stool. Back then some days were hard but not one of them was wasted. He looks away. The silence rises. He lifts hs glass but he cannot swallow.

'It was over the horse,' he says finally.

'The horse?'

Leyden looks at him but Brady does not want to go on. Even the mention of the horse is too much.

'What about the horse?' Leyden persists but then he looks away to leave Brady some room.

'I came home one night and she told me I'd have to buy food, pay bills. She told me I'd have to take her out for dinner.'

'And what did you say?'

'I told her to go fuck herself!' Brady says. 'I told her I'd put her horses out on the road.'

'That's terror,' Leyden says. 'Did you have drink on you?'

Brady hesitates. 'A wee drop.'

'Sure we all say things—'

'I went out and opened the gate and put her horses out on the road,' Brady says. 'She gave me a second chance but it was never the same. Nothing was ever the same.'

'Christ,' says Leyden, pulling away. 'I didn't think you had it in you.'

It is well past closing time when Brady finds the van. He gets behind the wheel and takes the back roads home. It will be all right; the sergeant knows him, he knows the sergeant. He will not be stopped. There are big, wet trees at either side of these roads, telephone poles, wires dangling. He drives on through falling leaves, keeping to his own side. When he reaches the front door, the bread is still on the step. The dog hasn't come home but he knows the birds will have it gone by morning. He looks at the kitchen table, the knife in the empty jar, and climbs the stairs.

He gets into the wisp and takes his jumper off. He wants to take his boots off but he is afraid. If he takes his boots off he knows he will never get them back on in the morning. He crouches under the bedclothes and looks at the bare window. It is winter now. What is it doing out there? The wind is piping terrible notes in the garden and, somewhere, a beast is roaring. He hopes it is McQuaid's. He lies in his bed and closes his eyes, thinking only of her. He can feel his own heart, beating. He closes his eyes. Soon, she will come back and forgive him. The bridle will be back on the coat stand, the cloth on the table. In his mind there is the flash of silver. As sleep is claiming him, she is already there, her pale hand on his chest and her dark horse is back grazing his fields.

Pixels

Molly McCloskey

1. Paris

He felt huge. As though he'd travelled from some pumped-up planet to schlep his ungainly way around this city. Everything was tiny here—the coffee cups, the pastries, the women, the cars. The cars looked compressed, like an accordion in its pushed-together state. He thought it impossible for a man to drive one and retain any kind of dignity. On the trains he felt like a grown-up on a school outing with a group of children: sinewy, swarthy, precocious children. The men seemed to list slightly—no matter what they were doing—while he stood upright, his feet planted solidly and just wide enough apart to keep him from pitching forward at moments of sudden motion. It was a difficult city in which to like yourself.

The heat didn't help. Sweat trickled down his back and his hands and feet swelled; he looked at his fingers and saw sausages, tumescent in their skins. Everybody who really lived here had gone away to escape the heat. Being here, he couldn't help thinking of himself as one of a thousand winners of a booby prize.

He and his wife were staying in an apartment loaned to them for six weeks by a friend of a friend. He sat on the balcony and listened to the neighbours, an act that couldn't quite be classified as eavesdropping because, for one thing, he didn't speak French and, for another, he really would've preferred that they be quiet. His discomfort was made worse by the fact that he couldn't tell if they were fighting or consoling each other or simply exchanging information—or even whether they were stupid or articulate. Not knowing the language, he never knew when to feel menaced, and nearly everything he heard sounded equally dramatic.

Once, when he'd been sure the neighbours were arguing, his wife said—though he hadn't asked—'Listen to them. They're talking about what to cook for lunch again.'

For a week, they went south, nearly to the Spanish border. They were sunning themselves one day on the pebbly banks of a stream where they'd stopped to swim. He let his head loll to the side. His eyes came to rest on a lizard about the size of his shoe, not two feet from him. The latter half of a fish protruded from its jaws, and both animals were glistening in the sun.

He nudged his wife and together they knelt transfixed in front of the scene. The lizard froze and was so bug-eyed that initially they thought the fish was stuck in its throat. But almost imperceptibly, the fish moved towards its vanishing point in the lizard's belly.

He searched for something to say that was both witty and knowledgeable. Why couldn't he just watch? But he couldn't; he was a language animal.

'It's odd,' he said.

'What?'

'He seems to think he's on television.'

She smiled and their eyes met. It was the year she was in love with someone else and sometimes when they looked at one another, the knowledge passed freshly between them and he felt it as acutely as he had the day she'd first told him.

2. London

London he loved, always had. He loved the order of it, the way so many things were red or black instead of green. You got tired of green. Also, there was something toy-like about the centre of London and even about some of the people, those who weren't rude, anyway. There was a quaintness that seemed a denial of the actual state of things. A prissiness, almost. Londoners were like practice New Yorkers, he thought. They were the ones God had to make do with before he dreamed up New York and got city people just right.

He was standing with his wife in front of a fish tank in Kensington. Or was it a pixel tank? They couldn't be sure. Couldn't be sure if they were real, the creatures whose noses bumped so believably against the glass, whose bodies whiplashed their way gently through the blue water—if it was water.

He thought they were marvellous. She thought they were fish.

'But how could they not be?' she said. 'Look at them.'

'I… don't… think…' he said, his own nose bumping the glass.

He put his arm around her as they stood there staring at the pixel fish, lingering in the aquarium warmth of each other, a little viscous-eyed themselves. His heart did something that wasn't quite a leap, exactly—it wasn't that much—more like it turned over in its half-sleep and sighed contentedly.

Side by side, as though they were kids at a World's Fair exhibit, their eyes followed the dimensionless swathes of colour on the screen (for he was now sure it was only a screen). But wonder was a thing that had been shrunk. They weren't looking at a mock-up of something that could traverse the heavens. This was computer-generated imagery, spectacular in its own way, but still. Sometimes he thought everything worth happening had already happened.

'Are you sure?' she said. 'Are you sure those aren't fish?'

'Pretty sure,' he said. 'Look, when they turn, for a split second, they don't have any breadth—or is it depth? Their bodies vanish, or just become a line.'

'I don't think I like it,' she said.

'What?'

She didn't answer. Instead she said, 'I like that word, though. Pixels. That's a word I like. Pixie. Pixie stick. Pinwheel. Pixel. It doesn't feel like a word that belongs in an adult's vocabulary.'

3. Aberdeen

Everything was made of granite, and it oppressed him. And yet when the mica sparked in the sun it seemed to him like little messages of hope, an SOS flashing from a place you thought there was no more life.

At night, all the young people were aggressively drunk. It wasn't their behaviour, per se, that was aggressive. It was the desperate and unhappy way they inhabited their drunkenness that seemed to befit people much older than themselves. People who were justified in being bitter.

'Do you think it's the Calvinist thing?' she asked the next morning.

They were walking along a stretch of beach beside the North Sea, the sand a funny orange colour.

'I think it's the oil,' he said. 'Mmm.'

'Any place built on oil money is bound to have a certain desperation about it. A paranoia. Everything you have is based on a finite, winding-down resource, so you're just waiting for the axe to fall. Even if it's not going to fall in your lifetime, you'd still click into the mindset.'

Driving south to Edinburgh, she gazed out the window at the lonely green countryside speckled with stone farmhouses and said, 'Home would look a little like this if it weren't for all the ugly bungalows we have.'

'Does it ever strike you,' he said, 'that everywhere is just a better or worse version of everywhere else?'

'I don't know. But it does seem like the older you get, the more everyone is just a composite of everyone else you've ever met. Except the people you've known for a long, long time. They're the sort of…'

'Prototypes?'

'Prototypes, yes.'

'So I would be a prototype for you? A kind of Adam?'

She smiled. 'Madam, I'm Adam,' she said.

4. Paris

Sometimes in the metro, he felt like he was dead. It wasn't just the fact of being underground, sunk in the stale gloom. It was the way everybody moved through the corridors without seeming to really see each other and the way, when they were on the trains, they all seemed ashamed and lonely, or else frightened, like he imagined people cohabiting in Hades would look.

The ascent to street level was always jarring and only served to reinforce the feeling that he'd been to the underworld. You'd be halfway up the grimy, piss-scented steps and lift your eyes and see a leafy canopy coming into view, dappling a blue sky, and beneath it, some limbs-entwined sculpture of two airborne bodies in a permanent, erotic swirl. He suggested to her, only facetiously, that the municipal authorities should provide an in-between place, some kind of decompression chamber between that hell and this heaven. She suggested in turn that the shock served a purpose, reminding you that you were never far from either realm.

They ate in French restaurants, looked at artefacts from Africa, and went to American movies. De Niro and Brando in a heist. The latter growing old like a woman, the way some men had the misfortune to. Lips the colour of bad ham, a soft, puckered face, all arbitrary dents like a potato. His girth so deliberate she had a theory about it. Rebelling against whatever had turned him, all those years ago, into pure sex.

'You don't just get that big,' she said, as they walked the canal afterwards. 'You have to want to.'

'You think he wants to look like that?'

'Of course. There was nothing in that body—his body when he was young—that suggested someone who'd get obese. It's kind of in your face. He's mad at us. He's mad at us for turning him into a thing. For having regarded him as perfect. Hollywood fucks you up. No two ways about it.'

'I'd never have done that,' he said.

'Done what?'

'If people loved looking at me, I wouldn't have spoiled it for them.'

'You don't know,' she said. 'Until the time comes, you don't know what you'd do.'

5. Dublin

When they were students together, in the long ago, they used to cycle down Anglesea Road. Looking up at the lights in the windows, he could nearly feel the warmth and had the urge to lose himself in other people's certainties. He felt a little lost, amidst every thing he was discovering, and he wondered why falling in love should be accompanied by such sadness. His only theory was that a state of perfection—being, like all other things, impermanent—necessarily contained the elements of its own destruction.

They settled in the city. And it was only when he ended up back in some spot they used to frequent as students and didn't anymore—Bray, for instance, or the Phoenix Park—that he realised how dense the city had become for them. In the beginning there'd been landmarks—places they'd first done this or that—but slowly all the spaces in between had been filled in. There were no longer any gaps, which meant there were no longer any landmarks, any ways of remembering how or where they'd been. When he looked back on all the years they'd spent together, what he saw was a tight weave, a kind of sprawl.

And then one day she told him. It was April, and everything about that evening—the precise time of her announcement, the clothes they wore, the yellow light on the lawn—stood out in a way nothing had for years.

The way she said, strangely: *Oh no.*

'It doesn't mean I don't love you anymore. *Oh no.*'

He didn't think he'd ever heard her use that expression before, not in a way that meant 'on the contrary,' and he wondered was it something she'd picked up from this man. Then he wondered if this was what his life was going to be like now: watching her movements, listening to her talk, looking for signs of some insidious infiltrator, as though the man were an illness advancing.

He was by turns enraged and dreadfully sentimental. He spent a lot of time wondering what would be worse: being left suddenly and without warning or watching their marriage die a slow death. He thought more about their student days than he had in twenty years. If they could see things fresh again, he thought (not the old things, of course, but just any things, anywhere, together), they might be okay, going places had always been good for them. So he convinced her to take those weeks off and they went to Paris.

6. Paris

The beauty of the city, he remarked, was in inverse proportion to the kindness of its inhabitants. This made sense to him. What could these people possibly owe you, anyway? You were here, weren't you? He looked around and saw beauty so flagrant and freely distributed that it struck him as promiscuous. At the same time, he became disproportionately grateful for whatever crumbs of decency he was tossed.

As a result, he went round feeling either awed or infuriated. Queuing in the post office, for instance, was a ridiculously time-consuming activity. But then they put such pretty blue seals on the envelopes. Things they printed out of machines that appeared to be full of information pertaining to your letter and yours alone.

'Why don't they just use a standard stamp?' he said.

'I know,' she said. 'I mean I don't know. Sometimes they do. But how can you get angry with a people whose idea of fast food is a crepe?'

When he made love to her those days, it was as though from afar. He thought of long-distance phone calls during which someone on another continent sounds right next door, and how the illusion is both comforting and disconcerting. This was the opposite of that. She was right there but seemed very far away or as though she were inhabiting another medium altogether, as though she were underwater and he could just barely make her out through the murk.

Of intercourse, she said: For a woman, it's like you've brought the outside world into you. So that afterwards, for a little while, you have a sense of permeability. Like the boundaries between you and the world have blurred. You feel precarious, but you also feel more connected.

He wanted to ask her how it felt then, switching between men, bringing two beings from the outside world in. Did they cancel each other out, like a double negative? Or did she feel twice as connected? He didn't ask, because he couldn't bear to hear the answer.

Mostly he wanted to know what she saw in the man. He'd met him. He was extremely seductive. But extremely seductive men tend to walk a fine line, always in danger of veering into the ridiculous. He suspected that was what women loved about him, that he was willing to appear ridiculous. He was a cheap trick who didn't fear his unmasking.

7. The West

The first summer, he grew runner beans and peas, red-leaf lettuce and onions, but his yield was always too much and he didn't know what to do with the surplus. He had neighbours, but their gardens were plentiful and self-assured. So this summer he'd opted for a more self-indulgent, impractical selection. He planted corn, of all things (a breed, the seed packet said, suited to the English climate, and he figured that was close enough to the Irish). He doted on the staked willowy stalks, marvelling at the sight of actual ears appearing. But in late July, the rains came and never really stopped. The corn shrivelled on its stalks and died and he felt as though he were witnessing the demise of weak pups in a litter.

Summer days, the tractors roared back and forth past his door. Colossal hulks, either empty, their malevolent-looking prongs exposed, or overburdened with bales of newly mown hay which passed within inches of his window. Having lived in the city for over thirty years, he felt menaced by the tractors. Other days, his neighbour herded cattle past the door, to the field beyond, where wild roses and blackberries grew tangled with the rushes.

He marvelled at the gravity of those beasts. How the earth seemed to pull them to it. It cost them such effort to lift their heads, as though they were labouring under a great burden of feeling. He liked to watch them sway in their slow, almost sensual way as they ambled up the road. He even liked to spy on them when they'd got free of their enclosures and were grazing on the roadside. The half-defiant, half-shamed look in their eyes suggesting that after having been shunted to and fro so often, they weren't quite sure how to feel about their sudden freedom.

The time of solitude is different, he read. And it was true. His life was like a concentrate. Space was different too, now that he was alone, or perhaps it was the way things occupied space. All his life, or all his life with her, he had experienced objects of any kind as simply things underfoot; he hadn't thought about them at all. Now he felt them pass in and out of relation with him. When a visitor entered his house, he could feel objects recede, only rising up again and regrouping around him when he was once more alone. When he went out for the day, he was conscious that his life, in the form of its things, awaited his return.

He'd come home from Paris alone. It turned out he was worrying about the wrong thing altogether, though there was no way he could've known this. Ironic, of course, that he had taken her there to repossess her only to lose her entirely and in the most freak fashion. Actually, it was unbearably common, it was the sort of death that took place on city streets the world over, but the fact that a few seconds this way or that would have altered things so profoundly gave such accidents their freak quality.

The only consolation was imagining all the catastrophes you must've skirted without ever having known it. All the times you'd lingered or left early or, at the last minute, taken a different route and made it through the day unscathed. Timing was important, it was life or death, but as there was no way you could foresee the consequences of your most trivial decisions, timing became—paradoxically—the very thing you couldn't stage manage. In fact, he thought, you would drive yourself crazy if you tried to minimise danger through such means. Still, he marvelled at the blithe way people took their lives into their hands every day and stepped out into the world.

There is no reality but in relation, he read. The problem was loving beings who changed or disappeared. Mourning to him was looking at the world and seeing a monochrome. Knowing that this was its true tint and that all colour was an add-on to delude the faint of heart, which pretty much included everyone.

But not even that lasted. In time, he saw blues and greens again. Today, for instance, the world is all flash. The mountains, the grass, the glittering, just visible sea. As though the elements are attempting to outdo each other. This is the liquid, hallucinogenic quality that will mellow, come evening, into a light he thinks of as tangerine. The air itself will acquire colour, will seem to hold it, the way a solid does. He does not know what conditions are necessary for such a thing to unfold. He doesn't know much at all about wavelengths or the atmosphere or how to read the sky; he can barely tell the direction of the wind with much accuracy. But he can see light in the making.

The Butcher's Apron

Lisa McInerney

Pup is indignant about the flag. It is indignation that swells and spills over and it provoked in him, in the fifteen minutes between then and now, a dreadful need of being with his own people. The tribe at Justy's do not let him down. They lift their heads; they share his shock; they call his pint. First he is animated. His indignation asserts itself in arms arcing through the pungent, carbonated air of Justy's, ten minutes to seven, Friday evening, late April. Then he is pensive. He is melancholic. He shifts in his bar stool, lugging its legs an inch over the tiles. He has relinquished the mass of his story but is momentarily lost in its absence. This is Pup. He is young and he is gangly and there is an awful lot he doesn't know.

Sparky luxuriates in Pup's ignorance with the imposed ecstasy of a condemned man tackling his last meal. Pup's constitution will one day match what houses it, but for now he lopes and leans and baulks and scratches. He is only just gone twenty-three and works in the warehouse of a place that sells UPVC doors. He is six foot two or three without the bulk to make it look right. He has a young wan in the housing estate on the arse of the town; she is rubicund and mostly sullen and whenever she comes to Justy's with Pup, Sparky asks her if she thinks she's on The Missions or what? Sparky would have plans for Pup if he thought the young wan would let him. Pup is sincere and possessed of a laugh that lays waste to everything around it.

Now Sparky tries to jog Pup from his gloom. He unfolds himself from his over-bar hunch, leaves one forearm on the counter and the other on his hip and aligns himself so that his belly shrinks. 'And they just have it flying there?' he says. He is loud and sure and his voice has the desired effect. 'Fucking unreal,' says Pup, and he uncoils also and looks around at his audience. 'Like it was always there. The fucking cheek. The fucking…' he doesn't know what.

Boom bust boom. There is an economic recovery, the news says; *in Dublin only*, the news will not concede. The management of Justy's—Justy himself being long dead—never knew the sound of a full till and so they do not know how hard a fall it was when the fall came; Justy's never attracted the kind of patrons susceptible to fiscal undulations. They have a day trade: no busy times, no lunchtime surge, just a steady current of the same old same olds. This allows for certain liberties. If the customers want a lock-in, there'll be a lock-in, during which the smokers light up. Clandestine services can be pitched in the beer garden, from two regulars in particular: the cur who sells the dope and the malkin who sells the suck-offs. If Sparky has a want of a bit of grub but no mind for the road home, he can bring in a snack box or a takeaway dinner from the hot counter of the Topaz on the lower road or even a cooked chicken from SuperValu and and eat it at the bar. Justy's looks after its own and its own murmur and tut at Pup as he relays his story.

He starts, as before, from the point at which his lift dropped him after work. He strolls in along the lower road towards the town square, considering the fresh weekend; he crosses at the roundabout; he spots to his left the gaudiness of it, its flashing in the damp breeze, its fucking audacity. He peers, shades his eyes, squints. He comes a little way up the path towards it. It flies to the right of the EU flag, which flies to the right of the Tricolour. It is a Union Jack, hoisted on a flagpole at the entrance to the Kilcreehy Castle Hotel. It makes no sense. It is like there is a glitch in his sky.

'What reason could they have for that, now?' ponders Cullinane from the cluster. A man of many scars and few head hairs, a pragmatic man. He submits that the hotel is to host a wedding tomorrow—is one of the families British?

'Sure someone must be going,' Sparky says. 'Someone must have been asked to the Afters.'

No one in Justy's has been asked to the Afters.

This wedding occupies the tribe for a small time—*who* is going, if they are not; who is signing the nuptial contract; where this British family get off tramping into the Irish heartlands with their inglorious cloth.

And the concession then to rationale—it might not be all that bad. As a gesture, y'know. As a nod towards friendship between natural foes. Perhaps it might have been a good thing, in another time. It is, the tribe at Justy's decide, just *too soon*.

Sparky is surest of all that it is just *too soon* to fly a Union Jack in Ireland; if it wasn't too soon then why did they all get such a shock on hearing Pup's story? It is not usual for groups numbering more than, say, five souls to share the one reaction. Sparky is a thinker, though he might not look it. He likes to believe that it is for this reason he's nicknamed 'Sparky'; *I'm not an electrician at all,* he laughs, often, *ah but I'm a live wire.* Those who ask about Sparky's nickname are rarely acquainted with those who know that Sparky is Sparky because Sparky was his dog's name when he was a boy. Nevertheless, Sparky is sharp enough. Fierce cute, even. He reminds himself often: *I'm no fool.* The thought that he *is* a fool and so too stupid to know that he's a fool gives him terrible anxiety.

'The Butcher's Apron,' he says. 'That's what they call it above,' and he flicks a thumb, as if Northern Ireland is the attic atop the manor where they might tuck away their loons and malcontents.

It is *too soon* and it is an affront and so action needs to be taken but the shock resonates and it's too strong to allow for thoughtful planning. And so tactics need to be charmed out, whetted by emphatic reminders of their history, of the ties that bind compatriots. Reminiscence is a virus hopping from host to host and strengthening; one by one they succumb to it, Pup, as the instigator, first. *My granddad was in the IRA.* Everyone's granddad was in the IRA. *My father's great uncle was shot by the auxiliaries. That Mass Rock up off Gogarty's Lane, that was our land one time.* They spin yarns from old battles. They lament hardships suffered by ancestors. They are connected by ambassadorial grief, and through the thickening fog—for they drink as passionately as they talk—Sparky feels loss. Like something has been yanked from his grasp. The loss of a birthright.

Talk turns to other invaders. The new crowd come not with pikes, swords or firearms but with impudence. They set up businesses and primarily serve their own. They send their children to the local schools and secure exemptions from compulsory Irish lessons. They drive taxis—*almost all the taxis,* keens the chorus. Sparky shifts in his seat. This kind of chatter always ends in cacophonous ignorance, each voice shoring up and adding to its precursor's woes; the predictability of it saps him.

'We'll go have a look,' he says, and waits to catch Pup's eye. 'We'll go have a look, will we?'

That he has stirred Sparky into action cheers Pup greatly. He swigs the dregs of his pint and belches, leaving his jaw swing for longer than is necessary. He stands, grinning now, as if he's forgotten the alien colours.

Their town is of an unremarkable layout: a spine of pubs, chippers and dentist surgeries, capillaries stretched out to a Lidl on the west, an Aldi on the east, sheathed by a vellum of pebble-dashed housing estates and fields patched with burnt circles and sodden depressions. There is only one route Sparky and Pup can take and so they take it mechanically, each locked into his natural gait—Pup to his bouncing, stretching getalong, Sparky to his heel-knocking, clipped swagger, like a man afraid to trust his own knees. And there is a clamminess to the wind and to their surroundings, dankness to the concrete under them: the earth is nervous.

The castle of Kilcreehy Castle was never more than a stone framework around which was propped and plastered the necessities of the hotel: the castle houses only the lobby and reception desk and two suites above, suited mostly to American genealogy enthusiasts. Sparky and Pup do not make it that far, their crusade interrupted at the eyesore on the flagpole.

Well, what do we do now? thinks Sparky and the thought's incompetence upsets him; he is not used to being useless, not inside his own head.

As if in sympathy Pup breathes, 'It's a shock, isn't it?'

The flag is lurid in artificial light. It is bold and mocking and in its overlapped crosses it clashes even with itself. It is, notes Sparky, an empire's flag, an arrogant thing. It is bigger than he thought it would be.

He knows the Tricolour should not be flown after sunset. He doesn't care so much for the other two but knows that reverence is meant to be extended to them as well: the cold new European empire, and the brutal old.

He walks away and Pup catches up and keeps pace.

'What do we do now?'

Sparky says, 'We ruminate, Pup.'

They do not return to Justy's. They head instead to a pub closer to the hotel. This is owned by one Terry Corrigan, who's twenty-four stone and mobile only in the gravest of circumstances, so Sparky and Pup are served by his son Darren, who inhabits the role of landlord with studied precision. He dispenses one-liners. He is fluent in politics, county rivalries and the Champions League. He is a master of ambiguous responses. He has walnut-coloured eyes and has never managed to grow a decent beard. 'Sarcastic fucker,' Sparky says, cradling his pint in the sweep of his right hand, and Pup agrees.

A band has just finished setting up and its frontman conducts soundchecks as Sparky and Pup get cosy. Sparky hopes for patriotism. The Wolfe Tones. Paddy Reilly. Songs about revolution, emigration, bloody fraternity. Pup fidgets and looks around, twisting over this shoulder, then the other, like a man trying to free himself from a mangled car. 'Will you calm your tits?' Sparky says—a wisecrack he learned from a nineteen-year-old niece—and Pup guffaws. The band start their set but they play 'Pumped Up Kicks', then Olly Murs. Little in the way of rumination has taken place but Sparky wants to move. 'Come on,' he says and Pup apes him, swigging back the final third of his pint and stretching ceremoniously.

Sparky is not yet drunk but he is itchy for it—the haze and the loss of heed, inhibition drowned; drunkenness feels like being submersed; he likes that. It takes time and effort to get Sparky drunk, because it's the one sport where practice makes the player worse. It means that nights out have become expensive, sometimes crushingly. Pup's nights out too, but for different reasons: Pup always buys rounds of shots at closing time.

The upside to the protracted sobriety that defines his fifth decade, Sparky thinks, half-bitterly, is that he can outlast Pup or any of them at funerals, christenings and weddings.

Which reminds him again of the flag.

'I wish,' he tells Pup, 'that they'd played some of the old songs, that band. It's all trendy these days. It's all fuckin…'

Pup knows what he means.

There is not much light left now. A smudged ribbon of cloud separates the sky from its khaki horizon. Sparky clears his throat.

He is less a singer than he is a chanter, his voice trained by tipsy nationalism and the camaraderie of Saturday afternoon football terraces. But he tries to give it meaning. He tries for sweetness, even. Soul sound. The way the monks mean it, or the Welsh.

I was eighteen years old when I went down to Dublin…

And Pup joins in, just as solemn and sincere.

There is a point where Sparky realises they might make each other cry, far as they are from intoxication. They are under the influence of the song or of what the song means, what any of it means... They are custodians of a history, Atlas to its weight, and the tune is just one of many, a sinew of great heritage, of a country, a family compelled by the border of sea, thirty-two counties, *thirty-two*, each as much part of the whole as the next.

Sparky and Pup slow their steps but the song ends; songs do not go on forever.

'What'll we do now?' asks Pup.

Sparky is loathe to return to Justy's. He has unfinished business with the enemy banner. He tilts his head to the right, to the door of another pub. Three houses down, four more to go—five if he counts the hotel bar, and he might yet. 'I haven't been in here in a long time,' Pup says as they cross the threshold.

They settle down by the soot-stained fireplace. They have two more pints apiece and Pup then moves to the vodka Red Bulls and gets even more fidgety, bouncing on the balls of his feet and watching the women. He is not old enough for fidelity, Sparky knows, and Christ, distraction is hard enough to come by, there should be concessions made. It's a small town and a big world and he knows that Pup is stuck here, that he has no mind for travel and even if he did, no fucking money and no chance of coming by it. He suspects that Pup's young wan is tolerant of occasional, whispered betrayal, so long as she's not poked on it, so long as he doesn't get anyone pregnant. She'll marry him some day; they'll get a mortgage; he'll quieten.

But Sparky isn't lax on Pup's wandering eye tonight. He is in need of attentive company tonight. So he says to Pup, 'Did you know that the Fianna are only sleeping?'

Pup is instantly and gratifyingly wide-eyed. 'How's that, Spark?'

'Fionn mac Cumhaill never died, they say. He's in a cave and he's asleep and the Fianna sleep around him. They'll wake again in Ireland's most desperate hour, and put what's wrong to rights.'

'You'd think,' says Pup, 'the Anglo thing would've gotten them moving.'

'Sure then there must be worse to come,' says Sparky with satisfaction, and while Pup sits enchanted and chewing his bottom lip he finds a two-euro coin and brings it to the jukebox on the wall by the bar and sifts through Metallicas and Rihannas for 'Uncle Nobby's Steamboat' and 'Carrickfergus' and 'Come Out Ye Black and Tans'. And so the magic is extended and Pup's eyes glint with clannish fervour and not with the notion that somewhere in this place is hidden the chance of a feverish ride against the back of the town grotto.

The lights are flicked off and on for last orders and Pup leaps forward for a couple of sambucas and, with Sparky refusing his measure, downs both.

They leave and move with purpose towards Mighty Bites where Pup orders taco chips and a chicken burger, and they sit outside so Sparky can have a fag, and there aren't many people out, it being only Friday and an unremarkable weekend, but they make a carbuncle to a small mass in their late teens. Sparky tells them the story of the sleeping Fionn, but they seem uninterested and he spots one of the girls smirking at another. 'You think it doesn't mean something,' Sparky says, trying to sound sage, 'but it'll mean something to you soon enough.' Where are the young people to go, he wonders, if not to London or Melbourne or Toronto? They are dressed too well for this town and they know it and it pleases them. He feels it like a burning in his throat. Or his gut. He'd like to lift a cheek of his arse to relieve himself but decides against it.

'How are things with you, Paud?' trills one of the girls and Pup brightens and tries to answer with calculated, masculine nonchalance, and Sparky winces on his behalf; the girl is seventeen or eighteen, glittered and spiced, and she has no interest in Pup beyond the pallid cruelty of deceit. He watches Pup sit straight and the girl sidle closer, watches her winch her neckline so that her breasts thrust for her chin, watches her eyes settle on the fleck of special sauce at the corner of Pup's mouth. 'Let's go,' says Sparky, and Pup blinks and says, 'Sure, you jog on if you like, Spark,' and there's a pang flipped in Sparky again. He reminds his friend that they're not done with the night yet, that there's a great impudence they have yet to challenge. 'Oh yeah,' says Pup. He announces darkly that they have something to take care of and doesn't notice that the young wan neglects to react.

So Sparky leads them back to the flags, and now in the early hours they are still slapping the breeze. And maybe, he thinks, swaying in queasy accord, if the hotel people had done their duty by the Tricolour and taken it down at sunset, and taken its rival with it, maybe he would have allowed himself home to bed. He's irritated, then incandescent that the protest's been pressed on him, after the week he's had, because the hotel people won't follow the rules, can't be bothered to do what's right.

He pushes on down the hotel driveway, Pup in tow.

The lobby light is dimmer than he expected, late and all the hour. There is a dark stone floor, brocade upholstered couches, mahogany. A broad-shouldered man in a gunmetal grey suit behind the desk, arms moving, hands busied with office implements. Laughter travelling from a distance, orphaned sounds, strangers' merriment.

Sparky lays his hand on the polished desk top and his hand looks pink and his fingers stubby.

'Do you not know,' he says to the broad-shouldered man; his badge sports no name over the embossed title of Night Manager, 'that the flag is supposed to be lowered at sunset?'

The Night Manager frowns. His actions slow. And then 'Oh!' and almost indiscernibly a breathy stream of *f* sounds; he stops what he is doing. 'It should have been done, lads,' he announces. 'Sorry about that,' but he doesn't look at either of them and Sparky's not sure whether this is out of curtness or shame but either way it emboldens him. 'Are you not going to do it now?' he says, and Pup to his left puffs his chest, a manifestation of Sparky's valour.

'I'll see what I can do,' says the Night Manager.

'And while you're at it,' says Sparky and his voice cracks, 'You can take down that other one and leave it down; it has no right to fly here; long enough we were trying to get rid of it.'

'Ah,' says the Night Manager. 'Well. We have a wedding tomorrow, lads; he's from England; it's a courtesy.'

'It's an offence,' says Sparky.

'Well it isn't,' says the Night Manager.

Not having the benefit of intoxication, how can this broad-shouldered man see the heart in Sparky's objections and travel, in his mind's eye, back to when this land was raw and the bloody rituals that birthed it appreciated? And Sparky, so usually persuasive amongst his own, has in fuelling this beautiful devotion tied his tongue: he slurs, and staggers once, and loses words. And Pup cannot help. Sure what would Pup know; he lopes and leans and baulks and scratches; he's young and weak and vulnerable; he is not even used to his independence.

They are defeated and insult upon injury they retreat back to the

Union Jack, that symbol of a great history denied to Sparky and to Pup, to all of them.

Sparky thinks, *how many of us died to send that yoke back where it belonged*? He imagines laid out before him a battlefield, he sees young men fall for honour, he imagines them clean-shaven, in dull grey waistcoats, in flat caps to a man.

He weaves between the flagpoles. 'Where's the rope?' he says. 'There's a rope to bring it down.' But the halyard is inside the pole, secreted behind a locked panel, and he cannot get at it. He steps back. He looks up.

'It flies there,' he chokes, 'as if it means nothing anymore.'

Sparky cannot bear the thought that he missed out on its meaning something. He has had a thorough education in its significance; he passed with flying colours Inter Cert History and Italia '90 and *Was It For This?* and he has travelled, Sparky, he has lived in Liverpool and Chicago, he has felt his Irishness, he has known meaning in it, and—

'Hold on,' Pup says.

He starts in the raised shrubbery in which one too many flagpoles were planted. His abundance of joints and limbs makes sense for once; Pup is lithe, Pup is a machine. Sparky stands into the shrubbery after him. He sinks a little into its soil as he cups his hands for a leg-up. Pup begins to ascend. He coils around the metal supporting the flag of the European Union, sticks out the sole of his runner and balances against the pole on which is hoisted the Union Jack. He strains, pants, and makes progress and Sparky is almost overcome.

A good lad, Pup. No cop on, but a steady compass, a sense of right and wrong, a willingness to learn, a heart unrivalled in the town. *And look*, Sparky laughs, *up he shimmies!* And when he reaches the flag there will be the feeling that a great deed was done in a small gesture, and Sparky waits for it.

But there is no gesture. There is no pride plucked from the sky; there is no evil vanquished. There is only a fall. Down he comes again in great disarray, limbs bunched, face to the dirt, and Sparky stands over him, 'Pup? Jesus. Jesus, Paudie,' but there is no answer, and he knows that's the end of it.

Night of the Silver Fox

Danielle McLaughlin

They stopped for diesel at a filling station outside Abbeyfeale. It was late evening, dusk closing like a fist around two pumps set in a patch of rough concrete and a row of leafless poplars that bordered the forecourt. Kavanagh swung down out of the cab and slapped the flank of the lorry as if it were an animal. He was a red-faced, stocky man in his late thirties. As a child he had been nicknamed Curley because of his corkscrew hair and the name had stuck, even though he was now almost entirely bald, just a patch of soft fuzz above each ear.

There was a shop with faded HB posters in the window and boxes of cornflakes on display alongside tubs of Swarfega and rat pellets. 'Fill her up,' Kavanagh said to the teenager who appeared in the doorway. Then he spat on the ground and walked around the back of the building to the toilet.

Gerard stayed in the cab and watched the boy, who was about his own age, pump the diesel. The boy was standing well back from the lorry, one hand holding the nozzle, the other clamped over his nose and mouth. When his eyes met Gerard's in the wing mirror, Gerard looked away.

Three months in and he was still not used to the smell. The fish heads with their dull, glassy eyes; the skin and scales that stuck to his fingers; the red and purple guttings that slipped from the fishes' bellies. The smell of dead fish rose, ghost-like, from the meal that poured into the factory silos. Gerard shaved his hair tight, cut his nails so short his fingers bled. At night in the pubs in Castletownbere, he imagined fine shards of fish bone lodged like shrapnel beneath his skin and tiny particles of scales hanging in the air like dust motes. The smell didn't bother Kavanagh, but then Kavanagh had been reared to it.

'Daylight robbery,' Kavanagh said when he returned to the lorry. He handed the pump attendant the money. 'Bring me out two packets of Tayto and have a packet for yourself.' He shook his head as he climbed back into the cab. 'Daylight robbery,' he said again, 'Four cents a litre dearer than Slattery's.'

Gerard didn't ask why they hadn't gone to Slattery's. Slattery's had stopped their tab a few weeks back and Kavanagh had been keeping his distance since.

Kavanagh hummed tunelessly while he waited for the boy to return with the crisps and his change. It was a fragment of a ballad he had taken up some time after they passed Gurrane, forty miles earlier, and he had not let it go since. Taped to the walls of the cab were pictures torn from magazines of women in an assortment of poses. They were mostly Asian and in varying states of undress: Kavanagh had a thing for Asian women. A photograph of Kavanagh's wife, Nora, taken at last year's GAA dinner dance, was stuck between a topless girl on a Harley Davidson and two dark-eyed women in crotchless panties. Nora had blonde wispy hair and glasses and the straps of her dress dug furrows into her plump shoulders.

'We're in Injun territory now,' Kavanagh said, when he saw the boy coming across the forecourt. 'These Limerick bastards would rob the teeth out of your head,' and he counted the change down to the last cent before putting it in his pocket.

It was almost dark when they pulled back onto the road. Kavanagh threw a packet of crisps across the cab. 'That'll keep you going,' he said, 'we can't count on Liddy for grub.' Four miles before Kilcroghan, they turned down a narrow side road, grass growing up the centre. Briars tore at the sides of the lorry. 'There's a man in Dundalk runs one of these on vegetable oil,' Kavanagh said. 'Did you ever hear anything about that?'

'No,' said Gerard, although he remembered reading something in a newspaper a couple of months back. If he let on that he knew anything at all, Kavanagh would have him tormented. Kavanagh had a child's wonder for the new and the strange. Each new fact was seized upon and dismantled, taken apart like an engine and studied in its various components. He had been bright at school but had left at fourteen to work in the fish factory.

Kavanagh shook his head. 'I don't think I could stand it,' he said. 'The smell. It must be like driving around in a fucking chipper.' Gerard glanced across at Kavanagh and tried to work out if he was serious. Kavanagh was watching the road, fingers drumming the steering wheel, humming to himself again. The light from the dashboard lent a vaguely sainted glow to his features. Gerard decided not to say anything. Kavanagh broke off his humming and sighed. 'You're all chat this evening,' he said. 'I can't get a word in edgeways. Are you in love or what?'

'Fuck off,' Gerard said but he was smiling as he turned to look out at the trees that reached black and tall from the hedges, their branches slapping against the lorry's window.

Gerard had first been to Liddy's mink farm back in August, six weeks after he started working for Kavanagh. He had not been able to shake the memory of the place since. It was partly the farm itself and it was partly Liddy's daughter. She was about seventeen with blue-black hair, eyes heavily ringed with black liner. When Kavanagh had gone inside with her father, she had taken Gerard across the yard to show him the mink.

The mink were housed in sheds a couple of hundred feet long, twenty or thirty feet wide, with low, sloping roofs of galvanised sheeting. The sides were open to the elements, wind blowing in from the mountains to the west. Gerard followed the girl into the first shed and along a sawdust path down the centre. In wire mesh cages on either side were thousands of mink, mostly all white, with here and there a brown one. They darted back and forth and stood on their hind legs, heads weaving, snouts pressed against the wire. Their eyes glittered like wet beads, and they twisted and looped, twisted and looped, hurling their bodies against the sides of the cages.

Gerard stood in front of a cage and poked a finger through the mesh. A mink stopped chewing its fur and looked at him, a vicious tilt to its chin. It sniffed the air, crept closer and snapped, grazing the tip of his finger. Then it backed away to stare at him from a distance.

The girl was a couple of paces ahead, watching. 'I suppose you think it's cruel,' she said. Her hair was tucked into the hood of her jacket and she had her arms folded across her chest.

Gerard examined his finger and shrugged. 'It's none of my business,' he said.

The girl had stared at him for a moment, saying nothing, her dark eyes narrowing. Then she sighed. 'It's what they're bred for,' she said, turning away, 'they don't know any different.'

It was dark when Kavanagh swung the lorry through a muddy entrance with rough concrete pillars on either side. The lorry lurched along an uneven track lined with chain-link fencing. In the distance, Gerard could make out the long, dark rows of the mink sheds, moonlight glinting on the metal roofs, and beyond them a huddle of outbuildings. 'Liddy hasn't paid since June,' Kavanagh said, 'so he'll need to come up with the cash tonight. I'll sort you out then.'

'It's all right,' Gerard said, 'it's grand,' although it wasn't all right anymore. Kavanagh hadn't paid him in three weeks and on his last visit home Gerard had to borrow from his father to pay the rent. 'I'll sort you out,' Kavanagh repeated as the lorry turned into the yard.

The farmhouse was a square two-storey building, its whitewash fading, weeds growing from crevices in the front steps. A cat ran across the lorry's path and hid behind a row of tar barrels. Liddy's mud-spattered jeep was parked in the yard, a back light broken. 'It would be easy to feel sorry for Liddy,' Kavanagh said, 'but what would be the use in that?' and they both got out of the lorry.

A light came on in the porch and Liddy himself appeared. He was a stooped, wiry man, a grey cardigan hanging loose from his shoulders, and his eyes darted from Kavanagh to Gerard and back again as he came towards them across the yard. His skin had the waxy, pinched look of a museum doll. It reminded Gerard of how his mother had looked in the months before she died and he knew immediately that Liddy was sick.

'How're the men?' Liddy held out a bony hand to Kavanagh who took it in his own vast paw and squeezed until Gerard expected to hear bones crack. Liddy's daughter had come out into the porch. She was slouched against the door frame, arms folded, her black hair pulled loosely into a ponytail.

Liddy looked up at the night sky with its shifting mass of cloud.

'The rain will be on soon,' he said, 'you might as well get her unloaded. I'll put the kettle on for tea.'

Gerard went to release the back of the lorry but Kavanagh held up a hand. 'Hold on a minute,' he said, 'if it was tea I was after I could have stayed at home. Tea is fuck all use to me.'

The girl, wearing tracksuit bottoms and a vest, was coming down the porch steps and across the yard. She had the same black-ringed eyes that Gerard remembered from before.

Liddy had already begun to shuffle towards the house. He called back over his shoulder to Kavanagh. 'Don't you know I'm good for it?' he said, 'have I ever let you down yet?'

Kavanagh didn't budge. 'That's three loads you owe me now,' he said. 'I've bills to pay. I've this young fella here to pay.' He nodded at Gerard who stood waiting by the lorry.

Liddy stopped. He gave a wheeze that shook his chest and caused him to bend almost double, hands on his knees. 'Sure what could a young lad like that want?' he said, when he righted himself again. 'A young lad like that would be happy sitting under a bush with a can.' He laughed then but Kavanagh didn't.

'Leave it for the time being.' It was the girl, her voice slightly muzzy as if she had been sleeping. She raised both hands behind her head and stretched like a cat. 'We can talk about it inside.' She turned and walked towards the house and the three men followed.

The porch was stacked with bags of coal and kindling. A plastic bucket and a yard brush stood in one corner, beside two pairs of wellington boots, caked with mud and sawdust. A picture of Pope John Paul II, arms outstretched, hung next to a calendar from the Fortrush Fisherman's Co-op, two years out of date, days circled and crossed in spidery ink. Beyond the porch was a dark, narrow hallway. Liddy faltered but the girl pushed open a door into a small sitting room.

There was a mahogany chest of drawers with ornate carvings that must have come from a bigger, grander house. Squares of faded linen were folded on top, next to a family of blue china elephants. The room smelled of things put away, of dust laid down on dust. The carpet was brown with an orange fleck and along one wall was a sofa in a dull mustard colour. On either side of the fireplace were two matching armchairs, their plastic covers still in place. A copy of the *Fur Farmers'*

Yearbook and a few tatty paperbacks sat on a coffee table.

Liddy took one armchair, Kavanagh the other. As he lowered himself onto the sofa, Gerard caught a glimpse of himself in a mirror above the fireplace. His skin was still lightly tanned from days spent on the pier over the summer. His shorn hair carried a hint of menace to which he had not yet grown accustomed. He took off his jacket and placed it beside him on the sofa, and as he did so, he thought that he caught a faint odour of dead fish. Through the open curtains, he saw the moon reflecting in the puddles that lay like small lakes upon the surface of the yard.

'You'll have a drop of something?' The girl spoke like a woman twice her age. Standing there, waiting for an answer, she could have been the woman, not just of the house, but of the farm and the yard, the dark rows of mink sheds and the wet fields and ditches out beyond.

Kavanagh shook his head. 'Tea's grand,' he said.

Her eyes settled next on Gerard who felt his face grow red.

Kavanagh looked across and chuckled. 'He's the strong, silent type,' he said, 'he has the women of Castletownbere driven half mad.' He winked at the girl. 'You could do worse.'

The girl, momentarily shy, gazed at the carpet and tucked a wisp of hair behind one ear. 'Tea's fine,' Gerard said and the girl smiled at him before going out of the room.

After she had gone, the men sat in silence. Kavanagh was never short of something to say and Gerard knew the silence was a shot across the bows: Kavanagh's way of sending a message to Liddy.

Liddy stared into the empty grate for a while and then, when there was still nothing from Kavanagh, he addressed himself instead to Gerard. 'What part of the country are you from yourself?' he said, 'and through what misfortune did you end up with this latchico?'

Gerard was a second cousin of Kavanagh's on his mother's side and Kavanagh had taken him on at the fish factory after he finished school that summer. It was partly Kavanagh's way of looking out for the boy after the death of Gerard's mother the year before. It was also because Gerard's father had lent Kavanagh the money to fix the factory roof after the storms the previous winter and Kavanagh had yet to repay him.

Gerard could feel Liddy's eyes on him, waiting for an answer. He was saved by Kavanagh breaking his silence. 'Isn't he the lucky boy to have a job at all?' he said. 'Every other lad his age is in Australia.'

'Luck is a two-faced whore,' Liddy said, 'there's people said I was lucky when I got this place.'

Kavanagh fell quiet and when he spoke again it was to enquire after a relative of Liddy's who was in the hospital at Croom. The talk turned next to football and greyhounds and, for a while, a peace of sorts settled on the room.

When the girl came back with the tea she had changed into a low-cut pink top and a short black skirt that clung to her hips and thighs. Her hair, freshly brushed and more indigo than black, hung past her shoulders. She was carrying a tray with the tea and a plate of Club Milks and as she bent to set it down on the coffee table, Gerard's eyes went to her plump, white breasts and slid into the valley between them. The girl was putting cups in saucers, pouring tea. Without warning she raised her head and caught him looking. She stared at him until, blushing, he returned the stare and he noticed for the first time that her eyes, which he had thought were brown, were in fact a very dark blue, almost navy. Then she straightened up, tucked the empty tray under her arm, and went out of the room.

Kavanagh unwrapped a Club Milk, took half of it into his mouth in one bite and chewed slowly. 'Well Liddy,' he said, 'what have you got for me?'

Liddy leaned forward in his chair. 'We had the activists a while back,' he said. 'Ten minutes with a wire cutters and I'm down a thousand mink. Next morning, I've a farmer at my door with a trailer full of dead lambs, all with holes in their throats.' Liddy shook his head and brought a hand to his own thin throat.

'Those fuckers should be shot,' Kavanagh said. 'Thundering bastards. I know what I'd do with their wire cutters.'

Liddy's hand left his throat and settled instead on his knee, which immediately began to jig. 'We had a cull last month: Aleutian disease.'

Kavanagh sighed and put his cup down heavily on the table. 'Listen,' he said. 'Do I look like Mother Teresa? There isn't any of us has it easy.'

'If I'd known what I was letting myself in for,' Liddy said, 'I'd never have come out here.' He seemed to be talking more to himself than to Kavanagh. 'I'd have stayed in the city and saved myself a lot of trouble.'

'Trouble knows its way around,' Kavanagh said, 'I've the bank on my case, I've the wife on my case, and I've this young fellow here to pay.' He pointed to the pile of Club-Milk wrappers that had accumulated in front of Gerard. 'Look at him, he's half-starved.'

Apart from the crisps in the lorry earlier, Gerard hadn't eaten anything since they had left Castletownbere shortly after four o'clock. He was about to open another Club Milk, but now he put it back on the plate.

'I'll have it in a lump sum next time,' Liddy said.

'You'll have it tonight, or I'll turn that lorry around and drive back the way I came.'

'I've a man coming for pelts on Tuesday. Call in the next time you're passing.'

A flush was edging up Kavanagh's neck, spreading over his cheeks. 'There's nothing for nothing in this world,' he said. 'You can pay me tonight or you can go to hell.'

'I wouldn't have to go far,' Liddy said, 'look around you.'

A sullenness had come over Liddy. The forced banter of earlier had disappeared and in its place was a sour obstinacy that hardened into bitter lines around his mouth. Gerard had a sudden vision of how Liddy would look laid out: his body sunken in a too big suit, a tie awkward at his throat, even the silk lining of the coffin pressing heavy on his arms.

There was a noise outside in the yard; the clank of metal on concrete. Kavanagh was first to his feet, the others following behind. The girl was on a forklift. She wore no helmet and the wind that blew across the yard snatched at her hair, snaking it in black tails about her face. She had released the back of the lorry and was unloading a pallet of fish meal.

Kavanagh crossed the yard like a bull. The girl stopped the forklift but didn't get out. Her face was pale in the light of the porch lamp. 'Fucking cunt,' Kavanagh was roaring and he started to swing bags of meal from the forklift like they were candyfloss. Liddy watched from a distance. Gerard went to help but the girl had been intercepted early and already everything was back on the lorry. 'I thought I'd make a start,' she said. 'It's getting late.'

'Do you think I'm some class of fool?' Kavanagh said.

The girl's voice was soft, measured, as if calming a small child. 'You're no fool, Curley,' she said. 'Come here and talk to me.' She patted the passenger seat of the forklift. Kavanagh looked away and shook his head. 'I've enough time wasted,' he said, and began to walk towards the lorry.

The girl called after him. 'Hey Curley,' she said, 'Don't be like that.' Her voice dropped lower. 'You can't go yet, you haven't seen the silver foxes.' She was leaning out of the forklift, her shadow stretching across the yard. 'We brought them over from England last month. They're still only cubs.' She was looking directly at Kavanagh, her head tilted slightly to one side, her lips parted. 'Come down to the shed and I'll show you. You've never seen foxes like these.'

Kavanagh had reached the door of the cab. He stopped, one foot on the step. In the forklift, the girl patted the passenger seat again and winked. Kavanagh appeared to be considering. Liddy was standing by himself, staring at the ground. For a while everything was very still and there was only the sound of the wind rattling across the roofs of the mink sheds and the cry of a small animal in the trees beyond. Then Kavanagh strode across the yard to the forklift and climbed in. They drove off, the girl at the wheel, the wind whipping up her dark hair, Kavanagh bald and stocky in the seat beside her. The forklift went to the far end of the yard and disappeared behind some outbuildings.

Gerard and Liddy were left standing in the yard. Liddy looked like a man who had been struck. He did nothing for a moment, then turned and began his stooped walk back to the house. Gerard was about to go to the lorry and wait when Liddy shouted to him from the porch. 'You might as well come in,' he said.

This time, instead of going into the sitting room, they continued down the hall and into a small wood-panelled kitchen. A table and two chairs were pushed tight against one wall, a cooker, a sink, and an assortment of mismatched kitchen units against another. There was a wooden dresser stacked with old newspapers and chipped crockery. The stale grease of a fry hung in the air. To one side of the back door, in a glass display cabinet, was a stuffed brown mink. It was mounted on a marble base on which was inscribed something Gerard could not read. The mink stood on its hind legs, teeth bared in a rigid grin, front legs clawing the air.

Liddy took a bottle of whiskey from a cupboard beneath the sink and wiped two glasses on the end of his cardigan. He sat at the table and gestured at Gerard to sit beside him.

'She's gone five years now,' Liddy said, pouring the whiskey. Gerard didn't understand at first. He had been thinking of the girl behind the outbuildings with Kavanagh. The white breasts, the dark eyes. Her mouth, wide and loose; her red lips and a stud on her tongue that had flashed silver when she smiled at something earlier in the evening. Then he realised Liddy was staring at a photograph high on the wall above the dresser. It was of a woman, tall and angular, with straight brown hair, her hand resting on the shoulder of a girl in a Communion dress. 'I'm sorry,' Gerard said because he couldn't think of anything else to say and it was what people had said when his mother died.

'Oh I'm not sorry,' Liddy said, throwing back his whiskey and pouring another, 'there's a lot I'm sorry about, but not that.' His weariness had been replaced with anger. 'She took herself off to Belfast. She told me she was going to stay with her sister but you can be sure she had a man waiting. It was always the same with that woman: she'd tell you that day was night.' His head jutted forward and Gerard smelled the sourness of his breath. 'I asked her to take the girl with her,' Liddy said, 'but she wouldn't.' He put down his glass and spread his hands wide, palms upwards, in supplication. 'What sort of life is it for a young girl out here, I asked her, but she left us to it, Rosie and myself.'

Rosie. The girl's name didn't suit her, Gerard thought. It was too tame, too domesticated. It was a name for a spoilt poodle in a wicker basket, not a girl with a tongue piercing who could drive a forklift. Liddy drank more whiskey. 'Rosie was twelve when she left,' he said, 'and what did I know about raising a child? A girl needs her mother. Boys are different, boys can make their way, but girls need mothers.'

Liddy fell silent, swirled whiskey around the end of his glass. Gerard wanted to get up and leave but he knew that he could not. It was a moment before Liddy spoke again. 'It was coming out here did it,' he said. 'She was always a flighty woman. She had one eye on the door from the day I married her, but we got along well enough up to that. A couple of winters here and nothing could hold her.'

Liddy was becoming more and more agitated, his hands moving incessantly, almost knocking over his glass. Gerard's own glass was barely touched. He thought of Kavanagh and the girl in the shadows of the outbuildings. He wondered if silver foxes were the same as ordinary foxes, only silver, or if they were some different creature entirely, and then he wondered if there were any silver foxes at all. He imagined the cubs in Kavanagh's rough hands and Kavanagh, awed and silent, turning them this way and that.

'Her mother, bitch and all that she is, would make a better hand of her,' Liddy said. 'Rosie's a good girl, a fighter, but what chance has a girl out here?'

Gerard knew that he should say something but had no idea what.

'Rosie will be okay,' he said, 'Rosie's a smart girl.'

Liddy stared at him, his eyes bloodshot. All of the anger left him and he sagged over the table. 'She is,' he said. 'She's a smart girl. And a good girl.'

He set his glass down on the table and buried his head in his arms. The kitchen was utterly quiet, nothing but the sound of the wind whistling under the back door. A strange sound came from Liddy, half cough, half sob. Then another that caught and lengthened until it became a wail. Liddy was crying, his shoulders quivering, the top of his head shaking. Gerard took a mouthful of whiskey, felt it burn the pit of his stomach. Liddy was bawling now, his head still in his arms. Gerard pushed his chair back and stood up. He went over to the sink and placed his glass on the draining board. He took one last look at Liddy crumpled over the table, then left the kitchen and went back down the narrow hall and outside to the yard.

When he got to the lorry he discovered that Kavanagh had locked it and taken the key. The night had grown colder. Gerard remembered his jacket, still in the sitting room where he had left it earlier, but he thought of Liddy weeping inside the house and decided to do without. A light was on in a prefab but the door, when he tried it, was padlocked and he took shelter instead beneath the overhang of the prefab's roof, next to a row of barrels. He wrapped his arms around himself and hoped that Kavanagh would not be long. Something warm brushed against his legs and he saw a cat dart from behind a barrel and streak across the yard.

He pressed his face against the prefab window. The walls were hung with pelts: thousands of headless, bodiless furs, their arms spread wide and pinned to wooden racks. On a bench was a machine with long silver-toothed blades and beside it, a pile of dead mink. He noticed a smell coming from the barrel nearest him and lifted the lid. Inside were the skinned corpses of the mink, pink and slippery and hairless. He dropped the lid of the barrel and stepped back from the window.

The wind carried fragments of laughter up the yard and he saw Kavanagh and the girl returning on the forklift. This time Kavanagh was driving, the girl beside him, an arm flung across his shoulder. They slowed as they passed the pelt shed and waved. Gerard stepped out from the shelter of the building and walked behind the forklift to the lorry. A drizzle blew in from the mountains, stinging his face. Kavanagh, flushed and sweating, jumped out of the forklift. 'Give us a hand,' he said to Gerard without looking at him and together they began to unload the lorry. Gerard shivered in his shirtsleeves but the cold, like the smell, didn't seem to bother Kavanagh.

Gerard felt someone touch his arm. The girl was behind him, holding his jacket. She didn't say a word but Gerard held out his arms and allowed her to slip the jacket on, let her zip it up and smooth it down over his shoulders.

Afterwards, as they turned the lorry in the yard, Gerard noticed Liddy standing alone in the porch. Gerard raised a hand and waved but Liddy didn't wave back. The girl was by the forklift, hands in her pockets. Gerard watched her in the rear-view mirror as the lorry drove out of the yard, saw her turn and walk towards the house, saw the light go out in the porch.

Kavanagh didn't speak until they reached the end of the muddy track and were back on the road. 'I'm calling on Clancy tomorrow,' he said. 'He owes me a few bob. I'll sort you out then.'

'It's all right,' Gerard said.

They drove in silence for a while, the only sound the relentless squeak of the wipers as the rain grew heavier. 'Tell me,' Kavanagh said, 'did you ever see a silver fox?' Gerard shook his head. Kavanagh let out a low whistle. 'Beautiful animals,' he said, 'beautiful. But why do you think their fur is that colour? Aren't they foxes at the end of the day?'

Gerard shrugged and looked out the window. Kavanagh kept talking, his voice becoming more animated, his hands restless on the steering wheel. 'They weren't silver exactly,' he said. 'You'd be expecting silver but it was more...' He paused and his eyes scanned the cab—his wife's photograph, the pictures of the Asian women, the collection of knick-knacks on the dash. When his surroundings failed him, he clicked his tongue in exasperation. 'They were a sort of blueyblack,' he said. 'White bits on their tails and faces. Little balls of fur.' He went suddenly quiet, as if he had embarrassed himself.

Back on the main road, the lorry picked up speed as they headed south. A few miles on, Kavanagh spoke again. 'What kind of life is it at all?' he said. 'Weaned at six weeks and shipped off in a crate?'

It was cold in the cab and Gerard pulled his jacket tighter around him. He put a hand to the inside pocket, felt for his wallet and realised that it was gone. Shadowy trees and ditches blurred past. The wind blew dark, shapeless things across the path of the lorry, things that might have been alive or might have been dead: tiny night creatures and flurries of fallen leaves. They drove on through small, half-lit towns, through dark countryside whose only light was the flicker of wide-screen televisions in bungalow windows. Kavanagh began to hum. It was the chorus of a country and western song, full of love and violence, and he kept it up until they reached Bantry and took the dark coast road for Castletownbere.

Bone Deep

Martin Malone

They found a woman's skeleton in a well at the Market Square. The well had been covered by a grey boulder I used to sit on while waiting for a school bus to turn the corner at the traffic lights. The council had moved in with bulldozers and donkey-jacketed men to put a new face with new EU money on an old landmark. But for that reason the skeleton would not have been discovered.

The expert on TV said that the skeleton was over a hundred years old, if not more. Experts never give precise answers to anything. They hedge their bets and in that way can never be totally wrong—never being wrong is extremely important to a lot of people. Especially experts. He also said that the skeleton probably fell in during the rising of 1798 and added that she might have been thrown into the well and left there to drown.

My father is tipsy. It is ten past nine on Sunday evening. He has been tipsy all day. He gets like this once a week. We are in the sitting room at the American oak table Mum's father left us. Earlier, Dad made ham and mustard sandwiches. None of us eat them; we don't like the thick fat he leaves hanging like curtain frills over the crusts.

Elly is eighteen; she is pregnant again but married this time. She lives with her husband in a mobile home in his mother's back garden. Ann is fifteen. She has a stud in her nose and a bar in her eyebrow. She talks about getting a tattoo. Terry is the twin who survived the car accident. He is sixteen, three years older than me. He cannot talk, nor move from the waist down. His blue eyes are clouded.

Mum is at bingo. She doesn't like leaving Terry and we don't like her leaving him either. His twin, Marcus, is with us in framed photographs on the mantelpiece.

'So, the skeleton made the evening news, eh?' Dad says.

He's a short round man with thick hairy forearms. His fair hair is coarse and badly cut. It is badly cut because he insists on going to Oscar Henry the poor-sighted barber on the main street. Dad goes to him because he never has to queue.

For months after the accident Mum and Dad didn't speak to each other. The anniversary is looming now and the brooding silence between Mum and Dad has returned.

That sunny May afternoon Dad said he was going to the Curragh Races, did anyone want to tag along? I hate horse racing, Ann too, so we stayed at home. We watched Terry and Marcus climb into Dad's car. Marcus ran his window down and said he'd bring us home a few bars of chocolate. Terry waved. They never made it home.

Mum wasn't five minutes in the door after having her hair done when the guards arrived, carrying the news in their grey faces: Marcus was dead and Terry was clinging to life in a hospital ward.

A week after Marcus was buried Dad arrived home from the hospital and told us all to pray for Holy God to take Terry. He said our brother was suffering too much. We started to cry and he changed his mind and said we'd to pray for him to live.

Ann and I look at each other. She wipes Terry's mouth. He can't keep the Rolos Dad buys for him in his mouth. He loves Rolos. Most of the chocolate gets on his chin and shirt. Terry has to wear a white-coloured shirt; he will not wear a shirt of any other colour. We don't know why this is so.

Ann wipes Terry's mouth again. She will do this a number of times. On each occasion she will scowl at Dad. She has told me that Terry is Dad's mistake and that he should be the one to clean his chin.

'Did you get to see the skeleton, Ian?' Dad says.

'No. I couldn't get close enough because of the crowd,' I say.

'I did. I'd say she was a young woman. She was very small. The archaeologist reckons she was fifteen or thereabouts.'

He is talking to me because Ann won't talk to him. She talks to him as little as possible.

'How do you think the skeleton got there, Ian?'

I shrug. I do not know, or care. It has nothing to do with me. Dad works as a machine operator in a factory on the outskirts of town. He lost the small finger of his left hand to a press. If he concentrated on his job and didn't drift off to places and matters not of his concern, he would not be a finger short. Perhaps he would not be a son and a half short, either.

His big round face expects an answer.

'Was the skeleton a skeleton before it ended up in the well?' I ask.

He nods, says, 'No.'

I try to sound like the TV expert and say, 'I think the woman got drunk and fell into the well. She was hidden from view by the water. The well was, of course, poisoned by her decaying corpse, and thus sealed.'

'That's very good. Very good.'

He looks at me with fresh respect. He is happy to be sending me to a private college. He says I'll do fine—I have his brains.

He sips at his beer. Sniffles. Sometimes he looks at Terry and there are deep creases about his eyes. He fell asleep behind the wheel.

'I wonder what colour hair she had?' Ann says.

'Dark haired,' Dad nods, 'I'd say dark hair... the odds are good that it was dark.'

'If she were pretty?' Ann continues.

Dad is under the impression that Ann is asking him, while in fact her questions aren't aimed at anyone in specific. She is more thinking aloud than anything.

'Yes, very pretty, the angle of her jawline, her teeth straight and all present, the slope of her skull, yes, she was pretty. Then who really knows?'

If I had seen the skeleton I wouldn't have tried to fit a face and a body to its bones. Instead, I'd have imagined myself as a skeleton.

'Did they find clothes?' Ann says.

'God, aye, they did,' Dad says.

'What exactly?' Ann is interested in clothes. She hopes to be a fashion designer.

'Black stuff.'

'Shawl, dress, skirt, what?'

Dad glances at me and shrugs, 'I don't know—they were in a Dunnes Stores bag.'

He laughs. His cheeks shudder.

A spasm crosses Ann's face, 'I'd say she was murdered.'

'Murdered. What makes you think that?' Dad asks.

'Look at all the women being murdered today—men are just animals. Animals then, and animals now.'

'Animals,' Dad muses.

One day I am sure he will draw her out. There will be a row and Ann will go to live with Elly. Then on bingo nights Dad will sit alone with Terry and wipe his chin free of chocolate. I'll stay in my room with the portable TV Mum has promised to buy me for my next birthday.

Dad stares at Ann, runs a hand over his hair, and pinches the grey at his temple. Ann ignores him and hands Terry the TV remote. I ask a question to divert his thoughts.

'What will happen to the skeleton, now, Dad?'

He likes it when his opinion is sought; it makes him feel important. He likes to feel important. He does not realise that we see him as the thorn in Daniel's lion, the ice that tore the Titanic, the driver who killed a brother, left another badly broken and crushed a mother's soul.

'They'll bring it to the...'

Ann says, 'The Zoo... for animals to lick the bones.'

Silence, apart from the TV, where Jerry the mouse is tormenting Tom the cat. The cartoon pair never talk. This sits well with Terry.

Dad's lips open and close but his words don't arrive. The can at his elbow is empty. The fridge is out of beer.

Finally, he says, 'You're breathing the word "animal" a lot tonight-are you in double speak mode?'

Ann's cheeks redden. She has a triangular face with pretty pursed lips you'd think were always poised to kiss.

'I'm sick of it!' she snaps, throwing Terry's chocolate smattered tissue at Dad.

It is too late to stop the argument. The only hope is for Ann to bolt for the door. He may or may not follow her. He won't if I tell him she's been acting funny all day. Then he will put her mood down to woman trouble and make allowances for her. He will shout up the stairs after her and tell her how lucky she is to be a woman.

Ann doesn't leave. She wants to fight, 'I think all men are animals. Drunken, lousy drivers of animals.'

TV Tom is bent over the mouse hole, fingers in his ears, waiting for the bang from a red stick of dynamite which he does not know Jerry has moved behind him. I try to focus on the cartoon and point for Terry to do likewise, but he is looking at Dad and Ann.

Dad's hands come together and his eyes fill with tears. All his rising anger has suddenly dissipated. Ann averts her glare, proffers the Rolos to Terry, but he sweeps them from her and they land with a soft plop on the fireside rug. She goes to wipe his chin but he angles his head away from her.

His wet eyes are on Dad's. He tries to talk. It is an awful sound to listen to. A half tongue flapping in a broken head. Ann sighs. She thinks he is being difficult because of the row that had been shaping up.

Ann leaves the room in a huff. And I follow, shutting the door. Ann pounds up the stairs to her bedroom. I just can't listen to Terry going on and on. But we want to escape from more than Dad and Terry. It is our shame at not being able to do what Terry has done—to forgive. The accident may have taken much from him, but it hasn't taken everything.

Dad and he are alone. I wait in the hall and put my ear to the door. I hear Dad say to Terry that he has another packet of sweets. Not to worry.

There's not so much as a peep from my brother. Sometimes we forget how close they are. Bone Deep.

Out of It

Lia Mills

TJ is a man with black eyes and a sweet smile and I know better than to trust him. His wife, Sharon, is the only friend I have in this city. His arms, roped with muscle and bristles of dark hair, make me shiver. The skin on the back of his right hand is puckered and silver.

'What happened?' I ask when it's long past midnight and we've been drinking forever and that scar is driving me wild.

'I was in a fight.' His gold tooth flashes when he laughs. 'Over a woman.'

'Over a woman? Or with a woman?' Sharon drawls, looking at me. She sends her eyebrows climbing up her forehead in a way she has that cracks me up.

TJ's mouth closes over the rim of his can. I can't help looking at the place where that silver track disappears into the hair at his wrist.

Sharon goes into the kitchen. 'We're out of beer.' She checks her watch. 'It's too late to buy more.'

TJ crumples his empty can. It crackles.

'Come back to our place,' Paul says. 'Stay over.'

So, in the middle of a sweltering Texas night, we pack up the children—their three and our two—and Sharon's yippy dog, Mitzi, and drive the short distance south on the freeway to the city limits, where there's half a bottle of vodka and some beer in our ice-box. It's not the first time we've done something like this to keep a party going.

TJ has a past. His past includes an ex-wife who tried to kill him and surly teenagers who sometimes come to stay. When these kids are around they pick their teeth and glare at us. The girls despise me and

Sharon. We're not much older than they are. The boy leers. We laugh at them. They don't stay long.

TJ is not the only one with a past but I've left mine behind. Seven years ago I left the cold, damp island where I was born to fly south and west, directions that appealed to me at the time. As soon as I arrived, I cut my hair and dyed it, threw my winter coat away—even looking at it made me sweat.

Coming to live here was a lot like settling in the murky bottom of a hot pond. The heat makes a person slow and irritable, a dangerous mix. It gets in the way of thinking. It makes your nerves twitch. Sharon says it can do that even if you were born here, like her. Most people are on their way to somewhere else. I've made it my business to adapt. I've grown lines around my eyes from squinting at the sun, my arms are brown, my legs are always bare. My feet are broader than they used to be and stronger. Freeways, flyovers, hypermarkets don't cost me a thought. I know shortcuts through parts of town where even Sharon never goes. Only my accent gives me away.

Once, when I was pregnant the second time and should have known better, I heard screams from a van parked at the mall. Pulse racing, I pulled the door open. Two young blondes, caked with make-up and fake tan, fell around laughing when they saw me. Thrilled with their little joke.

'You're crazy!' Paul was angry when I told him. 'Don't you know to mind your own business?'

Sometimes I forget. It's sweet that he worries about me, but I can take care of myself. As if he knew what I was thinking, he pointed at my swollen belly. 'There's the baby to think about.'

TJ, now, is the kind of person who might intervene in a brawl. If he felt like it.

Sharon leaves the room to check on the boys, all asleep in one room. I can hear the baby, already tucked in to the spare bed, stirring. Sharon's head reappears in the doorway.

'I'll go lie down with Jessie a while.'

She's not likely to be back. This is how these evenings often end, one person after another drifting off to sleep. Paul has crashed out in the armchair, snoring. I'm sitting on the floor, leaning against the sofa, where TJ is. The last can of beer is propped, cold, against my ankle.

Next thing, TJ's warm, scarred hand steals around my leg and lifts the can from my fingers. 'Don't be greedy.'

I twist my head to look at him. Something in that angle makes him loom larger than he is. Dark, with a halo of light behind him. 'Why not?'

He bends his head and kisses me. His mouth is warm and friendly and tastes of everything I need. Booze and cigarettes and late night conversation. Neither of us does more than breathe. As if we can't decide if we're ready. As if this can wait.

When he lifts his mouth off mine, my neck hurts. I bend away from him to rub it before unwinding to my feet.

'I'm going to bed.'

He shrugs the can to his mouth, still smiling.

'Later,' he says.

I wake Paul and persuade him to come with me.

'Goodnight, man,' he says to TJ on the way past.

That night I sleep on the inside, near the wall. It's too hot for the weight of Paul's arm across my hip. The fan stirs the soupy air. Through the window I hear music, sirens, breaking glass. A door closes. Someone laughs.

Sharon starts avoiding me. I think she knows. 'God, I was really out of it that night,' I say, testing.

She shrugs, as if she has other things on her mind.

'Weren't we all?'

The days get hotter. Paul's birthday is coming up.

'What do you want to do?' I ask him.

He pulls me closer. Petals of vivid colour in his irises shiver and flare, like those nature programmes about plants that eat flies. When Paul does this, it's easy to get distracted.

'Besides that.'

He wants a barbeque. A laid-back kind of day, drinking with TJ and Sharon. The kids can amuse themselves. It could be any other weekend, but if that's what he wants, that's what he'll get.

*

I'm not sure how it will be when I see TJ again, but when they arrive for Paul's party, his eyes are like they've always been. Mocking. Inviting, but quick, so no one else need notice.

The heat outside is crazy, but the house is shuttered and cool, all the fans spinning high.

'Paul's outside, lighting the barbeque,' I say. 'Go on out, if you can bear it.'

He swings a case of bottled beer onto the counter with one hand. Sharon puts the baby into the highchair and gives her a trainer cup full of juice. She twists the top off a cold, beaded bottle and passes it to me, then opens one for herself.

'I've looked forward to this the whole way over.' She takes a long swallow.

TJ loops the necks of some unopened bottles in his fingers and carries them out to the patio, where Paul is poking at the grill and the boys are digging in the sandbox. We watch them all through the window, while Jessie slaps at a mess of juice on the tray of the highchair.

'Anything strange?' I ask.

Sharon peels the label off her beer bottle with her square, strong nails. 'I think I'm pregnant.'

'Jesus, Sharon!'

'I know.' She looks gloomily at the baby.

'But—?' My voice trails off. She has plans to go back to work in a couple of months. How will she do that now?

Her face twists. 'You try saying no to a man like TJ.' She tries to smile, puts on a sultry voice. 'He's such an animal,' she mimics a TV commercial for aftershave that's playing a hundred times a day just now.

I don't laugh. We're teetering on the edge of something. I'm not sure I want to know what it is. Instead, I get a cloth and start to clean up Jessie's mess.

'I don't want another one, Una. I can't face it.'

'What are you going to do?'

'I don't know.'

The side door opens and the boys clatter in, begging for drinks.

Paul comes in behind them. 'It's too hot to eat outside.' His hair is plastered to his head with sweat.

I open more beers and pass one to Paul while Sharon pours juice for the kids. TJ comes in with a platter of food in his brown hands. His shirt is open. His dry, scarred fingers brush mine when he takes the bottle I offer. I smile a shallow smile and slide my hand away.

Later, we sit among the ruins of the birthday cake while the children watch a video. I stab the burnt-out candles into a mess of leftover cake and light them, watch them burn, blow them out again. I poke their edges with the used match. The others swap horror stories about guns. Two streets over, a man blew himself away while cleaning his hunting rifle. They argue about whether this was an accident or not.

'Anyone who's used to guns knows to be careful,' Paul says.

'For sure,' Sharon says. 'Where do y'all keep yours?'

I look up and laugh at the very idea.

'Una doesn't care for guns,' Paul says.

TJ strokes his upper lip with the index finger of his scarred hand. 'You don't say. What's not to like?'

I remind them that a kid in their neighbourhood was shot dead by his eight-year-old brother a month ago. They'd found their father's gun in a bedside drawer. They look at me as if I'm fresh off the plane. I put the sulphured end of a matchstick against a stubby candle. The match flares. I pull it away.

'I don't care for them much, either,' Sharon says. 'But I sure feel safer when there's one around. We keep ours way out of the kids' reach.'

The match sizzles in my hand. 'You have a gun?'

She shrugs. 'It's not loaded. The shells are locked away.'

How many times have my kids played at her house? The match burns down and singes my fingers. I drop it. They laugh at my shock.

Paul takes the plate of crumbs and wax and splintered wood away from me and carries them over to the sink on his way to the fridge. 'Una hates guns, but she'll play with fire.'

Sharon catches my eye and does her eyebrow thing. I smile but I don't mean it.

In the pre-school car park, Sharon tells me she's not pregnant after all. 'False alarm,' she says.

'That's great!'

She doesn't seem to hear me.

'Isn't it?'

'Sure it is.'

Late one night the phone rings. When I answer it, I'm confused by noise. Shouting and banging, popping sounds like a TV show. There are words but I can't catch them. Then the line goes dead. I hang up.

'Who was it?' Paul asks.

'No one,' I say. But when I wake, suddenly, in the middle of the night, my heart is beating fast, like waking from a dream of falling.

The next day, I meet Sharon at the school.

'Hey,' I say.

She turns sunglasses as big as plates in my direction.

'Thanks for sending the police around,' she says in her sarcastic voice, one I've heard her use before but not to me.

'What are you talking about?'

She takes the glasses down so I can see the bruise beside her eye. 'When I called you.'

I lean against her car. 'Was that you? What happened?'

'I asked you to come get me.' She adjusts the glasses on the bridge of her perfect nose. They make her look like a movie star.

'I didn't hear you, Sharon. I couldn't make out what you said. I thought—'

She tugs open the door of her car. 'Must've been the neighbours.' She arranges the baby into the car seat, fixes the straps, sits in behind the steering wheel. She hasn't met my eyes once in this whole conversation.

'Sharon—'

'I don't want to talk about it.' She drives away.

I go to my Suburban, sit in to it and pull the door shut. All around me, mothers are hurrying to their cars, on their way to whatever their lives are while their kids are in school. When I shut my eyes I can see Sharon's kitchen as clearly as if it's my own. The bright lights, a whirl of confused movement, struggle. The sounds I heard come from distorted faces. Crying. Yelling. The plastic toy box on the table in the corner tilts, spills wooden blocks on to the floor. TJ's hands reach for the phone and jerk it away from Sharon. Her hair flies around her face.

*

When I get home I try to call her but her phone rings out.

I have to do something, so I haul out the phone book and look through it for anything that might help, make a list of numbers to calm myself down. When I make the first call, I feel stupid, melodramatic. I don't know what to say. 'I have a friend,' I begin. 'I think she's in trouble.'

The woman at the other end thinks I'm the one in trouble. When I insist that I'm not, her best advice is to give Sharon their number.

After four of these calls, I feel like a liar and a fraud. Everyone I talk to says the same thing. They can't help unless Sharon calls them herself. The few things I can tell them sound stale and hollow from my mouth. I'm not sure of anything any more. Sharon and TJ had a fight. People do.

'You're way off base,' Paul agrees when he gets in from work.

'How do you know?'

'Don't go there, Una. You don't know what you're dealing with.' He pours two tumblers of vodka over ice and hands me one. 'It's the weekend. Here we go.'

The vodka does its thing. I breathe easier. 'But, she's my friend—'

'But nothing.' He pulls me close, his fingers cool on the back of my hot neck, his eyes intent on mine. 'Plus,' he says in his lazy voice, 'When you get right down to it, what do you know?'

Sharon blanks me. I see her in the distance, across the car park. Head down, always in a hurry, keys ready in her hand. She wears what might be a bandage around her wrist. Whenever I call her, she's busy. One time, she invites the boys around to play but I remember the gun stashed away in her closet and suggest that hers come to me instead.

It's TJ who comes to pick them up, but I needn't have worried. He's in a hurry, all business. He stays in the pickup, keeps the engine running and waves to his boys to *move it*! He flashes me a smile and drives off as if there's nothing wrong at all.

When the phone rings after midnight a few days later, I know it must be Sharon. This time, I'm ready.

'Come get me,' she sobs. 'Hurry.'

'Where are you?'

'The car park. The church around the corner.'

'I'm on my way.'

The streets are slick and brooding as I drive along. A wind picks up.
The traffic signals dance on their wires. It's hot. The air-conditioning is
broken. I have to leave the windows of the Suburban rolled down, even
though every instinct warns me not to. The storefronts are shuttered and
dark. There's no-one around, no traffic. It's like waiting for a storm to
hit. I have a creepy feeling that something has happened that everyone
knows about but me. An empty can rolls and skips along beside me for
half a block. It makes a hollow sound until it clatters down a drain.

I'm afraid that TJ will have got to the car park ahead of me, but there's
no sign of him. Sharon runs from the bushes behind the callbox and gets
in beside me. She has Mitzi in her arms, no purse. Her face doesn't look
right. Her nose is crooked, and blood clots on her lip. I look at the dog.

'Where are the kids?'

'I left them there.'

'You can't—'

'Just drive.'

Her eyes are dead. This woman is a stranger. I don't know anything
about her, or what I should do next. So I do what she says.

At a stoplight, a patrol car pulls up beside us. I want to lean down and
ask them to take her from me, but she knows what I'm thinking.

'Don't,' she says.

The dog licks her hand. She's left her kids behind and brought this
pink-nosed ball of fluff with her instead. I drive on.

When we get to my house I put the dog outside in the yard. I don't
care what Sharon says. I don't care if it keeps the neighbours awake all
night with its yipping. She sits on the sofa with her feet flat on the floor
in front of her and her empty hands in her lap, like this is a waiting
room. I boil the kettle and make tea. It gives me a chance to look at her,
to figure out what to say.

'What happened?' I ask her, when I bring over the tea. Weak, no milk,
sweetened with honey. This is how I've learned to drink it, here.

She shuts her eyes, inhales steam from the cup.

'You don't have to tell me anything,' I say, after a long silence. 'But
you have to do something.'

When she doesn't answer, I try again. 'What about the kids?'

'They'll be all right.' She tucks her hair behind her ears. 'He won't do anything to them.'

'How do you know?' She doesn't answer. 'What good will it do them to grow up watching him do it to you? What about the baby? Do you want her to think that's what she should expect?'

She shuts her eyes.

I bring her the phone and the list of numbers.

'Please call a shelter,' I say. 'Talk to them.'

She makes a face. 'Those people are crazy! They hate everyone.'

'You know that's not true.' I hold out the list again. 'They'll know what to do. Call them.'

'Okay.' She takes the phone.

I go down the hall to tell Paul what's happening. Sharon's voice is a low murmur in the other room.

Paul yawns. 'I thought I told you to stay out of it?'

He rolls over, turns his back to me.

I have never felt more alert and all he wants to do is sleep.

I go into the boys' room. The sound of their breathing steadies me. I slow their ceiling fan because it's making too much racket. It clunks a little, off balance.

When I go back out, Sharon won't meet my eye.

'Well?' I ask her. 'Are you okay?'

She nods.

The doorbell rings and my heart stops. This can't be good. The kitchen clock says 2.55.

'Get it.' Her voice is hollow.

I go to the door and squint into the judas-hole.

He stands back under the porch-light and lets me see his scarred hands, empty and harmless, at his sides

'It's TJ.'

'I called him.'

'But—the shelter—?' I stare, stupidly, at the list of numbers I made for her.

She gets to her feet. 'It's better this way, Una.' Her hair falls loose around her face. She gathers it up again and ties it as if there is nothing else on her mind. 'You don't know.'

228

I stand in front of her. 'I know you don't have to go out there. You can stay here. As long as you want.'

'Oh yeah? Is that what Paul would say? Where is he, then?'

The doorbell rings again and this time he knocks as well.

'Paul's asleep.'

'I bet he is.'

I don't know what to say.

'Una.' Her voice is flat. 'You just don't get it.' She steps towards me. 'Back off.'

I move out of her way. She goes to the back door and tugs it open, scoops up her dog and carries it past me, her head dipped into its fur so I can't see her face.

I fold my arms. I can't stop her leaving, but I won't open the front door. I won't make it easier for her to go out there, where he is waiting, his dark head massive against our porch-light.

She opens the door herself and steps through it without another word. She walks past him as if he isn't there. They don't exchange so much as a glance as she goes to his pickup and swings herself up into the cab.

TJ is in no hurry to follow her. He's not even angry. He leans against our wall, under the light he helped my husband install last winter. I stood right where I am now and cracked them both cold cans of beer. Laughing at some joke TJ told.

Now, Paul is where he wants to be, out of earshot, cocooned in sleep while TJ watches me. His look reminds me of all he knows: the layout of our house, our kids' routine, the hours Paul spends at work. The feel of my mouth under his. It's like the dream of falling all over again but I'm about to hit the ground. My heart grates, high and uneven, in my chest.

TJ is not interested in his wife, or what he'll do to her when they get home. It's me he's looking at. It's me those hands don't reach for.

The Day I Brought Water

Sinéad Morrissey

It's nearly night-time and it's summer so the sky is red and animal clouds are in it and moving quickly. Summer means fires on the estate, houses and mattresses and cardboard boxes. I'll find them on my way home through the back path, the whole sky full of smoke and boys running and when I go inside for my tea I'll talk about the new fire. Summer means Mum sunbathing out where the bins are, and earywigs all over our house, in keyholes and towels and beds, and the whole street skipping with one big rope singing 'On the Hillside Stands a Lady' until bedtime. Parents coming out in twos and fours then to bring us in and the last one tying up the big orange rope and going away somewhere else because he's lonely.

Nearly bedtime now but I want to watch the news, all by myself, so I'm taking my TV that rolls ducks and boats and the Tower of London across the front of it to *Row Row Row Your Boat Gently Down the Stream* out to the playground in the middle of the back path. I am setting it on a wall and winding it up and sitting down on one of the round stone seats by the round stone table in the living-room part of the playground. The big girls with tall black shoes are nearby and some of them come over to me.

'Can I brush your hair?'

They are sitting round me in a circle and when they've finished I get up onto her lap and I brush hers. I remember her. She was the baby-sitter once and we watched a film with pirates and ships and cannons and she laughed when Dad asked her if she wanted something to drink, laughed about it with her friend who came later, just before we went to bed. I'm telling her again how she looks like the woman I saw singing on TV.

'Who, Suzy Quatro?'

The girls are laughing. They are leaving together now, back down to the big road at the front. The sky is dark red now and the clouds are black. Boys are here in the part that's lower down than everywhere else. They're jumping on top of a blanket they've set on fire. They come up to the wall and knock over my TV. I'm running behind the wall to pick it up. I'm running home.

All sun. My brother leads us through bushes opposite our house and inside there's a space. Somebody's made chairs from planks and tyres and boxes and everyone is here already, the whole street, but we've missed it. It's stopping. So we come back out again. The bushes have the white squish berries all over them that kill you if you eat them. The whole street goes off together and leaves me and my brother and Richard. And now the three of us are far away from the back path and we've been walking for a long time. All sun. We see a dog with one eye.

Four men are lying on the grass under a bridge. We go over to where they are because they told us to. We're standing now, watching them. Mostly they do nothing but sometimes they spit. They're looking at their shoes. They only have vests on top and their faces are dirty.

'Will you do something for us?'

He's talking to my brother. They don't have shoes. They have big black boots, scraped away and white around the toes.

'What ?'

He's not smiling. He's not promising things.

'Will you bring us something?'

Before they promised sweets and I went with them. I saw chocolate bars and chews and rock so I followed.

'What?'

He's not smiling. He's not giving us anything.

'Will you bring us water?'

The last time was nearly night-time and the sky was red. Red for ages and ages. Now it's after lunch. All sun. They lie and spit and stare up at us, into the sun.

'Water?'

Only one of them is talking. Every time he speaks the other three laugh and roll about, pulling at the grass.

'Yeah, water. Four big pint glasses of water. From your house. Is your house close? Can you get there and back in ten minutes?'

They're all sun-tanned. Their hair looks wet. They push their fingers through it and it stays where they leave it.

'No. It's further than that. About twenty minutes there and back.'

The one speaking has curly hair. It's light. The colour of skin in pictures.

'Twenty? Well, lads, is it worth waitin' for?'

They laugh, far back in their mouths, as though they don't want to laugh at all.

'Jesus, Mick. Lay off it.'

He's looking up at my brother and his voice is a different voice now.

'We're thirsty. It's that simple. And we want four big pint glasses of water from your house, that's twenty minutes from here, there and back. So you and your two wee friends are going to go back to your house, get the glasses, fill them up with water, and bring them back to us, and you won't be any later than twenty minutes, and you won't spill any along the way. Okay?'

He's looking like someone else now. The tall one. The one with the I-Know voice.

'Do we get something?'

Sweets. Clove Rock and lemon bonbons and Curly Wurly bars, on the top shelf of a wardrobe inside a bricked-up house.

'No you don't. You get to do us a favour, okay? Christ. Kids today. Runnin' fuckin' businesses.'

He spits. The others roll away. They lie with their feet towards us and they look up at the bridge. He's staring at my brother. And we've whirled around and we're running into the sun.

They didn't move but we're moving now. We're running. My brother shouts out that we're running to beat the clock. I don't know the bridge where the men are lying but now we're in a street. I can remember it. I asked a big girl to tie my laces here and she did, but into a hundred knots instead of just one and they wobbled in a pile on top of each foot. I had to put my feet up one by one onto Dad's lap when I got in and I watched them all come undone under his fingers. And we're into another street now and from here I know the way. We come to the big road my brother sang Finders Keepers on, the road I always think of when I hear a Why Did The Chicken joke, the road me and my Mum and my brother stuck our thumbs out on to try and make cars stop when we missed the bus from town, though no car did and we walked all the way along the road until we got home. The men didn't move but we're moving now, so quickly I'm tired and I want to stop running but my brother is shouting how we've got to keep running to beat the clock. Past the school and the shop where I got the pink pretend jewellery set for my birthday. I watched it behind the glass every day until my birthday came and then I bought it and when Dad lifted up the earrings they dropped and smashed on the bathroom floor, so he bought me a whole new pretend jewellery set in blue. Down the back path and past the playground with the low part in the middle and the living-room where the two boys saw me sitting on the wall watching the big girls smoke cigarettes in their tall black shoes. The men under the bridge didn't move but the two boys did and I followed them. I walked behind them and they turned round to me very often and smiled. They promised and I went but when we got there there was nothing there. And the one who was tall and thin told me the whole time where we were going, where it all was, the things they promised, and he turned around as he walked and smiled at me the whole time. And it was nearly night-time and the sky was red. Past the playground and down the back path to the big wooden gates showing the way to the houses. And I'm tired of running but my brother and Richard are home already, so I keep running, right up to the back doorstep, and then I stop. I'm sitting and putting my head on my arms on my knees. I'm breathing quickly. My heart is loud.

Glasses of water appear beside me in the biggest glasses we've got. They come one by one and stand beside my thighs. I watch them from under my elbow. They're dancing in the sun. The sunlight goes right inside the water, and dances there, and I watch it through the glass. I think about the big shadow my brother and Richard run into in the hall every time they come out of the kitchen, holding another glass of water in both hands. When the shadow goes out into the back yard and moves across it in a line until all the squares are covered, the sky's already gone red. I sat on the back step one time and watched it move across. It was straight, like a ruler, and slow, and the sky was red and the clouds not turning black, just redder and redder. I sat there for a long time. Mum and Dad standing in the yard had no shadows. They talked in low voices I couldn't understand and then they just stood and didn't speak. Just looking at the two boys who came and stood in our yard. The two boys stood by the gate and didn't speak. It was quiet and the sky was red and I could hear my heart, still banging inside me. I felt the metal edge of the step hurt the skin under my leg and I watched the big shadow move across the yard, slowly, like the tide coming in in straight lines instead of in waves.

'I'll take two glasses 'cause I'm the biggest.'

My brother has stepped over the glasses into the yard. He's shaking my arm. I look up and the sun goes into my eyes. He's handing Richard one of the glasses. Richard is still standing behind me in the big shadow. One glass is still standing beside my thigh.

'Come on, you've got to take one too.'

I'm standing up and turning to the shadow and bending down to pick up the last tall glass with the sun inside its water. It's heavy and full. Richard steps past me into the sun and when I turn round we're standing together and all of the glasses are in our hands.

'We can't run this time, but we'll walk fast. If we run, it'll spill. Let's go.'

My brother and Richard are moving up and down in front of me, getting more and more ahead, like they're on boats. Their heads are down, looking at the glasses. Their heads go up quickly sometimes as they look at the path but then they go back down again. They're faster than me. I'm looking at them and I should be taking care over my glass, but I watch their heads instead and when they go round the corner at the end of the back path they're gone and I can't watch their heads anymore. The sky is blue. There's no one else right to the end of the back path and I'm beginning to hear my heart. I pass the last of the tall wooden gates and now I'm at the playground. I can't see their heads but the sky is blue. The sky was red and no one was there and I was in a wardrobe. I pushed against it and it opened and I ran to the window. Instead of glass there were boards and bars but part of the wood was broken. I saw so much red I thought new fires on the estate, new fires everywhere, and I was crying but nobody was there. I can't walk anymore because I can't see their heads so I'm putting my glass down on the ground. I'm sitting on the ground and bringing my knees up to my forehead. I put my hands around my knees because no one is here. I watch the colours that come when I push my knees into my eyes.

Someone is touching my arm now. He touched my arm and when I turned round there was a boy standing in the room and he was carrying my trousers. He helped me to put them on, held them out and I stepped into them, one, two, that's a good girl, and he took my hand and we found the front door and we walked out together. He held my hand the whole time and we walked along a long street and in every front yard boys were playing. I saw the tall thin one right away and the other was bouncing a ball against a wall and he said No but I said Yes and then he kept holding my hand and he brought me down a hundred steps and at the bottom there was the back path. My parents stood at the back door and he talked to them. Then he went away and he came back with the two boys and then he went away again.

'Come on. I'll take your glass too. You're too small.'

I look up and the back path and Richard's face have a purple colour that's changing to blue because I pushed my knees against my eyes. He's bending down to pick up the glass and I'm standing up and watching the blue go away from the ground until it's normal.

'But you've got to keep up this time or we won't beat the clock, okay?'

We're walking. I can walk with Richard easily this time and I watch the glasses as he moves up and down as well as forward and hardly any is spilling.

There are long dark shapes under the bridge so the men are still there. The one with the curly hair is looking at his watch. We're standing right in front of him now but he doesn't look up. One of the others is sleeping. The other two are slapping cards on top of other cards that sit in a pile between them. They don't look up or stop playing, even though we've come back with the water.

'Thirty-four minutes, children.'

'I know, I'm sorry. My sister fell behind and sat down, so Richard had to go back for her.'

He's looking at me now. I want to sit down again. Put my knees against my eyes and watch the colours. I don't.

'Your sister?'

'I'm sorry. She's only four.'

'Are you only four?'

I'm looking at my brother. His hands are full. I look back at the man and he's still staring at me. I don't speak. His voice is different again.

'Some cat took that child's tongue out.'

He spits. He drops the spit slowly to the side of his feet. Then he lifts one boot and stamps on the spit with his heel. He looks back at my brother.

'Did you spill any?'

'No.'

'Lads! Room service has arrived! Get your fuckin' act together! Sit up, you! There's a lady in front of you!'

He kicks the man who's asleep on his side, but he sits up so quickly I know he wasn't really asleep. The other two put down their cards slowly and turn their heads to us.

'Are we going to get those glasses, or are you just going to stand there holding them all day?'

My brother and Richard hand over the four glasses to the four men. They take them. Now they're all standing up. Looking down at the water in the glasses in their hands.

'Thanks very much.'

And then he looks up, looks at my brother the whole time, and he empties the water with the sun in it into the grass at the side of him, where he spat, looking at my brother. They all do it, one after the other, looking at my brother, four taps turned on and spilling into the grass, until the last glass is emptied and the sun's gone with the water into the ground. They're handing back the glasses. We stare. Richard and my brother take them, still staring, and the four men pick up their cards and walk away.

The Hill of Shoes

Kathleen Murray

So it had come to pass. The generation that were amoebic brothers to prefrogs, begat the generation that observed froglike creatures with eyes now centred. Eventually they begat a generation that co-existed with frogs, each species responsible for its own welfare. Finally they begat a generation who established a legal framework to protect and preserve the frog brotherhood.

Francis, working on fencing at the end of the Hollow, registered the sound of the motor in the vicinity of the house but made no move to return. The postman let himself in and took a certain amount of care, propping the parcel between a sugar bag and cup on the kitchen table. He took his time, throwing his eye over the pile of papers on the sideboard, bills and newspaper cuttings mostly. The body of the cat, stretched and stiffening amongst the boots and shoes beside the cooker, escaped his notice.

That evening Francis placed the cat's corpse in a grain sack, bending the stiff tail down before he opened the brown paper package. He knew by the stamp that it was from Elizabeth, from Canada. Perhaps some pictures. It was over a year since she had left; she had sent him one letter asking for her birth certificate and he had made a trip up to the city to get the document and send it on. This letter was longer than the first, describing her days, a library job, living in a city, Toronto, raising a son. And in the parcel a keepsake—the boy's first shoes.

He was sitting at the table looking at the shoes in his hand. So small, they both fit on one palm. He pushed them into the pocket of his overcoat, set off on his bicycle, the grain sack tied to the handles, a shovel tied to the crossbar. His mother used to inter small animal remains at the end of the garden. But in this case he felt compelled to think of a new place for the cat that had soldiered independently and in tandem with him through hard seasons. Maybe because this cat had been there in his parents' era—it probably was the last living creature on the farm other than himself who carried any memory of their times. Maybe because it was a spring day that felt like summer and Francis wanted to be on the move somewhere. The place he chose was near a small pond he had known as a boy.

After he had buried the animal beside the water, he took a few moments to smoke. Pulling the tobacco pouch from his coat he felt the shoes. He placed them on the ground beside the freshly turned earth as the dappled light traded off the water's slight agitations. The cat and the shoes, matters of life and the living of it; he needed time to settle with them.

The tadpoles, three in number, the only survivors of the many hundred frogspawn removed from the lake, were residing in a blue plastic bucket in a corner of a dusty backyard. After the death of the largest tadpole from over-exposure to the sun, the plan to dig a small pond in the yard was dropped. The demise of the frogspawn cloud in his care didn't cost the boy a thought, but Joseph Devine experienced a keen sense of loss, tinged with guilt, over the death of that one tadpole. He decided to free the surviving duo. They had suffered in the heat, taken on a lurid purple pallor and abandoned the fundamentals of tadpole life: swimming and bubble blowing.

Using a large silver soup ladle, he removed the pair from the bucket and placed them in a plastic bag. Although alive, one tadpole, permanently disabled by heat stroke, could only swim using the flipper on its left side. Every couple of flutters the roll would begin, until it would find itself executing a backstroke. Desperate tail-flicking and body spasms would occur, eventually resulting in a righting of the torso.

Joseph brought the tadpoles, not to the nearby ornamental pond in the local park but further afield, hanging from the handlebars in a plastic bag. Having concealed the bicycle under a hedge, the boy made his way through tangled riverside undergrowth, following a small stream until it reached a waterhole. He acted furtively, in the mistaken belief that someone might care about the edicts protecting frogs and he would be caught red-handed carrying two potential frogs. To cloak his fear he immersed himself in a fantasy of criminality involving the kidnapping of two frog brothers destined for princehood, protected by a royal praetorian of wasps that might appear at any moment from the skies. He gave no thought to the tadpoles, thrown back and forth in a bag of water with a steadily rising temperature, a situation to which their bodies had previously been unable to adapt.

Joseph was searching for the perfect spot to release the frogs, particularly the frog with the affliction. And a thought lingered at the back of his mind: if they were to grow to adulthood and spawn the next spring, perhaps he could return to restock, a chance to overlay the current experience with a more successful one.

A secluded place at last, a saucer-shaped incline where the water seemed to vanish into the earth. Although it was fed by the stream, it never became more than a pool, shallow to ankle height. The overhanging trees gave permanent shelter, the inaccessibility enhanced by a dense thicket of bushes along the last stretch of the stream.

Even now, just as Joseph should have emptied the bag into the water, he hesitated. He moved around the edge, rejecting this place due to an overabundance of weeds and that one because of a low branch, a potential perch for a hungry bird. Another spot was illuminated by shafts of sunlight—rays had already sounded the death knell—so he moved on. Sloshing the water from side to side in the bag to ensure maximum swimming action he continued circling the waterhole. Finally climbing over a fallen tree and pushing aside some vegetation he stretched his arm over the water.

As he knelt to release his captives (the first swimming furiously away, the second swimming furiously in a circle punctuated by loop-the-loop body rolls), his eyes focused on the surface of the water broken by the liquid pouring out of the bag, and then shifted minutely to the left, something catching his vision like a fish hook. Later, when required to recount his story, a story he was asked to recite again and again, this exact moment never submitted to the soapstone of memory and remained a blur.

The tadpoles were oblivious to the events unfolding at this point—they were already halfway across the pool, inconspicuous amongst weeds, distant from each other, prompted by the strong tadpole's instinct to separate itself from the weaker one.

Thirty years later, after his daughter died, a cot death, one scene stayed with Joseph, playing over and over in his mind's eye. He would remember just how it was when he had entered the bedroom, whistling under his breath a tune that was playing on the radio, taking in the dimness of the light after the brightness of the hallway, anticipating her sleepy smell and then the unexpected silence in places you hear the sounds of life: her mouth, her nose, her chest. And his face smiled into the cot as he had intended, coming whistling into the room, as if his smile could negate the scene. He could see himself smiling as if he were the baby looking up, waking up. Here too he experienced a moment where the scene was so unforeseen, so unheralded by all that went before, it had never quite lodged in his memory. But no one, not even his wife, asked him about this moment. What did you see first, Joe? What did you think?

It was three years later, when he was ready to repaint the nursery and pack the clothes, the blankets and cot away in the attic, that he came across the thimble. It had been a gift to the infant from an aunt, and on finding it, Joseph sat down on the floor and held it by the tip like a little finger. He set it down carefully beside him, meaning to do something with it later. Forgotten it rolled away under the dresser and fell through a gap in the floor boards.

Four decades on, the thimble reappeared. The young couple who purchased the house were locals originally, returnees from Australia. During renovations, the electrician who lifted the boards found the thimble nestled against the pipes. He held on to it and planned to visit an antique dealer to have its value estimated. However, knowing his guilt would increase in proportion to its worth, he never quite got around to the appraisal. He was a worker not a thief and he satisfied himself afterwards that he had stolen the thimble because it had appealed to him directly without knowledge of its origin or monetary value.

A number of descriptions of the scene at the waterhole exist: the police report, the local historical society journal, an academic thesis, the account included in a monograph written to accompany the Thea Ross exhibition.

But before all this was the original impression that formed in Joseph's mind. A pyramid of shoes. Whilst the concept of shoes is one grasped at an early age, the circumstance is usually the foot, walking, pairs. Context is the landscape of understanding, the horizon line of comprehension, and shoes in large quantities are to be found in shoe shops. So the little hillock of shoes appeared not as shoes to Joseph first off, but as feet, as if he saw through each shoe to its essential nature, the fit of a foot.

When Joseph returned home he told his mother what he had seen. There was some discussion between the two as to whether this was the type of matter that required the boy's father, the local sergeant, to take any official action. It was not, in and of itself, criminal to leave a pair of shoes or indeed many, many shoes outside. There was, however, the business of the tadpoles. Frogs were rare, a species protected by law and it was a small crime to collect frog spawn.

The next morning Mrs Devine went with Joseph to the site to verify the boy's story and it was clear to her that her husband should be informed. The empty shoes with no feet to occupy them (so many shoes—could there even be enough feet in the town?) carefully piled up in this odd, secret place. The upper layers rested on the lower deposits of shoes, boots, straps and buckles, laces merging with moss and rotting leaves that might be covering six feet of decomposed shoes.

Sergeant Devine realised that the preservation of a crime scene for forensic examination was paramount, but in this case the moment had passed. By the time he was informed of the shoe site and visited the scene, there was a well-worn path into the glade. Flowers, coins and mementos were attached to the branches of the surrounding trees. Although no one had touched the pile of shoes, they had clearly stood alongside it and even gone so far as to cut away the bushes and tangled undergrowth to facilitate closer inspection.

He made his visit late in the evening and passed a woman and daughter coming back along the river. They greeted him but he avoided eye contact, forestalling any idle prattling. He was on official business and having not yet seen the shoes, would not be able to respond authoritatively if the subject were to be raised in conversation. He made his way over to the tree trunk and as his wife and son had directed, turned left and found himself looking at the pile of shoes. Before his training forced a frame of reference on his experience, he felt his heart shift a little and his breath hold. He too saw feet, a mound of feet, flat feet, calloused soles, children's feet, elegant toes, nails.

Although the crime rate in his town was virtually nonexistent, Sergeant Devine had come across all variety of human experience in the course of his work. Because he knew most of the perpetrators and victims, their histories and circumstances, he was a man of measured judgement. He had a strong intuitive sense that there was no criminal intent inherent in the shoe pile. The new shoes were fresh growth repudiating the lower layers, sinking into the earth. The buckles might act as dental records, revealing the age and size of shoes that had decomposed. That was all he could think of; buckles like fillings loosed from their natural resting place.

As the shoes were one person's mark and the story of chance, no amount of detective work (and Sergeant Devine had put in many hours thinking about the shoes piled beside the water, even after his retirement) could have solved what at the end of the day went down in the annals of the town as a small mystery.

Bernard was preparing breakfast whilst Elizabeth sat in the living room, looking through the newspapers. Probably eggs and spinach, she thought, her son's speciality. The headlines focused on a significant drugs find and lower down the page a controversy that was brewing in the Canadian Olympic show-jumping team. The side panel to the left carried local news, a few lines that might draw the reader in—a thumbnail picture of firemen carrying a coffin, the tainted blood trial, a synopsis of a feature on credit card fraud, a storm warning for the Eastern seaboard. Turning over to continue the Olympics story, a photograph took up about a third of the second page. Initially, it appeared as if a child had stuck overlapping scraps of coloured paper on a sheet, an abstract collage framed by a fence on one side, metal blue, with a policeman in short sleeves at the back of the photo, a large group of people in the left foreground and a young man in a black shirt and pants looking across the scene, perhaps listening to instructions from someone just outside the frame.

Up To 1,000 Shi'ite Pilgrims Die In Stampede

Abandoned shoes and sandals, thousands of them strewn like leaves

242

across the bridge, mostly plain open-toed sandals, black and brown. Here and there they were broken up with children's shoes, gaily coloured plastic petals. The footwear in the foreground of the photo was in focus, the Bata brand name clearly visible on some, but with distance they merged into one solid, indistinguishable mass. Many of the sandals were upturned, their soles a caramel flesh colour.

The single biggest confirmed loss of life in Iraq since the March 2003 invasion occurred on a bridge in Baghdad. Trampled, crushed against barricades or plunging into the Tigris River, up to 1,000 Shi'ite pilgrims died yesterday when a procession across a Baghdad bridge was engulfed in panic over rumours that a suicide bomber was at large.

Why take off their shoes before crossing the bridge, she wondered. The smell of toast from the kitchen drew her back to the present.

The two-lane 2,300-yard-long bridge was littered with hundreds of abandoned sandals lost in the pushing and panic.

Can you die from a rumour? Elizabeth recalled growing up in a place of certainties, where fear could build up behind your back like a wind and drive you forward against your own will, where whispers were enough to inscribe your name in a ledger of death before your dying. Yes, she thought, sometimes what you believe might come true is enough to kill you.

Hamid Jassim, a doctor at the scene when the panic erupted, said most of the dead were suffocated or trampled.

Suffocated. She thought about that, trampled to death by human feet, bare feet.

Bernard stuck his head in the door, 'Come on, it's not the last supper, I'll be back this time next week.'

He was leaving later that morning for a week-long conference. He was an archaeologist; an ice historian is how she described him to herself. His speciality was as a materials conservator, focusing on historical artefacts found in ice fields and glaciers. She had visited him on many of his digs but during the excavation of the Sara Sara ice mummies she suffered a stroke and was confined now to their apartment in Toronto.

*

The week passed quickly for both of them in their separate spheres. Although bogs fell outside his main field of enquiry, Bernard had attended the conference in Galway to meet two scholars who specialised in the preservation properties of ice and bog and the parallels in the artefacts they held. It had been a useful encounter and had given both parties further lines of investigation to pursue.

Waiting in the airport bar for his flight to be called, Bernard wrote a postcard to his mother, anticipating his own arrival home before the post. The barman rubbing a cloth over the mirror remarked to Bernard's reflection, 'You'll never fall out with your own company.'

Bernard stared at his face in the bar mirror, imagining the flesh falling away to reveal the bones, a bone structure similar to his mother's, the skull, the jawbone. After the stroke a year ago, Elizabeth was left with some slackness on the left side of her face. The eyelid refused to close, leaving her eye permanently open. Initially she would tape her eye down each night with a small pad and a bandage wrapped around to keep it in place. Eventually her doctor recommended a gold weight implant. A small piece of gold was inserted into her eyelid and this ballast enabled her to close both eyes at night. Bernard imagined the coffin surrounding her disintegrating, leaving the skull staring not towards the sky or down into the earth, but turned to one side, a gold teardrop resting inside. In a thousand years, he wondered, who will be here to make sense of it all? This chain of thought led him back to a conference paper, on twins discovered in Austria, buried 27,000 years ago covered in red ochre under a mammoth tusk with thirty-one ivory beads. It was impossible to conclusively determine the significance of the bodies and artefacts; whether location was one of choice or convenience, the children a sacrifice or an offering.

A Garda Sergeant like his father, Joseph Devine rebuilt old tractors, and it was in this capacity he found himself visiting Francis. He'd heard the old man had a shed full of old farm machinery. The house was set well up the lane behind what would once have been an imposing entrance gate, now a solitary post on one side, a pile of stones on the other. Up along the lane, there were various implements thrown on the verge: engine parts, metal bars, churns. An enormous oak dominated and darkened the yard. He noticed a pair of scissors and a mug hanging from a lower branch and a large ball of tape resembling a hive attached to the bark.

He knocked on the porch door and pushed it in when he found it unlocked. Francis had lived alone his grown days and the state of the house reflected an austere life. Before Joseph broached the business at hand, a tractor Francis was looking to sell, the conversation travelled along a number of paths, one being the topic of collecting. In his day, Francis said, people collected all manner of items: stamps, insects, birds' eggs, teapots, cigarette cards. His own mother collected Toby jugs and he still kept them on the dresser, though he never added to them. As a child, he shared with her the anticipation of each new arrival and would study the catalogues carefully, even when he was alone. But after her death he could not recall what exactly his mother had wanted with the congregation on the shelves; he felt a slight unease remembering the care she showed the laughing faces of John Barleycorn and Sairey Gamp, dusting them with her own handkerchiefs and scarves.

That day as they talked about cattle and the late snow and Toby jugs, Joseph's mind slipped back to a time, maybe thirty years previous, a summer of frogspawn and shoes, of questions drifting in the long evenings, a mysterious season that doesn't always come around in a lifetime and can only belong to those who live through it, only be understood by its creators. And so the strata of lives laid down—a gold weight, a cat's spine, a shoe embedded in the sediment—fossils and footprints of their age.

Rustlers

Michael Nolan

I was turfed in the back with nothing but a toolbox to sit on. There were drawers full of screws that rattled as the van went, and it went all right. My da drove like a demon, chucking me left and right through every dip and turn. 'I need a piss,' I called, but he couldn't hear. I stood up, put my mouth to the gap in the chip-wood panel between the front and back and told him I was bursting.

'You've a bottle in there,' he shouted. 'Piss in the bottle.'

There was only backwash left in the two-litre bottle of coke so I stood up and undid my jeans. It was a rigmarole with the van belting round corners and me clawing out for something to hold on to while targeting my purple helmet in the hole and squeezing a drip. Ended up wetting my hand, but still near filled the bottle, the piss going a funny shade of black mixed in with the coke.

We stopped in a narrow lane with trees hanging down. The door slid open, hitting me with glary morning light sore in the eyes. My da was standing in boots and weather-all's like he was ready to storm a beach. 'Do you need to go?' he said.

I said I did and hopped out.

There were more fields, trees cuffing the fields and shabby looking hedges, a house across the way. One of those houses you see in the country with a pointy roof and slab-grey walls. I took myself out of my jeans and thought this is where we're supposed to be. But I couldn't see any sheep, not in that field or the one beyond where mist smudged the grass. A breeze tickled. I gave myself a nip.

'Watch out for them birds,' Bimbo shouted, twiddling his baby finger at me. He was cooped up in the passenger seat with the door hanging open. The van tilted down with the weight of him. He'd been my da's mate since before I was spat out and he got on like this was something he had over me. My da paced with his phone to his ear, his head tilted as if to hear.

'We're on the lane,' he was saying. 'We said nine o'clock. If these culchie bastards catch a whiff of us we're chinned.'

I sat on the ground with my back against a tree and stayed well clear. My da took his rustling seriously. Him and Bimbo were at it flat out every Sunday, and I was forever getting roped in because I stayed with him at the weekends and hadn't a choice.

The cow shite was the worst. The stink was everywhere and had me heaving. Bimbo didn't give a fiddlers. He sat there munching crisps, his greasy fingers burrowing into the bag. 'Gimme one,' I said, and he flicked me the finger. 'Go ahead. Just one.'

I didn't even want one. I was bored to the bollocks and trying to get a reaction from him. He slapped a handful into his mouth and offered the bag.

'There's nothing in it,' I said.

Bimbo grinned potato-pasted teeth and dropped it to the ground.

'Magill's going to meet us farther on,' my da said, slipping his phone in his pocket and pulling the side door open.

'Farther on where?' Bimbo said.

'Down the road. Get in the back, Gavin. We're going.'

I stayed where I was. My da wasn't much taller than me, but he was stocky and strong with shoulders that could charge a bull. He held the door open like he would for a lady, and I could see into the back; the manky floor cluttered with wire coils and carpet, the toolbox I'd spent half the morning wrestling to hold on to. For a mad moment I wanted to fight him.

Few more years, I thought, and patted the dust from my arse.

We met the fella Magill on another lane. There was a jeep parked up with a trailer large enough for horses, and Magill standing by with his country arms crossed. He was big and bald and looked at me with a gammy tilt of the head.

'I need you to give me a hand,' my da told me. 'Bimbo's back's playing up.'

Magill swiped gravel with a laced boot and stared.

'It's heavy, so be easy,' my da said, bending down to pull the trailer from the tow bar. 'Ready?'

I said I was, but the sudden unsteady weight caught me snoozing. My feet slid on the stones and Magill smirked.

'Wee bit to the left, Gavin. That's it. Take your time.'

I'd a good grip, but the bar was cutting the hands off me even though my da was taking most of the weight. I could feel it lighter on my side and was mortified. He swung the trailer round like it was nothing.

'That's us,' he said, hooking it to the van. I let go and checked the red lines carved across my palms.

'No messing about now,' Magill said. 'It needs to be done early.'

'What time does he leave?'

'Ten. He does the milk round.'

My da said happy days and they talked prices. The fields around us were hilly. Still it smelled of shite, a wet sludgy smelling shite that stinks your clothes for a week. My da would drop me home that night and my ma would look at me, disgusted, and kick me into the shower. 'Where's he had you?' she'd say, and I'd be tempted to tell.

Magill got into his jeep and farted back down the lane. My da stared. People said we looked like each other. We'd the same dark hair and eyes, and we both raised our eyebrows when we were talking like we were trying to see over glasses neither of us wore. Sometimes my ma would look at me and gasp, and I'd feel an awkward flush of pride.

'You all right?' he asked.

Before I could answer, Bimbo stuck his vending machine head out the window. 'Any chance? There isn't a sheep in sight and Gavin's mooching for a tussle, aren't you, kid?'

We drove along roads that were more like dirt tracks than roads, and it took us half the morning to find the place. By the time we did, my arse was aching from trying to stay on the toolbox without face-planting the floor. We pulled up by a gate on a leaky back road bordered with bushes, and got out.

It was ewes we were after, these ones with black faces staring across the field like burglars in balaclavas. We leaned on the gate with our elbows at our chins. My da was chewing at the bit to get going. 'We'll go left round the side of the field,' he was saying. 'Cut back across and filter them this way.'

Bimbo spat stringy gobs and joked about throwing a few woolly ones in the back with me. Then it was quiet. We were in the blunt-end of nowhere. The sky domed out and the stillness hung. The farmer's house was a few fields over. It was a big gaff with two chimneys and windows you could swim in. The car was still in the drive and I wondered how he'd react when he came home to find half his flock gone. The insurance will cover it, my da always said, and that the sheep were being raised for slaughter. If anything we were doing the fluffy friggers a favour, and their dopey-headed faces hadn't a clue.

My da straightened up. The car was pulling out of the drive. Too far away to hear, some sheep turned their skulls and chewed. 'That's us,' he said.

We broke the lock and opened the gate wide, pulled the trailer round and set the ramp down. There were a few testy baas. One looked at me like I'd dumped in its garden. My da was whispering, 'there now. Good and slow, lads. Take her easy.'

A big mummy sheep came tearing forward, and stopped. We moved slowly towards them, me and Bimbo fanning to each side while my da spread his arms like a preacher. The sheep started backpedalling. They never knew what to be at when we came for them like this. They bunched up with worried eyes and put me in mind of fish in a tank; when they moved their wool puffed and they could've been floating.

'Easy now,' my da said.

We had them yards from the gate. They were bumping into each other trying to find a way between us; we closed in fast. They panicked and squealed and made a run for it. Some squeezed between the gate and road while others got halfway up the ramp and took a tumble in the tussle. Black legs buckled like burnt matchsticks and we were there, grabbing muckles of clumpy wool and shoving them in.

We got the trailer closed and locked. The road was clogged with sheep babbling between the hedges. 'That's the ticket,' my da said, while Bimbo held his knees and coughed to catch his breath. I slapped his back.

'You all right, fat boy?'

He spat between his feet, too puffed out to speak.

'C'mon,' my da said. 'We need to split.'

I held onto the toolbox under me as the bottle of piss-coke rolled across the floor. The rush had me giddy. We had at least twenty, and we were like bandits tearing across the country. It would get even better when we sold the sheep and my da laughed his whooping laugh and slipped me a few quid to keep me sweet. I listened to Bimbo and him bantering in the front and wished I was sitting between them, all three of us buzzing off each other with the sheep in the trailer wondering what the hell had just happened.

Then we stopped. The front doors screeched and closed with a crack. My heart slipped. I tried to open the side door and it was locked. 'What's happening?' I said, and didn't get an answer. I tried to see into the front and couldn't make anything out. There were voices. I imagined my da running one way and Bimbo the other; me left in the van surrounded by silver Skodas. I banged the door.

'Daddy. Daddy, where are you?'

The door skimmed open. My da looked flustered. 'I need you to stay here and mind the van,' he said.

We were parked on a road at the back of the farmer's house we'd just done over. There was a field between us and it, and the heady musk of hedges hung in the heat. 'No way,' I said. 'I'm not staying here.'

I was scundered red and not for letting him see. He glanced at the ground, then at me hunched under the roof. I hadn't called him Daddy in years. The guilt was in his gammy face and I felt bad for it.

'We have to be quick,' he said, and stepped back to let me out.

We made across the field like mercenaries. The grass squelched and we kept low, dodging the breeze that cupped the field and the trees all around it. Bimbo was panting behind me, and when we got to the bushes and forced our way through the sticky smelling branches, he had to stop.

'I'm gonna puke.'

We pushed through to the back garden. A gnome was fishing in a pond and there was a swing set by the shed, a football net in front of the stables, and all sorts of dainty looking flowers snuggled up to the house. My da tried the back door and was surprised to find it locked. 'Look,' he said, and pointed to the conservatory. One of the windows was hanging open.

He climbed through, knocking an ornament of a woman in a dress to the floor. I glanced back towards the van, but couldn't see it through the bushes that were smattered with sun. 'You scared?' Bimbo said. I told him nah, and he looked at my legs as if he could see them shaking.

The back door opened and my da was there, beaming. In we went, through the kitchen and into the hall. Our footsteps echoed. That's how big it was. They echoed. The floors were wooden and glossed to a sheen, and a glittery looking chandelier dangled above us.

'Keep dick, Gavin,' my da said, pointing to the front room.

Him and Bimbo headed upstairs and I did what I was told. The curtains hung to the floor, and I could see to the end of the driveway and nothing much else. You'd think a farmer would have a humble wee gaff with a sitting room and a fireplace and a few scenic paintings on the walls. Maybe you'd catch a whiff of boots, or dog, but not here. It smelt of leather and dusty picture frames and made me think of a library. The ceiling couldn't be reached with a brush pole, and there was a piano in the corner by the bookshelves. A music book on the stand was opened at the page of a tune called 'Für Elise'. It made me uneasy. They were taking ages upstairs. I was about to call up when my da came waltzing into the room, his neck hanging with gold necklaces that blinked in the early morning light simpering through the window. He'd a rucksack full of stuff slung over his shoulder, a paddy cap on his head. 'What do you reckon?' he said, puffing his chest out like a man in a portrait. Then he took the hat off and slapped it on me. 'There you go. Farmer Gavin.'

Bimbo stomped in with another rucksack and they looked around the room, but nothing tickled their fancy. 'We need to head on,' Bimbo said.

'What about the stables?'

'Fuck the stables. We've enough.'

My da checked the time. He wasn't ready to give over. 'Yous two take the stuff back to the van and I'll meet yis there.'

'I'll stay with you,' I said.

He handed Bimbo his rucksack and I waited on him to say no, but he didn't. When we got outside, Bimbo lumbered his way towards the bushes and I followed my da to the stables. It was only when we got close that I heard a radio playing classical music. The stables had been divided into pens and there were dogs in each of them; black Labradors that danced on their hind legs and stuck their snouts through the railings for a sniff.

'No good,' my da said, then stopped at the last cage and clapped. The dogs loved this and howled. 'Is there a lead?' he said, before spotting one hanging by the door and grabbing it.

I didn't feel right about this. I glanced towards the house, then at the football net in the garden making shadows on the grass. A breeze groomed the flowers and the gnome at the pond was blushing. My da opened the cage and a border collie stepped out, smiling. 'Look at him,' he said. 'He's a cracker, isn't he?'

I heard a gentle crunching sound and thought it was the radio. My da was scratching the collie's chin. 'This fella's going to make our job a lot easier,' he said.

I peeked out of the stable and saw a car mowing across the driveway. 'Daddy,' I said, and hated myself.

He heard it too. He straightened up and shushed me. 'Wait,' he whispered, and stood with his back against the wall to see out. When he looked at me again and saw my face, he nearly choked. 'It's all right,' he said. 'Take it easy.'

He turned away like he couldn't cope. The dog stood by him and I was raging at his giddiness, and the dog's happy obedience, and my own humiliating panic. I wanted to lock myself in a cage and pray to God the farmer would feel sorry for me when he found me. My da was in kinks laughing. 'You're pale as a plate,' he said, and covered his mouth with his hand.

The engine knocked off. A woman on the radio was wailing her lungs out. Tails slapped the ground.

'Soon as he goes into the house we bolt for the van, right?' my da said.

'Right,' I said, and as soon as the word left my mouth, we heard the gentle click of a door closing and were away like stink.

The collie bounded between us, its tongue loping out the side of its mouth as we broke through the bushes and into the field. The necklaces were still clattering about my da's chest as I held the beak of my Paddy cap and hoped the farmer wouldn't have the sense to look out the window and see us bailing across the bleached grass towards the van where Bimbo had the engine started.

I dove into the back and the dog leapt in with me. The door slammed and we hammered up the road the way we came, left onto another road so crooked and rutted the dog was struggling to keep its feet. He looked at the drawers full of screws like he couldn't understand why they made such a racket. We were tossed up and down and the trailer full of sheep hurdled along behind. I couldn't see us getting away with it, yet we were. The jittery potholed roads soon gave way to tarmac. We were on the motorway. My da and Bimbo were giving it stacks in the front while I cuddled the shaky dog between my legs.

I checked its collar. His name was Butch.

We drove for so long Butch boked on the floor and it smelt like something pulled from a hole. I scratched him behind the ear and he tilted his head and sighed. Every time I stopped, he'd nudge my hand with his soppy nose and rest his chin on my thigh. He was always smiling, even while he boked, and kept looking at me like he was mine. I didn't know how to tell him he wasn't.

I tried to sleep but my stomach was going bucko. I couldn't be sick. It would only give my da something else to laugh at. He'd look at Butch's sick and my sick and chuckle at my luck. So I gulped and breathed. My ma swore by breathing in your nose and out your mouth, and the thought of my ma made me sore.

When we got to where we had to go, my da let me out and I plonked myself on the ground. We were by the sea, and the grass was dusty with sand. The fields sloped down to the water and the water was blue to the horizon. Behind us was a cottage, and beyond that were fields and cattle in the fields. No trees. Barely a bush. Only the road we came from, and the green fields under the sky.

I sat with my legs crossed watching Butch sniffing and pissing every few steps. My da and Bimbo looked into the back of the van and winced at the stink.

'Jesus Christ,' Bimbo said. 'What'd you eat?'

My da got wipes, climbed into the back and started dabbing. I don't know why him and my ma broke up. I was too young when it happened for anything to be made of it. All my ma ever said was, 'he's your da, and I'll not stop you from seeing him.' Like it wasn't up to her. Even when he forgot to pick me up from school and I had to sit at the gates with a teacher I could tell was mooching to get home. Or when he ditched me in his flat until stupid o'clock in the morning, then came wailing in the door with a woman in heels that scraped the floor.

He dropped the sick-stained wipes out onto the grass. Bimbo stood by chewing a straw from a carton of juice he'd guzzled just before. 'Some craic that was,' he said. 'Never seen your da run so fast in my life.'

My da was on his knees in the back of the van, face still pinched with the smell. He told Bimbo to go see the fella down the road. The bald fella who gave us the trailer. Magill. He was leaning with his back against a gate, watching us.

Bimbo went on his way. Butch followed with a curious wiggle, and my da was stuck with me. An uncertain bleat quavered from the trailer. My da went to the passenger side door and got some air freshener, sprayed it in the back and stuck his head in to make sure the sickly smell was gone. Then he trudged round to the driver's seat and hoked about for something. When he came back, he stood with his hands buttered to his pockets like he didn't know what to do.

'So do you like the dog?' he said.

I said I did, and he asked me what I wanted to call it. 'His name's Butch,' I said. 'He's got a collar.'

'Sure that doesn't matter. You can call him anything you want.'

'You can't just change his name. That's not how it works.'

'But he's your dog now.'

'No he's not. He's not coming home with me, is he?'

I sounded more dramatic than I'd meant to, but stealing sheep was one thing, this was someone's dog. My da took a step back. He hadn't a clue how we'd gotten onto this. Neither had I, yet it seemed more important than anything. 'Your ma wouldn't have a dog,' he said, like she was to blame. 'But sure you'll see it at the weekends, won't you?'

'I don't want to do this anymore.'

His face softened and he bent down beside me. 'That's okay,' he said. 'Don't worry. Sure you can come stay with me on a Friday and I'll drop you home on Sunday morning. That would work all right, wouldn't it?'

I shrugged and said it would, not knowing how to say what I was trying to say.

'Don't get me wrong,' he said. 'I'll be gutted not having you with me. You're good at the rustling. But if it's not what you want to do it's okay. We can work round it.'

I knew he was trying to make everything better, but I felt like I was taking a weight off his shoulders. Bimbo called out. He was coming up the road with Butch strutting by his side like his work for the day was done. My da straightened up. 'That's us,' he said. 'Come on. We did good. A wee smile would go down a treat.'

He poked me in the ribs, playfully pulled the Paddy cap down to my eyebrows. I slapped his hand away. 'Stop it,' I said.

I hit his hand with more force than I meant to and he looked hurt, then torn, like he couldn't decide if he should shout at me, or apologise.

Instead, he left me sitting there and went back to the van. Him and Bimbo got in. Butch ran alongside them trying to chew the wheels as they reversed down the road. There was nothing else to look at. The land was flat and green and quiet. It was no different from anywhere I'd seen before, yet I felt weirdly alone. I watched them climb out of the van and say a few words to Magill. Butch was put on his lead and the trailer doors pulled open.

For a second, I thought the trailer was empty and that the sheep had disappeared. I could imagine my da's face paling and Bimbo's stupid mouth falling open, them both turning to me like I had something to do with it. I wished that I had. I could've left the trailer open and let the sheep tumble out as we made our escape down the motorway. They'd bounce between cars like fleecy pinballs causing all sorts of havoc as my da drove on, clueless.

But the sheep hadn't gone anywhere. Out they came with their coats all scraggly, hobbling down the ramp and across the field on woozy legs. I could hear my da's voice. He was on his tiptoes pointing things out to Magill. He patted Bimbo on the shoulder like he couldn't have done this without him, and I made up my mind. I didn't want to see him anymore. The next weekend he phoned, I'd tell my ma I didn't want to speak to him. I'd tell her the same thing the weekend after and the weekend after that until he stopped calling and I didn't have to listen to him at all.

When the sheep were in the field and the gate was locked, the van came hankering up the road to get me. The windscreen was glazed white in the brightness, and I could just about make out the shape of my da at the wheel and Bimbo stuffed into the passenger seat. Then I saw a little head; Butch squeezed between them squinting in the sun. The horn beeped. 'Hurry up,' Bimbo said, but I wasn't for moving. He said something to my da and my da got out and came round the front of the van. His face was dripping. He wiped the sweat from his eyes with the back of his arm and pulled the side door open.

'Have you coke left? I'm choking for a drink.'

'Behind the toolbox,' I told him, and he knelt in and lifted the bottle that had darkened in colour and cooled in the shade. He looked at me as he unscrewed the lid. Bimbo watched, and Butch sat on his lap and watched with him. I stayed where I was. The breeze lapped my ears. Somewhere at the other side of the road, a ewe bleated. My da held the bottle to his lips, expecting me to stand up. I could smell the sea. It smelt like piss.

I waited.

The Beast

Philip Ó Ceallaigh

Two old men were standing in a vegetable garden. One of them was very big, and you could tell by his full head of grey hair and particularly by his grey moustache, long enough to curl at the ends, that he had a good opinion of himself. Ion could dress up and go into town and not let himself down. He always wore a shirt. When he worked by himself in his garden behind the house he might unbutton it and let the sun on his big gleaming bronzed belly. Only when it was very hot would he take his shirt off entirely. Ion liked to work in his garden. He had grapevines and plum and pear and apple trees. Then there were the vegetables and at the end of the garden was a stand of poplar trees, the leaves of which flickered in the sunlight when the breeze brushed through them. Beyond the poplars was the field of corn his son had planted with the tractor. Ion was standing with his friend Mircea admiring the progress of the beans, tomatoes and the other plants.

Mircea wore shorts. He was the only man in the village who wore shorts. He was bald. He wore a white T-shirt with 'Freddy Mercury' written on it. There was a faded picture of Freddy.

—You're dressed like a twelve year old, said Ion. Makes you look like a scarecrow.

—Is that a fact?

—And you don't even know who Freddy Mercury is.

—A singer from France.

—He's neither a singer nor French.

—If I had jugs like that I'd keep my shirt on.

—When you walk down the road...

Mircea seized Ion's wrist. He was pointing at a creature not more than ten paces from them, nibbling at the dill.

Ion had seen just about everything. As a young man, after the war, he had to sign away ten hectares of fine land outside Timisoara to the collectives. Then he cried. When they shot the dictator he laughed. By then he was too old to work it properly. But his son, who lived in the city, bought a tractor and planted corn, and returned on weekends and holidays to the land.

But Ion had never seen anything like the creature that was in his vegetable garden that evening.

They were very still. They expected the animal to flee at any moment.

Mircea pointed to a net by Ion's foot. It had been for protecting strawberries from birds. It was June and the strawberries were finished. Ion picked up the net and gave a corner to Mircea. At the same time he didn't take his eyes off the creature. They advanced slowly through the rows of beans. They could not help feeling dramatic as they did this. This was hunting. They went very slowly. They were both nearing eighty and tended not to rush things anyway. But, in this case, with stealth called for, and under pressure, they managed to move with uncommon grace.

The creature looked up at them. It did not seem interested in escape. Perhaps it was a very stupid animal. The net fell on the creature. It continued watching them, twitching its nose. Ion leaned down to seize it behind its neck so that it could not bite.

—Careful, now! said Mircea.

The creature offered no resistance. They went to the yard beside Ion's house and disentangled it from the net and put it in a box and had a good look.

It was hard to explain. After all, they had both lived in the area nearly eighty years. In a hundred and sixty years you could expect to see just about every animal there was, even the rare and shy ones.

The creature had little ears like a mouse, and walked more or less like one, and had hair rather than fur. But it was the size of a young rabbit and had no tail. Its face was neither rabbit nor mouse. It did not seem upset at being captured.

—Maybe it's a cross between two animals, said Mircea, speaking what had crossed both their minds. Like a mule.

Ion harrumphed.

258

—Like a mouse and a rabbit? Don't annoy me. Maybe a mouse and an elephant!

They both laughed. This referred to Mircea's favourite joke. Mircea had no memory for jokes so he held onto just one, which he would repeat whenever he was with someone new and a joke was called for: A mouse is in love with an elephant and tricks her into letting him have his way. During the act a branch falls from a tree, striking the elephant, who cries out in pain. Take it all, baby! snarls the mouse.

Ion always considered this an inappropriate joke from a small man who had a very large wife, but had never said this to Mircea. Some things you could never say. Ion's wife was herself rather frail, so the conjugal beds of each of the friends took roughly the same cargo. Finally they became tired of standing and the strength had gone from the sun. Mircea walked home to eat, down a dusty dirt road striped with the shadows of trunks of trees.

The bed creaked when Ion got into it that night. It creaked every night. It was that kind of bed and he was that kind of man. He was troubled. It was only a matter of time before Mircea started blabbing and his yard was full of people wanting to see the creature, all standing about and gawking and chattering like monkeys and him expected to provide food and drink for everyone. He would have to be there to keep an eye on things and would never get any work done. The gypsies from the other side of the village would come over his fence in the night and try to steal it. If they stole fruit off the trees at night they would be interested in a strange animal too. One that might be of great value. Of interest to scientists, perhaps. There might be a reward involved. A quite significant sum. Ion got out of bed and brought the cardboard box, which contained the creature, from the living room into the bedroom and set it on the floor at his side of the bed. He stroked the top of her head. She seemed to appreciate the gesture, lifting her head and twitching her nose. A gentle smell of warm hay and fresh droppings rose to his nose. It really was a placid, affectionate little thing, and possibly quite intelligent.

—There now, Brigitte.

He got back into bed. The name had come in a flash of inspiration. He had always been good at giving animals names. It was one of his talents. It was after Brigitte Bardot, a great star of his younger years and, furthermore, a great lover of animals. She had visited Bucharest a few years before, concerned about the stray dogs, and had even adopted one and brought it back to France. She was on the news about it. Still a fine-looking woman, Ion thought.

Along with the creaking of the bed, there was also always much groaning and grunting before he settled. But this night there was too much going around in his head and he was unable to sleep. As well as all his other concerns, Mircea was troubling him. In fact, the truth was that Mircea had been troubling him for over seventy years, since they were boys. Even then Mircea had been rather spindly and awkward and had tended to get in his way whenever there was something serious to be done. They had had their disagreements through the years. There had been patches when they had not spoken for months. But Ion did not consider a month or two a particularly long time. Certainly it was a shorter period of time than it had been when he was twenty. Yes, thought, Ion, there was something flimsy and unreliable in Mircea's character. You could see it in the way he dressed. Who wanted to see his scrawny legs? And the way he spoke about Brigitte, as if asserting his rights as proprietor. He was probably already thinking about money.

—I don't know if we can trust him, said Ion to his wife, who had been drifting asleep.

—Who?

—Mircea. He's not the kind of man who you can entrust something important to.

—You shouldn't have drunk coffee after dinner. Don't pester me.

Ion lay awake for what felt like a very long time. His mind whirred unpleasantly. A man could find himself burdened with responsibility when he least expected it. Then, just as he was drifting off, he was shocked into full consciousness by the strangest noise. It was a high-pitched birdcall. Coming from Brigitte's box. He turned on the lamp and the noise ceased. His wife sat up, squinting in the light, her face crumpled with sleep.

—What was that?

—Brigitte! She sings!

The world was getting stranger.

Mircea, too, slept badly. He was troubled by Ion's attitude to the animal. It was clear to Mircea that the animal was half his by rights and it would have been nice if Ion had acknowledged that. Ever since they were boys Ion had wanted to be the boss. Ion had been a year older and much bigger and they had always played the games he wanted. And Ion's family had owned more land. Even after the land was taken away the better families remembered who they were. Usually Mircea did not mind Ion taking the lead since there was no point arguing over every little thing. But in this case Ion would be figuring that the strange animal might bring in some money. Or, perhaps, attention from the media. Ion would stand in the garden in his best shirt telling the people from the television how he had caught the beast.

As usual, Mircea woke far too early because he had to get up and go outside to relieve his bladder, but on this occasion he was unable to get back to sleep. It was already bright outside. He rehearsed the argument he would have with Ion. It was like playing chess. When he says that, I'll say this, then if he says...

At one point Mircea spoke aloud:

—Are you telling me straight to my face that...

His wife opened one eye and looked at him.

He got up and boiled some milk for his breakfast and after he had drunk it he fed the chickens and the pig. It was still too early to go to Ion's house so he fixed the fence around the vegetable garden where some of the smaller chickens were getting through and attacking the tomatoes and peppers before they could even ripen.

—Up early! said Ion heartily, when Mircea appeared in his yard several hours later. Rather too heartily, thought Mircea. He's a little too eager, thought Ion, determining not to tell his friend that the beast sang. They walked back towards the garden where they had first found the creature, circling around the subject, each waiting for the other to begin. Finally, Mircea came out with it.

—You know, I've been thinking. Perhaps we should involve the authorities.

—Authorities? What authorities? What are you talking about?

—I mean the animal.

—Brigitte?

—Brigitte, yes. Since we don't know what we have on our hands here. We have to go to town. Go public. The press. Or some government department which deals with unusual phenomena. And, of course, as you well know, there may be a sum of money along the line.

Ion, tight-lipped, dug his toe into the earth by the vines.

—We? What we have on our hands? I might have known. You probably didn't sleep a wink all night, thinking about reward money.

—Don't tell me it hasn't crossed your mind too.

Ion cleared his throat.

—I've always been happy with what I've got. This is a scientific discovery, not a lotto ticket. But if I receive any payment you won't be forgotten.

—How can I be forgotten? said Mircea, his voice rising. She's half mine and you know it! It's only fair!

—Don't get excited now! See this land? Mine! My father gave it to me and his father gave it to him. I had to wait forty years to get it back. And I caught her here so that makes her mine.

—I saw her first and then we caught her together, with that net there. So it makes no difference where she was caught. Under the law she's mine.

—I know the law. If my neighbour's apples fall on my land then that makes them mine. So she's mine, one hundred percent, and if you get a penny it will be the result of my generosity. At right this moment I wouldn't count on it.

—We'll see!

—Indeed we will.

Ion escorted Mircea to the gate, where they parted.

—Guinea pig, said Ion's youngest son, who had driven out from the city, where he worked as a schoolteacher.

—Doesn't look much like a pig. She squeals though.

—They're from South America. The Indians in Peru eat them. Maybe that's it.

—Really? Think she's worth anything?

—No. And she's a he. Look.

—That would be a guinea pig tool, I suppose. What can I say, you've let me down, Brigitte. Or whatever your real name is, you Peruvian piglet.

Ion put the 'pig' back in the box.

They went inside for lunch. It was Saturday. It was always nice when one of the boys came home. Ion's wife became very lively and it was a good excuse to sit around and have a good feed and some plum brandy. Then Ion would lie on the couch in the afternoon, listening to the chickens scratching, and fall asleep.

Mircea was angry all day but by late afternoon he ran out of energy and was merely depressed. He turned on the television but was not interested in anything so he turned it off and sat quietly in his chair while the sun grew swollen and low over the fields, and he did not turn on the light, so the only light was the fading light through the window. In all probability the creature was Ion's by law. But it was Ion's arrogance which offended Mircea more than the money he would lose. The way he had been dismissed from consideration. A little bit of good luck and Ion could not bear to share it. So much for friendship.

He heard the gate clacking shut. They were the footsteps of a woman but lighter than those of his wife, who was visiting relatives in the neighbouring village. A head appeared around the door. It was Ion's wife. She told him that Ion wanted him to come around for a glass of wine a little later.

Mircea perked up immediately. He had been right to be assertive, to show that he would not be walked over. It was the right approach to take with one such as Ion, who tended to get puffed up very easily.

As Mircea walked down the road the houses and trees were silhouettes. The branches of the trees in particular, having surrendered depth and colour, now stood out as an intricate black lacework against the sky. Or if he looked at it differently, the light appeared as that which was solid, a mosaic of a million irregular bright shards. You might live forever and such things would amaze you, because always you forgot. You could never really know things, because always you were forgetting. If a man wanted to paint such a thing it would be impossible. He would never have enough time. He would get hungry, become sleepy, and finally discouraged at his lack of ability. Behind the high wooden fences he could sometimes hear sounds. The voices of children. Music on a radio. The clank of a metal pot as a woman got a meal ready.

The sounds behind the fences were peaceful sounds. He saluted a neighbour taking a tethered cow back to its stable after its last feed by the roadside. He passed a boy and girl. They had been kissing and he had disturbed them. They separated and greeted him politely and did not resume speaking until he was safely passed. They were both perhaps sixteen. He knew the families they came from, knew more about their grandparents and great-grandparents than they knew themselves. But the knowledge of their grandparents meant nothing to them.

The old were fading and disappearing and the world needed to be discovered again, for the first time. Only kisses on warm summer evenings, the first ones in the history of the world, were real to the young. And the young were right, he felt. Kissing a girl under a tree and looking at the road and not knowing or caring what it meant. Then you blinked and you were an old man, walking down the same road.

A bat flitted ahead of him. Or perhaps more than one bat. It was more a movement than a shape, an agitation in his field of vision, gone before he could focus on it. He had no wish to be elsewhere in the world. He did not know very much but somehow he felt it was enough. You were born, you died, and meanwhile life was often strange. He had a presentiment that he would die before his wife and he felt a little sorry for her. She had got very used to him. And Ion would die too. One of them would die first and then the other would be unable to visit, to drink wine and talk. There were other houses but it was not the same.

Ion met him at the gate and shook his hand warmly. So they were still friends and equals in any dealings concerning the animal. It was not about money. It was about respect. They sat down at the wooden table on the porch. Ion poured red wine from a jug. It was a better batch than the year before. They sat and listened to the crickets and talked of inconsequential things. Talk of the creature could wait.

—I'm peckish. You'll join me?

Ion brought out a pot and plates and Mircea cut a loaf. They ate in silence until they were both full. Then they ate a little more. It was a fine stew of various meats and even some smoked sausage which had softened nicely in the cooking. It had onions, garlic, green beans, peppers, tomatoes, and thyme and bay leaf and dill and parsley—everything from the garden—and the sauce was rich with black pepper and paprika and sour cream had been stirred in at the last moment. Mircea mopped his plate with bread and took a good swallow of wine to wash it down and leaned back in his seat and burped without restraint. Ion refilled his glass. Nothing better in life than to sit at the end of the day with an old friend and share a meal and a few glasses and talk.

—About Brigitte, said Ion.

—Yes?

—Everything you said. Quite right.

Ion leaned over and put his hand over Mircea's and clasped it, looking him in the eye.

—Fifty-fifty, said Ion, smiling.

—That's fair.

—Shared! Right down the middle!

Ion leaned back. He began laughing silently, his hands on his quaking belly. He looked ready to burst. His face was bright red. Then he laughed aloud until tears rolled down his red cheeks.

Mircea looked down at the little pile of bones on his plate. His mouth fell open.

The Boy from Petrópolis

Nuala O'Connor

I listen to the waltz of Lota's heart under my ear—*babumf, babumf, babumf.* The plump of the years when she might have borne children has fallen away. She is slender now, angular. I have not had a child either and so, between us, we own two wasted wombs, a pair of houses built but never occupied. I often wonder who is worse off—a motherless daughter, such as me; or the daughter who fails to become a mother, the one who ends the line. Also me. I am badly off on the double, perhaps. I lift myself off Lota and out of the bed. She will sleep on.

The new boy is outside the window when I enter the kitchen; the wheat of his hair is just visible above the sill. I open the back door.

'We gave you a key,' I say. 'You did not let yourself in.'

He stares at me and shakes his head. I repeat myself—my Portuguese is not sharp—and he shrugs. The boy is one of those sallow, green-eyed Brazilians, startling to look at. I didn't think anybody outside of fiction had such eyes but here he is, as green-eyed as a cat, or something more exotic—an ocelot, maybe. He has Germanic skin, smooth and healthy, the skin of someone who gets fresh air. His name is Tito da Silva, though he has half a dozen other names too, like everyone here.

I hand the mop to Tito and he sets off with it slung rifle-wise over his shoulder. I have no idea where he is going but I don't call him back or quiz him. He will settle, I think; it won't take this one long to know what is what around here. I go through to my desk and sit. I poke at one typewriter key and watch its leg kick up and down like a can-can dancer. I look out the window; the milky blue of the sea is my constant

266

distraction and this morning is no different. The water makes me long for the sway of a boat under my legs.

Something about Tito has set off a ripple in me and already I know I will not write a word. I gaze out the window, my chin cupped in my hand—like a *namoradeira* statue waiting for her lover—and watch the eddy and gush of the waves. The horizon sits high here, something I mull over often. Lota says it is to do with proximity to the equator and she is probably right. I imagine fish swishing down from that lofty horizon and crashing onto the shore on their bellies; shoals of fish, biblical and silver. I imagine myself among them.

'Madam, you did not give me a bucket.' Tito startles me and, when I turn to reprimand him, I see that he looks abashed so I swallow my annoyance.

'It's Miss,' I say, 'not Madam. Please. Follow me.'

He trails behind me to the kitchen, head down. I hand him the bucket and he smiles. I sing: *'There's a hole in the bucket, dear Liza, dear Liza, there's a hole in the bucket, dear Liza, a hole.'* Tito steps away from me as if stung. 'It's just a silly old song,' I say. He stands, still and contained, looking at me as if indulging the half-mad. 'Go,' I say. 'Go mop.'

Back at my desk, I watch a lizard skitter down the garden path; it stops and tongues the air. I hope the cat will not saunter by and see it; he wouldn't hurt it but he likes to paw at lizards, toy with them. I wonder if it is the same lizard that found its way into our bed last week. It sat, a little regent, on Lota's pillow. I wanted to screech but knew that Lota wouldn't appreciate that; I squeaked and pointed.

'Come, friend,' she said, and carried the lizard, pillow and all, to the back door and set it free. The lizard ran, jerky and plastic, down the path.

I think this may be the same fellow; it certainly looks identical to our bedroom visitor. I watch the lizard's gait along the stones, its purposeful stop-and-start meander. Tito appears from nowhere, grabs the creature's tail and tosses it over the wall. The lizard hurtles through the air and I gasp, knowing the long drop on the other side, anticipating the crush of its body on the paving below. Tito saunters on, sees me in the window and salutes. I return a static wave then let my hand fall back to my side. The morning has collapsed; I need to get out, I need to walk.

There is no sign of the lizard outside the wall. I search up and down and am relieved not to find it. 'You landed safely, friend,' I say.

*

The Copacabana sand is cold when you dig your toes under its surface. I relish that cold; it brings to mind Nova Scotia and the antediluvian chill that place holds. I go to Great Village in my dreams and sit on Grandmother's lap and we chatter together, though I cannot hear the words. Those dreams make me lachrymose but they also bring peace— the profound joy of good memories works on me like balm.

I have the beach to myself and I push at hairy coconut husks with my feet to see if there is anything underneath. I scrabble in the sand for stones and shells. The ocean here does big work—the sand is powdery—so I rarely find anything unusual on my beach-combs. At home on my desk I have a treasury of sand dollars, lima bean stones and architecturally crosshatched Venus shells. This morning I find a wedge of green sea-glass and it brings to mind Tito and his variegated eyes. The squally colour of the glass delights me and I pocket it.

I pass the huddle of beach shacks that sits up behind the tide line. They are made from driftwood and burlap sacks and even in winter they must swelter. Sometimes a boy sits outside the end shack. I say 'a boy' but he may be a man, it is hard to tell. He is retarded, this boy, his head is too small for his body, but he is beautiful because of it. This boy, with his long torso and tiny head, has a sweet, inquisitive face. '*Bom dia*!' I always call, but he never replies.

I notice the smell of damp every time I re-enter our home. If there is such a thing as a national scent, then mildew is the smell of this land. Its moist fingers curl from the corners of every house and store and restaurant; a clay-like smell hovers everywhere. I call out for Lota.

'In here,' she bellows, and I find her in the kitchen. She has already drunk the neck and shoulders off a bottle of whiskey. It is Irish whiskey— she claims Scotch tastes like tea. 'Top of the mornin' to you, Cookie,' Lota says, raising her tumbler.

'I doubt if Irish people actually speak that way.'

She grunts. 'That new boy won't last.'

'Why's that, Lota?'

'Well, already he has you running from your desk, and I'm drinking and it's not yet noon.' She squints at the wall-clock.

'None of that is his doing,' I say.

'There is also the problem of his idleness. I found him asleep under the coconut tree, stretched like a lord, farting and snoring.' I laugh but Lota continues. 'I won't have it. He is lazy and we do not need another lazy boy.' She sallies on like this for a few more minutes, it being the Brazilian habit to keep explaining things—particularly uncomfortable things—long after you have understood.

I cut across her eventually. 'This week I have chosen to read not write,' I say, a plan that has just occurred to me.

'Surely you have read the bookshelves dry,' Lota says, and plunges the cork back into the top of her whiskey bottle.

'Where is he now?' I ask.

'Who?'

'Tito,' I say, and she looks at me quizzically. 'The *boy*, Lota. The *boy*.'

'How should I know?'

I sit at my desk and read with dismay the lines I typed yesterday. Who was the woman who wrote them? And what foolishness made her believe they were worth a thing? I have been pulling and slapping the same poem into shape for months now and it will not behave. The words sit still on the page. I poke my finger through the dish on my desk that is filled with my favourite shells and stones; the piece of green sea-glass sits in its centre, winking at me. I snatch the sheet of paper from the typewriter and stuff it into the desk drawer. I will do what I told Lota I would do: I will read. I select a volume from the shelf—some friendly sonnets—and head for the yard.

Tito is kneeling on the path, bent over the bucket I gave him earlier, gazing into the surface of the water. I stand and watch him looking at his reflection like someone trying to find answers from the moon.

'Are you enjoying what you see?' I ask. Tito startles. 'Your face. Do you find it handsome?' The boy jumps up and backs away from me. 'It's okay, Tito, I'm just making fun. Teasing.'

He closes his green eyes and purses his lips; he shakes his head, grabs the bucket and stomps off, water sloshing over his bare feet. His slender body retreats, rigid with annoyance, or embarrassment, or who-knows-what. I am beginning to wonder if Lota is right about Tito; if he will not last with us at all.

*

Sudden, blasting rainstorms are the order of August here; the sea and sky go from zinc to turquoise in the space of moments. The rain falls in televisual lines and clouds roll like demons along the horizon; the tide roars and complains. But when the storms end, the air is breathable and it is then I love to wander the beach to see what has been left for me.

Today I hope to find driftwood, lots of it. Tito has agreed to construct a bench to go in our yard and, for weeks now, he has been appearing with lengths of wood for my approval. I want to contribute some pieces too. This is our project, his and mine.

The sand is already dry by the time I walk it. Before long I spot a beauty: a stubby plank painted red with scatters of yellow showing through. I flop onto my knees to admire it, thrilled with its grain, its carnival colours. It will make a perfect armrest on the bench. I lift it and shake off the sand. From the corner of my eye I see someone approaching from the shacks above the tide line. But when I look up, ready to greet them, I see that they are not coming towards me at all, they are dancing. Outside the end shack two people are dancing to a drumbeat, two young men. They roll their arms like windmills and dip their knees up and down; they shimmy around each other and kick their legs with solid grace. The drumbeat rises from a small girl who is beating out a rhythm on a tin can. I realise I recognise the young men, both of them: it is the retarded boy and it is Tito.

They dance on, circling each other fluidly as if this is something they have rehearsed. The girl's drumming gets wilder and the boys dance in a frenzy, their heads shaking voodoo style. In the end the rhythm is too crazed and they fall in a tangle of arms and legs onto the sand, laughing. I want to approach them but their joy is so intimate, so carefree, that I daren't break their spell. I take my piece of painted wood and lope on down the beach.

Tito is pleased with the piece of driftwood. '*Belíssimo*,' he says, rubbing his fingers over it, front and back.

'I saw you on the beach,' I say, 'dancing.'

'And I saw you,' Tito says. 'I see you often—gathering things.' He tilts his head and grins; he looks like a toddler when he smiles, which is seldom.

'I love that stretch of Copacabana,' I say. 'Is that where you're from?'

'I'm from Petrópolis, but I live on the beach with my brother.'

'You must miss the mountains, both of you.' I imagine a place where clouds clutch at peaks.

'We miss our mother,' he says.

For a moment, I am surprised by what he has said—I'm so used to the people here being occupied with the present and not the past. But he is only a boy, of course, and he needs his mother.

'She's still there, in Petrópolis?' I ask.

'No, Miss. She is dead.'

I put my hand on his arm. 'My mother is dead too. We're the same.'

'No, Miss,' Tito says, gesturing at the garden, the house, the half-made bench. 'We will never be the same.'

'They are orphans, Lota. We must help.'

I have been building up, explaining, re-explaining, trying to be Brazilian in my approach, but Lota is unmoved. She puts her hands on my shoulders.

'Cookie, they are practically grown men. I wanted a boy to help around here. I did not want the full catastrophe.' Lota slips out of her slacks and tosses them into the hamper.

'They live in a hut covered with sacking. Did you hear me when I told you that? Don't you care?' Tears are hurting my throat.

Lota shrugs and buttons up her pyjamas. 'I'm tired, Cookie, and I'm finished discussing this.'

She slides into our bed and turns her back to me. I stand over her, boiling and confused.

'For a woman of causes you surprise me. You're hurting me.'

Lota does not turn around and eventually I creep in beside her, holding my body rigidly away from her side of the bed.

In the rich geography of dreams, Great Village and Rio de Janeiro collide; winter in Brazil becomes a Nova Scotian summer and, in my grandparents' house, I am the old woman in the rocker and Tito is the child at my feet. I run my hands through his hair, soft as rabbit fur under my fingers; I croon a song to him. Outside the window, snow shrouds the beach.

I wake, grappling with this new reality, to find the bed empty beside me. Business has taken Lota away early; I will be alone for the day. A company of parrots raise their pandemonium in the yard and I listen to them argue back and forth before rising to go to my desk. I sit there and mull over how best to get Lota to help Tito and his brother. Perhaps if I spoil her a little, I will get my way; she responds well to devotion. We are a harlequin pair, for sure—Lota is mighty and spontaneous; I am naturally cautious.

Tito is out back, lining up pieces of wood for the seat of the bench; I watch him concentrate and configure. That he was mine in my dream has only increased my affection for him. He purses his lips, frowns, arranges the driftwood in patterns, then changes his mind and moves this piece here, that there. I go to the kitchen and stand by the door.

'*Bom dia*, Tito. Come have some iced maté with me.'

He hesitates but then joins me at the table and sits in silence while I prepare our drinks. Tito holds the straw delicately as he sips; his long fingers are stained and rough. I look at his face; the green eyes, the wet mouth. I still feel the dream-softness of his hair under my hands; I feel like a grandmother, like a mother, like a lover. I smile at Tito.

'Miss?' he says.

'It's nothing, Tito. Nothing at all.'

I put my hand on his arm; he closes his over mine and squeezes. I let my lips fall to his fingers, kiss each one in turn. When I raise my head to gaze into his eyes, they are closed. Tito takes back his hand gently, stands and leaves the kitchen for the yard.

I put on a jazz record and prepare a supper of beans and rice with shortbread to follow. The candles I have placed here and there cast their cheery gloom. Lota comes in, all nerves, all light, chattering about what she has done for me, what she has done for Tito. I go to speak and she shushes me; she needs to get her words out before I can say a thing.

'I've found a position for him, with my old friend Gabriela in Petrópolis,' she says. 'She will be patient with Tito, being an idler herself. There is a small house on her land; he and his brother can live there.' She kisses my cheek. 'And when we build *our* house above Petrópolis, at Samambaia, maybe he can come work for us. There now, Cookie. I hope you are pleased.' She stands and smiles, triumphant.

I take Lota in my arms just as a samba rhythm bursts from the record player; I spin her out in front of me and make windmills of my arms. Lota laughs and does the same. I dip my knees and she follows me. We shimmy around each other and kick our legs. Later, in our bed, I cup her small breasts in my hands and kiss her neck. Lota has a special heat; she is warm as Rio, warm as Paris, warm as Great Village on a high summer Sunday.

Tito and his brother come to say goodbye. They are polished and quiet in neat white shirts, alike despite the brother's rolling eyes, his too-small head. Tito holds his brother's hand, anchoring him to his side. Lota will drive them to the train and they will travel on alone to Petrópolis.

'I will miss you, Tito da Silva,' I say. 'I will miss your sweet face. Thank you for my bench. For everything.'

He nods and holds out his hand to me; lying in his palm is a piece of green sea-glass, the match for the one I found on the beach. I take it from him and close my fist around it. I embrace Tito quickly and his brother lets out a raucous squeal of delight.

When they are gone, I go to the dish on my desk and take my green sea-glass from it. I pop it and the piece Tito gifted me into the breast pocket of my shirt. Now I carry Tito's eyes with me everywhere and my heart knocks against them in an eternal, maternal waltz: *babumf, babumf, babumf.*

During the Russian Blizzard

Mary O'Donoghue

The Ingushetian was a man with skills that flicked out like a Swiss knife. That was my aunt's valediction when he finished coving her guest bedroom ceiling and tiling the rinkydink en-suite. She wasn't sure if it was Ingushetian or Ingusheti, she said, and she'd hate to be as ignorant as her colleague who referred to Pakestinians and Iranis. Then he fixed a few other things, free gratis he insisted, shaky drawer handles and gutters throttled by leaves. He even lopped a bough or two. They were elbowing menacingly onto the back roof, and in a storm would crush the kitchen, he assured her. I'd seen that kitchen in photos. It was a furlong of chrome and white shutters. She told him she couldn't let go such a capable man. She researched and found the term to be Ingush. She offered to rent him that guest bedroom.

It was all above board, she told me, when I turned up in Boston that September, it was all entirely above board. I was at the kitchen island drinking her tea. My face was a blind oblong on the fridge door. After graduation I'd expected to get a big bite out of life, but nothing big wanted me. Everyone I knew had hied to Australia. I did the books for a ten-seater terroir bistro in Dublin. Its potatoes came from Kildare and somewhere in Mayo there was a pig. It was always about to fold. I went out with the head chef, half-slept a night on the tussocks of his old futon, and decided to take the hoary year out. I bought up for Boston and my aunt's guarantee. Two months fact-finding would get me a job. Besides, she said, there was nowhere better than New England in the fall. We drank from porcelain mugs and she made me take a second French pastry.

The Ingush man was somewhere in the long garden that fell down to the sea. My aunt was a radiographer who'd put her learning and time into work, developing and rising until her nose touched the surface and she was Chief Radiologic Technologist at a hospital where she'd screened, she estimated, some thousands of breasts. One Christmas, three Benedictines, and she told me and my sister big or small they all looked like sliced meat on the photo plate. Carpaccio, she said quietly, then a second time, more slowly, surprised at her description. We looked down and folded our arms charily. She was my father's sister. She had bouts of imperiousness and grand generosity. Largesse arrived during lean college terms. There was repeated advice to never travel the world with boyfriends. We used to feel sure she'd rescue us into a brighter life someday. I suspected she looked in the mirror some days and turned away in disappointment.

His name was Ruslan and he was proud of it, he told me first thing, because it was the name of the best and most peace-keeping president of his country. He met me at the airport, *ADELE FROM AER LINGUS* held across his chest. Shaping up for forty, he was square of face and smooth-haired as a Pantene ad. He smelled of pleasant herbs like sage and lavender. You knew he would do things well and carefully. He cursed once in the snarled airport traffic. He said sorry. I said it was a thing of nothing. He laughed at that, a thing of nothing. I had a happy presentiment he'd start using it and keep using it until it came to annoy me.

We picked up speed on the road to the south shore. I'd been this way once before, two weeks in Cape Cod with a crowd from college, but I'd bypassed my aunt's locale. Now I was curious, impatient even, to see the road and the house and the rooms where she'd always seemed so content. Something rattled under the Honda's ribs. Ruslan said he was deliberately choosing to ignore it. I flicked through the CDs. AC/DC. Bruce Hornsby and the Range. Enya. In an effort to resurrect the banter lost somewhere along Pilgrim's Highway, I said AC/DC were due for a comeback. He said they'd never left, so they were not due for a comeback. He said I was probably too young to have followed their arc.

I asked him if Enya had been big in Ingushetia. He took the CD and looked at it a long while. He probably took the same serious slant to every topic. He probably measured everything with a set-square. His left hand on the wheel was steady and relaxed. Garbed in velvet and peeping like Bambi, Enya was now in his crosshairs. It made me wonder if he'd been a sniper at some stage. He had the look of militia, dark flak zipped under his chin. I couldn't remember if Ingushetia was a warry hotspot. I was suddenly disgusted by how little I knew or cared about world politics. Ruslan would surely be conversant in every Irish pitched battle and failed rising.

He left Enya aside and said he was glad, glad in the cockles of his heart, that such an angel had never made it to his country. He called it a toilet and a cauldron. He pointed out new shingles loosened on a church cupola, trees taken down here and there, all by last week's high wind. He never stopped smiling, right the way to turning up a steep driveway, a house on a hill, my aunt waving us on with a straw hat.

In the first week I drank lots of flavours of tea, hibiscus, Darjeeling, the green leaves my aunt steeped with a virtuous grimace. I put in time on her slim silver laptop, job searches, dating sites. My sister said I should post a profile as soon as I fetched up in Boston. It's what people did, she said, when they moved somewhere new. Hung up their clothes, sorted their money, and gave themselves a nickname, some outdoor pursuits, and the best smile amongst all their photos. No convert like my zealous sister, who met her fiancé across a speed-dating table in Ringsend. I perused profiles. Grinning, tanned and hopeful, they made me nostalgic for the scruffy Lebanese chef.

I replied to an ad for an entry-level accounts receivable analyst. I got told I was too qualified. I answered an ad for a bookkeeper. Growing firms wanted comptrollers! the ad said. A Cambridge start-up called me for an interview. An hour on the line ended in a vague tip-off about another start-up that might be willing to orchestrate the visa they said I'd need, but it was a long shot, because nobody wanted to pay for a visa in the tight economy.

I took a phone interview for weekend job. Tutor wanted, College Student. Accounting was his nemesis, he said, but he needed it to become an entrepreneur. He had big plans, he said, he saw opportunity everywhere. We agreed to start the following week, three hours on Saturdays, two on Sundays if they were needed for impending exams. His mother telephoned to cancel. She was concerned my Irish training wouldn't transfer. No hard feelings, she assured me. None, I said. I postponed the job search and committed myself to self-improvement.

I researched Ingushetia. I studied its history of upheaval. It rose against Russia, against Communists, against Northern Ossetia, and lately there was trouble biting round the border with Chechnya. Suicide bombings, high-profile murders and kidnappings. Years ago they had a beautiful female sniper who had never been captured. Everything from its ancient three-handled pots to all the boxers and wrestlers it claimed as famous people made me sad not to have known Ingushetia sooner. An elderly woman sat with me in the small library. Together we ticked book after book for interlibrary loan. A lot of them had Ingushetia nested in studies of Russia and Chechnya. Many titles were in the Ingush language, parades of vowels umbrellaed by long accent marks.

I settled on an English book about counterinsurgency, disappeared persons and human rights. The librarian said it would take ten days. She ran after me with another reference, a John le Carré spy thriller containing an Ingush renegade, and the library had it. I went home with the paperback. A man's silhouette stood in a door looking out on rocky escarpments. The sky was crimson melting to pink. It looked pulpy and compelling.

I fixed on the climate as a question for Ruslan. He reported it as summer beauty, sometimes brutal in winter. His father used to say, and he pardoned himself for relaying it, a person put their balls in a lunchbox in the freezer or they let January take them. I was sitting on the back deck watching a wasp disco round his arm. He was putting a new handrail on the steps and the deck. My aunt was in the rose bushes. Below the rose bushes the sea slurred and intimated. It was evening, the last Saturday in October. A dead blow hammer, Ruslan had told me proudly. Filled with lead shot, it struck hard and heavy but didn't mar the surface surrounding the nail. A beautiful idea, he said.

Earlier that morning he had assembled a new bed in his room. He was all for slats, he said, instead of the base they call boxspring, because slats kept a bed cool, and they looked cool in addition. His bedroom was at the back of the house. A mini-foyer, with a one-drawer desk and a mirror, separated it from the kitchen. When Ruslan was finished, my aunt made the bed with new sheets, also cool. I helped her smooth corners and tuck under. I wanted to press my face into the waffle pattern. Then lunch was made around me at the island. Shrimp asleep on spinach leaves. Ruslan knew precisely when to fluff the cous-cous. My aunt suggested opening a bottle, just for the nice day that was in it. Ruslan took only half a glass. He had bookshelves to assemble. Allen wrenches dangled like sycamore keys from his thumb. My aunt offered to drop me to the train into Boston.

The train was full of Saturday spiritedness. Young parents held children to them and asked enthusiastic questions about what they might see at the aquarium. Did they think there would be a. Who was looking forward to the. Strangers talked about the weather. Two backpackers were told they'd certainly picked their dates. A tropical storm was brewing out there, said an old man, and he waved his hand behind his head as if the sea were in the window. Another man joined in to say he'd heard it all before, it always got downgraded, it was part of weather porn to keep everyone in a state of high anticipation. He goggled his eyes like he'd just witnessed something stunningly wicked on a screen. He patted the backpackers on their JanSports and told them to have a good one and not let the begrudgers grind them down.

I held on to his bonhomie when I reached downtown. I treated myself to a lipstick at Macy's, fajitas from Fajitas & 'Rita's, and a book about Jackie Kennedy's clothes from a cart in the breezy, brick-walled yard of a bookshop. A man asked if he could take my photo while I was browsing the carts. He said it was because I looked so absorbed, and he needed that look for a photo. I said yes. Then I hurried for the street, sharply lonely and disappointed in myself at having been found absorbed.

My sister once tromped in on her best friend's parents. To all intents and everyone's purposes, the girls had set out for the beach at Liscannor. Something was forgotten, a magazine, goggles, and then the scoot back to the hotel. Rooms with connecting doors. She says they were in her sights before she took it all in. There followed a long evening, dinner at different times, skulking, nothing said to her best friend. But I tugged the details from her like a tapeworm. His hairy back. Soles blacked from sandals. The gentleness and how everything was strangely, wrongly, accompanied by her best friend's mother's caterwauls. In college there was the obligatory walk-in or being walked-in-on.

And there was my aunt, hoiked up on the island. Her legs were slung over Ruslan's shoulders. My aunt had good legs, lean from walking and cycling. Always a little bit tanned. Ruslan was truffling between them. His feet stood one in front of the other. In the race blocks. His hands gripped the brink of the island. He was still in his clothes. Jeans and a navy-blue shirt. The shirt was only a bit slackened, as if my aunt had given up bothering to untuck him and rushed instead to her own skin. I saw them from the French doors. There was no sound. I stepped back and down the steps. I hugged the hedge until I reached the rose bushes. The pink ones were blowsy, ready to be snipped. I took my aunt's private path to the beach. I toed dead crabs and swore at a seagull. The Atlantic didn't give a damn.

That evening Ruslan finished the handrail and grilled trout for dinner. My aunt read aloud a *Daily Mail* story about a boy who'd pretended to be the dead son of a rich family. Ruslan said the family must've known all along. They were desperate to have their son restored to them. Any son would do. He spoke with the same concentration and curiosity that went into cooking the trout, the capers and sliced lemons stuffed in the belly. A young policeman, his cousin, had been killed in Ingushetia, he told us. Hundreds of policemen were being killed by Islamist militants at that time, and his cousin was killed by four bullets. He said his aunt and uncle took in another cousin and named him after their son. They gave everything to that boy, Ruslan said, and he used it all for drugs. Now they were trying to find him in the streets of Magas. They wouldn't stop until they came upon him, Ruslan knew, because that was the kind of people they were.

We read about bad weather on the way. My aunt brought armagnac in tiny glasses. Istanbul, she said, flicking her nail at their gold lace collars. Ruslan went to his room for Skype. His sister, in California. A research assistant, he said proudly. A team making headway into motor neurone disease. The door was shut when I passed by. I wondered if my aunt thought wife, thought children, but refused to pay it mind.

On that Sunday morning I asked Ruslan to tell me more about that cousin of his shot by the police. He said there wasn't much more to tell about him, except that he had lived one neighborhood away from his parents and been a good young man and a large crowd of friends cried at his burial. They were all like him, tall and sad and handsome. He said there usually wasn't much to tell when someone had been good and kind all their life. They left a light mark.

I asked him to tell me about the bad one. The imposter. Ruslan was punching keys on his new mobile phone. He set it on the island by his coffee mug. He braided his fingers and set his chin on them and looked at me levelly. Why, he wondered, was I interested in that chap. Ruslan was given to Britishisms, and they came out when he was at his most serious. Gosh. A bitter pill. Agog. Tight as newts, he said of drunk roarers on the beach. I pictured a small musty bedroom, teenage posters, a single shelf stacked and bowed by Jeeves and Bertie. I told him I was fascinated by charlatans. The Pan-Am pilot and the Six Degrees chap. Ripley. Ruslan maintained his gaze and said there was nothing interesting about straw men. He told me I should turn my attentions to real people, their real accomplishments. As with carpentry, he had a way of fixing his final point so it couldn't be tested. I should get out and about more, he said, meet a nice Boston boy or a Harvard scholar. I should enjoy the freedom before I started working again.

It was the working again that vexed me. He thought I was living off the fat of my aunt's coastal home, then, and from the stock of her fridge and the quilted toilet tissue printed with daisies. Since I'd been there Ruslan had gone to work each morning in a small blue van. My aunt slipped from the house before dawn, quiet as a black-op. He lingered over coffee, the newspaper, email. We passed things to one another, milk, butter. We were as wordless as a long-term relationship. He shaved after breakfast, waved from the van before it rafted downhill. But for all I knew he played Keno all day. I'd seen those lost souls when I passed by bars and coffee shops. Old men for whom the counter was home, and the screen of jinking numbers. He rarely came home before my aunt, and he always looked as though he had done a day's work but found time to smooth himself out, because that was the kind of man he was, because those were the standards he held to.

Sunday evening and my aunt went out to meet her friends. They congregated every week, but this week everyone was summoned in special honour of the hurricane. Sandy had gathered strength and was bowling for the east coast. They said it now had an eye. It might not hit until Tuesday morning. It might not hit at all. I fell in love with the word landfall. My aunt threw it to one of the friends, said she'd be making landfall at the restaurant round eight. She left a scarf of perfume in the air. Ruslan watched her from the porch, shouted he would tie back the trellis just in case Sandy showed up overnight. She shouted back not to wait up, she might even stay over at Suze's. There were cucumbers growing on the trellis, he told me, a new venture on her part, and what rotten luck to have them destroyed.

As soon as he got to work I asked him about the civil war in Ingushetia.

I sat in a garden chair, thick cotton and wood like a film director's. Had he been involved in any way. No, he said. And yes. Because you had to be involved in a country that small. You couldn't dodge involvement. He cut and tied thread as he spoke. He said I must mean killing. Which he didn't. But he gave money and the use of a shed to two of the rebels. One of them was shot dead within a month of the war. He knew the cousin of a suicide bomber. He said he was glad I called it a civil war, because so many referred to it as an uprising. They got that bit between their teeth, he said, and they wouldn't give the country its war.

The sky was ragged and turning for night. Ruslan stopped finicking with the trellis. He sat in the chair across from mine. He was in angry torrent about uprisings and the Arab Spring and his own Ingushetia ignored. He knew when I stopped listening. He must be boring me stiff, he said, he must have mistaken my interest. It happened to him a great deal. He would one day learn to keep mum. He sat back dejected. His chair creaked and the cotton looked unsafe beneath him.

I'd gone into the garden without underwear. Under shorts I was bare and open. It wasn't that I wanted him to intuit it. It was enough for me to know, all through the sermon about Ingushetia overlooked in the grand scheme of the world. I left my seat and walked to his. I took his hand. It was poorly done, a hand sent up a shorts-leg. I had to jemmy things along. He looked upset at where he was drawn. He said it was a mistake on my part and I would regret it. He said he'd done his level-best to avoid any such thing. Even the top of his head felt melancholy when I kissed it.

We stayed there a while. His hand deliberated and did its job until I fawned on his shoulder. He said we should call it a night. He smoothed my shorts and walked me to the French doors. He went back to tying the trellis. I heard him secure the whole thing to the fence. Short dull thuds like sounds inside a box. Later I heard my aunt's car take the hill. Then a low burr of kitchen chat. Then doors. Later still I strained to hear slats trying to be quiet.

In the early hours of Monday he went about battening the house. The forecast was deadly serious. By then the President had declared an emergency. My aunt conscripted me to make leek soup and a lamb stew before the power went out. She was sick of news-talk about hunkering down, but still we should be prepared. We watched walls of waves on other coasts. Window by window, Ruslan hammered boards to the back of the house. We watched the sea rush under homes on stilts. We watched people Ruslan called bloody fools tying themselves to piers just to say they'd weathered Sandy. One man screamed into the camera. He wasn't going to let that bitch take him alive!

The kitchen was dull like a cellar. Four triangles of light came through the French doors. Ruslan hadn't enough timber to board them fully, so he made an X and said it should hold. The power stayed on. The lights gave one long hiccup in the late afternoon, that was all. I called my sister and mother. They were full of terminology like batter and storm surge from the nine o'clock news. I told them everything was grand, that Ruslan had storm-proofed the house. When they asked who that was, to say that name again, I told them I had to go.

My aunt and Ruslan went to bed for the storm. They tried to behave like it wasn't inevitable. She said she should get through a backlog of emails, maybe hem the new curtains, now that she had this free time. He went in and out of his quarters, sometimes closing the door and speaking to the Skype entity. It might have been the Skype entity that set my aunt drifting from her laptop to the coffee machine and back, then from the coffee machine to his door with a thick blue mug. The door closed behind her. I couldn't tell if she'd closed it or he.

I poured coffee into a mug that said Floating Hospital. I sat at my aunt's screen and went through the open tabs. Holiday homes in Croatia. Her credit card bill, payment accepted. *Marie Claire*'s advice on how to maximise one's best feature. My aunt was vain about her hair. I could tell by the way she tossed it or crossly ponytailed it in one hand as though about to chop it off, then dropped it on one shoulder, all forgiven. She had an abundance of hair, it's true, and it held on to its russet tones somehow. I imagined Ruslan liked to drag his big hands through it. I left the laptop for upstairs and I ran myself a bath and I looked for parts of myself. I made a little noise, my mouth pressed to the high bath wall. They wouldn't have heard, all the way down there, far inside the din they were making and trying to cover up.

He was probably a terrorist in Ingushetia, or at least a thug, and she probably knew. He was probably married, with a gang of stolid dark-haired kids. But like my granduncle who willed his home to a younger woman, the painter from Sussex, and caused all manner of acrimony, it didn't really matter when that stranger from somewhere, wherever, put in front of you what you so badly wanted all along.

My aunt stayed cooped up with Ruslan all day long. I got nauseous from soup and stew. I made popcorn for watching television. Now all the talk was about high tide. Someone said the worst was yet to come. The ominous phrase caught on, and someone said it every ten minutes. I turned on the radio, and its people chirped about high tide too. They sounded ebullient, those radio people, bright and excited about the worst that was coming. They'd been the same that morning, telling one another what they'd made for the freezer and how excited their children were to have a day off. They seemed happier chatting with one another than addressing a listenership. A buoy off Cuttyhunk Island recorded wind speeds of eighty-three miles an hour. I said the name Cuttyhunk over and over. I found that it was south, near Martha's Vineyard. I researched wind speed. Anything above sixty-four counted as a hurricane. At sea, the air filled with foam and waves topped forty-five feet. Cuttyhunk saw it all.

I thought to go out and see the fuss. I wanted to slip down past the rose bushes and find a whole sea turned white. From a triangle of French door I saw the rose bushes flattened like horses had galloped through. Wind was all around the house, and rain. I'd heard things flung, paint cans, branches, but still nothing out there seemed perilous. The back door was a problem, all those battens fixed in place by the dead blow hammer. I'd have to go out by the sheltered front and press myself along the walls until I got to the back of the house. The college crowd who went to Australia posted photos of mammoth surfing waves before they got sixty-hour-week jobs. They commented on one another's photos, phrases like hot shit, shit hot, holy shit, no shit. I wanted to stand buffeted by whatever shit hit Cuttyhunk, just to film it, just to put it up for all to see.

It didn't come to that. I was buttoning my phone into a coat pocket when my aunt made a showing. She wore black silk, a cami and panties edged in lace. Her face was miserable in segments, a downcast eye, a line notched more deeply between her nose and mouth. One of her cheeks was red, like she'd been lying on that one all day long. She wasn't alarmed to be caught out. Behind her Ruslan's bedroom door was open a sliver.

In spite of being brought low, she was candid. The rest of the night would only work, she said, if I joined. It was Ruslan's suggestion. He wasn't like that, she said, only it was something he'd seen years ago in a film. It might have been Russian. There was a blizzard. A hotel was cut off from the world. A room where a lonely man had gone to drink and coke himself to death. He was joined by two strangers. They knocked at the connecting door and slipped into his room and they all spent the storm together. When the snow subsided, everyone in the hotel was executed, but that was beside the point, according to Ruslan. By then I was sitting on the chair next to his bed. The room smelled metallic and soupy. My aunt was cross-kneed at the bed's edge. She looked bored and a touch embarrassed by Ruslan's speech. His eyes were large on something in another dim bedroom. He wore a pale blue T-shirt and tight black boxers. He couldn't remember why everyone in the hotel was gunned down. It was a Russian film, after all, and he knew Russia for indiscriminate violent happenings and thoroughly bad lots. But the film's ending was a puff of smoke, he said, a bagatelle compared to the tenderness of those women. They lay either side of that man and comforted him.

The scene felt familiar. I'd seen something like it, minus the massacre. In the scene nothing happened except that a solitary man was kept warm. He was lonely for a wife and a child. Or for a dead wife and a dead child. He was an emigrant who could never return home because everyone there awaited success and all he had was fiasco and debt. Or who'd burned all his bridges after some bad thing done years before. I tried to remember that solitary man's back story. The en suite gargled. High tide, dark water backing up the gulley traps and pipes. My aunt's hand tapped my elbow like a soft okay. She was behind Ruslan's back, her arm enclosing his chest. I was in front, held back from the bed's edge by Ruslan's arm. I was still in my hoodie and jeans. Soon a hand might come pecking for buttons. I hadn't even taken off my boots.

I dozed in and out. The pillow was plump and sweetly scented, as if he'd been breathing his fruit tobacco into it. I tried to get back to that film. In his film things must've gone on. In mine, nothing but a hand held, maybe a calming word. The bath hawked and spat. My aunt breathed steadily enough to be asleep. I waited for the moment I'd know what happened during the Russian blizzard.

Japanese Row

Aiden O'Reilly

I would feel the faint warmth from her glazed parted lips as she holds my arm in hers, and I would slip it lightly through, up to the elbow, then my hand against her lower ribs, her fingers on my shoulder, to steady or resist, and my hand curled round to the tense bow of her back. And then she would turn to face me, my hands curved round her waist, fingers shifting pressure on her hips, her chin jutting onto my collarbone. I would know how to appreciate this, and not grasp her or squeeze her breasts. Anyone else would look at her and might as well be looking at a city sycamore. I look and think: That's nice, a well-turned ankle, an interesting arched eyebrow, a nice way to fill the space inside a skirt.

Even with the fairest of them I do not lose composure. I'm quick off the mark with some ready wit to let them see I'm no Quasimodo with the manners of a dog. There's one just past the steps to the maternity clinic, another oasis of contentment and reprise. I've spent many hours there on those broad well-swept steps. But she can't be seen from there, she's further on, on the side wall of the tenement building. She sits there looking seraphically at her toes—each toe a little darling bud. I would know the measure of their soft resilience. She white-gazes at her toes; she can just see them over her knees. With her the feet are the window to the soul. Each part of her is sufficient in itself to look at—the round knees, the line of the chin, the nose a delicate shellfish. The larger curves give me a feeling of fullness. It's a pleasant sense of solidity. When I look at her back curved and her knees drawn up I feel a fluid strength.

*

No one else would have dared address her. No one else would have smiled first at her. The bus conductor was instantly at a loss, it was plain as day, but he has learned in his job how to pretend not to see. Others find it harder. But I had acquired that confidence from my bravery and the purity of my vision. And because I can already feel how her underarms might be to touch.

I stood up from the bus-stop bench where I'd been warming myself since dawn and said, This is the way to the school you are looking for. She was holding a folder with the bands of blue and the crest on it. Behind me Mallin doubled over and cackled. His laugh-wrinkles fissured his weathered face.

—You won't find it so easily, I explained, everyone who looks for it comes back this way after an hour of searching. She held me in her suspicious regard and I, not down-faced, held her in mine.

—I'll walk you there. It's no trouble, I'll carry that dunnage.

She edged her bag away from me with her foot and then picked it up. She took a few tentative steps towards the crossroads.

—It's all right. This direction.

I darted in front of her. She looked about her at the road signs and took a few steps in the same direction, as though she reached this decision with no regard to me. I kept ahead of her then, across the intersection and down the so-called industrial road. She kept a strict five paces behind. Looking about her at the road signs and door numbers.

—Is it far?

At last she had given over the pretence that by pure chance we just happened to be going the same direction.

—Not two minutes, but it might as well be an hour, I answered.

—Why an hour? How far is it could you tell me?

Anxious voice now.

—It's an hour if you don't know the way. But it's two minutes the quick way.

Her hip bones pushed out the taut fabric of her dress so a crease appeared first one way then the other, switching to and fro. If the curve of the waist is beautiful, the face will be beautiful too. One glimpse of an ankle indicates the whole. A blur between two passing lorries is enough. Even through watery eyes, dust-blinded and sun-scarred, the way they move, once you're attuned to it. A shadow on the ground is often sufficient. Later I can confirm the first glimpse at leisure. It's unfair really, that beauty is not dispensed in parts. They even smell nicer.

Sometimes even the word 'she' dropped by a stranger in passing sets me in a receptive mind. 'She' is a word full of itself.

I listened gratefully to her footsteps behind me. Click clack click clack.

These are my guardians, these pretty pretty ones with pneumatic surfaces. When I concentrate on them I feel I can do no evil. I immerse myself in every glossy image, every sky-wide billboard. I would know exactly what to say to them. Why are there none like these on the streets and in the queues? Only the most exquisite, the most spiritual beauties appear on these glossy pages. Their beauty pierces me. In this it does not lie. There is no faking, though all the world sets its value at nil. Beauty reigns.

Full curves fill with osmotic pressure. The tenderiser is a shaved triangle.

We passed the empty storage bay where I spent most of '98. On no-man's land I can at last feel at ease. It may be a bus stop. It may be the wind-sheltered side of a warehouse. Here I can breathe. Here a thought is my thought, I owe nothing and am owed nothing.

There is also Waldamir, who once ice-skated to the provincial championships and carved furniture from rosewood for his mother. There is Bull, who could never get away in time. There is Alex, who knew the insides of valve radios like the faces of old friends. I have seen him pull an old Robertson's out of a skip and croon over it, taking the valves out one by one and shaking them close to his ear, sleeping with it for several nights running until at last it went missing on a night of special brew.

They have great pity for me because I cannot drink enough: it disagrees with my stomach. Once in a while I clear out the system with a bottle of vodka. I sweat my pores dry without feeling the least bit more jolly. Then they cheer me and become better friends. It's not my fault I can't keep up the pace. They're annoying and repetitive when they're drunk. And though the stuff helps them sleep soundly, the next day they'll have muscle cramps. But they know that too.

She was not perfect, my elegant teacher. The skin below her eyes had a smooth puffy look to it: too much cream, too many worries. A face needs something startlingly attractive about it to get away with black hair. Eyes that bore in and core out. You can tell to the nearest millimetre what they're looking at. Lips that tremble exposing water-painted teeth. She didn't have that, but she had a fine look of nakedness about her. Her bare shoulder blades, the soft collagen and blue-tinged tracery of her neck, a little hollow at the base of her throat, the pallor of skin unused to the light. She was beginning to draw me in.

—A teacher is it you are?

—Yes, she said shortly. Again she consulted her folder and looked at the squat white box houses. Not for nothing do we call it Japanese Row.

—We should be almost there by now.

—Indeed we are. Knox Road, she said, leads off the end of this.

My knowledge reassured her. She even attempted the ghost of a smile. My dear, why do you fret yourself searching for the right thing to do? What I appreciate is naked personalities. Continue to treat me as a dog if you wish, only let it be from the heart.

The school at last. Not mine, though I remember. I was the silent one in class, and when I spoke the sound seemed to emanate from the centre of the room. This annoyed the teachers and gave me a lone-ranger status in the schoolyard microcosm. I had no jokes, I was no good at sport, but I could drive the teachers to insanity. I kept it up for six years. After school I didn't train to be a commis chef. The benches are full of those who once trained as commis chefs. I don't even know what the word commis means. I trained as a photo-lab assistant. At that time my fatal weakness appeared.

Eight or ten or twelve years after leaving school, in some local pub with chance friends I would mention how old Leary had once called me a reprobate; O'Reagan the reprobate, he called me.

—Remember that time he put Stokes up at the top of the class and told us he has an excuse because he comes from a troubled family? Leary was such a fascist hypocrite. And remember when he shouted at Lysaght, stop masticating. And Lysaght pulled his hands out of his pockets like he was bitten?

Their faces took on pained expressions and they exchanged

knowing glances. Oh excuse me, I've made a bloomer. What taboo have I broken? Whose toes have I stepped on? I dug up the past, that's what. We're all so mature now. Beyond it all. We have our own lives now.

—What you talking about, O'Reagan? said one of them. This is 19__ (any year later than 1988). Okay, it might be funny to mention if we just met after twenty years, but we meet each other every week. Come on, times have changed.

—Did I tell this story before? I asked, thinking perhaps I might have told it a few nights before.

—No, maybe not exactly that one. But you're always going on about school and things that are just over and done with... and we've moved on.

He frowned, puzzling over how to express just precisely what it was that annoyed him so much. But I knew what it was. The schoolyard haunts us. We pretend we have escaped it. But it is ever there. The laughing scorning voices we left under a corrugated roof.

I never grasped that handy trick of letting time heal all wounds. Never copped that I'm supposed to smirk indulgently at all that was real to me as a teenager. I have remained ever and the same. I stuck to my guns, and didn't do the memory wash.

—Why school? Why can't we talk about something more recent? We didn't have a clue back then.

And this from someone who is only a bus driver. What has he learned in the intervening fifteen years? How not to blush. What wisdom does he have? The successful transference of habit. With me, for better or for worse, the imprinting failed. I was left unguided. I failed to follow mamma duck's waddling arse and went my own way.

That bus driver was Gilchrist. He was the last to let me go when I cut the ropes. The last to speak to me like we used to in the old days. We sat in a huge tin shed with our backs against enormous rolls of paper. A bare light bulb burned dully overhead. A bag of sugar and loose teabags lay across a rack of fuses. Was this the antechamber to normality? Was this my last chance?

—When I lost my driver's job I was at a loss too. But see! I picked up a handy number here. You can do the same. I can have a word with the boss. Regular working hours will get you back in form.

He spoke convincingly, he really wanted to help. In a few words he sketched out his plans for me. Sit there night after night among the rows and rows of paper, skip with the wage cheque down to the bank, and I'd soon be back in the ranks. Meeting friends and inviting people home for dinner to a one-bedroom apartment in Drumcondra. I laughed out loud. It was sad to disappoint him. He really and truly believed salvation lay in a warehouse job. I cherish him for that. Though he is in league with powerful forces, I cherish him.

And I would have taken that job too, it was that close, but the gods interceded and the bus broke down on the way to the interview. I never rang them back.

My little darling, do you know who made you? Gave you your accents and your graceful figure? That well-bred walk and those pretty shoes? That nice clean smell? Who was it?

—You don't really have to help me, she said. She has a nice toothsome way of pronouncing her 't's. We were approaching the caretaker's door.

—I've nothing better to do. There's no one knows the area as well as me. Doesn't look like there's anybody here, does it? You can wait in the library. It's only two roads away. Give it one more buzz, he might be on out the back.

Her mouth was stretched thin as she rang a second time.

—No, I can't wait. It might be closed for the day.

She crouched to push a folder through the low letter box. At the level of my knees. I could see how her bra fell forward from her breasts.

—You know I could roll you over on your back now and see your panties under that skirt, I said.

She sprang up.

—You think I didn't think of it? I asked surprised. She edged around me clutching her remaining folders to her breasts.

—Help, she shouted half-heartedly, then, a little more reasonably, *Go away*.

She backed off fluttering. Am I a tame puppy who never thinks to bite? Is thought a crime? But she's a charming butterfly who can't behave any other way. She's no more or no less than what she was brought up to be. Make no surprising moves. Say the right things. Act relaxed, and she'll flutter onto the palm of your hand. Go away, you, you more than half a mechanism. Watching you is like watching a drowning puppy.

These in the white-walled houses would be nothing without their mummy and daddy and hurry hurry. I owe nothing, I'll say it again. Here where I am are made the silent decisions that keep them inside of love. I am a harmless old beggar, fuck. Or do you think less of me because I stop short of the deed?

I ambled back to the bus-stop corner. Mallin doubled over and cackled with laughter. He slapped his thighs and pointed frantically at a departing bus.

—Pipe down, or I'll give you a crack across the jaw, you ignorant leech, I said.

All Day and All of the Night

Sean O'Reilly

Exactly a month after Siobhan had been told by a good friend of ours that I was having an affair with a leggy flat-chested doe-eyed singer, I was allowed to move back into the house. In the meantime, I'd been staying at my sister's, on a mattress in the games room, lying awake all night with the French doors open, listening to the birds in the trees along the river, big sounding creatures I'd never heard before. It was the beginning of another summer. When word came through that I'd been granted a reprieve and could go home, my sister Melissa gave me a lift with my gear, which amounted to one bag and my guitar. I suppose I was nervous as hell, my head busy rehearsing all the things I would need to say and do to save my marriage because when the car stopped, I jumped straight out, went to the boot for my stuff and had the guitar on my shoulder before I realised we were actually parked on the street right outside the house we had grown up in.

Would you look at the state of it? Melissa said when I sat back in. Look at the roof. Look at that letterbox—you wouldn't put a bloody court summons through it. And those are the very same curtains if you ask me. They are.

Our curtains were green, I told her. Big long pale green velvet things. Wee Auntie Lou made them. I remember having to go out to the back shed to get the step ladders to put them up. And remember how scared I was of the back shed?

You were scared of your own shadow most of the time. You were. Melissa lit up a cigarette, holding it out the open window. The houses seemed to have shrunk and the street was as narrow as a country lane. Melissa was parked well up on the pavement. We stared uneasily at our old front door like we were waiting to see ourselves come charging out. It was tilled. No number on it now. A saucer on the window ledge. Melissa ditched her smoke and began her spiel: Listen to me, Marc, okay. I just want to say this one thing more to you and that's all. You're doing the right thing. You are. I know I've said that already but we all think it, all of us, the entire family... but I just wanted to say this one thing more to you, just between me and you so don't take my head off. But if you need anything, a loan of any money or anything, then you should just ask okay. It's just money. Don't be bottling it all up okay. You see what happens when you do? Don't be driving yourself mad with worry. You were always so useless at lying anyway.

There was a strange thump on the car's back window. A young woman who couldn't get by along the pavement with her pram the way we were parked. The child started crying, screaming. Do you hear me, Marc? Melissa said, starting the engine, paying the young mother no mind. She had steered the pram into the road, giving us a die-slow look through the glass as she passed.

Graham will divorce you if he catches you smoking again, was all I could manage. There were many other ways I could have replied, and not all of them would have been kind or grateful for the offer of money but Melissa had taken me in for the last month, fed and watered me, kept the wine flowing and stayed up late with me, even got out her old fiddle one night. Then again, it was around her dinner table, Melissa presiding, that the rest of the family gathered to work out what was to be done with me, all eight of them rolling up in the driveway after work and before lunchtime at the weekends. It was an official family crisis. My marriage needed to be saved. Melissa would report back on her conversations with Siobhan, the shrewd delicate negotiations, and it would be agreed by a vote what my next step should be. And it was Melissa who went to see Greta. Cornered the warbling hippy home-wrecker after a gig, threw the bus timetable for Dundalk at her, as I found out later.

Back home again, still unpacked, and sitting at the kitchen table with Siobhan after our dinner, it was me who brought up the idea of getting out of town for the weekend, to do whatever talking we needed to do down the road in Inishowen. Siobhan's people owned a place down there, right on the coast. Siobhan had bought them out a few years back. We had put a lot of work into it since. Siobhan loved the time away, from the city, from me too, I suppose. Anyway, she laughed off the suggestion to start with, saying, You hate it down there sure. You never know what to do with yourself. No? When was the last time then? You haven't been down there since around last Christmas and that, which didn't escape my attention, was only because we brought other people with us. All I have to do is mention Inishowen and a look of dread appears on your face. Sure, you haven't even seen who moved into the big house in front of us, the big house you gave out about for to your friends blocking our view and then never mentioned again since. Strange, don't you think? Well, there's people moved in now full-time. Year round I mean. A middle-aged couple with their children. He's some hotshot accountant. Or he was.

The weekends are tricky you know, I said.

Really? Why's that I wonder? She looked at me, her head to the side, suffering in one eye, anger in the other, and then she let me off the hook with, Well, the weekends are all I have, Marc. Will you please try to get that into your thick skull for me? Will you? Whether you like it or not. And it's not going to change either.

No doubt about it, Siobhan had studied and worked hard since we had made the move home from London. A full-blown cliché like it sounds, she stopped to talk to me one Mayday morning when I was picking my way through an old Kinks' floor-filler on the steps of a squat near Holloway prison. She'd heard the accent. She came in for a cup of tea. She was easy with everybody. She left for the tube and came back again ten minutes later. She stayed the night. And now she was a solicitor. Right from the start, she said she felt aimless in London, bored, guilty, and she wanted to go home to try to put something back in, to do some good. She persuaded me that it would help my song-writing. Get back to the source, she'd plead with me and soon enough it was the mantra I began to use on myself. Less than a year after meeting her, we were driving up through England and Scotland to the Stranraer ferry with all our possessions, most of them hers, in a car that wouldn't start again when it was time to drive off at Larne. People got jumpy, they thought it was a bomb, the cops arrived. Siobhan and I were questioned for hours. She threw away a lot of her clothes afterwards.

Back at the kitchen table, I took hold of my wife's hand and ran my thumb in circles around the underside of her wrist, round and round over those prominent branching blue veins. Come on, Siobhan. It'd be good for us. Sea air. Walks. Your garden. The beach. Swimming. It'd be good for us.

Will it now? Will it really? You who never goes near the water.

I'll be the first in. I'll wear the wetsuit even. Promise. Come on. A change of scene.

Isn't this just typical of you—all this sudden haste? These brief enthusiasms. And then you change your mind at the last minute. She was mocking me, and fairly too, but I could see from the way she was blinking rapidly that she was thinking the idea over.

Friday tomorrow. I can get away by two. But you see, Marc, if you even so much as—

I'll have the car packed by two, I said, my right hand up to God.

It was gone four, and after a stop at the garden centre for a few bags of compost, before we were on the main road out. The traffic was good. The music was good. The weather looked good. Siobhan had had one of her major soap-opera days, the cops had to be called to remove a man who had chained himself to the railings after being barred from seeing his children. Me, I had been sitting around the house, playing old CDs and reading letters I'd sent to my as-then fiancée when she had gone to New York for those last few months of her brother's life. I pulled into the car park of the supermarket just before the euro-zone border and asked her, Remember the thunder and lightning on the drive up from Dublin airport with your brother?

Siobhan looked at me—aghast has to be the only word. An empty expression which filled quickly to the brim with rage. The hackles were up. How…? Why would you even? She couldn't get the words out. Her neck reddened down into her cleavage. I did my best to apologise as we went up and down the aisles of the supermarket, Siobhan acting as if I was invisible which only made me more desperate. I was trying to tell her how great it felt to have her back, that I'd missed her, just like when she came home after nursing her brother. She wouldn't look me in the eyes. With Siobhan, the trick is you leave things well alone. You don't mention the shit unless there's a damn good reason. Otherwise you are being negative. I'd touched one of her sore spots and it would be a while before she'd get over it. People noticed us, me anyway, a man blocking a woman with a trolley in the toiletries section, then the tinned goods. We didn't manage to buy one complete meal. We forgot all the basics. Then she sent me off to buy the alcohol, which I took as a punishment. Siobhan didn't drink much. She didn't like to go beyond two glasses of wine. Buying the hooch alone meant I was entirely responsible, before the fact, for the amount I would drink that weekend. Three bottles of wine I bought. Once we had packed the car, she put out her hand for the keys. I was relegated to the passenger seat.

There was one other thing that happened before we turned off the main road and headed inland. We had forgotten the bottled gas. We pulled into a garage right on the shore of the lough, the summer ferry on its way across to Magilligan. I went in for the gas. As I was waiting for a stoned teenager to open the multiple locks on the cage where they keep the bottles, I noticed Siobhan was out of the car and talking to a man on the forecourt. He was a big guy, darkish, the gentle giant sort, late forties, with a huge Adam's apple. A bag of shopping in one hand and wiping his mouth a lot with the back of the other like somebody had decked him for no reason. Siobhan put out her hand to touch his shoulder and he took a quick step back, nodded in agreement to something and flip-flopped away towards a green Range Rover, spitting on the ground before he got in. Siobhan, hands on hips, stood shaking her head until the big tank roared out across the cattle grid.

Who do you mean? she said when I asked her a few miles down the road.

Was he one of your clients or what? Your man back there with the bad taste in his mouth.

What? She glanced at me, sighing.

I'm only having a laugh, Siobhan. The man you were talking to. You were seen in close dispute in the parish of Moville with an unknown entity. How do you plead?

There was no dispute.

Let's not quibble over words. Will you identify this man for the court or not?

Siobhan flipped down the sun-guard and checked her face in the little mirror. That's Padraig, she said, rubbing balm on her lips. And Padraig is our neighbour.

We turned off the coast road and into the interior while she told me a bit more about him. He'd made a packet during the years they call the boom time for some and lost it all again at the beginning of what they call the recession for all. Millions maybe. It was well known he was in big trouble. The lights were often on in the house all night long. And she had overheard a few big rows. But he was nice, she said, he wasn't the over-privileged sort, he had worked his way up out of nothing, and he doted on his kids. I sang a few lines of 'Luck Be A Lady Tonight' as we slowed for the turn just after O'Doherty's bed and breakfast. Another four kilometers on a road no more than a gulley between hedges and electric fences before we'd get our first sight of the sea.

Siobhan got straight to work in her dungarees on the vegetable garden after we'd settled in. She would be at it for hours so I tried to relax, to do nothing but just be there. It could take a fair while for me to acclimatise. I tuned the old Gibson Hummer, the very same guitar I was playing when I met Siobhan in London, opened a book about the history of the townland, destroyed the homes of so many spiders I felt sick, cleaned the barbecue, tightened the clothes line, and still only forty minutes had passed.

I got back into the rocking chair with the guitar, strumming, listening for a secret between the chords. The main window was a picture of pink-stained sheep in the field and the waves rolling in from the blue fathoms. Along the horizon, the freight tankers like moving targets. A speedboat as well. The sky was nearly pure. And off to the left was the new neighbours' ranch house. The raw concrete back had eight windows. A short busty blonde woman came out the back door with a bag of rubbish. I saw her turn around suddenly and it was because Padraig was in the doorway, speaking to her. She waved the bag in the direction of the wheelie bin. Padraig stepped outside, and approached her with his hand out. He wanted the bag. He was given the bag. He pointed her back inside and she obeyed. I watched him untie the binbag, inspect the contents, close it again and put it in the bin. For another few minutes he stood there looking at his own house, like it was an animal he was going to take on, or a mountain. He cast a long range gob of spit towards a rook on the wall. Then he went back inside his castle.

Siobhan and I sat outside to eat that evening, sheltered by the gable from a wind fresh from the northeast. As the cloud moved in overhead, we ate burgers and I drank some wine. Our conversation was mainly about the house, the many jobs needing to be done. Siobhan wanted to extend the vegetable patch. The ground would have to be turned, the stones picked out by hand. It sounded like a job she might allow me to do. The weekend was already mapped out in her mind. She liked to keep busy, especially in the daytime. Up with the birds and to bed after the evening news. Well, it was her way of getting through and it worked. I said it to her, I love the way you get things done. You just go right at them immediately they appear. You don't put things off the way I do. And that's brilliant.

Maybe, she said. But I'm a bit of a control freak though, aren't I? I am.

I hadn't expected that from her. It was rare to see Siobhan expose her own doubts. I got out of my chair and squatted down in front of her. I took her hands, turned them over and kissed the blue veins. I'm so sorry, I told her. This is all my fault, not yours. Genuinely.

Maybe our lives are going in different directions, Marc?

I don't believe that for a second.

How can you be sure? You've turned into a liar, haven't you? And I've turned into this woman who… I've never felt so on my own before… I never knew this kind of loneliness even existed.

That's why we have to stick together, Siobhan. That's what the world is like. I got it into my head you didn't really need me any more. And that I was holding you back. I wasn't thinking straight.

Am I cold Marc, is that it? I know I'm mad busy and tired to pieces when I get home and just want some peace… but I thought you were happy enough doing your own thing. Your music. The band and all that. Were the signs all there and I just didn't want to see them? Hell, I feel like such an idiot.

We took a walk down to the shore before it got dark. On some stretches of the road we had to run to escape the swarms of insects. The hedges were almost too ripe with berries and flowers and nettles and a hundred different birds shot out of every space singing and whistling and showing off around us. Only the downstairs lights were on as we passed the neighbours' house. All the windows closed and the curtains drawn. The Range Rover out front. I thought it was a bit unusual on a fairish evening to see smoke spraying out of the chimney and I even pointed it out to Siobhan but she was preoccupied with trying to explain to me how the ground had moved under her feet the morning that good friend of ours stormed into her office to tell her what type of man I really was. Farther down the road at the bend, I thought I heard footsteps behind us, someone running, and maybe I did see a shadow crossing the road behind us when I looked back or maybe it was only a fox or a clumsy bird.

The big soup was coming in fast. The water swelled up under the seaweed, throwing the tentacles high between the rocks. Way out on the cliffs the young gulls were playing their bone whistles. Siobhan and I sat in our usual spot on a bed of soft heather on top of a black crag. Crab shells broke under me as I leaned in close to kiss my wife and got the brush off. I need you to understand what it was like, she said, meaning the month we had been separated, how she couldn't get the images out of her head of me and some other woman. She went on to describe the scenes in so much detail even I began to forget they weren't real. I could almost feel them, the wild lovers, hear their salty bodies sliding together. Until they were worn out, their souls, long before their bodies stopped.

Of course, I tried to cut in but Siobhan needed to tell me everything, frame by frame, while the sea bulged and bubbled and burst against the rocks. I wanted to tell her the truth, how nothing had really happened between Greta and me because no matter how hard I tried to put it to the back of my mind, I was just too flooded with guilt about what we were doing. Those orgies of passion my wife was meticulously inventing lacked any resemblance to what had actually gone on. Most nights I saw Greta in her B&B on Spenser Road, sneaking up to the room like a teenager, and lying beside her on the plastic-covered mattress and talking about music and books, her own poetry and anything that entered my head to delay the moment when I would have to prove myself. Talking became a way to avoid touching. Words were there to stave off the other words, the real words. Or to cover over the gaps where there is nothing. But Siobhan didn't want to hear any of that.

One night down here by myself again, guess what I did? she goes to me, biting her lip.

So it was funny then?

Not really.

You don't have to tell me, I say, which brings on a bizarre fit of laughing.

I want to, she says. To tell you... Okay, I'll pull myself together. But again she's laughing and I play the waiting game, watching the bloated seaweed lolling about in the soup.

Finally she tells me, There was this one very bad night, worse than the rest, I felt so poisoned by it all and betrayed and worn out. I dragged myself into bed somehow anyway. And after a while, I got up and opened the window. I lay there just listening to the silence. Not a peep out of the waves or the wind. And there wasn't a car on the road anywhere—you know how you can just about hear them at night? Even those damn gulls were quiet. Just this total silence pouring in through the window and it getting deeper and deeper and deeper. Like I was on a boat and it was sinking.

You like silence, I said and got shushed immediately.

So that's how I must have fallen asleep. Okay? But when I got up in the morning what did I find? The front door was open too.

Fuck, you mean somebody broke in?

Again I seemed to have said the wrong thing. She elbowed me. No. You're not listening to me. It wasn't a break-in, nothing like that. You know as well as I do that I've never left a door open in my life. You know what I'm like about security. I double check everything sure.

There's a first time for everything, I said.

Jesus, Marc, why are you being so...? I didn't forget to lock up. I must have got up in the middle of the night and went down the corridor into the living room and opened it in my sleep. Me. And went back to bed. I've thought about it and thought about it since but I don't remember doing it. But I sort of remember the feeling of doing it. Does that make any sense? The feeling of doing it but not really the act itself. I think it was me, Marc.

Whatever it was about what she was saying, and the waves and the seaweed, and the crab shells and the lights of the freight ships on the horizon, I couldn't take another second of sitting there. The mozzies are eating me alive, I told her and got up. Siobhan told me to go on, said she'd follow me in a few minutes, she just wanted to sit there by herself for a while. I didn't argue with her. I thought nothing of leaving her. I hurried back up the road. Going by the neighbours', I saw a flash of flame in the car. Padraig was having a smoke. It might have been a pipe. The driver's door was open. The house in darkness. I waved to the man but it was too dark to be sure if he returned it. As soon as I got in, I was searching for my phone. I took it back outside to under the oak tree, the only spot where you had a chance of a decent signal, and checked my messages. Three from my sister, and one from Xavier in the band saying we might have a gig at a festival. And one from Greta asking me to meet up with her.

I decided to take a bath. It was an excuse to keep by myself. I'd had my fill of talking for one night. The bath, salmon pink and shallow, a made-for-two jacuzzi. Think of a big shell, an oyster shell maybe from one of those Botticelli paintings the round-breasted goddesses hover above. Siobhan and I had dreamed of spending cold winter nights in the bubbles. The thing arrived wrapped in horse blankets on the back of a lorry from Strangford Lough, three dour midgets in the front cabin. I poured in lots of bath oil, watched the foam expanding, replicating itself without sense. When I opened the window I could see Siobhan and Padraig clearly talking together in the vivid flat light from the car's interior. I shut off the taps, then the light, and waited to hear or not hear what they were saying.

The next morning there was a flower on the pillow.

The simple truth about me that Siobhan would never admit to for her own mysterious reasons was that somehow or other I had basically become a kept man. Siobhan kept the roof over our heads and the kitchen table from losing its purpose. Greta was actually the first person to say it to me. Her and me deep in the gloaming of another one of those off-side palsied bars we had to use to hide ourselves away from scrupulous eyes. Another evening of talking about the band as a means of not talking about anything else. The evening she said to me, I don't think you really want me. The small red ink stain on the hem of her denim skirt. Long dark silky hair getting caught in the corners of her mouth. I think you want to want me but you don't really. After we'd had a few, and I was probably rehashing my theories of what had gone wrong in my life, of what was stopping me making a real go of things, Greta came right out and said I sounded as bitter as a kept man. That's what other people say about you too, she added, taking my hand. We had a bit of an argument about it. I denied it. Refuted it. Annihilated it. Then I sort of broke down. She put her arm around me, whispering,

You're not trapped, Marc, you're free. There's no children involved. You can do what you want. Make music. Just let yourself be free. I hadn't broken down in a long time, not like that, crying in front of somebody. Head in my hands, elbows on the table, and Greta lying across my back, talking through the options. So when I looked up and saw three angels across the table it seemed right, a show of mercy and I bowed my head. Greta did the talking. Three women in angel costumes, wings and wigs and wands and ballerina tutus, collecting money for some addiction centre. How was I to know a good friend of my wife's was among them? A week later, after doing some cute intelligence gathering, the woman's duty was clear to her.

You're what, a kept man? Siobhan frowned like it was old news. I had jumped out of bed that second day and told her I was going to get my act together once and for all. I was sick of feeling ashamed of myself, of holding her back, us. I would wise up and pull my weight and take that offer of guitar teaching in the arts centre. Siobhan seemed more interested in the taste of her coffee. Only a bra on under the dungarees. I stood there in my Sex Pistols boxers.

We're partners, Marc. Partners. Things will work out. Trust me.

It was a gorgeous morning. A warmish breeze cleared the mist from the fields and then the hills behind us. I brought out the old guitar and played a few of her favourite songs while she chopped up the earth. She was in good form. She sang along with me on some of the tunes, shook her booty around to our own Kinks song, and slowly the rocks and stones filled the wheelbarrow.

I was at the back of the house, using the stones to repair the loose sections of the low dry wall. Out of nowhere, a Garda squad car rolled down the lane and parked outside the neighbours'. The blonde woman, the mother, came out and ran towards the car to embrace a boy who got out of the passenger seat. Padraig stood in the doorway with his arm around a teenage girl. I went inside to tell Siobhan. She was flicking through one of her gardening books.

Oh good was all she said.

Oh good what?

They found him. He ran away or something or…

Or what?

Whatever boys do.

When?

She shrugged.

Did he tell you that, Padraig, I mean?

She nodded like it was obvious he had. Then she said, He's done it before loads of times. He's a bit of a handful it seems. Not fitting in and behavioural problems. Rebellious.

Rebellious? The word sounded wrong to me. There should have been a different word. But all I said was, You didn't tell me.

Tell you what?

That some kid was missing.

What are you on about now, Marc? Why the big concern? It'll probably happen again next week. Padraig's got enough to worry about by all accounts. He's lost everything he had. Do you know what that means? Hell, the bank are after the house now too.

I don't care about his bloody house.

What? Why not? No, actually forget it. I don't want to know. And sure they found him now anyway. He was probably in the town somewhere sniffing petrol or whatever they do. You're getting all stroppy about something that didn't even happen. What's the matter with you?

Nothing.

What? Because I didn't tell you, is that it? Did I keep it a secret, is that what you mean? That I lied to you. Huh?

Later on that afternoon, the squad car gone as suddenly as it had appeared, the two of us went for a long walk. I'd fallen asleep on the sofa for a while and woke up groggy and irritable from a bad dream. The road took us high over the ridge and down steeply to a small cove of white sandy beach. It was a small oasis on that hard-hearted coastline. Few people knew about the place. We had it all to ourselves. Siobhan, as per usual, wanted to get into the water straight away but I wasn't bothered. We sat on the sand together for a while, her teasing me about never going in. She stripped down to her black swimsuit and I watched her running down the beach, from the white sand to the wet sticky sand and splashing into the whitest foam and I thought, what the hell is wrong with you kid and stripped off myself. I bombed in after her, bollock-naked as they say. It was freezing but we played about together along the soft ledge where the floor took a nose-dive. I managed to get her swimsuit off, headed in towards the shallows with it in my jaws thinking she was chasing me. She had swam way out instead. She was a strong swimmer. Siobhan swam every morning in the leisure centre and was home before I was awake. I ran up the beach, started getting my clothes on. The wind had lost any warmth. I was bored as soon as I had my shoes on. I was never mad about beaches. The sight of this group of lads with a ball and Frisbee and an icebox of beer must have given me the idea what to do next, where else could it have come from? Because when Siobhan had swam back in and waved to me as a sign to bring her swimsuit down, I waved back to say I was going to join in the football. My wife swam off again. I really didn't know how far I would push it before I gave in and brought the swimsuit down to her, the tiny scrap of sleek black skin. When she came back in again about ten minutes later and waved again, and might have slapped the water in frustration, I decided to make her sweat for another few minutes, just for the laugh. The ball was kicked high and bounced on the wet sand near some driftwood and a crow lifted off. Reluctantly, one of the lads went after the ball. He was taking his time about it. Then he seemed to have stopped dead. Siobhan was coming out of the sea, first topless and now completely naked, and with her head held high she did a stunning walk up the beach towards me. She put out her hand for the swimsuit. The lads cheered.

Siobhan said, And you know what was strange about it, well, unexpected anyway, for most of it I could only see myself from above. If it was exciting for me at all, that was the memorable part of it.

We were on the road back, at the crest of the ridge. We were holding hands.

Even the gulls were cheering, I said.

Seriously, Marc, I was looking down on myself for most of it. You know, I could see every detail close up, every face but it was like an aerial view. And you know what I was thinking as well? About the splitting of the atom. Seriously. All those male scientists. You know, in some ways it actually felt more like a kind of out of body experience than a…

Not for me and the boys it didn't, I said and Siobhan pulled her hand free as though she was angry and marched ahead.

Siobhan?

She stopped, turned around and she was smiling. She was as beautiful as I had ever seen her and as I walked slowly towards her I wished I would never reach her. And when I did finally stop in front of my wife, she put her arms around me and kissed me, deeply too, a very deep and intense and salty one.

I was still feeling the thrill of that kiss hours afterwards. I was outside at the table, footering with some song lyrics in the notebook. Trying to put the warm energy to some good use. Capture the moment. The grace. That was the intention but the dream from earlier kept distracting me and I gave in and thought writing the damn thing down might shift it. How in the dream I'd been watching Siobhan out in the water and a boat comes along and slows down beside her and she is talking to whoever is on board. Then I see her pulled right out of the water like a big fish and the boat speeds off around the headland with her. The beach is empty. Vast. White like a desert. I get the panic, run for ages through hot sand clouds until I see one of those lifeguard towers. A face looks down at me and it's nothing like him but it's Padraig. I try to explain what happened but he is very suspicious of me. He doesn't believe me. Call the police, I shout up to him. He points out at the water and says, The police can't help you out there, lover-boy. His saliva drenches me. Then he wants to know about the boat, what kind it was, and that's where it all becomes unbearable because I can't describe it, I can't find any word other than boat. Just the one word, boat. Boat. Boat. I was trying to write this down, to do it justice when the man in question came walking across the field towards our house, the real Padraig walking through the real pink-dyed sheep who refused to get out of his way. Wearing a suit like he was going to work, and wellies, he was carrying something that might have been a television aerial. I put a stone on top of the notebook to keep the wind from blowing it away and went to meet him at the wall.

She's not in, I said, right at him.

He nodded meekly. A dollop of foam on his earlobe. A whiff of aftershave on the breeze. He was a bad colour. Tired blue eyes that wouldn't meet mine.

She's away to get some seaweed for the garden, I said next, deciding to give him a chance. She lays the stuff down as fertiliser. It's full of minerals, supposedly. I shrugged and rolled my eyes like it was all beyond me, these women and their attachment to their gardens.

I waited for him to join in. What he did was turn towards the shore and say, The sea will have it all back again if we're to believe the environmentalists. It's where we all came from in the first place, supposedly.

Well, we escaped, I said, and science or no science, I'm not going back. I like it up here on terra firma.

It's all about survival, he seemed to agree.

For the laugh I said, I don't know about that. I'm not at all convinced the best are the ones who have survived. The fittest for what anyway? Power and destruction? Greed. Waste. Murder.

He did more of the wise nodding. Somedays, yes, you're right, Marc, it does look like the bad guys have won. You're right. But what is it they want in the end? What's the long-term plan? He put the machine on the wall between us and wiped his mouth. It was some kind of strimmer. The sheep went on eating and the tide went on going out. Him and me hadn't even been properly introduced but there we were philosophising in a field. He was looking up at the skies now, the broken cloud moving fast. Just then the bathroom opened. I could hear Siobhan humming a song, The Kinks again. If Padraig noticed, he didn't let on.

I hear your wee lad went walkabout? I said, maybe to distract him from the obvious.

They're too young to understand. I try to tell them how much I love them. But you can't explain to them what love is. How deep it goes. What you wouldn't do to protect them. Boy, they're that keen to shed their skin and change, they don't want to know about love.

We were silent for a minute or two. The horizon was extremely busy with traffic. Did he hear Siobhan drop her brush in the sink? Glancing at him, I saw the dollop of foam blow off his ear.

Moderation in the service of the survival of as many as possible, was his next thought aloud. That's the binding myth from what I can figure out and what's the alternative? Sure. But there's always a part of us, hidden sure, secret sure, which doesn't want to listen. Which wants something else completely. It doesn't sing along with the choir. You know what I'm talking about, Marc. The grass is never greener, is it?

I looked at him, wondering.

He spat into the field behind him, wiped his mouth. But try telling all that to a teenager eh, Marc? He tapped the machine lying on the wall and set off across the field. About halfway he stopped, turned around and shouted, Give that to herself from me. You can hold on to it.

What happened later that night, I didn't even tell the police properly. Neither did Siobhan apparently although we never discussed what we would say or not. We didn't try to get our stories straight. They interviewed us separately, then together, a few days later in the front room of our house in Derry. A joint force of plainclothes PSNI and Irish Gardaí. Somehow our stories must have matched enough. Maybe the reticence, the years of native suspicion of any type of uniform, saved us from any foolish notion of getting involved. Then again, there's stuff you just don't want to tell the cops, any cop, whatever it is that has happened. Private stuff. How could I possibly have told them what went on between Siobhan and me for the rest of the evening and into the night? Like the weird way she started to look at me, staring at me like she was hypnotised, unblinking, the colour drained from her face, miserably almost, as we had our dinner that evening, and how I thought she had heard me say something to Padraig or that she had changed her mind altogether and now couldn't find it in herself to forgive me any more, to give me that second chance. How she stood speechless in front of the oversized fireguard, shivering, while I begged her to tell me what was wrong, what I had done? All she could do was shake her head. She had gone mute, the way she gets sometimes if she's hurt. Tell me to go then and I will, I shouted at her, shaking her by the shoulders. And how we'd begun to kiss and make love right there in front of the fireplace, and on the floor, the sofa and all over the room, you can't tell that to the cops. Particularly because it was a different kind of love-making than what we were used to. They'd want to know exactly what you meant by different and you'd instinctively know you don't talk about your wife like that to anybody, never mind the new ambitious detectives of the PSNI. How it was cold and fierce and rough and loud and extraordinarily tender and nearly violent and like worship and acting and fighting and what was said and what was broken and it seemed to have no end, there was this unique deepening fear behind it all that it mightn't ever stop, it could go on and on.

I told the cops I had chatted meaninglessly with Padraig at the wall when he gave me the loan of a strimmer and I hadn't seen him again until the next morning when they were putting him into the squad car. I didn't mention talking to him under the oak tree which had to have been before he did what he did. I was out for some air, a breather. The half-moon was up. The wind silent, even up in the branches. My hands trembling—I had a glass of wine with me—and the muscles down the front of my legs wobbling like stretched rubber. I suppose I was trying to collect my thoughts about what we had been doing to each other inside, what it meant. Suddenly, and it scared the life out of me, the phone went off in my pocket. Greta texting to tell me she was seeing somebody else. The screen cast a spooky pool of light around me and when I heard someone clear their throat and spit on the other side of the trunk I used the screen-light to find the figure of Padraig standing above me.

You know, he began, I never had a musical bone in my body. The whole lot of us were the same, the ten of us. Tone deaf is not the word for it. Now I look at my own two and they've instruments lying about all over the house. You're tripping over them on the stairs. Trumpets, violins. Portable pianos. You name it. They're just naturals at it. It's just in them. Some of us, however, have to work hard at everything just to keep going. Naturals.

It comes and goes, I said. And all they want to be is DJs these days. Loads of kids have talent but it just gets lost.

Exactly. They can't concentrate, he said. The phones, the computers, the TV, all the distractions. The temptations. Buy this. Buy that. They don't see the fight going on for their minds. And the wife, she takes their side too much. They're the image of her too. They're a unit. A team. I don't stand a chance against them sometimes. They look at you as if to say, who the hell are you when you're at home? Even when I met her, she was well out of my league. Boy, I didn't think she'd look twice at me. Her parents weren't too happy either. She'd been off abroad to university and there's me only an articled clerk with an agricultural outfit on the wrong side of the border. They're long gone now, too. I'd no ambition either though. That was my problem. No dreams. It was her who made me go for it. Made me believe in myself. Some men are nothing without the right woman.

Too true. We all need a bit of straightening out. Ask Siobhan in there.

Sure, he said. It's easier to ask her forgiveness than her permission, isn't that what they say. We've all heard that one.

How do you mean? My neck was sore looking up at him.

Sure, he said, wiping his mouth, ignoring me. But you know some women will never forgive you, not really. Not deep down. They pretend to all right, and go through all the motions. But they're just waiting. Nobody hides a thing like a woman. Then one day you can't imagine life without them. Boy, you reach that day and there's no hope for you. You have to protect them. That's love now, that's what we were talking about earlier. Hell and back. Once it gets a grip on you it can grow completely out of your control and take you over until you feel the pain of it with every breath. Like you're breathing in fire. That's love for you, Marc. And if you're lucky, very lucky, one day you might get the chance to show them it… Do you mind?

As he took the glass from me, I smelled oil or petrol. He downed the rest of the wine, handed me back the glass and walked away quickly. I heard him clear his throat again and spit in the darkness. Don't miss your day, he called back to me. I think I went back in almost straight away. I had something to say to my wife. She was drinking the wine, lying out on the sofa in her robe, and she had a CD playing loud but I sensed a commotion in the room, like she was pretending, like she had thrown herself on the sofa when she heard me come in. Maybe she had been dancing. She just stared indifferently at me again when I told her I had been having another barmy talk with Padriag outside, stretched out her arm and her near empty glass and ordered me to fill it. I played along. There were a few other funny orders before we were back in the bedroom again.

I heard the first shot and laughed. The second shot, maybe a minute, maybe ten minutes later, filled me with a sudden burst of energy, like a shot at the start of a race. The third came like it was an echo of one or two of the others, maybe real, maybe not, and I'm sure Siobhan heard it too because as she was sitting on me, sweating, gasping, amazing, she mimed being shot in the back by something delicious, and there were no more shots I heard. I didn't hear any sirens at all. Maybe I have a memory of flashing red lights but that could be just gap-filling after the fact. I couldn't tell you anything but what was going on between my wife and me and that same dream again with the lifeguard and I wake up choking for air and there at the window is a guard in a peaked cap, his black gloved hand thumping on the glass.

Padraig Griffin had shot his wife and his two children. He used a shotgun. A quantity of petrol was found at the top of the stairs but it had not been used. After the shootings, the boy was first, followed by the daughter and lastly the mother, and before he was supposed to put the shotgun in his own mouth, and a match to the petrol, Padraig had a sudden change of heart and called the guards. He said to the guards, he didn't want to go to hell. Not only was he bust but it came out later that he thought his wife was going to leave him.

Siobhan did what she does and went very quiet about it all. She'd get into one of her rages if I tried to talk about it. Every day she had her swim and left for the office and came back late. She carried on as normal. I barely left the house for a few weeks. I was afraid to get in the car because I knew where I would end up. One night I forced myself out of the house to show my face at a friend's birthday party and there I kissed Greta again. I told Siobhan the next day, that it wouldn't happen again, that it was like a goodbye kiss. Siobhan accepted what I said very calmly. We were both very relaxed about it, the way it can be when the truth is out in the open. We were in the kitchen, a Saturday evening. I was making a stab at telling her that not much had ever gone on between Greta and me anyway. She was listening to me this time. Look, I'm just glad it's over with her, she said and it was then I asked her something about Padraig.

Why do you keep going back to it? she shouted, banging the table with her fist.

Back to it? We're not even allowed to bring it up. Back to it?

All you do is go on and on about it. What good will it do?

I haven't said a fucken word about that or anything to you in weeks since it happened. And all I was asking you was, did you tell Padraig about me and you?

What? About me and you what?

Did you?

I didn't tell Padraig anything, she said. I didn't tell Padraig anything about bloody anything.

You sure?

What? She went appalled. What did you say to me?

You heard me. Siobhan, right, he seemed to know a lot more about me and you than some total stranger if you know what I mean. All those weekends you spent down there by yourself?

Are you serious?

Well you knew him better than I did.

He was depressed.

Was he?

What? You think there was nothing wrong with him?

Of course I do.

But what?

I didn't know what I meant any more.

But what, Marc? You see you don't even know. You need to get yourself a job you know that. Get out of the house more. She left the kitchen. The bedroom door slammed.

I waited downstairs. I fell asleep on the sofa, drunk, hours later. I woke to hear the stairs creaking and Siobhan coming down. I wanted us to make love, roughly, to grab her and push her into a corner. But she didn't come in. I got up and opened the living-room door and saw her fiddling with the chain on the front door. I called her name and her body seemed to stiffen. Siobhan, I locked it, I said. It's locked. She kept her back to me, then turned around, pretending to yawn, a slight smile maybe, and she goes to me, I was just checking.

Jeopardy

Nora Pyne

'For $400, this president was assassinated while attending the play, *Our American Cousin.*' 'Lincoln,' says Muriel, not bothering to look up from her crossword. That was the softball easy question. She knows the other answers already; there are only so many assassinated presidents. You either know them or you don't. The contestant on the TV, a postal clerk from Lexington, Kentucky, looks like she might. 'For $600,' the host asks, 'this president was assassinated at forty-six, making him the youngest president to die in office.' 'Kennedy,' says Muriel, pencilling *Madras* into the spaces on the crossword, but writing *Madrid* in the margin, just in case. She and the postal clerk keep going. 'For $800, this president, assassinated in 1901, was the last US president to have served in the Union Army during the American Civil War.' Good clue, thinks Muriel to herself; 'McKinley,' she says to the TV. The postal clerk gets the answer. 'For $1000, this president, assassinated in 1881, was shot just four months into his term as president.' 'Garfield,' they both say, while Muriel writes the word *komatik* in the crossword. The show goes to commercials and Muriel gets up to make her tea.

'For $1000, this Roman emperor was both the great-great-grandson of Julius Caesar and the star of this 1979 cult film.'

The 1979 Northwest Lutheran Women's Convention was held in Billings, Montana. Over thirty ladies from Muriel's church alone, more than any other church in town, enough so that they had their own bus for the drive across the state. She packed the freezer with three days' meals for her husband, Chester; the last of their children had just left home for

312

college. The ladies on the bus told jokes and sang the old songs the whole way from Parkton to Billings. The trip alone was enough for Muriel; she loved the picnic lunch at Glacier National Park, all those rolling hills of wheat and the bison grazing near Great Falls. The convention theme was 'Women and Family' and the worship uplifting. Pastor Boffmann, the keynote speaker that year, had the ladies energised by the end of his closing address. All those bake sales and layettes for the poor, and education packs sent with the missionary service to foreign countries, that wasn't empty; it was humanity. Muriel was proud to be Christian.

The other ladies felt it too. It was all so good and happy and honest, in the old-fashioned sense of the word. Norma Bonquest suggested they go paint the town red after dinner. 'No husbands and just us gals!' Norma had said, and Muriel felt as free as a teenager again, walking arm in arm with her best chum to the Saturday matinees or going to an afternoon tea dance with the gang. They met in the lobby, a few ladies from other churches coming along. It was a June evening, Muriel remembered, warm, and crickets chirping outside. Ellen from the church choir was still alive; the cancer had started, but no one, not even her, knew that yet. Muriel and Ellen had always gotten along so well; their kids were the same age and the two families shared Cub Scouts and Brownies, traded skates as kids got bigger, and went to the lake together in the summer. Muriel and Ellen could walk into each other's kitchen without calling first. It was Ellen who was next to her on the sidewalk that evening, and Muriel can still recall the smell of the flowery perfume Ellen took from her purse in the hotel lobby, spraying just a little on her wrists and rubbing them together so her warmth would hold the smell. When Ellen died the next summer, Muriel tried to find that smell again, going the morning after the funeral to the big department store downtown, and walking slowly around the perfume counters with her mouth tight, aware the salesladies were carefully ignoring her, but Muriel didn't care one bit.

On that evening in Billings, everything was still perfect. Kay Mayes, up front, told her joke about Saint Peter and the Norwegian pastor from Seattle, and when she messed up the punchline, they all laughed anyway. Ellen slipped her arm in Muriel's and they walked the rest of the way to the ice-cream parlour like that, Ellen and her perfume, Muriel and her happiness.

313

It was still only seven thirty when everyone had finished their ice cream; some headed back to the hotel to finish packing and get to bed, but Muriel was thankful when Norma Bonquest said the night wasn't over yet.

Later, when Muriel told the story to her bridge club, she stressed that not one of them had known. 'We thought it was a historical drama,' she said. 'It was such a nice theatre and just across the street. With a title like *Caligula*, what would you expect?' The other three women paused, cards held close. 'So,' said Catherine, 'what was it?' Muriel leaned forward, giving the words the seriousness they deserved: 'A porno.' 'No!' they had all said, shocked, and Catherine, subbing for Betty who was having her cataracts done, said 'What did you do?' 'We sat through it, every last bit!' Muriel said, still indignant. 'We had paid for our tickets and the manager refused to give us a refund. What else could we do?' The other three women, all young brides during the war and each knowing the value of a penny, nodded their heads in agreement.

The winter has been a long one and it is still only February. Joe, her son who never married, came home for Christmas, so she had some company for a few days, but her other kids had all moved away years ago, and they had married and had kids in their new cities, and now even those kids, Muriel's grandchildren, were starting to marry and have their own children. Everyone was so far away. They were good, her kids; everyone took a turn coming to visit Muriel for a week or so every couple of months. She thought they must have a script they shared, each one always saying the same thing; 'Mom, don't you think you'd be more comfortable in Riverview? They can look after you there.' But no, she didn't think she'd be more comfortable in Riverview. She had her things and her things were in her house and her house was in her yard and her yard was in her neighbourhood and her memories were in all of those places. In Riverview you got a room, and a room wasn't big enough for a life's memories. Riverview was for old people ready to die, and while she was old, she wasn't thinking about dying anytime soon. Better she stayed where she was. The young couple next door got her groceries each week, and now that the man had retired, he kept her walkway shovelled in the winter and the lawn mowed in the summer. Church sent the minivan on Sundays, the driver coming to the door, helping her carefully across the porch, out to the waiting van and familiar faces. No, she was fine, thank you.

She likes the evenings best, when she knows the whole street is settled in at home, houses warm, supper dishes cleared away, and TVs turned on. It is a comfort to know that each house is doing the same thing. Muriel sometimes looks out through the curtains across lawns to her neighbours' houses, driveways filled with cars and everybody home, porch lights on.

Muriel pulls the TV tray closer to the sofa, gets up and carefully walks to the kitchen, doing the trip in small goals of sofa to television to armchair to kitchen door to counter to oven. She makes herself a cup of tea and takes her time carrying it back to the living room. *Jeopardy* is about to start again. Tea on the TV tray next to the crossword and pencils, carefully easing back down onto the sofa, reading glasses on, TV volume turned up high. For thirty years Alex Trebek in her living room nightly, asking questions while she finishes the crossword and has a cup of tea.

The postal clerk picks the next question. 'Triplets for $1000,' she says, choosing the only unasked question in that column. 'For $1000, these three bones make up the hip.' Muriel looks up.

Chester had been a good husband. He hadn't asked too much of her, didn't have any radical thoughts, accepted that the house was her domain, and worked a steady job. They'd married just before he shipped out for Europe, had children when he got back, and when they had enough children, he knew to stay on his side of the bed. He didn't talk about the war and she didn't ask. Chester died a few years after he retired. They'd been able to travel a little in those last few years, and, all in all, he'd been happy with his life.

Things were different during the war. With the men gone, women went out to work. During the four years Chester was overseas, Muriel worked as a shipfitter in the Tacoma shipyards. She loved it. She loved the noise and clang and excitement, she loved the sense of urgency in the work, she loved feeling that she was part of the big effort to win the war, and she believed that what she did was helping to keep Chester safe somewhere over in Italy. When it came time for the harvest back on Chester's folks' farm, she always got special leave to help out Joseph and Agnes for the month. She liked that too. With most of the hired men gone, it was just Chester's mother and father. Chester's brother enlisted and was killed in the South Pacific in May of 1943, but that August his widow Louisa still took the bus from Portland to lend a hand.

For three generations the farm had been in Chester's family, homesteaded by his great-grandparents. It had been tough to keep it going through the war years, but it was tough for everyone, so there was no point in complaining. They were all up with the sun, Agnes cooking for the family and the few hired men too old or too drunk to go to war, everyone out in the fields to bring in the wheat. After supper, the men might spend an hour out in the barn repairing equipment, while in the kitchen, Muriel and Louisa, talking about their lives, put up bottles of preserves and jams from the fruit trees planted long ago outside the kitchen window. Before going to bed, the family sat together in the parlour, Agnes reading the evening prayers. After the final Amen, it was an effort for Muriel to climb the stairs on sore feet, change into her nightgown and brush her hair before collapsing in the old double bed, Louisa next to her. 'No need washing two sets of sheets,' Agnes had said, putting them in together to share.

The days and nights moved one into the next, with no sense of where they were in the week, only that there was wheat and sun, then jam and dark and sleep, that the war kept going outside the farm and some or all of their men weren't coming back. Late in the night, two or three weeks into the 1943 harvest, the house had settled into still quiet, except for the sound of her father-in-law, Joseph, snoring in the next room. Muriel had fallen asleep right away, but now lifted hazily awake, thinking someone was calling her. It was Louisa whispering Muriel's name, Louisa's hand at the back of Muriel's shoulder, and then, after a pause, Louisa quietly closer, hesitant in kissing her neck. Muriel woke into alertness, but with a sense of uncertain panic. She didn't know what to do.

Muriel had prepared for her wedding night carefully: she read all of *The Rules and Etiquette of a Married Christian Woman's Life*. 'Between husband and wife there is a special relationship; the duty of a wife is to be patient, understanding that men have certain needs.' In the dark, Muriel thought Louisa smelled of plums, and Louisa's mouth was soft on her neck in a way Chester's had never been. Louisa said Muriel's name again, and moved even closer, her stomach and breasts against Muriel's back.

'A woman has a role as the guardian of the family. Men have physical needs, and women need to be accepting.' Louisa's fingertip traced the line of Muriel's collarbone, shoulder to throat. She whispered in Muriel's ear 'This is my favourite part of you.' They were alone in the dark. Muriel, sick with fear but urgent with something she'd never felt before, took a breath. She rolled over to her sister-in-law.

If the night had been cloudy, things would have ended differently. If the moon had been lower, Muriel would have been lost. That night though, the moon was high, with light enough through the window to see shadow. Muriel lay back against the pillows, her nightgown pushed up above her waist. Louisa, naked, her feet dangling off the bottom of the bed, rested her head on Muriel's thigh, the taste of Muriel still wet on her mouth. Muriel was about to whisper 'thank you' when she saw the doorknob turn.

In that split second, Muriel saw everything that would happen. She knew what Chester would have to do, and her parents, and her friends, when they found out. Muriel chose to save herself. She kicked Louisa as hard as she could. Louisa tumbled to the floor as Agnes opened the door to check on the muffled noises she'd heard through the wall. Agnes's eyes saw Louisa sprawled naked on the floor, then a second later, Muriel, sitting up in bed, frantically pulling the quilt to her chest over her nightgown. 'It's her! It's her!' sobbed Muriel. Agnes turned back to Louisa, her eyes filled with revulsion, and she slowly said, 'You whore, you filthy, dirty viper. Pack your bag and get out.'

In the morning, Louisa was gone. Agnes never told Joseph, but she told Muriel to always remember to forget what had happened. It was the Christian thing to do.

Muriel was confused amid all the smells of Nordstrom's perfume counters that morning after Ellen's funeral, confused and lost. It was all so big and so busy. The different perfumes layered heavily in the air as she walked between the counters, a saleswoman at each one, pert with thick make-up. Muriel couldn't pick out the individual scents; she couldn't find anything close to Ellen's flowery smell. Burning, musky perfumes for women with shoulder pads clouded the air, closing in, and making it hard for her to concentrate. The funeral had been awful, Ellen's husband silent and unmoving in the pew, so the casket procession couldn't leave the church, and afterwards everyone crowding Muriel to say how sorry they were. Muriel couldn't go to her usual little perfume shop near the neighbourhood grocers. She needed anonymity; she couldn't bear the thought of someone being friendly or familiar or kind to her right now. The perfume section at Nordstrom's was the best idea, but now that she was here, she just couldn't breathe.

Kennedy's assassination in November 1963 held Ellen to Muriel's memory. Christmas was subdued and then New Year's Eve arrived. Ellen and her husband hosted the party, determined they would all have fun. Thirty couples squeezed tight into the living room and den, some dancing to a Perry Como record, drinks in hand. Anyone walking in the front door would have said the house smelled like a good time: hairspray, Brylcreem, bourbon, and the midnight buffet, nearly ready.

Ellen was in the kitchen at the stove, carefully transferring cocktail meatballs to a polished chafing dish with the exaggerated concentration of a woman who has had too many highballs. Muriel next to her at the counter, had a small tray in one hand, crackers arranged around a seasonal mousse, the recipe from the latest *Ladies Home Journal*. 'My feet are killing me. Pass me the toothpicks, will you?' said Ellen, reaching across Muriel and taking them herself. Ellen eased out of her kitten heels for a second, shoeless feet stretching on the kitchen floor. In the dining room, people were talking about the pictures of Jacqueline Kennedy in *LIFE Magazine*, her brothers-in-law Bobby and Edward at either arm, walking her down Pennsylvania Avenue leading the funeral cortege.

Ellen and Muriel were doing the same, Muriel picking up her drink. 'Imagine it for the poor children, a father gone like that, and Jackie losing a baby only in August.' Muriel knew Ellen was still a bit lost herself after a miscarriage in the spring. She had spent most afternoons that April sitting at Muriel's breakfast table crying. As she spoke, Ellen's hands stopped arranging toothpicks and cubes of cheese. Muriel turned to her friend; this wasn't the time for tears. 'You know what? This girdle feels like I'm trussed up in a python,' said Muriel, and Ellen laughed.

The midnight countdown started on the other side of the kitchen door. 'The girdle's worth it; you look a million bucks in that dress,' said Ellen, and she stepped gingerly back into her heels with a little unsteady sway, reaching a hand out to Muriel's hip for balance. 'Especially here,' she said. 'This is my favourite part of you.' In the other room the midnight cheers started, and impulsively, Ellen, smiling, leaned over, and kissed Muriel's lips. 'Happy New Year,' she said, and Ellen turned to take the cheese tray out to the party, Muriel following a minute later, one woman walking out to kiss her husband, the other to let herself be kissed.

At Nordstrom's, that morning after the funeral, Muriel couldn't find Ellen's smell, and she felt herself getting angrier and angrier.

Leslie Bower had started her new job in Cosmetics that morning, perm glossed into place, silver eye shadow arched high. Leslie had not an ounce of common sense but enthusiasm in buckets. That's why the manager sent her out on the floor with a handful of perfume samples. She was the one who stepped in front of Muriel. Leslie sprayed her with the latest signature fragrance. It's difficult to say who was more surprised at what happened. A few minutes later, locked in a cubicle in the ladies room, arms wrapped around her waist, Muriel sobbed in choking gasps, wanting to wail but trying to be quiet. Muriel had slapped the saleslady with the sum of her fury at every bit of unfairness in this life: Ellen buried this morning at Fairmount, and Chester sitting at home reading the newspaper, waiting for Muriel to come home and make his lunch.

'Ilium, ischium, and pubis,' says Alex Trebek on the TV, and Muriel, half a century later, can still feel the weight of Ellen's hand on the curve at the top of her hip, the force pushing down.

Lay Down The Dark Layers

Deborah Rose Reeves

Claret

The piece is perhaps a landscape, certainly not a portrait or that of a figure, but briefly she imagines she has happened across a corpse in the bathtub, not a painting. Specks of crimson and claret spatter the white enamel, in which an easel looms, its subject flayed and seeping russet, red ochre, raw umber, burnt umber.

She runs the tap until it steams then rubs between her legs with a rough cloth. There is no soap, only a clutter of brushes in a can of turpentine. She cleans her teeth with her finger and stares into the mirror. Her mouth is still plum from the wine they drank. I am a landscape too, she thinks, scratching at the crests and valley of her top lip.

Insects And Grass

Scrabbling for her shoes in the gloom, she cast short glances at the man asleep in the bed. She'd known him to see. The rest of the details were dim—only his hand on her thigh and the winking lights of College Green as the taxi rounded onto Pearse Street and tore through the night towards the docklands.

She had not been this downriver since her father had brought her and her brother to see the tall ships passing through. She couldn't believe that people lived here now, was bewitched by the reflection of the water on so many new windows and, once inside the apartment, she held her head so she could see the silvery stillness the entire time she was there until she was walking out the door again.

Outside she began to run, looking this way and that for a roaming taxi to take her back into the city or home. There was no urgency, she had no place to be, but she liked the image and how she believed she must look to anyone who might see her—glassy-eyed, sparkle-dressed, a girl running wild in the predawn.

Crossing onto Lower Mount Street she was stilled mid-flight by the copper fur of a fox beneath a streetlight, its green eyes regarding her from amidst a litter of peelings and scraps. She had heard of urban foxes, of the den by the Dáil, how they scavenged for whatever they could get and would eat insects and grass if nothing else were available. But she had never seen one in real life.

What Happened To You Anyway?

In the morning she looked into the mirror and the face of girl stared back and winced when she saw what she had not felt. Her fingertips rose to her cheekbone, beguiled. Her eye was a perfect plum with streaks of black mascara and specks of fine glitter that she washed away. Then, pressing nearer to the glass and considering it more closely, she took in the pretty print of fuchsia, mustard, grass, and periwinkle. Last night's clothes lay scattered all around.

In the kitchen, her flatmate regarded her from behind a cigarette and a French press.

I see you got home okay then, she said.

I couldn't find you. When I got back from the toilets you weren't on the dance floor.

I must've been off looking for you, she said, stubbing out the half-smoked butt.

That's so weird. I looked all around. I'd got a drink for you.

So you went to the bar or you went to the dance floor?

Jesus, I don't know. God.

They sat in silence with coffee and an ashtray between them, picking at their little bowls of plain yoghurt and fruit.

What happened to you anyway? asked her flatmate, finally.

Oh this? she said. I'm not really sure.

At work the women in the break room gathered around her. Let's just say there was a headboard involved, she said, and they all whispered Jesus through their teeth.

Does he have a brother? said Margaret who was like a mother to them. Or a father? And they cried laughing then went back to their desks and thought the day would never come to an end.

Don't tell mam, she said to her sister on the phone.

I can't believe he gave you a black eye, said her sister. Who is this person?

That's the thing, she said, touching her fingers to her face again. She was tired and the night before seemed long ago. It's everything but black. It's all these other colours.

Portrait

Barmen called him by his name and knew what he wanted to drink. He paid for his first drink only but was never without a glass before him. He was not ashamed for a woman to ask what he was having and he stood unconcerned in the face of a round. It was the rare man who interrupted when he was speaking. Often a girl would grab her coat and leave in a hurry, while others would linger until just after he'd left, pretending not to notice him from evening until closing. He was despised by many but repudiated by no one.

There is a man like this in every pub and corner of the country.

And The Thing Is

She'd say to people, I hadn't even thought about him that much.

Though she wasn't in the habit of them, she was very understanding about one-night stands: things happened, they didn't mean anything. Sometime later, though, she had popped into Hogans after work and caught his eye at the other end of the bar. Dublin is a small town—she offered what she thought was a knowing but mollifying smile and expected that to be the end of it, in that she expected him to offer her something similar in return. Rather, he looked at her as though to say, The fuck you lookin' at me for?

And the question opened what had been closed, revealing a space that a part of her rushed to inhabit. And this left its own space and that, too, generated a void. And this accounted for the shame and longing that emptied and filled her as she waited to pay for her drink, and the thirst with which she drank it, and the apparent nonchalance with which she ordered another.

And later, during a chance meeting on the stairs in which words were exchanged, she was so relieved by what she now assumed had been her own misunderstanding that she did not object to him pulling her into the ladies' bathroom and pressing her up against the wall.

I'm On My Way

Pale blossoms followed the bright berries of winter and fell away, too soon. The shimmering mirage of summer: diaphanous rain. The days and months moved on and she imagined she moved in pace with them. But here we see her in September, a barman is calling last orders please and she is saying goodnight to friends and waiting for a message that asks is she around. She is. She is always around, or can be. She is in the same place. The place that answers I'm on my way. It is the same night as the first night, the same night as the last. A hundred and one one-nights. The light and the breeze and the blossoms bend around her as they press on.

Their Situation

She enjoyed the sensation of stepping into a museum or gallery—parquet floors announcing her arrival and passage from room to room where high ceilings amplified all things, from the tickle in her throat to the timid stirrings of her soul. It was a small joy, available to anyone, and costing nothing, which was perhaps why they were so often very empty and she herself had only thought to pay a visit once she started sleeping with the painter on a regular basis.

Sleeping with an artist was different than she thought. She had pictured so many sketches of herself, scattered in a light-filled place: reading a book, stepping into a bathtub, removing an earring, seated, standing. She imagined what it would be like to pose for him, saw him lean in to fix a falling hair, moving her this way and that, though she supposed he did in his own way.

Still, she hoped they might sometimes do other things together too, but she didn't know how to invite him to join her without giving the wrong impression. She wanted it to be clear that she understood their situation. So she would only sometimes mention that she was thinking of going to such and such exhibition, and she would never say that she had been—unless to say she had been there with a friend—so that he wouldn't think of her as someone who was often alone.

Sometimes she thought of herself alone in those long, tall rooms, her face raised to the rows of gilded frames, and it was beautiful. She liked this unexpected life. Her eye fell upon new shelves in bookshops and she sought out others in the library. She began to acquire a new vocabulary and way of seeing things; yet this, too, presented a problem. Having finally found something she might say to him, she found she could not say it. A sudden allusion to Caravaggio might strike him as peculiar. *Pentimenti* is an awkward word to work into a sentence when somebody has an idea of who you are already.

3AM

Whatever happened to your painting? she asked into the dark.

Why? he said, after a few seconds.

I was just thinking about it, she said.

It's late, he said.

A few minutes later he sighed, turned on the lamp and left the room. When he came back with the canvas under his arm she sat up and clapped and he shook his head. He climbed back into bed and set it between them. It had not changed much since the first time she had seen it. Her fingers hovered over it.

Don't touch, he said.

I know, she said, though she did want to place her hands on it and feel the thin scratches and depressions that textured the surface. Several times, she could see, he had painted a layer, then waited for it to dry before taking to it with something rough. In a few trace places he had scratched through the deep browns and iron reds to reveal the canvas beneath. Dark mottling suggested rocks in a fallow field but it was not discernibly of anything.

She looked at him and smiled through sudden tears.

Is it finished? she said.

No, he said. He picked up the painting and set it on the floor. First you lay down the dark layers and then you add light. It can take a while. He switched off the lamp and turned away.

Her eyes adjusted again to the gloom.

Hey, she said.

What? he said.

Thank you.

Her Sister Said

What happened to his teeth?

And she said, What do you mean?

He's missing two of his teeth, she said. She tongued her top and bottom teeth, counting and thinking. It's like this one, and this one, she said, placing the curled tip of her tongue on one tooth and another.

I don't know, she said. I never noticed it.

She said she would look the next time she saw him but the next time she saw him she forgot to look.

Her Old, Dear Friend

Her old, dear friend set his glass on the table and kicked at the legs of the stool she was sitting on across from him.

What the fuck? she laughed, but his eyes did not return her smile.

You're always looking over my shoulder, he said.

What?

When we're out. When I'm talking. You're always looking just past me.

No I'm not, she said. Am I?

He's not even here, said her friend and picked up his drink and looked away.

They sat like this for what seemed a long time, looking around the room and into their drinks. Finally, she kicked at the legs of his stool and made a sad face to see if he would smile.

Patronage

For a third week the rain was preventing him from working. For money he painted houses and nobody had their doors or windows done in this weather.

Fuckin' rain, he said. What could he do?

She asked him about the insides or other odd jobs, bar work maybe.

Sure nobody's the money to be painting their kitchens every five minutes anymore, he said, taking a long drag from a joint and passing it to her. They're stuck with their fuckin' persimmon now aren't they?

She supposed so.

C'mere to me, he said.

In the morning, before she left for work herself, she set two tens between the teabags and the sugar. She thought to leave more but this way he might think it was his own that he'd forgotten. Either way, he never mentioned anything about it.

A couple of weeks later he was shy of his rent.

It's not like he asked me for it, she thought, licking the envelope. He was just talking and I was just there.

Thank you thank you thank you, he said.

She spoke to her father whose mother's house was sitting idle. It might sell quicker if they had a bit of work done—she had a friend who could start right away.

She thought of him in his paint-spattered overalls in her nana's old kitchen, listening to the small portable radio, milky tea pouring from the teapot, so familiar.

Her sister sent her a message when she was at work. Dad was going mad. Globs of paint and plaster were ground into the floor. The sink was clogged with the stuff. There were dirty dishes on the counter, brushes and rollers stuck to trays of dried paint. He's not going to pay for this crap, said her sister.

I've already paid him, she wrote back. I'm on my way.

She called him from the taxi and tried to explain things from her father's point of view. How it was his mother's house, and what that meant to him, so it was hard to see the place just left that way. He said he was sorry, he'd planned to go back and clean it up but had got a call about another job and couldn't turn it down.

You know what it's been like, he said. What could he have done?

Her father and sister had cleaned the house and gone by the time she got there. She let herself in and stood in the small kitchen, transformed completely from her memory of it. The windows were bare of their faded net curtains. The grimy wallpaper had been stripped spare. He'd filled in the parts in the walls that had crumbled, painted them a delicate colour she would never have thought of. It was brighter and more open, as she'd hoped. It was good work.

On George's Street, An Encounter

She wandered into Dunnes and placed in the basket the makings of a meal: stewing beef, onions, carrots, russets, crusty bread and butter, wine. She tried to picture his kitchen, what might or might not be in it, but could only see her hand around a glass and the cold tap running in the middle of the night. She picked up a box of salt and considered it then replaced it on the shelf and walked away. She returned the wine and chose a different bottle then went back for the salt and noticed, on the way, a large pot on sale that got her thinking about utensils.

Standing in the checkout line, she composed a text but was called to pay before she could send it. Out on the street, she fumbled with her bags and phone when he appeared through the arch of the old shopping arcade and down towards her. A girl was walking with him. He touched her hip and steered her across the traffic to the other side of the road.

On the bus home, she looked down at her boots surrounded by paper bags filled with dresses and books and thank you cards and chocolate and something for her sister and all of the food for dinner and the big pot. And she felt a little sick from the fumes that come from the engine under the back seat but it is also warmest there and it was the beginning of winter.

Salt

An uncommon snow fell in November, softening steeples and iron railings, pillowing cobblestones and filling the cracks. Low clouds leached into rooftops, grey as the gulls that screeched from deep within them, displaced. They skittered on the air, wanting to settle but wary and resentful. The intricate expanse of streets and alleys was from afar a frozen lake, sighs and speculations echoing from its fissures.

People walked as though for the first time, hands stretched to steady them, ready to slide. Delighted at first, strangers smiled at each other in mutual commiseration. They laughed nervously or were quieted with wonder. The air was still and time appeared to stop but when life continued to make demands of them they became impatient and anxious for salt to arrive from Europe. They soon remembered the last year's unexpected cold snap. You'd think we'd have learned something, they said.

Desideratum

From desire, she murmured beneath her breath, her fingers following the small font across and down the soft, translucent page of an aged dictionary. From the Old French, *desirrer:* wish for, long for. From Latin, *desiderare*: long for, wish for, but also meaning demand, expect. Her eyes hovered over the words then continued down the page. Original sense was perhaps 'await what the stars will bring', from the phrase *de sidere*, 'from the stars', from *sidus*: star, constellation, heavenly body.

She set aside the heavy tome and scanned the article she'd been reading. She couldn't remember the sentence she'd paused upon, her reason for needing the dictionary in the first place. Distracted, she couldn't say how she'd got from there to here, not in so many words.

When she left the reading room, the clock in the front square struck the quarter hour. It was hardly past six but so dark as to seem deep night. It was strange to see that the day was not nearly done, that she had more time than she thought. She walked across the cobblestones, illuminated by the lamps in the arches of the college chapel and the campanile. She had not a single idea but that Dublin was loitering beyond the gates, waiting for her. Passing through the wooden entrance of the west door, she ignored the noticeboards overflowing with events fliers and invitations to various clubs and societies, and stepped out into the city and nowhere in particular.

The Coach & Ferry

There was nothing to be done. He would have to go to London. His flatmate had asked him to leave, a rancorous end to what had been a friendship. Sides had been taken in Grogans and The Cobblestone: he owed everybody something. Twice he had moved back home but he couldn't be himself— they knew him too well. Where else can I go like?

You could stay with me but you know what my flatmate's like, she lied. She took him out to dinner and, later, lay in the crook of his arm, face pressed to his bony ribcage, rising and falling to the dull rhythms within, lulled to sleep by a long list of betrayals that thankfully didn't include her.

She did not know where he spent his last days and nights in Dublin. She had given him some little things for fun but they seemed foolish now when she thought of him on the coach and ferry—a string bag of chocolate coins in golden foil, and a small box of paints and a set of postcard-sized watercolour paper. She wrote her name and address on the first one and asked him to send her a little painting from somewhere better. When the postman came, and there was nothing for her, she was relieved to have been so soon forgotten.

I Am Here For You

She was the kind of girl that people unburdened themselves to while waiting for a bus. She found it difficult to extricate herself from the recounting of a grievance and often she settled into her seat, accepting that she was here till the end of the line with this one. She became frightened of being old. Women shared more resentments and men tended towards regret, though not remorse.

One night, a man stumbled up to her and asked if this was the stop for Rathmines; he thought he was staying at a Travelodge there. He didn't need to tell her he was on a stag weekend from England—a short-sleeved shirt on a winter night said it all and she hoped he would wander away again but he leaned against the wall beside her.

It was a rare night out for him, he said, and she smiled politely but looked away, waiting for the bit about the ball and chain. He was a night watchman at a hospital, he continued, and she commiserated about the strange hours, surrendering to being sucked into his life for a while. The hours were strange, he agreed, but he had chosen them. He was avoiding his family, he told her, a lovely wife and a daughter.

He loved them in his head, he said. He knew he did. But he felt nothing—nothing. Not even when the girl was a child. He knocked back a couple of cans every morning when he got home and slept into the evening. He didn't know what else to do. She didn't know what to tell him.

When the bus came he preferred to stand but he looked her way every few minutes until she nodded that this was his stop. He looked in through the window as the bus pulled away, as though to say now what? She pointed straight ahead, on your left, and watched him follow her finger up the street of a place he didn't come from.

Midwinter

She wakes in the dark and lays there. A thin light flits and shrinks below her door as her flatmate makes her way to and from the bathroom.

Outside, the suburbs groan but rise obedient. Taxi lights blink on and off—a new day for some, a winding down for others who see bright yolks spitting in the pan and mopped up with bread before bed, or second jobs. In town the streets are dark still but expectant; lights beneath bridges bleed into the river; the clinking chorus of steel kegs on the cobblestones. And far beyond the city, in a country field, a single ray of light slips between a crack, creeps a darkened passageway, and is greeted in a tomb by reverent gasps.

Her feet are on the floor now but the rest of her is slow to follow. Where is there to go? Without standing, she bends forward and draws the heavy drapes. The white wall flutters and sways with leaf shadows and the lighter shadows of the spaces between leaves, like some pacing piebald creature. She reaches out to pet it and it is gone.

Lute Player

There are two versions of *The Lute Player* by Caravaggio. One is in The Hermitage in Saint Petersburg; the other is part of the Wildenstein Collection in New York City. In both versions, what looks like a child—doe-eyed, pink lips slightly parted, thin fingers strumming on the strings. On one of them, some fragments from a madrigal on the lute player's sheet music say: *Voi sapete ch'io v'amo. Vostra fui.* You know I love you. I was yours. The other does not.

Horizons

He was not long coming back on the boat. He called her. Poles had got there first, he said. Better the shambles you know. London is a joke. He hung up and texted her the address of the place he was staying.

She stared up at the steel door, its rusting hinges and bolts, standard delinquent scrawl, and a keyhole where a handle might ordinarily be. Shivering in the grey light, waiting for him to come down and let her in, she saw that she had not broken any of the habits she thought she had: they had only, briefly, been impractical to keep. Two men crossed the road and whistled through their fingers at another up the street. She held her handbag tight. She stood her ground as they sauntered on by.

Dark stairs led to a small flat. In the hallway, his painting rested against a wall with a couple of black bin bags, a pair of work boots, and a bicycle frame. She thought to say something but his head was already bent low and away from her, focused on his tins and rolling papers.

The painting had changed since she'd last seen it. He had introduced a middle ground with a distant mountain range, folds of auburn and vermillion shadows. Above them, clouds hovered low in a pumpkin sky—soft, curved strokes of cornflower, rose, pale lilac, lavender. If the intent had been to add depth, the effect had fallen flat. The original dark foreground dominated the eye, the bright sky imparting not perspective or a counterpoint to the darkness, but seeming torn from another painting altogether.

C'mere, he said.

She turned towards him and saw the painting sitting in the hallways of many places to come.

I read that Degas practised cloud formations with a crumpled hanky held up against a lamp, she said.

Just come here, he said.

He was stretched out on a low windowsill, smoking. In the street below, a kid balanced a football on his knee and an older youth restrained a pit bull. He offered her the dregs of the joint he was smoking.

I have to go to back to work soon.

Suit yourself, he said, and looked away down at the boys and the ball and the road and the dog. He rested his hand on her thigh and she let him so he moved it in between her legs and rubbed at her jeans with his thumb.

Don't, she said.

He arched his hips and pulled his pants down around his thighs.

I have to be back at work soon.

Please.

I can't.

Then what the fuck are you here for then?

A Light In The Darkness

They come every year, the last days of January—tall ships, passing through. So much that was sworn has already been forgotten, so much that was promised abandoned. Still, there is a chance again, at least, to wander on up to Merrion Square and take a look at Turner's watercolours, stroll through the park and make a day of it.

The paintings were known as a light in the darkness and she thought of them that way though she had never seen them. She thought of them trembling gold in their dark cabinet the year long, their whispers building to delirious song, pining for that month when light is at its lowest and they would be released. She approached them as a bright assurance, the room aglow with glass and spotlights. She had been waiting for this day too.

The shipwrecks, then, the looming cliff faces, grey-green squalls, and blue coldness of so many scenes struck her as bleak, and she moved through these paintings quickly, seeking the warm sunsets and rises of her expectations. She liked those landscapes that were mere suggestions of a thing and not too much the thing itself. She did not want detail or reality. She only wished to dissolve into the faint washes of peach and rose reflected in still waters.

Soon she had completed a circle of the room and seen everything she had come to see, glanced over the rest. It had not taken very long. She looked around to see what other people were looking at and lingered on, wondering what they were seeing that she had failed to appreciate. She did not want to leave yet, to go back out there.

Is this it? she asked, sinking and rising on the answer.

Andy Warhol

Keith Ridgway

I am standing still, smoking a cigarette, staring at Marilyn Monroe. This is Dublin. In the mid-1980s. I am waiting outside the Gay Men's Health Clinic, or whatever it's called, on Haddington Road, off Baggot Street. Marilyn is looking at me. And I'm looking at her.

And I am walking with a semi and a cigarette through the Upper East Side of New York City. And it's a few months earlier. And I am staring at Andy Warhol, wondering if that *is* Andy Warhol, if it is *really* Andy Warhol.

I'm twenty. In both places, all the time.

Marilyn is huge, on an advertising hoarding, sitting or half-lying, her head and shoulders thrown back, her legs stretched out, chest pointing upwards, one hand touching her hair. She's wearing a one-piece swimsuit. She's smiling a big sweet smile, and her legs are long and her body is perfect, and her face is beautiful and she is looking at me like I'm beautiful too. The picture is black and white. Except for Marilyn's lips, which have been touched up in blue. She has blue lips. They match the label of the beer bottle that sexy, dead Marilyn is advertising with the slogan 'SOME LIKE IT COLD!'

And there I am, smiling under a dollop of sunshine in New York City, so pleased with my clever self, my skin so warm, doubling back to stalk Andy Warhol, and approaching him when he stops outside a fruit store and stares at a crate of oranges. I walk straight up to him like New York is mine as much as his, and he catches a glimpse of me and we're eye to eye.

—Excuse me. Mr Warhol?

I'm staring at Marilyn and thinking about necrophilia. Maybe advertisers know us better than we know ourselves. I wonder what my interest in necrophilia amounts to. And I wonder, as I stand there smoking my cigarette, waiting to go into the clinic, putting it off, I wonder again about New York. And I number my fears to myself, and I know that death is in the wrong place. And I know that there are things on the list that should not be there. And that the list is too long and too stupid. And I wonder whether there is, in the prospect of death, a place to shelter from being alive. I wonder about that, in all seriousness, I do. Look at me. With my wispy beard and my Dublin coat and my head to one side, wondering. Like I am the only person in the world. And I wonder if there is a way of talking about this that does not involve me. And there isn't.

—Hi, he says. Brightly. With only the most minor of hesitations. I think he looks old. He's in slippers, house-shoes, something like that, and he has a stack of magazines and a string bag and yellow baggy trousers like pyjama bottoms, and a blue jacket, also baggy. And he has his silver hair and his glasses and he is about the same height as me. And there is something about him that makes me feel tentatively happy and I don't know what it is. He smiles and looks in my eyes for the briefest of moments before looking elsewhere—at my nose, my throat, my shoulder—shyly. Maybe it's that.

—Can I have your autograph?

I don't know why I've asked for his autograph. It's because I can't think of anything else to ask him. I think I should ask him how he is, if he'd like an orange, if he'd like to go for a walk, have a coffee. But I am stupid. I don't even have a pen on me.

—Sure, he drawls. Let me write it on one of my magazines. These are my magazines. You can have one.

—That would be great. Thank you. I don't have…

—I have a pen. Oh my.

I don't know what the 'oh my' is for. He rummages for a pen, comes up with a big black permanent marker. I want to make conversation. But I am tongue-tied. I want to ask him about film, art, the twentieth century, New York, beauty, love, car crashes, death, but I just stand there dumbly and he glances at me.

—Oh my. I'm doing. Oh there. Okay. Let me see. It's warm today.

—Yeah. It's lovely.

—Oh. Where are *you* from?

—Ireland. Dublin.

—Oh my. I'm from Pittsburgh. It's near there.

He mumbles that last bit, and I spend a couple of seconds trying to untangle it, but I'm pretty sure that's what he says. And meanwhile he's writing his name across a copy of *Interview* with Stevie Wonder on the cover. And I'm saying nothing, because I am stupid.

—There you are. I make this magazine, you can have this.

—That's really great. Thank you so much.

—You're welcome.

And I think of something to say.

—This is a good day for me. I just got a job. My first job in New York. And now I meet you.

—Oh that's so great.

—So thank you.

He smiles at me again. And he flicks his eyes for one last instant onto mine.

—Thank you for asking.

He shuffles off. I light another cigarette and I look at his name and I'm smiling, and I mouth 'Thank you for asking' to myself, as if it's the nicest thing anyone has ever said to me. And I decide that New York will make me, and that I will be open and warm and happy here, changed, and I will live in the city and the city will live in me and I will welcome everything and I will be fearless and alive.

But I am twenty. And stupid. The two do not necessarily go together, but I happen to be both.

For a while I live in Washington Heights, reading Russian novels at a kitchen table in someone's apartment—some friend of a friend. I sweat and drink tea. I listen to phone-in radio shows and talk all night with people who come and go. I don't know anything about anything but people seem to like me. We have enough money to go for beers, but we look too young for a lot of places, and feel too young for a lot of others. I make a half-hearted effort at finding gay bars. I don't. New York, I decide, doesn't have any gay bars. It's okay, I'm not even really thinking about it.

When I get my job I move to somewhere up in the Bronx. I move in with another guy I know from Dublin, and his girlfriend, and someone else. I don't like any of them. I read more Russian novels. People don't come and go anymore. Everything settles down into something that begins to feel boring. I take the subway to work. I work as a doorman in an apartment building on Park Avenue, up in the 70s. Wealth. I buy a book of Frank O'Hara poems. I have never read Frank O'Hara before. He reminds me of sex. I haven't had sex yet in New York. I start looking at men on the trains. I follow a guy once because he looks back at me. Nothing comes of anything. Work isn't hard but the hours are long. I am bored. New York, I decide, is boring.

I am paid nine dollars an hour basic. This is more than any of my friends are earning. They start expecting me to buy the beers. I have a fight with the people I live with because they want me to pay more of the rent than they do. Even though I am sleeping on the sofa most nights. I stop telling them about tips and overtime. Whenever I call home my family has bad news. My exam results are awful. My father is ill. My sister has been bitten by a dog. I want something to happen. I am in New York and I am unhappy, and I have forgotten what I promised myself after I met Andy Warhol, and sometimes I suspect the reason they want me to pay more rent isn't because I am earning more but because I am masturbating all the time, on the sofa.

I see less and less of my friends. I avoid the people I live with.

The building where I work is tall and wide and deep and filled with millionaires who have maids and servants. Like in the Russian novels. I find it difficult to tell the residents and their staff apart. Some maids wear pinafore things, but many don't. Some nannies are very well dressed—they just look like rich young mothers. Part of my job is to take deliveries up to the apartments via the service elevators. The elevators are operated with a handle, a lever, and they can be stopped anywhere, so there's a skill—that I never master—in getting the floor of the elevator level with the floor where I'm stopping. I keep tripping into the kitchens of the wealthy. Maids or residents let me in and take the bags or whatever it is, or get me to take the stuff to the kitchen table or the kitchen counters or to put them on the floor somewhere. Sometimes I get a tip. Sometimes kids let me in, and they are always rude. Their parents can be rude as well. Maids are never really rude, just impatient or abrupt or hassled.

One day a woman in a dressing gown gets me to put her half a dozen bags of groceries on the table while she watches me. *Put that one on the floor*, she says at one point, standing behind me. Then, *Put another one on the floor. Carefully.* When I'm done I look at her and she looks at me and lets her dressing gown fall open and asks me if I'd like a tip. I say *No, you're okay thanks*, and trip back into the elevator. When I get downstairs one of the other doormen looks at me and laughs.

Another time I get stuck in one of the elevators with a guy who is doing work on one of the top floors. The elevator is always getting stuck. You have to fiddle with it and if that doesn't work you have to use the intercom to try and rouse someone downstairs and the building super does whatever it is that gets it moving again. It's never stuck for very long. It doesn't bother me. It doesn't seem to bother the guy either. We chat while we wait and he tells me that a kid like me must be drowning in pussy in New York City. He tells me that with a peachy little Irish ass like mine I must be fighting off the faggots in New York City. I just smile at him. He starts rubbing his crotch and goes quiet for a while, and I fiddle with the elevator lever. And then he says *I really want to cum do you want to cum too*? And I say *No, you're okay thanks*, and he says, *Well, let's see*, and he takes his cock out and starts stroking it and looking at me. *Come on kid*, he says, *I can see you're hard. What's the harm*? He drops his trousers and his shorts and gets into it. I don't know where to look. I think I should probably tell him to stop but I don't. I'm worried about where he's pointing it, but when he comes he turns slightly and it goes all over the floor. *I enjoyed that*, he says, gasping. *I'm glad you enjoyed it too.* When we get down he steps out and takes the super aside to talk to him about something. I get a cloth. When I stand up the super is there with his head stuck into the elevator, sniffing. He doesn't say anything. At the end of the day the guy gives me a hundred dollar tip and his card, with his home number written on the back.

I decide that people in New York like sex after all, and that some of them might like sex with me, and I decide to work out ways of making that happen.

*

337

It is always hot. The long streets shimmer and I pad down them, across them, and I look for shadows and I start to hate my job and I check the magazines and I traipse all over the place when my shifts are over, and I start to find dark air-conditioned bars and clubs and sex shops and porn cinemas and I begin to look different. I research. I work out what I need to do. I look at other guys, how they dress and behave and what they end up with, and I work it out. I get a fake I.D. and some new jeans and T-shirts and I buy a couple of pairs of shoes and I buy some good shirts from a discount store somewhere, and I get contact lenses and aftershave.

I realise that it's easy. I watch and learn. I learn what people learn.

So there I am, new to myself, standing with a beer in the corner of a bar, and men look me over, and come over, and buy me a drink. Or there I am loitering by the video cabins in a Times Square basement, men gesturing to me, flashing their stomachs or their cocks at me, inclining their heads like serious little puppies. Or there I am getting into a club with a wink from the doorman, and looking at the dance floor until someone looks back at me, and walks up to me and says something, or doesn't say anything, and touches me.

The first time is with a guy from Brooklyn. He is about the same age as me and he kisses me in a bar and asks me if I'd like to go back to his place for the night, and I say okay, and we go to the subway and the train takes a while and all the time he talks about cars, about which is the best car, which car he's going to buy when he graduates, where he's going to buy it, what he's going to do with it when he has it. He's handsome but he's annoying. I worry that he'll think I'm weird because I don't really talk. But he doesn't seem to think anything. At his place there are some other people in the living room eating and we just go through to his bedroom and when we're naked he just wants to jerk off and nothing else, and I try to suck him or get him to suck me, but he bats me away and tells me *No, no man, we have to be careful now you know*? And eventually he comes and then I come and he doesn't say anything about me staying and I don't want to stay anyway so he sees me to the door, past the people who still seem to be eating, and I get lost trying to find the subway and walk all the way back over the bridge and go home to the Bronx, and all the way I curse the guy and his stupid cars. What an asshole.

*

I smoke all the time. I smoke and I don't make friends. I see the same faces in bars or clubs, and especially in the sex shops. Sometimes people nod at me. For a while I stick to the sex shops with their video cabins, because if one guy turns out to be an asshole you're not stuck at his place before you find out, and there is always someone else. I find out that older guys are better. They are more relaxed. They do more things. So I prefer them to be older. In the video cabins there is never much talk and I like that. And I like the porn. And I like to suck guys off through the glory holes. Glory holes seem like a really good idea. And I like that I am sometimes not sure that the cock in my mouth belongs to the good looking guy I saw outside a minute ago, or whether it belongs to someone else. And I like to put my cock through those holes and cling to the top of the partition and arch my hips and stare at the cheap wood at the end of my nose and I love that cheap wood, those partitions. They are the face I want, most of the time, they are the face of New York. They are a beautiful nothing. Chipboard and hard plastic, red usually, bloated flat. I spit at them. I head-butt them and come. I wrestle with them and fight them and I want them to buckle and break and crumble, but I don't want what I want.

In the bars I have to talk more, work harder. But I find out that if you hook up with a guy in a bar who is good, and who maybe has a nice place, then you can have a really good night. But it is always hit and miss. And I make mistakes. And I try to stop making mistakes by not making decisions, by not caring, by allowing myself to drift through men, letting them talk to me if they want to, letting them like me or not like me, letting them make decisions about me, a series of decisions and calculations about me as if I'm a problem that they try to solve and they give up or keep at it and really I am not much of a problem and I usually go home with whoever asks first.

I don't make friends. If someone just wants to talk or be nice to me I move away. Guys my age. They look into my eyes and they want me to talk. Beautiful ones, ones that make my heart gulp—I avoid them. I steer clear. All I want is the men who want me.

And these men live everywhere. They take me in cars and cabs and on the subway to places I have never heard of, sometimes very far away, into New Jersey or out to Long Island or upstate somewhere.

And they lead me into buildings, and I follow them with my cigarettes and I get to see apartments and houses that are plush or seedy or ordinary or strange. I let myself get fucked by these men and most of the time they use a condom but sometimes I don't really check or know or care, and sometimes I know full well that they're not using a condom. And I like to fuck too, and I fuck these men with a condom unless they ask me not to. Because he says it's okay, that he's clear. Or because he tells me that it's all bullshit, that they're just trying to scare us out of fucking because they hate us. Or because he tells me that he is immune, that he gets his blood changed once every three months in a Swiss clinic, or that he's a virgin. *Well, I'm not*, I tell him. And he says, *I don't fucking care*. What I like to feel is like a body. Just a body. What a body feels. That's all.

Once or twice I get scared. Several times, I get scared. A man who stops his car in the middle of nowhere and wants to go into the trees. A man who ties me up and then someone else is there. Sometimes I find myself walking home. Or just walking, at dawn, lost somewhere, and I find myself crying or cold or unsure of what I've been doing. Sometimes I'm bruised. One time I don't know about it until I turn up at work and someone winces at my face and I turn out to have a black eye.

I get scared but I stamp down on it.

In one man's house I see a lot of medical paraphernalia. Some men won't touch me without gloves on. Won't go near my cock unless it's covered by a condom. In the bars sometimes I see men who look sick. They have friends. I notice that they usually have friends, sitting with them, chatting, holding their hand. I don't want friends. I am closed. I am not gay. I am not queer. I am not anything. I am not Irish. I am not in New York. I am not twenty. I am not doing any of the things that I am doing. I press my head against the board.

I lie awake on the sofa and I count them and stop. And I think that when I get back to Dublin I will be finished. That will be the end of it.

I am in a bar in Midtown, I don't know why. I haven't been here before. Someone told me about it. I'm tired. It's my day off and I am tired and I am thinking about going to the cinema. And there is this guy at the bar. He is quite feminine. He's dressed in jeans and a shirt, or a blouse maybe, and he's not much older than me, and he is wearing mascara and some lip gloss but his hair is short. And I don't really know that I'm staring at him until he winks at me from his barstool, a sort of ducked-head, half-smile, up from under his brow wink, which makes me blush, and I realise that he is blue-eyed and pale skinned and beautiful and drunk. And coming over.

He totters to my table and stands for a moment swaying slightly and I just smile at him, and he says, in a voice that is from somewhere else entirely...

—What you looking at kid? Are you enamoured? Are you enamoured of me?

I don't talk to people.

—Kid? I say, trying to drop my smile.

He sits down beside me.

—Well I haven't seen you before, he says. So you get to be kid for a week.

I don't want him there because I like him. But he stays there because he likes me. And I don't want to talk to him but he asks me if I'm a hustler and I am so embarrassed at this idea that I bluster and blush and stammer out all sorts of denials. And he is laughing at me, his head ducking down onto my shoulder, saying, *Oh don't worry about it, I'm kidding you, don't worry, you're cute, look at you, where are you from?* And I tell him Ireland and he looks at me for a moment and stops laughing and then he kisses me on the cheek and tells me that he just knew it, and that he loves Irish guys, and that he knew this Irish boy once and, well... and he trails off. Then he stands up and goes to the bar and comes back with another gin for him and a beer for me and he tells me that his name is Paulie and that he is the worst drag act in Manhattan.

We talk. I forget that I don't talk.

I am smiling.

He has problems. There is his drinking and it is such a nightmare and he doesn't know what to do about it. There is his rent and his sister who is just insane and there is the money he owes and there is the bar that owes him for two shows from last month when he didn't get a penny, and there is this and that, and I have nothing very much to give back to him.

—You're a fucking doorman? A doorman? Jesus. Look at you. Tell me your name. Tell me about you. What are you doing in a stupid damn bar like this? On your own? Why are you on your own? I don't mean a date, I mean your friends. Where are your friends? Where? Are? Your? Friends?

I don't have any friends, I tell him.

—What are you talking about you don't have any friends? Honey. Please. What sort of cute damn Irish doorman boy has no goddamned friends?

And I tell him no. And he asks me what I do all the time I'm not working and I don't know what to tell him and he looks at me and arches his eyebrows like he can guess.

—Oh boy. You're a hustler alright, you just don't charge.

And I buy more drinks. And we keep talking. He asks me if I have a boyfriend back in Dublin and I say no, I do not have anything back in Dublin. Nothing at all. And he calls me by my name and he is tactile, relaxed, and he lays a hand on mine or an arm on my shoulder. And then he goes to the bathroom and comes back ten minutes later and seems to forget that I'm at the table waiting for him, and I feel drunk and weird, and he goes to the bar and is talking to people there, and I get up to go, but he comes at me across the room.

—STOP RIGHT THERE.

And he drags me around the bar on his arm introducing me to people as his new boy: *My new boy, meet my new boy, isn't he cute, say something, wait for the accent, say something, oh go on, oh he's so shy isn't he adorable, isn't he the cutest thing?* And I don't know why but all of this is okay. It's funny. He's funny. And he looks so good, and I am happy to be with him, and I remember something interesting that I can tell him.

But when we sit down again straight away he whispers in my ear that he is not after my ass. He is, he says, *incapable*, he is *like an old man*—he *can't get it up no matter what*. He hasn't, he said, had an erection in a month. *Don't flatter yourself kid. Not even you. Not even your sweet little Irish tush.* And he gives me his ducked head low-brow wink again. And I have a hard-on. He doesn't know, he says, what it is, and he reels off a list of drugs so packed with ridiculous names that the recitation is like some sort of poem, so it reminds me of poetry, and I ask him if he likes poetry, and he looks at me silently and says nothing for a minute, and then he kisses my cheek again.

He knows so much more than I do. We talk about Frank O'Hara. He tells me about Ginsberg. Berryman. John Ashbery. I talk shyly about Yeats and MacNeice, trying to remember what I learned at school. And I tell him how I love Anne Sexton. And he tells me about Rimbaud, and he speaks a poem of his for me in French, close to my face, and I don't understand the words but I look into his eyes while he says them, I don't take my eyes off his, and when he stops I have nothing so I kiss him. I kiss him on the lips. And I feel his body minutely, in the course of this kiss, tense and tremble and relax. And I know, I know completely that what I am doing is something good and right and beautiful and that I am really drunk and if I am not careful I am going to cry and tell him every stupid thing I have done wrong. He takes my hand and holds it.

I don't really know what happens after that. I am inside myself feeling cold and I cannot understand what I am doing, and I am baffled by everything I say because it seems to be true but I have never heard it before. And I hear shouts start up in my mind. I hear panic and alarms. And I know that I have put myself at risk, that this is a bad situation, that this could kill me, this could kill me. I leave when he is next in the bathroom. I walk out and I walk for a long time. I pass the building where I work. I walk up the spine of the island and I look at people and at cars and buses and I look up at buildings and I explain to myself that I have had a lucky escape. A close call. I explain it to myself in detail and I enunciate the potential for disaster and I berate myself for my stupidity. I take a cab to the Bronx and I shudder in the heat and I sleep on the sofa.

A week or more later. I'm on the night shift, on the front door in my stupid blue suit with a guy called Barney. And Barney says to me:

—Here's that tranny again.

—What?

—There, see? By the trees down the street. Was here last night too. Just staring at me for about twenty minutes. Probably harmless but hey.

Paulie is wearing a black dress, a slim-fitting dress, and he is wearing high heels and carrying a tote bag and he is still swaying, and he's squinting at us. I go to the bathroom and stay there for a half an hour. I suppose I told him where I worked. More or less. When I get back he's gone, and Barney is pissed at me.

The next night I am on again, and this time Barney goes off somewhere and I'm there on my own and Paulie appears out of nowhere, in jeans this time, and a shirt and jacket, still some make-up, and his hair is different, longer.

—Hi.

I just look at him.

—Where did you go?

—Beg your pardon?

—That night. You just left. You know. I thought we were doing good.

—I'm sorry, I don't know what you're referring to.

—Huh?

—Maybe you're mistaking me for someone else.

—Oh come *on*. You have to be kidding?

Barney comes back.

—We okay? he asks.

Paulie ignores him.

—Don't do this.

I look at Barney and shrug as if to say *I have no idea*.

—You looking for something buddy?

—I'm just talking to my friend here.

—I don't know you.

—You fucking *do*. Jesus.

—You're confusing me with someone else.

Barney just stands there.

Paulie looks at me hard, and then his shoulders crumple and he looks down. And he sighs.

—You are one serious fuck-up. And that's a shame. That's a stupid damn shame.

He takes something out of his pocket and holds it out to me. I just look at it.

—Oh take it, you dickhead.

I take it. Paulie walks off.

He's handed me a folded-over piece of paper with my name on it.

On the inside is his full name and his address and his phone number and beneath all that he's written lines from a Frank O'Hara poem:

> *It's a summer day,*
> *and I want to be wanted more than anything else in the world.*

Barney watches me tear it up into little pieces and throw it in the flowerbeds.

One night I am with three men in a loft apartment in Queens and they are taking turns fucking me and in the middle of it all I start to cry. I just lose it. And they stop, and they are freaked out, and I tell them that I think that I have had enough now, and I get dressed and I go.

It is weeks before I remember that I had something I could have told Paulie. That I met Andy Warhol. I think about going back to the bar. But I have a list of fears, and at the top of the list is love. So I get ready to leave New York and I think about Paulie all the time.

I stare at Marilyn and I smoke my cigarette and I wait to hear if I'm sick. We just do things. We do one thing and then another. That's all. There are only the multiple pinpricks of living, and the tiny scars they leave, and if you look at them in a certain light they can look like constellations. But the stars are senseless too, dead or dying, and their light is a memory.

Body Clock

Eimear Ryan

Sometimes I'm shaken by the intense feelings you can have for a stranger. The sudden rush of affection for a kid in a supermarket hiding from his parents, or for an old man in a coffee shop, blessing himself after finishing a muffin.

Sometimes it's a pointless rage: towards the teenage girls on the bus with the mocking laughs, or the guy who asks you for a light when you're sitting outside a café having lunch with your friends. Yes, you'll light his fag, and he'll lean in and cup your hands so it's weirdly intimate, but all you want to say is: 'Call yourself a smoker?'

By the next day you've forgotten these people, but for a few moments they overwhelm you, short the circuit boards of your brain.

Right now, I'm on the train going from Logan Airport to the Back Bay. I'm in the standing space, trying to shrink, make my suitcase look smaller than it is. Passengers trying to get past keep stumbling over me. I wait for the sighs of impatience, the muted glares, but the people here don't go in for that much.

If I was anyone else on this train I would hate me.

I'm sitting on the broad back of my suitcase in Copley Square. If I tilt my head back as far as it will go, I can just about see the top of the John Hancock Tower, looking like a beaker filled with lagoon water. It's autumn, hot, and I wait, feeling my skin heat up and harden, watching teenagers ollie past No Skateboarding signs.

I'm waiting for Orla, who is seventeen years older than me, four inches shorter and thirty pounds lighter. She offered to meet me at the airport, but I like Boston. I want to experience some of it alone.

I see Orla when she's about fifty yards away. We experience that awkwardness where you sight someone from a distance, and have to maintain the enthusiasm until they're close to you. When is the right time to wave, to call out? Twenty yards? Ten?

'Hey Jules!' she yells from fifteen yards. She always knows the right time.

She is wearing all black on a scorcher of a day.

Her smile would be a beautiful one, if not for the stains. It's the smile I'll probably have in twenty years. I have a sudden wish to have Orla around all the time, just for that smile: it's the one thing that could wean me off smoking.

We cross the square to a café where Orla knows the owner 'quite well.' Sure enough, we get a complimentary bottle of wine. She looks across the table at me, sizing me up. To avoid the eye contact, I check the bottle's label. '06 Rioja. It means nothing to me, but Orla seems put out by the wine's vintage and origin. She fusses and apologises, and pours large glasses, adding 'I've got better stuff at home.' I'm buoyed by her slight discomfiture, and don't bother to tell her that my rough palate makes no distinction between seven euro swill from Spar and a swanky restaurant's house wine.

I should point out that I am not a bad person. I want her to come away from this visit believing that we bonded. I just hope it doesn't take too much out of me.

After we order, Orla clasps her hands and sighs in a way that is meant to evoke deep satisfaction. 'So!'

'So,' I reply, dutifully.

'How is Niall?'

'Good form. You know Dad, like.'

'Yes. Irrepressible.' She rolls her eyes, trying to disguise it by leaning forward to sip her wine. 'And—oh, who was that charming friend of yours at your eighteenth? Dermot?'

'Diarmuid. Yeah, can't wait to get back to college. We're gonna be living together again this year.'

She stops sipping. 'Ooooh. Are you sleeping together?'

'Oh God, no.'

'Why ever not? He's cute. And you, honey, you've got that certain appeal.'

'It isn't like that.'

'Like what?'

'This is gorgeous.' I spear some of my prawn salad, and offer her some, but she just looks at me, and won't let me take the conversation off on the tangent I want it to go. 'Thing about Diarmuid is, he sleeps with everyone he knows, except me. It's like his mark of respect or something.'

'Is he gay?'

'Not exactly.'

She smiles again, briefly flashing those nicotine teeth. I should photograph those teeth.

'I thought so,' she says, dropping her voice. 'At your party, you know, we both went to the back kitchen to fetch your cake… oh it was nothing really, a silly thing, the candles wouldn't light and he made some stupid joke… but I thought he was flirting with me.'

I am reminded that, though I don't see her too often, and though we are often mistaken for sisters, these are not the reasons I sometimes forget she's my mother.

We get the tram to Cambridge, to her new place. She moved out of Latest Boyfriend's apartment last month and she's a little sketchy on the details. I quite liked Latest Boyfriend—what I heard of him, anyway. She seemed less jokey and apologetic about him than the others. She was breathless and fretful, and it astonished me that someone could make her act that way.

We walk down a broken pavement that's littered with blue and red frat party cups. I kick them out of the way. The wheels of my suitcase get stuck in the cracks in the path. She doesn't help me haul it out.

'Here we are,' she says, fumbling with keys. 'I have to warn you, it isn't much.'

I guess I could have anticipated that Boston apartments don't come furnished.

We have a glass of the 'better stuff', which I secretly enjoy less than the café bottle, and lean against the counter, chatting intermittently. Eventually I cry jetlag and retire to my room. The windows don't have curtains yet, so I know I'll be woken in a gust of sunlight at 7AM. Best way to adjust the body clock, I suppose.

I climb onto the inflatable mattress in the corner and curl up.

*

I wake at 3.30AM. There is clearly no talking to my body clock. My throat feels shrivelled—I need water. The mattress hisses and writhes as I stumble to my feet.

In the kitchen, I put a glass under the tap.

'Oh—you're here,' comes Orla's voice, dully.

I jump slightly, turn and see her outline, a lotus position in a corner of the dark living room. Her face is lit eerily by the glow of the computer on her lap.

'Hi,' I say. 'Just wanted a drink.'

'Sure.'

I know I have to ask why she's awake and on her computer at half three. I go and stand beside her, but I feel huge and imposing so I get down on my knees.

'Everything okay?' I ask. Her eyes are huge and very black.

'Just got an email,' she says, fingers flexing on the keyboard. 'From Mark. He's back with his ex.'

'I'm sorry.' I know I was told Mark's name, but it's as if I'm hearing it for the first time.

'Yeah. He's rather... to the point.' She sighs. 'I had high hopes, you know? I'm not getting any younger and... it felt like a chance to settle down. Start over.'

There it is, then. She wants another go at family life. I don't say anything.

'Do you have a guy you love, Jules?'

'Umm, no.'

'You ever been in love? There's so much I don't know about you. We should talk about these things, really.'

I have a sudden rush of panic. She forces out a giggle.

'Hellooo? Earth to Jules? Ever been in love?'

'Sadly, no,' I sigh dramatically, going along with the jollity.

'Course not. You're too smart.'

I bristle slightly. I've been called smart before, though not always in a complimentary way.

'I do have feelings, you know,' I say, and I'm surprised at how petulant it sounds, the only full sentence I've spoken.

Her face crumples in the greenish laptop light. 'I'm sorry,' she says. 'I didn't mean—'

'No, it's okay,' I say, embarrassed for us both. I want to change the subject before I end up apologising too.

'I'm sorry… I don't always know how to talk to you, honey,' she says, her voice smothered in unshed tears. 'It's hard—we're not around each other much.' She laughs a tiny laugh. 'You even call me by my first name, for God's sake.'

'Yeah—that's…'

'You don't have to explain.'

We sit there a while, my leg going to sleep under the weight of me, no sound except the low gossipy noise of late-night traffic on the street below.

She says: 'I remember the last time you called me "Mam", actually. You were nine. I was visiting you and your father for a few weeks, and Kitty Kiernan— you remember her?'

'Course I do.'

'Yes, well, we were sitting outside, on that bench that used to be at the gable end. Really hot day for once, we needed the shade. And Kitty Kiernan got a hold of a mouse, just a few metres away from us. She was playing with it. Letting it go, and the mouse's little legs going, trying to carry itself away. And then Kitty Kiernan would just pounce on it again. Do you remember?'

I don't, but I say: 'I think so.'

'Anyway, you started crying, burying your face against me. You said "Mam, how can Kitty Kiernan be so cruel?" I was at a bit of a loss. I just babbled away. Eventually I said: "Oh honey, it's just nature, you know? Like in the Serengeti," and of course that got your attention, because you were all into David Attenborough at the time. Like I said—smart.' She paused. 'You stopped crying then, and you got brave enough to watch the whole thing, wide-eyed. And Kitty Kiernan finally finished the mouse off, and your little body just gave this heave of relief.'

We're quiet for a while.

'I'm sorry,' I say, because it's all I can think of to say.

She shakes her head. 'For what?'

I know that maybe I should have called her 'Mam' just now. It would have been a meaningful moment. But a part of me cringes and balks at those moments that most people, maybe rightly, regard as being the stuff of a good life.

Still, I look at her face—honest now, not trying to project anything—and I feel ashamed, remembering my resolve to cruise through this visit on autopilot.

I should maybe hug her, but it's too awkward in this dark unfurnished room. I'd be groping into a corner, losing my balance, hitting edges.

'Do you—want a cigarette?' I ask, trying to find something we can share. I remember I left my handbag on the kitchen counter. I jump up and pull out a cigarette and light up, wishing I hadn't, knowing my shaking hands are making the lighter's flame hover in the air, like an uncertain bug.

'No thanks, honey,' she says. 'I've quit.'

I laugh nervously. 'Congratulations.' I take a drag from mine, letting the smoke dribble from my mouth, then impulsively go to the sink and stab it out.

'Go back to bed, Jules. You need your rest.'

'Okay. See you in the morning?'

'See you,' she says, sounding strangely loud, as if closer than she is.

I climb back into my bed, bury my face in the pillow. I want to drop off, but I'm filled with a longing I can't name and I can't get comfortable. I try a few positions, on my belly, even the foetal position, but my body just aches. I finally flip onto my back and try to keep my spine stiff and straight.

I stare at the ceiling till the light spills in: sunrise.

Three Love Stories

Cathy Sweeney

I

In the hallway of the house where I live there is a reproduction of a painting of Alexander the Great by the Italian artist, Pietro Rotari. It is a poor quality reproduction and hangs in a gilded frame. The painting depicts the first meeting between Alexander and a young woman he would later marry. When Alexander was a young man he had fallen in love with his childhood friend, Hephaestion. Years later when Hephaestion died, Alexander's grief was uncontrollable. He ordered the manes and tails of all his horses to be cut and on the day of the funeral gave orders that the sacred flame in the temple be extinguished; something normally done only on the death of a king.

When I was young woman, I too fell in love with my childhood friend. That was a long time ago. Now I live in one room above a shop. The walls are painted green, but they have been painted so many times that when they chip it is blue underneath. The glass in the windows is thin. I have my own toilet but share the kitchen with other people. The kitchen is on the floor above my room and I go there in the afternoons when everyone is at work. I wipe the surfaces clean and then cook stew or goulash with dumplings or pork with rice. I eat some of the food and leave the rest in the fridge. The walls of the kitchen are painted yellow.

Alexander the Great was educated by Aristotle who, in his later years, fell in love with a boy. I imagine the boy as smooth and beautiful; soft eyes and hard arms, a boy bathed in the kind of stereotypes that never go out of fashion. The pottery of the time depicts such relationships—an older lover fondles the genitals of the beloved while holding his chin and looking into his eyes. The beloved's genitals are unmoved. He remains a perfect child in a perfect dream. Of course, this is art and not reality. Maybe Aristotle's lover was a muscular teen infatuated with his girl-cousin.

The food I leave in the fridge is eaten by a young woman from the country with yellow hair and green/blue eyes. She is a librarian. She told me this one day in the hallway. She would like to tell me more, but I pretend to be in a hurry. I live here because I have no money, not because I want to hear stories. One day the young woman knocked on my door to tell me that she was going away for the weekend with her married lover. She asked me to feed her cat. I told her I was busy. I am tired of people with their dot-to-dot fantasies.

After Hephastion's death Alexander the Great was warned not to enter Babylon. He went anyway, fell ill there and died; his death helicing back through all the events of his life. My childhood friend died many years ago. During the time I was in love with him many things happened, but in the end everything happened on one afternoon of green leaves blowing back and forth against a blue sky. This visual is attached to some particular memory, but I no longer know what. Alexander the Great is said to have been fair skinned, with a ruddy tinge to his face and chest, but Plutarch said that he had a pleasing scent.

After the young woman returned from her weekend I met her in the hallway. She told me that her married lover was going to leave his wife and that they were going to rent an apartment together. I expressed the sorrow due to anyone who gets what they want. In the fading light the young woman's eyes were charcoal and her hair was grey. A few weeks after that she moved out. I stopped cooking and took to eating in cheap restaurants. I rarely think of the young woman, but sometimes, when I am in the hallway, I experience an intense but shortlived desire to begin my life again.

II

After my father died I craved tranquillity—not the soft kind, but steady firmness of mind—what the Greeks called euthymia. My father was a hollow man. He plumped himself up with stuffing, but in the end I could see right through his eyes and out the back of his skull. At night the waves of his breath beat against my door and in the morning I cleaned spittle from the sheets.

Democritus was the first to write about euthymia. He explained it as the state of being in which the soul is freed from all desire and unified with all its parts. Democritus believed that euthymia should be the final goal of everything we do in life, and that is why I need to tell you about my lover, but first let me say this. I held my father's head in my lap as if it was the head of a gold baby. Time passed. I found stuffing in the bed and on the couch and in the toilet. Time passed. I held my breath when I kissed him. Time passed. My eyes turned into wolf eyes. Time passed. I fantasised about death, sometimes his, sometimes mine. Time passed. Nothing.

When my father died I went to see a priest. The priest told me that no one can be happy unless they live a virtuous life, not because virtue is good in itself, but because it leads to the absence of pain. I did not know this. He also said that many of the bodily pleasures brought with them pain. I did know this. As a child I had taken a bite from a glass and crunched it into a thousand red pieces. The priest's hands were warm but when he touched me my stomach growled. I had not eaten.

I will tell you more about euthymia, but first I must tell you about my lover. He is an old man, tightly contained within himself. His hair is white and his eyes are mercenary blue. He lives in the marshlands in a bungalow built from a plan in a book. It is the worst place in the world to live. The brickwork around the door is the colour of a giraffe's neck and all the rooms face north. Rubbish has gathered by the gates. The first time I went to the bungalow my lover held my hair and made love to me as though I were a man. Afterwards he changed the sheets, tucking the corners in, and I slept against his back in a deep moribund ache.

Before I met my lover I was stuck in a dance with desire and had no way of distinguishing waking life from dream. I was unhappy. That is a lie. Sometimes I was happy and it lasted for years, but then I was unhappy again and blamed the dance, and then I fell in love with the dance in the ferocious way we love things we do not like. After my father died I wanted to make peace with death, and that is where euthymia comes in, and I'll tell you about it, but first I must tell you more about my lover.

I go to the bungalow every two weeks and stay for two hours. When I arrive my lover sets a timer and we make love on the sitting room floor. The carpet is rope and I get scorch marks on my knees and lower back. I observe the dust that has gathered under the sofa and the chipped paint on the architraves. My lover makes no concession to the fact that I am a woman. Once, when I talked too much, he hit me in the face and made my nose bleed. Of course, I was not always delighted with physical pain. I used to shout 'How dare you?' and 'Bastard' and run out the door, until my lover bit my nipples and they blackened like berries.

My lover insists that I reach orgasm because he hates to owe anyone anything. When he works his fingers inside me, his eyes never leave mine. He will not tolerate a lie. Afterwards I am calm. My thoughts are sentences. If there is time left on the clock we sit together in the kitchen and drink coffee. The mugs have worn pictures on them and the windows are smudged opaque. I tell my lover things from newspapers and then the clock buzzes and I leave. I am getting closer to telling you about euthymia.

The last time I went to the bungalow my lover was sick and I sat alone in the kitchen. It is an old kitchen, veneer presses and dots of mould in the corners of the ceiling. Everything is neat. My lover stacks the dishes beside the sink and folds the bag of sugar tightly at the top. I make coffee and it tastes like his breath. He has no toaster, so I grill bread in the oven. It makes a spinning noise and I am afraid it will disturb him. There is no butter, so I use jam. I bring some coffee and bread to my lover. He eats the bread and, as I leave, I hear the coffee filtering through his chest.

And now I will tell you about what the Greeks call euthymia. At night, when I walk the city streets, metal clouds obfuscate the sky. There is tremendous weight in their mood, but it falls as virga, never reaching me. I possess tranquillity, not the soft kind, but steady firmness of mind.

III

Seneca was born a long time ago. He believed that the greatest obstacle to living is the expectancy we hang upon tomorrow. Because of this we lose the present, while all the time the future remains uncertain. This is the story of a woman who wasted a great deal of time (a) expecting her married lover to leave his wife (b) expecting her single lover to propose to her. Of course, in the end something entirely different happened.

It was an ordinary day. The woman got on a tram destined for the city. She had broad shoulders and was well dressed. She was neither young nor old but had a rich sexuality. Above her bra her breasts bulged and her hands seemed to be forever feeling their way in the dark. The woman had spent the night with her married lover, a short man with a compulsion to oppress things that were already oppressed. In the morning she was anxious to be gone but the married lover always booked rooms in industrial estates where there were no taxis, so she got a tram.

The tram was one of the newer kind and had no conductor. The woman dropped in coin after coin at the driver's booth until a ticket came out. The seats were narrow and the window was shrouded in dust. The woman did not know where she was, so she did not know how long it would take to get to the city.

This was the first stop on the tramline and people sat far apart. The tram moved as though in a dream that woke each time the doors flung open to let people on. Soon the aisles were full and the woman breathed the breath of strangers. Rain spat against the glass in hard little spits that carried no weight.

The woman checked her phone. Her single lover would call soon and sigh loudly to denote emotion. He was young and could not understand why poor people had children or why intelligent people took harmful drugs. Through the window the city passed in a frieze of odd angles and tower blocks and statues of giants in grimaces.

A child sat in the seat across from the woman. He was three or four years old and sucked on a soother. He saw something out the window and bobbed in his seat, pointing and sucking hard on the soother. Nobody responded. The woman looked out the window and saw a plane flying low to land. 'Aeroplane' she said to the child, 'Aeroplane'. The mother of the child pulled him onto her lap. Her skin was dead from smoking too much and her jeans were empty. She looked at the woman as if to say, 'Mind your own fucking business' or 'Get your own child, bitch'. The woman was unmoved. She did not want children.

The child wriggled free and stood beside the woman's legs, staring at her. His cheeks were glossed with snot and his hair was thin on a flaky scalp. The woman looked out the window at grey buildings merging into grey sky. She could smell bed wet. When she turned back the child was still staring at her.

Seneca said that every condition can change, and whatever happens to one person can happen to anyone. But when things change people want the past back. They want to relive their old life, conscious this time that it was not so bad. The woman, however, was not such a person. When her life changed, she realised that the past is just a random sequence of images.

On a busy street in rush hour the tram crashed into a bus. The bus driver thought the traffic light was green. The front carriage of the tram buckled as though made of foil and the next carriage turned on its side, broke away from the rest of the tram, and skidded along the road, slamming into the front of a pharmacy. In the end the death toll was eleven. People asked, 'How can something like this happen?' The woman was uninjured. When the crash happened, she had picked up the child and held him to her. Against her blouse, he felt like a bag of dough. She remained holding the child when she saw that his mother was dead. She held the child at the police station and in the courts and on visiting days, and in the end she held onto the child forever.

The married lover was inspired by the woman. For a short time he remembered that he too had children, and ended the affair. The single lover was repulsed by both the desire for the child and the child itself. Soon afterwards, he married a woman with a perfect hip-to-waist ratio. Seneca died in great pain. Ordered to commit suicide, he opened his veins, but either he didn't do a good job or his veins were too old. It took ages for him to die.

I Bought A Heart

William Wall

I bought a heart. It was a sheep's heart. I intended to stuff it with bread, onion and thyme. It was raining outside but the market was covered. My jaw hurts more on wet days. It was killing me now. The butcher was watching television. It was a small screen set on the wall to the left of the counter. Look at the fuckers, he said. Jimmy, I said, you shouldn't say fuckers to customers. Sure you're hardly a customer at all, he said, all you buy is fucking hearts, Jesus if I was depending on you for a living. He pointed at the television. Look at the bastards, after screwing us for ten years and now we're supposed to feel sorry for them. The sound was turned down. Do you know what I heard this morning, he said. Did you ever hear the expression stockbroker sentiment? Sentiment my arse. Put me down for two hearts next Thursday, I said, I'm expecting company. He wrote it in his book. Then I went away. I did not have an umbrella. I walked as near to the wall as I could because it's drier there. There are awnings overhead from time to time. I thought about a quick pint but realised I didn't have the money. The heart broke me. My mother is coming out for the day on Thursday and she still likes hearts. This is something I don't understand. She doesn't know my name. She doesn't recognise me. She doesn't remember that she has a child. But she still likes the taste of meat. She even *remembers* that she likes the taste. I sometimes think that the stomach has its own brain. When the rain got lighter I made a run for it. The pain in my jaw stopped when I ran. That's a good one, I thought, if I could keep running I'd never get pain any more. But you can't. Running would kill you quick enough.

Crossing the bridge the heavens opened. It was that straight down rain. It came down under my collar and through my clothes. I stood into the doorway of the funeral home. The rain made the river smooth. Then it stopped and in a minute the sun came out. That was when I noticed that she was behind me. She was crying. Are you all right, I said. Look, I said, I have a heart. She just looked at me. I'm going to stuff the fucker, I said. I don't know why I said fucker. I suppose that was Jimmy coming out in me. Jimmy is a big influence. Even when we were kids my mother used to say you were out with that Jimmy Canty again, the tongue he has, I can hear him in you. The woman came forward. What kind of a heart, she said. Sheep, I said. I'm going to stuff it. Lovely, she said, do you cook yourself? I do. Good man, she said, I'm all for that. I said, Did someone die on you? My husband, she said. I'm sorry. No, we were estranged, I haven't seen him in a while, he's in there now, I just thought I'd nip in before the new family arrives and say goodbye, funny thing is I never cried when I said goodbye before, I suppose I'm sentimental. Is he open for viewing, I said. I don't know, she said, I didn't go in yet. I'm just sheltering from the rain. So I see, she said. What did he die of? A stroke, at his age, you wouldn't expect that, would you, except he was a workaholic, of course, that can't be good for you, he had no life. I said I could go in and have a look at the corpse with her. She looked at me without saying anything for a bit during which time it started to rain again. Then she said would I? I said I would. We went in and had a look. We had to ask someone in the office because there were three corpses in three different rooms. He was lying in a nice-looking coffin with silk lining and what I thought were probably gold-plated handles. He was stone dead and he looked it. I saw the way my father looked. People said he looked beautiful because all the lines in his face were gone but I preferred him with the lines. They said death took forty years off him. That was no good to me because death took everything from me. We ticked gold-plated handles on the menu the undertaker gave us. We ticked hardwood. We ticked marble headstone. We gave him everything but when he was in a hole in the ground nothing made any difference. He was just gone. Everybody said it was a great send-off. That didn't make any difference either. I said that to the woman and she said it didn't matter to her because the new family were paying for it, she wasn't even notified except a friend saw it in the deaths. She started crying again. That was the way he looked, she said, he was a handsome chap, he was gorgeous really. Then she spat in his face. She did it twice. Missus, I said, what are you doing, you can't do that. That's for everything he did to me, she said. Then she said to the corpse, How do you like it now you fucking dead bastard, much good your fucking fancy woman did you. Come on, she said, I need a drink.

She bought the drink. I told her how the heart took my last euro. I'm totally stony, I said. God help you, she said, so am I but at least I have the price of a drink. Where there's an undertaker there's a pub. I asked for a pint of Guinness and she bought it for me. I don't know what she was having herself because she mixed it at the counter. It looked like a glass of water with ice in it but it wasn't. In my experience women like vodka and gin and you can't see either of them. She told me the story of her life. It was quite interesting. The relevant part was where her husband came home one night and she could smell the other woman on him. She went ballistic. Totally ballistic. Up until that minute they had never had a serious row and since then she often thought that it was a bad sign. If they had rows it meant they would have something to fight about. Did he admit it? He did eventually. What did he say? I can't remember, that's the kind of thing you want to forget, it wasn't nice, what did I ever do to him, I ask you. She went up and ordered another Guinness and another glass of invisible alcohol. I saw my orthodontist come in. As soon as I saw him the pain in my jaw started all over again. The glass of water had a little Chinese umbrella in it. So, I said, what are you going to do? She drank half of her glass. When she held the glass up the Chinese umbrella slid against her mouth. The removal is in ten minutes, she said, so we have to get ready. Then she finished the rest of the glass and went for another one. She came back with a whiskey for me and another umbrella glass. Down the hatch, she said. There was something like a dead smile on her face. I said, That man is my orthodontist. What do you want an orthodontist for, I thought you were broke? I had major reconstructive surgery, I said, after an accident. Down the hatch, she said. We drank our shorts together. I cycled into an articulated lorry, I said, I was coming down the hill, he backed out, to tell you the truth I wasn't looking. Jesus. They fixed me up in the hospital and then they sent me to him. He identified an overcrowding problem. He screwed up. He's a crap orthodontist.

I said, I'm going to tell him he ruined my life. When I stood up I was a bit shook. I'm not used to drinking so fast. I sat down again and finished the whiskey. Come on, the woman said, I'll go with you. We went up to the orthodontist. Excuse me, she said, this gentleman has something to say to you. But I couldn't say it. I just stood there. I wanted to say, After what you did to me I can't hold down a job. I got fired because I was sick and now the company is gone too. He didn't recognise me. Orthodontists probably only recognise teeth. I opened my mouth. I tried to open wide but the joint doesn't work a hundred per cent anymore. He looked away. I could see he was embarrassed. I can't say I blame him, this fucker with a wired-up jaw opening and closing it in your face without saying a word. He probably thought I was a maniac. He may or may not have remembered something. He pretended to be looking at the news. It was Sky. A line along the bottom said, Fed buys AIG. Jesus, he said, this is big.

Come on, the woman said, it's time for the removal. She pushed the orthodontist's arm which spilled his drink onto the counter. You ruined his life, she said. Then we went out and saw that there was a respectful crowd at the door of the funeral home. Right, she said, don't let me down now.

I said, I left my heart in the pub.

Fuck your heart, she said, come on. She pushed through the crowd and I followed. It started to rain again. We turned in the door and I saw the coffin ahead. I could see that her shoulders were shaking. I thought she was probably crying or getting very mad. There was a priest and a young family. I could see the new wife. She looked beautiful the way sorrowful people do. There were people in suits. There was an old woman who looked like my mother. She was looking at us. I could see she didn't know what was going on and she wasn't happy about it. I tried not to look at her. In my mother's world now something terrible was always going to happen. Even in her bed in the Home she was fretting. There wasn't enough of her left to be happy and happiness is the only defence against fear, I know that. I saw the same thing in that old woman. I couldn't do it then, whatever we were going to do. I turned around and went out.

My heart was still where I left it but the orthodontist was gone. I went home. There was bread there, and onion and thyme. When it was cooked it was delicious. I watched television all evening. I remember exactly what was on.

AFTERWORD & ACKNOWLEDGEMENTS

I hope you have enjoyed the stories in this book.

Setting up *The Stinging Fly* magazine in late 1997 felt like a good and necessary thing to do. Keeping it going since then has mostly felt good and necessary, too. Twenty years is a long time. It hasn't always been easy. I don't know what else I would have done.

There are very many people who helped along the way, too many to mention here. You know that I know who you are. I do want to name these names (colleagues and friends), all of whom have had hands-on experience working with me on the magazine down through the years:

Aoife Kavanagh, Gwyn Parry, Eabhan Ní Shúileabháin, Brian MacSweeney, Aiden O'Reilly, Maria Pierce, Maria Behan, Fergal Condon, Katie Holmes, Brendan Mac Evilly, Philip Bellew, Tom Mathews, Nessa O'Mahony, Emily Firetog, Claire Coughlan, Thomas Morris, Sean O'Reilly, Dave Lordan, Aifric Mac Aodha, Nuala Ní Chonchúir, Jonathan Dykes, Billy Ramsell, Lily Ní Dhomhnaill, Fiona Boyd, Mia Gallagher, John Patrick McHugh, Gavin Corbett, Lisa McInerney, Ian Maleney, Sara O'Rourke and Sally Rooney.

Thanks to all the magazine's readers. There'd be little point in doing this without you. A special thank you to our patrons and subscribers, some of whom have been supporting the magazine since the very early days.

Thanks to the Arts Council and particularly its Head of Literature, Sarah Bannan, for the ongoing support. Thanks to all our colleagues in the wider literature community in Ireland and beyond.

Thanks to all the writers in this book for letting us take their stories out for another spin. Thanks to all the writers who have contributed to the magazine. Thanks to all the writers in anticipation of your story or poem landing in with us someday soon.

Declan Meade
Dublin, April 2018

NOTES ON THE AUTHORS

Colin Barrett is the author of *Young Skins* (The Stinging Fly Press, 2013) for which he was awarded the Rooney Prize for Irish Literature, the Frank O'Connor International Short Story Award and the Guardian First Book Award. He has also had stories published in *Granta* and *The New Yorker*.

Kevin Barry is the author of the short-story collections, *There Are Little Kingdoms* and *Dark Lies The Island*, and the novels, *City of Bohane* and *Beatlebone*. He lives in County Sligo.

Sara Baume won the Davy Byrnes Short Story Award in 2014, the Rooney Prize for Irish Literature in 2015, and the Geoffrey Faber Memorial Prize in 2016. She is author of two novels, *Spill Simmer Falter Wither* and *A Line Made by Walking*.

Maria Behan is a fiction writer, political columnist, and journalist. She lives north of San Francisco these days, but she left her heart in Dublin.

Claire-Louise Bennett has written fiction and essays that have appeared in various publications, including *The White Review, gorse, Winter Papers, The Irish Times, The New York Times, Harper's,* and *Frieze Masters*. Her first book, *Pond* (The Stinging Fly Press, 2015), has been published in thirteen countries. It was shortlisted for the International Dylan Thomas Prize in 2016. Claire-Louise has received bursaries from the Arts Council of Ireland and very much appreciates their support.

Jennifer Brady is a writer and book lover from Dublin. Following on from her participation in the Stinging Fly Fiction Workshop she was a winner of the inaugural Irish Writers Centre Novel Fair Competition in 2012 and received a literature bursary from the Arts Council. She is a hands-on author, editor, proofer, project manager and publishing person working with authors and publishers worldwide.

Lucy Sweeney Byrne is a writer of short stories, essays and poetry.

Colin Corrigan's short fiction has also appeared in *Day One*, *The Fiction Desk*, and the anthology *Surge: New Writing from Ireland*. In 2018, he received a grant from the Elizabeth George Foundation to complete work on his debut novel. He lives with his wife in Ann Arbor, Michigan.

Mary Costello is from Galway. *The China Factory* (2012) was nominated for the Guardian First Book Award. Her novel *Academy Street* (2014) was short-listed for the International Dublin Literary Award, the Costa First Novel Prize and the EU Prize for Literature. It won Irish Book of the Year 2014.

Leona Lee Cully was born in Uranium City, Canada, grew up in Westmeath, and lives in Dublin. Her fiction has been published in *New Planet Cabaret*, *The Wild Word Magazine* (Berlin), *Penduline Press* (US), and *Carve Magazine* (US). She has collaborated with artists on films exploring urban space (narrative and voiceover). In recent years, Leona was invited to read her work at, as well as respond to, live art performances hosted by Live Stock and Dublin Live Art Festival.

Kevin Curran is the author of two novels, *Beatsploitation* and *Citizens*. He has also published short fiction in *Young Irelanders* (New Island) and has written for *The Guardian* and *The Observer*. He is the recipient of a bursary from Fingal County Council's Artists' Support Scheme.

Carys Davies is the author of two collections of short stories, *The Redemption of Galen Pike* (Salt) and *Some New Ambush* (Salt). She is the winner of the Frank O'Connor International Short Story Award, the Jerwood Fiction Uncovered Prize, the Royal Society of Literature's V.S.

Pritchett Memorial Prize, the Society of Authors' Olive Cook Short Story Award, a Northern Writers' Award and a 2016/17 Cullman Fellowship at the New York Public Library. Her debut novel, *West*, is being translated into six languages and will be out in the US (Scribner) and the UK (Granta) in 2018. Born in Wales, she now lives in north west England.

Danny Denton is a writer from Cork. His first novel, *The Earlie King & The Kid In Yellow*, was published by Granta Books in February 2018. He has also written for *Granta*, *The Guardian*, *Funhouse*, *Southword*, *Tate Etc*, and *The Irish Times*. He is currently the writer-in-residence for Cork County Library.

Wendy Erskine lives in Belfast. Her writing appears in the anthology *Female Lines: New Writing by Women from Northern Ireland*. Her debut short-story collection is forthcoming from The Stinging Fly Press in September 2018.

Oisín Fagan won the inaugural Penny Dreadful Novella Prize for *The Hierophants* in 2016. *Hostages*, his first collection was published by New Island Books in the same year. He is a recipient of a Literature bursary from the Arts Council of Ireland, and is represented by Lucy Luck at C+W Agency. 'Jessie' was his first story to be published.

Michael J. Farrell authored, for example, the prize-winning novel, *Papabile*, the Everyman/Aquarius anthology, *Creative Commotion*, and the short-story collections, *Life in the Universe* and *Life Here Below*. He lives in middle Ireland.

Nicole Flattery's fiction and non-fiction has also featured in *The Dublin Review*, *The Irish Times* and on BBC Radio 4. In 2017 she was the recipient of The White Review Short Story Prize and a Next Generation bursary award from the Arts Council. Her short-story collection is forthcoming from The Stinging Fly Press in 2019.

David Hayden was born in Dublin and lives in Norwich, England. His writing has also appeared in *Granta* online, *The Dublin Review*, *gorse* and *PN Review*. A debut book of stories, *Darker with the Lights On*, was published by Little Island Press in the UK in September 2017 and will be published in North America by Transit Books in May 2018.

Desmond Hogan was born in Ballinasloe, County Galway. He has been the recipient of the Hennessy Award (1971), the Rooney Prize for Irish Literature (1977), the John Llewellyn Rhys Memorial Prize (1980) and Irish Post Award (1985). Hogan has become one of France's most highly regarded literary writers in translation, with *les feuilles d'ombre* (Grasset) being nominated for Prix du Meilleur Livre Étranger 2016. The Lilliput Press have reissued his early novels, *The Ikon Maker* and *The Leaves on Grey*, and published his most recent short-story collection, *The History of Magpies*.

Grace Jolliffe's first novel, *Piggy Monk Square*, was shortlisted for the 2006 Commonwealth New Writers Prize and was broadcast that year on RTÉ's *Book on One*. Grace is not quite the full hermit, but she does live quietly in Galway. Her novels, *Sweet Little Things*, *When The Sun Shines* and *The Sunshine Girl*, are available on Amazon. www.gracejolliffe.com

Claire Keegan is the author of two award-winning collections of short stories, *Antarctica* and *Walk The Blue Fields*, and of *Foster*, which won the 2009 Davy Byrnes Award. Her work has been published in *The New Yorker*, *Best American Short Stories*, *Granta* and *The Paris Review* and it has been translated into fourteen languages.

Molly McCloskey is the author of two short-story collections, two novels, and a memoir, *Circles Around the Sun: In Search of a Lost Brother*. Her latest novel, *When Light is Like Water*, was shortlisted for the Irish Novel of the Year Award in 2017, and was recently published in the US as *Straying*. Her work appears in the *Guardian*, *The Irish Times*, the *Los Angeles Review of Books*, and elsewhere. Having lived for 25 years in Ireland, she now resides in Washington, DC.

Lisa McInerney's work has featured in *Winter Papers*, *Granta* and on BBC Radio 4. Her debut novel, *The Glorious Heresies*, won the 2016 Baileys Women's Prize for Fiction and the 2016 Desmond Elliott Prize. Her second novel, *The Blood Miracles*, was published in 2017.

Danielle McLaughlin's debut collection of short stories, *Dinosaurs On Other Planets*, was published in Ireland in 2015 by The Stinging Fly Press, in the UK and US in 2016 by John Murray and Random House, and most recently in Slovakia by Inaque.

Martin Malone is the author of seven novels, a memoir, three short-story collections and several radio plays. His first novel, *Us*, won the John B. Keane/Sunday Independent Literature Award. He is a winner of RTÉ's Francis MacManus Award and was nominated for the 2012 Sunday Times EFG Short Story Prize.

Lia Mills writes novels, short stories and essays. Her most recent novel, *Fallen*, was the Two Cities One Book festival selection for 2016 (Dublin and Belfast).

Sinéad Morrissey has published six collections of poetry: *There Was Fire in Vancouver* (1996); *Between Here and There* (2002); *The State of the Prisons* (2005); *Through the Square Window* (2009); *Parallax* (2013) and *On Balance* (2017). Her awards include the Irish Times Poetry Now Award (2009, 2013) and the T S Eliot Prize (2013). In 2016 she received the E M Forster Award from the American Academy of Arts and Letters. *On Balance* received the Forward Prize in 2017. She has served as Belfast Poet Laureate (2013-2014) and is currently Director of the Newcastle Centre for the Literary Arts at Newcastle University.

Kathleen Murray lives in Dublin. Her stories have appeared in anthologies such as *Davy Byrne Stories* (The Stinging Fly Press) and *All Over Ireland* (Faber and Faber) and in other journals, including *The Dublin Review* and *Granta* online.

Michael Nolan is from Belfast. He is the fiction editor of *The Tangerine*, and is currently studying for a PhD in Creative Writing at Queen's University, Belfast.

Philip Ó Ceallaigh has published over forty stories, many of them collected in the collections, *Notes from a Turkish Whorehouse*, for which he was awarded the Rooney Prize for Irish Literature, and *The Pleasant*

Light of Day. Both volumes were published by Penguin Ireland. He is also an essayist and translator, including of Mihail Sebastian's *For Two Thousand Years*, published by Penguin Classics. His work has also featured in *Granta*, *The Dublin Review* and on BBC Radio 4. He lives in Bucharest, Romania.

Nuala O'Connor AKA **Nuala Ní Chonchúir** was born in Dublin and lives in East Galway. Her fifth short-story collection, *Joyride to Jupiter*, was published by New Island in 2017. Penguin USA, Penguin Canada and Sandstone (UK) published Nuala's third novel, *Miss Emily*, about the poet Emily Dickinson and her Irish maid. It was shortlisted for the Bord Gáis Energy Eason Book Club Novel of the Year 2015 and longlisted for the 2017 International Dublin Literary Award. Nuala's fourth novel, *Becoming Belle*, will be published in 2018. www.nualaoconnor.com

Mary O'Donoghue's short fiction has also appeared in *Granta*, *Guernica*, *Georgia Review*, *Kenyon Review*, *The Irish Times*, *The Sunday Times*, *The Dublin Review*, *Short Fiction*, and elsewhere. She grew up in County Clare, works in Boston MA, and calls Tuscaloosa AL home.

Aiden O'Reilly's debut short-story collection, *Greetings, Hero*, was published in 2014. He studied maths, and has worked as a translator, a building-site worker, a mathematics lecturer and a property magazine editor. His fiction has also appeared in *The Dublin Review*, *The Irish Times*, *Prairie Schooner*, *3:AM Magazine*, *Litro Magazine* and in several anthologies.

Sean O'Reilly is the author of the short-story collection, *Curfew and Other Stories*, and the novels, *Love and Sleep*, *The Swing of Things* and *Watermark*. His latest collection of stories, *Levitation*, was published last year by The Stinging Fly Press.

Nora Pyne is a writer living in Ireland. 'Jeopardy' was her first story to be published and was written in Sean O'Reilly's Writing Desire workshop at the Irish Writers Centre.

Deborah Rose Reeves was born and raised in Dublin. She is currently settled in rural Oregon and working on her first novel. 'Lay Down The Dark Layers' was her first published story.

Keith Ridgway is a Dublin writer currently living in London. He is the author of the novels, *Hawthorn And Child*, *Animals*, *The Parts* and *The Long Falling*, and the short-story collections, *Never Love a Gambler* and *Standard Time*.

Eimear Ryan's writing has also appeared in *Winter Papers*, *Granta*, *gorse*, *The Dublin Review*, *Town & Country* (Faber and Faber) and *The Long Gaze Back* (New Island). She is co-editor of the literary journal, *Banshee*.

Cathy Sweeney lives in Bray, County Wicklow. She has been published in various other journals including *The Dublin Review*, *Meridian*, *Banshee*, and *The Tangerine*. Her short story, 'Three Stories on a Theme', is included in *Young Irelanders* (New Island).

William Wall has published four novels, three collections of short fiction and four volumes of poetry. His next book will be *Grace's Day* (New Island, Dublin, and Head Of Zeus, London, August 2018). He is the first European winner of the Drue Heinz Prize. His work has won many prizes and been widely translated.

NOTES ON THE EDITORS

Sarah Gilmartin is an arts journalist who writes a weekly column on debut fiction for *The Irish Times* and also reviews for *The Sunday Times*, *Sunday Business Post* and *Irish Examiner*. She lectures in feature writing at Dublin City University and Dublin Business School.

Declan Meade is *The Stinging Fly*'s founding editor and publisher. He also runs The Stinging Fly Press and has edited a number of anthologies.

PERMISSIONS ACKNOWLEDGEMENTS

Colin Barrett: 'Let's Go Kill Ourselves' originally published in Issue 14 Volume Two. Copyright © 2009 Colin Barrett. Reprinted by permission of Colin Barrett.

Kevin Barry: 'Last Days of the Buffalo' (originally published in Issue 5 Volume Two) from *There Are Little Kingdoms* by Kevin Barry, copyright © 2007 Kevin Barry. Reprinted by permission of Kevin Barry.

Sara Baume: 'Fifty Year Winter' originally published in Issue 26 Volume Two. Copyright © 2013 Sara Baume. Reprinted by permission of Sara Baume.

Maria Behan: 'Grace at the Wall of Death' originally published in Issue 9 Volume One. Copyright © 2001 Maria Behan. Reprinted by permission of Maria Behan.

Claire-Louise Bennett: 'Finishing Touch' (originally published in Issue 29 Volume Two) from *Pond* by Claire-Louise Bennett, copyright © 2015 Claire-Louise Bennett. Reprinted by permission of Claire-Louise Bennett.

Jennifer Brady: 'Ten Days Counting Slowly' originally published in Issue 10 Volume Two. Copyright © 2008 Jennifer Brady. Reprinted by permission of Jennifer Brady.

Lucy Sweeney Byrne: 'Danny' originally published in Issue 33 Volume Two. Copyright © 2016 Lucy Sweeney Byrne. Reprinted by permission of Lucy Sweeney Byrne.

The Stinging Fly magazine was established in late 1997 to seek out, publish and promote the very best new Irish and international writing. We published our first issue in March 1998. We have a particular interest in encouraging new writers, and in promoting the short story form. We now publish two issues of *The Stinging Fly* each year: in May and November. It is available on subscription from our website. Subscribers receive free access to our complete archive of back issues.

The Stinging Fly Press was launched in May 2005 with the publication of our first title, *Watermark* by Sean O'Reilly. In 2007 we published Kevin Barry's debut short-story collection, *There Are Little Kingdoms*; and in 2009 *Life in The Universe* by Michael J. Farrell. *The China Factory*, a collection of stories by Mary Costello, was nominated for The Guardian First Book Award in 2012. *Young Skins* by Colin Barrett won the 2014 Frank O'Connor International Short Story Award, the Rooney Prize for Irish Literature and the Guardian First Book Award. In 2015 we published *Pond* by Claire-Louise Bennett and *Dinosaurs On Other Planets* by Danielle McLaughlin; and, in 2017, *Levitation*, a new collection of stories by Sean O'Reilly.

We have also published a number of other anthologies as well as new editions of Maeve Brennan's *The Springs of Affection* and *The Long-Winded Lady*.

All Stinging Fly Press titles can be purchased online from our website. Our books are distributed to the trade by Gill (IRL/UK) and Dufour Editions (USA).

If you experience any difficulty in finding our books, please e-mail us at info@stingingfly.org.

visit www.stingingfly.org

Thank you for supporting independent publishing.

'... God has specially appointed me to this city, so as though it were a large thoroughbred horse which because of its great size is inclined to be lazy and needs the stimulation of some stinging fly...'

—Plato, *The Last Days of Socrates*